Also by Jaimee Wriston Colbert

Wild Things
Shark Girls
Dream Lives of Butterflies
Climbing the God Tree
Sex, Salvation, and the Automobile

Praise For *Wild Things*

Brace yourself for Jaimee Wriston Colbert's *Wild Things*. These linked rural noir stories unfold their wings near the Susquehanna River in a landscape graced by wildlife and haunted by lost prosperity, "business after business failing, padlocking their doors, factories with their boarded up windows, just another has-been town slowly shutting down." Those left behind must navigate the meth labs and broken families and their own oversized yearning. "Abstinence may lead you to god," says one of Colbert's women, "but it's hunger that'll get you fed." These characters sing their hunger and dance their hard-won wisdom. These brilliant, surprising stories defy gravity and take flight.

— Bonnie Jo Campbell, *Mothers, Tell Your Daughters, Once Upon A River,* and National Book Award finalist for *American Salvage*

Jaimee Wriston Colbert has written a book of deeply affecting elegies to the scattered remnants of wilderness, the some few wild things we still live among: blackbird, brown trout, reef shark, teenage girl. By turns luminous and razor-sharp, in landscapes as diverse as a shimmering beach in Oahu and a crumbling mill town in upstate New York, these characters find comfort, not only in the "peace of wild things" but also in their scrap and bite, their tenacious urge toward survival in an absurdly hostile world.

—Pam Houston, *Contents May Have Shifted* and *Cowboys Are My Weakness*

Colbert hones her clarion vision of the interconnectedness and vulnerability of life in this edgy, knowing, situationally complex, and emotionally intricate short story collection. .... Colbert's divining sense of brokenness and our longing for wholeness makes for extraordinarily incisive, stirring, funny, and haunting all-American stories."

—Donna Seaman – Booklist, Advanced Review of *Wild Things*

Colbert has created a masterpiece of short stories in which the vulnerability of all life is exposed and loneliness reigns supreme. ... An original collection of stories that captures the essence of what it is to be human in the 21st century.... Colbert writes past the limits of despair and soars through the skies of hope, giving her readers a unique gift that heals our hearts and nurtures the wild in each of us.

—Katie James, *American Book Review*

A tremendous new collection from a writer with extraordinary powers of observation and an empathetic understanding of the thorny, heartbreaking human condition. There's so much reverence for the world in *Wild Things*, so much intelligence and beauty on every page. A stunning book.

—Christine Sneed

Praise for *Shark Girls*

Colbert has created an edgy and lush gothic tale laced with outlaw eroticism and barbed absurdities, and propelled by a powerful undertow racing beneath every alarming scene, bitterly funny moment, and strange twist of fate. From women battered and haunted to "throwaway kids," rock-and-roll burnouts, and quixotic quests, Colbert summons a world as volatile as Hawaii itself, with its cycles of volcanic destruction and slow repair.

—Donna Seaman, *Booklist* (Starred Review)

This novel is so original and strange that it's hard to put a label on it, yet it has the lively detail and bold characterization and compelling plot that always make a good novel. I was captivated by the bold twists and turns, as well as the sharp and inventive language, and I was drawn in by the fascinating lore and setting of Hawaii.

—Bobbie Ann Mason, author, *In Country: A Novel*

Colbert's *Shark Girls* is a mesmerizing novel, vibrant with eroticism, myth, and mystery.

—Madison Smartt Bell, author, *All Souls' Rising*

Praise for *Dream Lives of Butterflies*

Dream Lives of Butterflies is full of startling wisdom and high-flown humor. Jaimee Wriston Colbert's characters are complete originals; full of sass and attitude, they struggle with the cultural tension between worlds and lives. Readers will love following these people on their full-hearted, rambunctious adventures.

—Diana Abu-Jaber

Jaimee Wriston Colbert's words are like magic. Colbert gives voice to those pushed to the margins of resistance, of sanity, of survival - and what a voice it is! Lyrical, imploring, humorous, and heartbreaking, the stories contained here take us out of dreams and into the reality of lives whose truths are both strange and familiar. It is her brilliant exploration of that no-man's land between what we desire and what we must live without that defines Colbert's deep empathy for her characters. We feel ourselves being drawn into the plight of the characters with such startling recognition that we feel our own lives teetering on the edge of something wondrous.

—Kim Barnes

Jaimee Wriston Colbert's Dream Lives of Butterflies is a stunning collection, heartbreakingly funny and sad at the same time, the tonal complexity underscoring at every turn her deep and abiding compassion for both character and landscape. Nothing appeals more to me in serious fiction than the kind of fundamental human dignity that lives and breathes in each of these beautifully choreographed linked stories. Jaimee Wriston Colbert is one of

the most fiercely talented writers I have read in a long, long time, her voice as emphatic and gorgeous as it is brave. A remarkable achievement.
—Jack Driscoll

Praise for *Climbing the God Tree*

A debut novel set in a haunted Maine town. Eerie, understated, and deft. Colbert uses atmosphere the way David Lean uses scenery.
—*Kirkus Reviews*

The scope of Jaimee Wriston Colbert's storytelling is impressive, with no fewer than 16 central characters delineated in intricately overlapping narratives... The stories stand on their own as sensitive and unsentimental evocations of unrelieved loss.
—*The New York Times Book Review*

Jaimee Wriston Colbert looks deeply into the ragged places in our psyches - into the parts of us torn open by loss and by failed love - and reveals our humanity in all its beauty and imperfection. Here is a writer who, in powerfully linked stories, movingly evokes both our craving for the sacred and our tenacious embrace of the profane.
—Dawn Raffel, Judge, Willa Cather Fiction Prize

Vanishing Acts

Jaimee Wriston Colbert

Fomite
Burlington, VT

ISBN-13: 978-1-944388-25-6

Library of Congress Control Number: 2017952868

Fomite

58 Peru Street

Burlington, VT 05401

www.fomitepress.com

For my Dad, Arthur James Wriston, Jr.,
who first taught me the magic of story

"What's madness but
nobility of soul at odds
with circumstance?"
—Theodore Roethke

"But most of all I shall remember the monarchs."
—Rachel Carson

PROLOGUE

1977

ON A LUMINOUS SPRING DAY after a night of storms that pummeled the island with slashing wind, driving rain, explosions of thunder and a blitz of sheet lightning, a giant swell bore monster waves to the Hamakua coast, and Jody Johnstone carried his surfboard into a pounding sea, never to go home again. He became a kind of silence in the family he left behind. Everything that was their lives before snapped apart, like the halves of his surfboard the police brought back. When life was finally reassembled it had become something else, like settling into someone else's world, trying to make it your own.

Gwen was eight and a half after "the incident" as Madge, her mother, came to call it, and already living her life in memories: her last walk with her father on the Devastation Trail gathering olivines for a school project, the pale green stones, "Pele's diamonds," glittering in his hand like miniature blades of grass. Her favorite memories were of the years they lived on O'ahu before things became strained, before they moved to the Big Island. Those days she ran wild on Kawela beach, bare and brown. "Ahiu, wild thing!" her father belted as she hurtled into his arms, a horse galloping the yellow sands.

That's when she felt like she belonged to Hawai'i. Life in motion, the ocean out their back door rolling, swelling, trade winds swishing through the palm trees, rustling the ironwoods whose tiny brown cones prickled her feet as she ran. Running, always running is how Gwen would remember it, a life whose mysteries awaited her, hiding from her cousins behind the Ironwood thicket, or holding their breaths, her father's arms around her in the aqua sea, eyes strained open watching parrot fish drifting like umbrellas over the reef below. When they swam back to the beach her mother, still smiling in those days, wrapped a towel around Gwen and held her close, Madge's warm body, her skin smelling of sun and papaya lotion.

Jude Canada, Gwen's grandfather, sat at the helm of life on Kawela Bay. His family had been missionaries from the Church of The Living Waters in Connecticut. Jude was an insistent man, spine straight as a yardstick. Life was serious business, you *buck up* and live it well, and in the end you get your reward. He married a part Hawaiian girl, Ana, who bore Gwen's mother then died when Madge was still a child. This too a silence.

Jude liked to drive his big green Pontiac, fins swimming through the traffic like sharks. He drove fast and was intolerant of any slower car that shared his road. In later years, cataract vision, it must have seemed like those other cars were coming at him, snail's pace, floating menacingly out of the shadows of his limited eyesight, aiming to get in his way. Jude squealed the Pontiac around corners, cursing other cars, stop signs, "Lord almighty, when'd they put *that* one up?" he'd howl. In the back seat Gwen and her friends from Rainbow Elementary tittered, sticky hands pressed against their mouths, they'd let their small bodies crash into each other like waves, the jerking motion of his turns.

When the law took away her grandfather's license he was devastated. "I don't have to see a road to drive it," he roared, "must we see God to believe?

I know Kamehameha highway like I knew my own wife. I can *feel* the damn curves!" That's when Jude Canada grew old. He spun into a "decline," as Madge put it, and then he died. Madge bought *Art's Alive*, an arts supplies store in Hilo for her husband to manage, and a house in Volcano, with the money Jude left. She had some paddlers on an outrigger row her out past the Kawela breakers, where she scattered her father's remains beyond the reef.

Big Volcano cabin is high up in volcano country above a long, jagged gash at the property line, a gaping volcanic fissure running across the land like a wound. An old rift zone, sight of ancient eruptions, there are cracks and crevices and unstable lava tunnels that can cave in, falling sixty or more feet down into the earth. In the distance Mauna Kea and Mauna Loa, the two largest mountains in the world if you count the miles below sea level, rise like purple ghosts—or white sometimes depending on the season, a good storm pelting them with acres of snow. It was isolated then and for the most part still is. Which is how things can happen and nobody knows. How Gwen's mother lived there and slowly began to lose her mind.

A year after they moved, his new business failing, Jody Johnstone walked into the giant surf. Violet Johnstone Stuart, Jody's sister, called it suicide. Madge said her husband *disappeared*, then she wouldn't talk about it. Violet's daughter Kiki claimed she had a dream and saw how it happened. Bony horsey little Gwen clamped shut her mouth, stuck her fingers in her ears, shrieking, "Odd man's it! Odd man's it!" when Kiki tried to tell her. "He didn't mean it! Don't you get it? Your dad didn't mean it! Honestly, don't you get it, you lolo girl? He was looking for a great ride, not to die! Nobody around here wants any kind of truth."

Madge would not believe he drowned, snarling at the Hilo Police when they brought her the pieces of his board. "Without a body where's the proof? Show me flesh not fiberglass!" Then she came apart. And then she came back together again, only different. The smiles were gone, her sun-smelling skin turned cool and odorless. Conversation in their house became a punishing chatter whenever Madge spoke to Gwen, until Gwen could hear only this tattle inside her mind, her faults, her inadequacies, her *should-haves*, harping at her like a relentless twenty-four hour news channel.

Eventually Madge rebuilt her husband's store into a thriving business. "Isn't that Mrs. Johnstone smart!" the other shop owners in downtown Hilo remarked, grateful not to have failure among them, "so *akamai* that *wahine*." But during the long evenings she waited for him to come home.

Part I

Spring, 2011

1

Buddy

ONE OF BUDDY'S EARLIEST MEMORIES has to do with death. He's a little kid about three or four, still those marshmallow legs and he's running ahead of his mother on the jetty in Rock Harbor, Maine, that noses its way out a mile or so into the harbor, ocean the slick color of a dime all around them, small waves sucking at the sides. He dates his memories this way: PM for pre-move, and AM for after their move from Maine to Hawai'i, because that's when everything came apart. It's like he's going backwards now. Instead of his life ahead of him the way it's supposed to be, things to look forward to, he's slipped from a bright mid-morning back into some dank dawn. AM. After move.

But we digress. That's a word his mother would use, *digress*. Gwen likes big words, Jesus, red wine and Xanax, but not always in that order—she likes to mix it up a bit. She also believes there's a *perceivable* chance the world will end in September 2013. She's talking apocalypse: earthquakes, tsunamis, the dead crawling out of their graves. Most Christian Fundamentalists, new ageists, Mayan calendar enthusiasts and their ilk set their sites on December 21, 2012, but she's rooting for the following year on the Virgin's birthday, September 8. It makes sense, she said, that God would pick a special day for such a significant event. She thinks there's a good chance those right wing Jesus-freaks got it wrong, she told Buddy; she'll cut them off at the knees.

In the time of Buddy's memory, the jetty and he and his mom heading toward the lighthouse at its end, she was different. Had a bit more *something* inside her, less trouble on her face. There they were on this breakwater, she's strolling along and he's running out in front of her, silver sea, silver sky too because the fog's blowing in, and suddenly out of this mist there's a figure moving toward them, opposite direction. Probably he's just got on an oversized sweatshirt is all, dark colored hood and it's pulled up over his head and part of his face to protect him from the damp fog. The thing is they can't see his face. It's an empty place under the hood, like a shadow you could put your hand through, come out clean the other side. Buddy stops running and Gwen catches up to him, tugs on his arm, yanks him back beside her. They're both staring at this hooded, faceless walker coming toward them, his long stride that's kind of slow, like liquid, like he's pulling his own legs along through water, no feet, maybe tentacles instead. She hugs Buddy against her, leans down and whispers, "I've heard it said, son, if you look Death squarely in the face, what you see is the face of God."

NOW BUDDY'S LEGS HAVE GROWN into the sinewy, stretched-out length of a teenager, and he and his girlfriend Marnie Lo are steaming down the Volcano Highway in her mother's Plymouth Fury, her slippered foot plastered like a cement block to the accelerator when they hear the shriek of a siren behind them. "Sonofabitch!" mutters Marnie.

He whips his head back, sees the flashing blue lights circle round and round blinking OINK, OINK (he knows a pig when he sees one; his father's a warden for a maximum security prison). The voice on the megaphone orders them to move over to the side of the road. "Side-a-the-road!" roars the voice. Soft shoulders this road once had, sliding volcanic soil. Pull over and half your car would immediately sink. Like stepping into one of the puka ferns his mom warns him about, long hairy trunks disguising lava tubes shooting down to the middle of the earth.

"Sonofabitch!" Marnie wails for the second time, kind of rolling all the letters into a spit-it-out type of a word. "Shut-up and let me talk, OK? I'm good at this kind of thing."

What Buddy notices first is the cop's legs when he gets out of the PIG-mobile and struts over, meaty thighs crammed into his blues. He bends down and peers into Marnie's window. "You know how fast you were doing?" He glares at Buddy, like Buddy's the one driving. He's a haole cop, German maybe, looks like a Nazi. So maybe this won't go too good for them, Buddy's thinking, the way this Nazi is staring at Marnie, flat eyes the color of Mel Gibson's eyes giving her the up, down, then back to her own yellowy-brown eyes, skin the color of a honeybee. Marnie's half Caucasian, *hapa-haole* they call it in Hawai'i, the honeybee half is all kinds of things, Hawaiian, Chinese, Filipino. No German to speak of. How he knows the color of Mel Gibson's eyes is because the night before they watched one of her stepdad's ancient DVDs, *Man Without A Face*, sprawled out on the Lo living room's shag-carpeted floor, her mother's cats taking up all the furniture. One side of Mel's face looked like an avalanche rolled over it, but the other side announced he was still Mel Gibson. "Your basic hottie, blue eyes, tan skin, sexy smile and that goddamn adorable butt," Marnie proclaimed, "the dude is *fine*."

"Old," Buddy said, "the dude is old."

"So maybe I'm into old guys, huh?" she snapped.

Old guys, all the ways Buddy's not what she's looking for. He's mud-eyed, skin white as bleach, barely a butt to speak of on his jangly, long-ass frame, not old and not much to smile about these days. He stares straight ahead at the Fury's windshield where a small white moth lights down. The glass is still damp from the rain forest drizzle they just high-tailed out of, little clumpy sparkles like wet salt. "Flew," the cop whines, "you flew down this highway at eighty miles per! You're on the Big Island for chrissake, 45 miles per hour, did you think it was NASCAR?" He hooks a slab-sized thumb under his polished belt, then grins into Marnie's face at his own cleverness exposing vampy canine teeth.

The moth sticks its proboscis into the moisture. Buddy knows about moths and butterflies, the order Lepidoptera. This moth is thirsty for special chemicals, nutrients, salt. He knows another kind of moth that drinks tears from the eyes of cows. It flutters against the cow's eyes, using its long mouth parts to sweep across the animal's eyeball making more tears flow, which the moth then drinks. It's a mutually satisfying relationship, the moth is fed, the cow's eyes are dried. He appreciates this about nature. Everybody gets something. But the moth's the clever one. If it wasn't there in the first place, batting its wings at the cow's big eyes like some bitchy flirt, the cow wouldn't be crying. Buddy's mother said his father was like that. "Had me convinced our survival depended on him," she said. "What do you know, here we are in Hawai'i without him."

At sixteen what Buddy likes most is entomology and the idea of having sex with Marnie. Because at that point he still believed it could happen any day, that any moment she'd reach out, those olivey arms, undo his jeans, slide her tender tongue down. What he likes least? That's easy, his parents and Grandma Madge. Sometimes his mom forgets about Buddy, but she never forgets Grandma Madge. "Grandma wakes up with a howling inside and she thinks it's hunger," his mom said, "but I think it's the person she used to be just falling away." Buddy's grandmother has TIAs, what they call shower strokes. Her mind dies a little after each one.

"Well," Marnie hesitates, sighs, her voice sweet and sticky as a doughnut. She's peering up into the cop's looming face, rolling her yellowy-brown eyes. "The thing is we got stuck behind a tour bus at Volcano. You know how that goes." She yawns and squiggles the top half of her body into a slight, slow stretch, runs her tongue across her lower lip.

The cop shoots up a wormy brow, slides his gaze down and narrows his eyes. "You're not toying with me, are you young lady? Because if you are I'd have to give you a ticket, just on the principle of the thing." He grins and Buddy groans, faking a cough.

Marnie says, "Oh no, I wouldn't do *that*. I'm just like, putting out a little something to consider here. See, if I was speeding to make up for having to go so slow before, in a way it evens up, huh?"

Putting out? Buddy's thinking. That's retro guy talk for when a girl had sex with you and you didn't have to buy her food or take her to a movie. Mostly he doesn't go for guy talk, or even hanging out with guys much. He never felt he was entirely one of them, nor girls neither. Buddy wasn't sure where he fit—what he wants is to fit with Marnie. That's why he likes the insect world, they don't question these things. You do what you're born to do.

The cop shakes his massive head. "You won't find logic like that in the laws of the highway, miss. You got any idea how much speeding tickets are up to these days? It's a lot of babysitting change I'll tell you."

The cop's posture's gone from rigid to lounging, his chin thrusting its way inside Marnie's window like it's independent from the oversized face it's attached to. Surveying that blackened stubble, Buddy thinks how he must have to shave three times a day. Buddy barely shaves at this point, once a week about does the job. He tugs at his shiny chin and watches Marnie ferret out a purple marker from her purse, scribbling a number onto a gum wrapper. He feels that aching inside, that punished, helpless hurt. The moth finally wheels away in a gust of wind, and Buddy misses it like a lost friend.

"We're on our way to the airport," Marnie informs the cop who could double as a steroids poster-boy and who looks only at her now, Buddy might as well be in another time zone. "And FYI I'm no babysitter. Like, do I look the type to hang out with some bratty little kid? I'm a model. I got a gig in Honolulu."

"Well Miz Model," the cop straightens, stretching his stuff, "I know what it's like trying to catch a plane, wouldn't want to blow your *gig*. So today I'm calling this a warning." He finishes writing something on his note pad, tears it out with a flourish and hands it to Marnie. "But you better watch that speed, because next time I'll give you that ticket." He winks at her then struts on back to his cruiser, slips inside and peels off. Marnie rearranges her tank top that she'd tugged down when the cop first appeared, displaying more than just a shadow of cleavage. "What a major creep!" she says.

Buddy memorizes that cleavage. Takes a mental snapshot to drag out during his sleepless nights with his other imagined photos of her body parts, slipping them together like a jigsaw puzzle. "So why'd you give him your phone number then? You like told him your life story practically. And *BTW*, letting a pig peek down your shirt to get out of a ticket is pretty cliché, don't you think?" He has to be careful. When Marnie gets mad she snubs him for days. She's on his mind all the time, an itch under his skin, a popping, burning inside.

Marnie rolls her eyes, aims the Fury back onto the highway and in minutes they're flying again, past ginger groves, fern forests, skinny waving papaya trees, palm trees, small houses with corrugated roofs and lava gardens, then further down the mountain toward the sea gleaming like a sheet of stretched out aluminum. Six months ago when Buddy's mother hauled them from Maine to Hawai'i, she pointed from the plane at snow-capped Mauna Kea and announced, "They can ski that mountain in bathing suits." As if that would mean anything to Buddy. As if his life without his father in it could be a life. He thinks about his dad, picturing the way he looked the last time Buddy saw him. He memorized what his dad wore when he drove them to Portland Jetport, silence thick as the fog hanging over the road like smoke. His dad was wearing his red flannel weekend jacket, the one he wore *every* weekend, the one that drove his mom crazy. "Sign of an unimaginative person," she said, "a creature of habit." His dad once put that jacket around Buddy's shoulders at a Patriots game, a light rain blowing in sheets across the bleachers and he's shivering beside Buddy in his t-shirt. It's the only game they ever went to, and Buddy didn't understand why they kept sitting in that cold rain; did it feel to his dad like something that had to be finished? His dad didn't care about the Patriots, neither did Buddy. The flannel was still warm from his father's shoulders.

So why couldn't his parents just live together like roommates, they wouldn't have to even share a bed. "Good-bye Richard," his father said. Buddy's real name's Richard but nobody calls him that. Hitter Harrison, third grade Little League pitcher nicknamed him Bucky on account of his big teeth, and the name stuck for a while, then eventually became Buddy the way nicknames do, migrating from one form to the other, no remembered connection between the two. Bucky, Buddy, he doesn't mind. Richard would sound moronic in Hawai'i where guys have names like Poi-dog, Barracuda and B.B. (for Big *Brah*); it would set him apart even more.

His mother wanted to put braces on them but his father said wait. His father's the warden for Rock Harbor Adult Correctional and his motto is, Wait And Be Ready. He once told Buddy, "Never question what you think you know. If you question things you lose the advantage of being right." So they yelled at each other, his mom and his dad, about his teeth, about how his dad always waited on things and thought he was right. Their house in Maine became a cold house, like it was always winter.

Buddy misses that house, an old house in a neighborhood of old Rock Harbor houses, big yards, trees that blossomed every spring. He misses the sense of permanence of his life in Maine, even though he knows now it was all a lie. "Our house is on the market," his mother announced a few weeks after their exodus, her lips pinched tense as guitar strings.

"Bud-o, what you don't know about life," Marnie says now. "*Hell-o*? You hear me tell that loser I'm going to get with him? Like, did you actually think I'd give some cop my cell phone number? He was so busy mouthing off about the laws of the highway and eyeballing my tits he didn't think to look at the number on my license. Even if he did he'd call my house and get a date with The Sleaze!" Marnie tosses back her lava colored hair and roars.

Buddy laughs too. The ringing in his ears morphs into a mantra, *tits, tits, tits*! When he thinks about Marnie's breasts it makes him buzz all over, like he's plugged in, like he's electric, like he could turn on and shine. He doesn't like the word *tits* as much, too bovine. Breasts, a good word. Marnie calls her stepfather The Sleaze. None of them live with their real parents, at least not both at the same time, not Marnie, not Buddy, not the others they hang with sometimes. Marnie says if people were meant to have mothers *and* fathers men would also get pregnant. "You can tell God's a man," she says, "because if he was a she *guys* would get periods."

Buddy slides his hand over the distance of seat between them, over the torn fake leather upholstery, up and under her arm hanging loosely on the steering wheel. "Guess I'm just a jealous kind of guy," he says in a husky voice, trying to imitate some actor they watched together on some cable station movie. Tentatively, heart hammering, he slips his hand up under her top. Marnie has been letting him do that; she ignores him when he does, like he's not really doing it at all. A thrill shoots through him, a hot, pounding, jumping sensation like his blood's on fire, like he's burning up inside.

He closes his eyes, rubs her hard little nipple between his thumb and forefinger like a marble. *Nipple*, another highly agreeable word. The Fury cruises down the Volcano Highway, air like a steam bath leeching in through the windows, its verdant, mossy smell. Buddy inhales, stifles a yawn. Marnie squirms and Buddy reluctantly pulls his hand back, eyes still closed. The motion of the car under him is like the spinning of the world, too fast to jump out, too late to turn back. Never mind that he stole money from Grandma Madge's room so he and Marnie could fly to Honolulu. His grandmother won't know the difference. Never mind that his father sends money in the prison's blue envelopes so he can go to a private school he hates, not even a 'How *are* you!' scrawled inside for Buddy.

Was it Buddy's fault his parents couldn't stand each other? His giant teeth? Migraine headaches that slammed down the brakes on ordinary life for the three of them? "You always manage to grow a headache at exactly the worst times," his father complained, as if his headaches were toadstools, persistent and useless in their front yard, something to wipe out with the lawn mower, the weed whacker. Tried to convince himself he couldn't care less. Marnie said parents are basically useless. She said her own father beat-feet out of their life almost as soon as her mother could stand after squeezing her out. Then her mother screwed around for a few years, Marnie said, a major *ho*. One night she brought home The Sleaze. He was in her mother's bed the next morning and the morning after that, weeks, months, going on years now. "Guess she screwed him into something permanent," said Marnie, "like a socket maybe. Because then she goes and marries the dude."

Hilo Junior Academy is for retards, far as Buddy can tell, a school for "exceptional learning styles." He's there because he has a sort of brain chemical imbalance that causes migraines so bad he fantasizes taking a knife, cutting them out. Brain chemical screw-ups are rampant in the Canada-Johnstone-Winter clan, we've got the mood-disordered depressives, the nut-job demented, delusional alcoholics, and then there's Buddy. Family tree. He was absent from school as much as he was there. Well what difference did it make, wasn't he numbed into a state of brain-dead whenever he went? The neurologist his mom sent him to said Buddy needed a change in "attitude," that he was too tense, a powder keg. Only instead of firing off a couple rounds in a school assembly he blew up in his own head.

HJA is where Buddy met Marnie Lo, in his culinary arts class. He'd noticed her around campus, who wouldn't? Mane to her waist, most of the time black though sometimes she dyed it different colors, purple haze, Halloween orange, always her tight black clothes. He started dressing in black too for a while, and their cousin Kiki called it a *death thing* on account of the breakup between his parents.

D.J., Buddy's food prep partner, whispered, "That chica's got anger issues, hold on to your balls!" The teacher was barking out a recipe for luau chicken, and Marnie hacked away at the raw carcass on the high silver countertop like she was murdering it, like she had some major grudge against it; vicious swings of the knife, as if the poor bird wasn't already weeks dead and previously frozen, flesh, bone, all of it confetti under the glint of her silver blade.

"What you staring at haole boy?" she asked Buddy. "You never seen someone cut up chicken before?" She tossed the microscopic remains into a bowl of coconut milk, grinning.

He shrugged, face pink. "You have some bones in it."

"Got a problem with that? Bone's good for you, calcium you know. Like it keeps the body hard." She winked and her eyes traveled the length of him the way guys check out girls. "Don't your mommy ever cook chicken for you?"

"My m...m...mother (since his parents separation Buddy had developed this unfortunate habit of stammering sometimes when he talked about them), my mother can't cook pork and beans." *Yikes!* You get the picture? There he was babbling like some moron to the most *babelicious* girl in the school, maybe the whole state, about beans! He blushed violently, skin the color of those bloody chicken scraps quivering like jello under her knife.

"Pork? You called it *pahk*. What kind of talk is that? Where you from, anyway?"

He told Marnie about Maine at lunch that day, the two of them lounging on prickly crab grass under a banyan tree, its exposed airborne roots scraggling down around them like an old man's beard, sharing a plate of fried teriyaki tofu from the cafeteria.

"So you're a coast haole from the *east* coast? I never met somebody from the east coast."

"My m-m-mother's from here. She grew up in Hawai'i. Her grandmother was Hawaiian so that makes her part Hawaiian and me too a little, if you do the math."

Marnie shook her head, leaning so close to him that a hank of her black hair grazed his arm. He felt a chill like a cold wind breeze up his spine. "Thing is, Buddy Winter, I effing hate math. My subject's recess. Anyway, if you're not born here it doesn't count. It's like you're renting Hawai'i."

"They think like that in Maine too. You're not a Mainer unless you're born into it and live your whole life there. The way some talk it's like they evolved from amoebas into their own living rooms."

Marnie grinned, her mouth so close Buddy could smell the tang of teriyaki on her breath. "Well damn, haole boy, I guess that means you don't belong nowhere, huh?"

Buddy swipes angrily at the sudden tears in his eyes, thinking about the truth of this now, how he really *doesn't* belong anywhere. Humid air pours into the car windows as the Fury burns to a stop at the first traffic light they've seen for miles. "Hilo-town," Marnie announces. Buddy nods, then shoots his arm up and over the seat, around her tight little shoulders, hoping she won't notice the wet on his cheeks. There are moths that drink mud, blood, anything. He imagines sinking his mouthparts into that sweaty place on Marnie's neck where her fine hairs wisp like curls of smoke. He'd attach himself there and never let go.

AFTER ABANDONING THE PLYMOUTH ALONG the side of the orchid and lava-lined road leading into Hilo Airport they're standing at the Aloha Airlines desk, trade winds whipping through the wide open terminal, stirring up a mean scent of flowers from the nearby lei stands. The wind messes with Marnie's hair, and when she lifts her arm to push it off her face her top slides up, revealing a golden slice of belly, flat as the TSA information card she's waving at Buddy. "Dude, we need to pay!" She tugs at the sleeve of his t-shirt that says *Maine Lobster Fest*, pretty dorky but he's a kid at this juncture. Clothes are bought for him.

He shoves his paw reluctantly into the pocket of his jeans emerging with the fistful of twenties he scrounged from his grandmother's room, handing them to the ticket agent. Buddy feels a wave of nausea. How low can he go? He found some under her bed, and he doesn't mean the mattress, lying loose on the floor. He discovered a couple fifties (Marnie doesn't know about these) stuffed inside a pair of glittery stiletto shoes wasting away at the back of her closet. "Grandma was a world-class beauty and quite the dancer," his mom told him. These days she wears pink canvas athletic shoes, some cheesy bargain brand. The tens were in a dusty fish bowl filled with pencils, sea shells, poker chips, clots of cotton balls stuck together every which way like molecular models, half used lipsticks the color of dried-up roses, twisted scraps of tissue and ancient ticket stubs. Concerts, cool ones too like The Dead, when Garcia was alive. Her mind dies a little each day, Buddy reminded himself as he pocketed her money.

"I'll most likely get paid this time for modeling," Marnie says. They're lined up between two ropes like a herd of cattle, waiting to be loaded onto the plane.

"Will it cover the cost of these tickets? I'm just wondering because, you know, it's my grandmother's money." He avoids her yellowy-brown stare.

Careful, he thinks, it won't work having Marnie mad at him in Honolulu. A big city where being alone could get pretty ugly.

The line's finally moving and Marnie clutches Buddy's hand like he's her little kid, lugging him along behind her as they troop out onto the tar-smelling tarmac then up the 737's steel steps. He doesn't mind. The way everyone stares because she's so hot, they can't help but notice she's chosen him. "So what!" Marnie shouts over the roar of the engines. "Your grandma's *pupule*, yeah? Crazy people don't need money, they can entertain themselves."

Flying out of Hilo Airport the plane circles above Mauna Kea. Six months ago there had been that snow, skiers darting about like beetles below. The wings of the jumbo-jet made a shadow like a pterodactyl on the glaring whiteness, and staring out the window at the strange land he'd felt dead inside, pulled apart, an insect without its wings. "It's the best thing, Buddy," his mother had said for the tenth time that day. "Grandma needs me. My cousin called, said she's not doing well living on her own anymore."

"Give me a break! This is about you and Dad," he snapped.

"Yes, OK, in part, but I'm her daughter, dammit. I'm all she's got."

He had turned toward his mother then, his glassy stare. "So what do you want me to say? Should I swear too, goddammit? I thought you God-freaks weren't supposed to swear. It's against some law isn't it?"

"At the moment I don't give a damn. Just don't shut me out. Besides, as long as you don't put *God* in front of dammit it's not swearing. Look, I haven't been the world's worst mother, have I? I didn't beat you, lock you in a closet, starve you. Don't I pretty much give you what you need? Talk to me."

He made that strangled sound like he was choking down a too-big bite of meat, mumbling *yeah right* under his breath. "Fine. My topic is butterflies. Butterflies have four stages in their life cycle. This allows them to adapt to a wide range of climates, even climates like the tundra or the arctic.

They can live in severe cold, in a resting state known as diapause. They don't need to respond to outer stimuli, because inside they're quietly surviving." Then he pulled away from her, closing his eyes until the plane touched down. "Aloha and welcome to Hawai'i!" a flight attendant announced. Maine, his history, erased.

Now it's June and the volcanic ridges and craters stick out like pock-marks on the craggy face of Mauna Kea. Buddy feels alternating waves of guilt and exhilaration. He stole money from his grandmother, and his mom thinks he's spending the night with a kid from his English class. But he's free. He's in charge. He could start a new life with his girlfriend. She'd let him feel her breasts and then the rest of her. Maybe they'd even be in love.

Buddy lifts a urine-cup sized specimen of guava juice off the flight atten-dant's tray and hands it to Marnie, who's pawing through a magazine, then take ones for himself. He yawns, rubs his eyes. He hasn't been sleeping well. Keeps having the same weird dream that began in Rock Harbor right before they moved, and he's been dreaming it in its various incarnations since. Last night's version, he's walking along the rim of Halema'uma'u crater and he notices a body lying on the lava-strewn side. An awesome body, naked as rock, skin the color of vanilla ice cream against the black lava, curled up like a S. Her hand was reaching out.

The dream pretty much unfolded that way each time he dreamt it, a woman's body, dead. Buddy didn't have a lot of experience with death then. His dog had died and that sucked. His grandmother was dying he sup-posed, though his mother shook her head when he asked. "Of course not! They're just *baby* strokes."

He settles back against the seat, steady thrum of the plane's engines like some rap song, just enough rhythm you ignore the words. Marnie sticks her iPod's earbuds in her ears, chomps down on a wad of grape bubble gum, scrutinizing an ad for the "creamiest" coconut shampoo in *Aloha* magazine.

Buddy runs a hand through his own dark tangle of curls framing his sallow face; like a halo his mom used to say, sliding her cool fingers through his hair. Closes his eyes. For a runaway he doesn't feel too bad.

2

Gwen

HER MOTHER SITS IN HER rocking chair by the plate glass window that looks out at Mauna Kea and Mauna Loa. Inside their single level pine house the walls are unpainted, post and beam, dark, wood-scented corners with numerous shelves and a lifetime of clutter, but near the giant window there is light. This is where Madge is when she's not wandering about. Where she is now, in limbo, waiting for some cue to set it all in motion again, scrutinizing the mountains as if she expects them to do something, instead of merely looming, snowcapped or not.

She wandered again last night. Gwen looked out her window before going to bed and saw her down in the yard, arms up, white nightgown flapping like some ragged gull's wings. "OK, Magic Man, you're an artist!" Madge shrieked, as Gwen approached her slowly, like coming up on a wild animal, fretting she could bolt at any moment. "You might at least *call* me an artist," her father once said to her mother. Madge just laughed. Gwen remembers how her father walked out of the room, the slope of those wiry-hard shoulders.

"What on earth are you doing out here!" Gwen scolded, leading her mother back inside.

Madge shrugged. "So what's it to you?"

"What's it to me? What's it to me!" Gwen lifted her shoulders angrily, dropping them back into place. How could she tell her if Madge had stumbled into the rift and fallen through geological time it would be one more notch in Gwen's desertion narrative—Father walks into the surf; husband demands a divorce; Mother plunges into the earth.

She remembers how after they arrived at Hilo Airport, she had expected to see her mother at the bottom of the escalator that leads into the terminal, waiting with leis like everyone else's family. Gwen had imagined her appearing elegant, not exactly young anymore but at least yanked and forced and coddled together, which was always her way. But she wasn't there. The air was damp and tropical, cloying scents of pikake and plumeria mingling into the spicy fragrance of maile from a recent rain shower. Gwen had forced a breath through her lungs, pointing Buddy toward the spinning carousel. "Wait for our luggage. I'll go look for Grandma."

Then she spotted her. "Mother?" Gwen whispered. She was wandering through the magazine stands, violent red hair wild about her shoulders, a Bozo-the-clown halo around her head, plaited with streaks of white in two bands to the right and left of her part like Siamese skunks. Madge Johnstone had dyed her hair since the day she found the first strands of grey lurking malevolently inside her natural auburn, brushed her hair one hundred strokes daily, and in later years wound it into a neat twist at the nape of her neck. Now her face, usually so purposefully made up, was bare of even lipstick. She used to caution her daughter, "If you have time for nothing else, take a moment to put on your lipstick. A woman can get away with most anything if she has on her lipstick." What a disappointment Gwen must have been to her mother, skimp haired and monochromatic beside her.

"Mother!" Gwen had gripped Madge's shoulders until her mother's face stared up into her own. She was foggy eyed and for a moment Gwen wasn't sure her mother recognized her.

Buddy, silent as stone appeared with their luggage. Madge gave him a bewildered, bird-eyed glance, then turned back to Gwen. "Isn't this one a bit young for you?"

"For heaven's sake that's Buddy, Richard! Your grandson?" Gwen shot him her *don't say a thing* look.

Buddy glared at them both, plunked the two overstuffed suitcases down and rubbed his eyes. Tears sprouted in the corners of Gwen's own eyes and she blinked them back.

"Well good, let's get out of here," Madge announced. "Where's the car?"

"The car? Mother, we've just come from Maine! The question is where's *your* car?"

"You don't have to shout, Gwenyth. We can always take a cab. Here, you!" She spun around, clapping her hands at a local teenaged boy slouched against a pole, thumbing through *Mad* magazine. "Are you a cab driver? We want to go home now."

The boy shot Gwen a resentful look, avoiding Madge's frantic gesturing. Gwen grabbed her mother's arm, tugging her away from the magazine stand. Was this someone's idea of a YouTube photo-op, the chic Madge Johnstone's awkward and pathetic daughter watching her mother come undone? Her mother didn't look so chic anymore!

"What for chrissake's wrong with her?" Buddy hissed, opposite side from where Gwen was lugging Madge along. He'd hoisted their luggage over both of his shoulders, making a not too pretty face.

"Don't you dare talk like that! I've told you, when you use Jesus' name you call him Jesus Christ, and you say it with respect. Not Christ and sake in one damn breath for heaven's sake!" She kicked her leg out at him but it didn't make contact. Who was she upset at anyway?

Gwen herded her mother and son into the parking lot, counting her steps under her breath. She used to do that as a child trodding reluctantly beside Madge, who's lecturing her about some thing or another, warning her, threatening, admonishing—thirteen, fourteen, fifty-nine!—as many numbers as it took. "You still have the Mustang, Mother?" Gwen prayed that she did, imagined sinking into its leather upholstery and shutting her eyes.

"What? Oh yes, wild horses wouldn't drag it away."

"Then do you have a clue where it's parked?"

"Where what is parked?"

Gwen had let go of her mother's arm, reared back and stared at her. She was wearing a burnt orange mu'umu'u with bright pink sneakers, pink the color of a cat's tongue, insides of a rabbit's ear. With orange! There was a time when Madge Johnstone wouldn't even own a mu'umu'u. "They're so tenty," she scoffed, "the blubbery woman's shroud. If you've got a shape, flaunt it."

"Mother?" Gwen whispered.

"I brushed my hair with my toothbrush," Madge confided. "Can you imagine? What was I thinking? It didn't work but I kept at it."

Gwen had held out her hand and Madge immediately grasped it, as if she was accustomed to holding her hand, as if Gwen was the person who made the world safe for her; as if between the two of them, mother, daughter, it was Gwen who must now bear this weight.

And this has been their life since, time measured by the weeks when things seemed to be growing worse, Madge forgetting how to dress herself properly, screaming at Gwen when she tried to help; then days when she was her mother again, shrewd, petulant, in control; followed by the long hours when she's a shell of a person, depressed, lifeless.

Gwen's cousin Kiki, who isn't a fan of doctors, admitted taking Madge to one before Gwen arrived, after Madge tried to "heat up" the iron by putting it on a stove burner, turning all the dials on high. But Kiki wouldn't accept the diagnosis, Transient Ischemic Attacks. "It's just a fancy name for people growing older. They don't want to deal with old folks so they tell them they have a disease. Disease my ass! She got a fever? Fighting for breath?"

Gwen took her mother back to the same neurologist, Juli Alvarez, pink cheeks, agreeable eyes, a female sensibility. "We can't always be sure what's causing these mini-strokes. They used to be thrown into a catch-all label, hardening of the arteries," Dr. Alvarez said.

"Sure, the package deal. How about telling me what's *really* going on," Gwen pleaded.

"Basically there's a narrowing of blood vessels, inflammation and spasms of the small arteries in the brain. A lot of times the brain returns to normal after an episode, but not always, which seems to be the case with your mother. The concern is that these shower strokes can be a precursor to a more debilitating stroke."

"Aren't there any, oh I don't know, *cures* out there for her condition?"

Dr. Alvarez sighed. "There are drug trials, of course, but this has progressed pretty rapidly in Madge and it's doubtful she'd qualify. I think the best we can do is keep her on blood pressure medication and aspirin, then wait and see."

You sound like my husband, Gwen thought, though she didn't say it. She had a hunch she would need an ally down the line, a medical steward of sorts.

So Gwen set up house, her son moving sullenly in and out like a shadow. What else could she do? Until a few years ago she was a middle school teacher in a withered town, middle of Maine, not even a Wal-Mart within a hundred miles. Taught social studies to three grades in one classroom, the history of the world to kids who would never get the chance to see any of it. They came to school in the dead of winter with no coats, spent their lunch money on opiates, which seemed easier to score than decent textbooks.

There was nothing she could do.

One afternoon, a couple months after their move, Buddy had roamed into the living room, Madge dozing in her chair and Gwen lingering beside the counter that divided this room from the kitchen, contemplating another glass of wine, fingering the bottle perched there. "Can we call it happy hour?" she said to him brightly. "I'll pour you a soda and we'll break out the macadamia nuts."

"This is messed up," he snarled, glaring at the bottle, Gwen, then at his grandmother who had slit open her eyes at the sound of his voice. "I don't fricken belong here." He shrugged in disgust then headed back to his bedroom.

"You think you belong with your father?" Gwen had shouted at his retreating back. She phoned Rob the week before about taking Buddy for the summer. "My mother's about all I can handle," she'd said, choking back tears. Rob said he didn't think it was "appropriate"; that it might be "confusing" for Buddy.

"Well? So where *do* you belong?" she shrilled and Madge scowled. "Answer me, son, just who do you think you are!"

He turned around at the end of the hallway, frozen stare, his dark hair glowing in the pale light steaming down from the two skylights over his head. Gwen's father had loved those windows, a glass sky! he said. "You really want to get into it, Mrs. Winter? Fine, you asked. The praying mantis sits very still. It looks like it's praying with its front legs held up, but in fact it's waiting to pounce. Its legs have numerous sharp spikes. When a smaller insect comes along the mantis' legs shoot out, the spikes dig into the insect, trap it and the mantis bites off the insect's head. So go ahead Mrs. Winter, pray for whatever it is you think you deserve, to whoever you think can give it to you. And have another drink with a Xanax chaser while you're at it. It's what you do, isn't it?"

"Drink?" Madge had peered down the hall at her grandson, a piercing, almost lucid gaze. "You, young man, are too young to drink and you"—she stared back at Gwen long and hard with more clarity than Gwen had seen for awhile—"you better quit while you're ahead. I dated a drinker once, did I tell you? Used to line up all his empty beer cans by the door in a pyramid shape so if someone came inside during the night they'd make a racket. Why would he worry about such a thing, you might ask? He was afraid someone would steal what's left of his *un*drunk beer. You hear me, daughter? It comes to this."

3

Madge

SHE CAN'T ALWAYS FORM THE right words anymore, but listen! She can tell it on the inside. If she tells you her story, Madge will remember who she is. Moments from her story are like rain. Tiny drops, these fine memories, brush up against her, misty and cool. Then they evaporate, sucked up into those clouds. But rain isn't lost. Comes back as snow, a river, the sea. Remember this: Madge is never completely lost

She was beautiful, do you believe it? The Artist adored her. Hair red as a hibiscus, skin the silk of its petals, breasts round as two moons. Her body was magnificent, The Artist said it. Though her mother was the color of polished wood, Madge is fiercely, foolishly white.

Now she is growing old. Breasts, hips, flesh runs down hill, stopping only where her belly thrusts out in a ledge. How can this be? When did this happen? Inside her head is still that beauty, but on the outside she's an old house sagging in on itself, her roof caving in at the middle. Laws of gravity dictate this, when you're old you return to the center of things. And she's wrinkled. She catches *her* in the window when the light's on the glass, watches the mountains and sees *her*, dried-up stream beds, trenches, claw marks as if from some persnickety cat. So her face is now.

She asks Gwenyth, What's happening to me? Madge took care of her when *she* was sick. Fixed her guava juice. Helped her blow her nose. Warned her about boys. Taught her lipstick. She has Madge's mouth, her father's thinness. Madge was jealous, she admits this, the way Gwenyth captured his heart. *In the end, could anybody hold on to him?*

It's like this: she's in the middle of a field of waving pili grass, fruit trees, berries, flowers and trilling birds. Starts of color and air shimmering as if the light will never end. But suddenly it's night. Moonless, black, occasional pricks of starlight. She knows she's in that field, can smell the flowers, feel the grass around her ankles. She can hold out her hand, touch the trees, slender stalks of plants. But she can't always name them, even remember *what* they are, where they are. Or where she is. She knows these things in her heart, but not in the place where language must happen, naming them, making them real.

Until the sun lights her again. Which it will, if she can just remember it.

4

Buddy – Honolulu, First Weekend As A Runaway

MARNIE SITS BESIDE HIM ON The Bus, her tight little thigh shoved up against his, vibrating to the throb of the engine. This gets Buddy thinking about sex. Not something he's managed to get much of so far. Stares out the window at Honolulu flying by, white buildings, red tile roofs blazing in the sun, eruptions of flowering trees swimming through steam and exhaust, Ko'olau mountain range like a giant green worm inching up behind. The concern du jour: Did he really run away? Almost an entire weekend gone and his mom hasn't claimed him. He'd lost the charger for his phone, then forgot the phone in his other jeans, on the floor of his bedroom, so she can't call him. He kept imagining she might appear anyway, her face snarled up into that put-upon look she gets. She'd pray, need a drink, pop a Xanax. But she'd be here.

"Well?" Marnie pummels his shoulder. "You didn't answer me from before about the motel. Couples in the movies always get a motel."

Couple? His heart hammers. Are they? They spent Friday and Saturday night on the floor at Marnie's uncle's house, the room lit up by a bare blue light bulb, a retarded old song from the sixties, "Spooky," playing over and over, *Spooookiee*. "He was in Vietnam," Marnie said, like that explained it. A motel? He slides his hand inside his pocket, the twenties are almost gone. Turns toward her, her yellowy-brown stare, then looks away. Tripler Hospital receding in the back window, a pink giant of a building where on Friday Marnie had "modeled." Today they had returned to collect her pay, a Zippy's gift certificate.

"Assholes," Marnie grumbled, "like that's what this awesome *bod* is worth? Two hamburgers, fries and an extra-large shake!"

"A hospital?" Buddy asked her when they first arrived. "What kind of hospital uses models?"

Marnie shrugged. "It's for Army guys. Probably half of them are missing body parts. It's a Christmas-in-June pageant. Like I'm supposed to parade around and look sociable. So shoot me, Buddums, don't you guess Heidi and Kate started somewhere? They weren't *born* on the catwalk."

Thinking about this now gets him thinking about Christmas. The idea of it, even the word comes back with a sick feeling, and he grabs his gut like a fist squeezing him there. Got a migraine once just listening to "Deck the Halls" in Longs Drugstore. Bright lights lit up like a tree behind his eyes, sparkle, flash, boom! roar of the chainsaw making kindling of his brain. Christmas was the end of his parents' marriage, the start of his mother's evacuation plan, uprooting them to Hawai'i.

Christmas Eve day he and his mom had driven to Portland, some last minute shopping at the mall. Heading home it was that late afternoon December dark, skeletal tree branches, the wind rose and snow spun across the road. Buddy had his learner's permit so he's behind the wheel, and his mother's sweating bullets beside him. "You learn by doing," he reminded her—her own clichés rattled back whenever they suited him. Mostly they were silent, except for her periodic, Slow Down!

Then, all of a sudden she turns toward him, says, "You know what, son? When I was a kid my mother and I drove out one night to see the volcano erupt. The sulfur was so thick you couldn't see a thing in front of you or around you, not a thing. My mother, your grandmother, was scared. Now there's a woman that doesn't scare at anything, nerves of metal. She never prayed. Not that I knew of anyway. The sort of person who just took it for granted she'd do the right thing at the right time. This time was different. She was really scared. She told me she was afraid we'd plunge right off the road's soft shoulder into the rift. I'd never seen my mother scared. Even when my father didn't come back she wasn't scared. She was mad as hell, but not scared. I'm not sure it occurred to her to *be* scared, worrying how we would live without him. This wasn't a man who would buy something so mundane as life insurance. He was an artist and a magician! Amateur, my mother called it, the sensibilities of a thoroughly impractical man, she'd say. Anyway, you couldn't see the road from all that thick sulfur. It was like driving in space. Like handing the wheel over to fate."

Buddy's mother shook her head and laughed, a sharp unhappy sound, more like a bark. In almost the same breath she said, "Well honey, the thing is I'm not sure your father and I are going to make it together. This is what I have to tell you. Do you understand? Things, pressures have been sort of building between us and it seems we've reached some kind of impasse. Turns out he's an expressway sort of guy and I'm the back roads. What I'm saying is, I don't think we can leave it up to fate anymore. *You'll want to be with me, won't you, Buddy?*"

He sat hunched over the steering wheel, hollow as pumice; *sulfur*, he's thinking, *volcano!* staring at the snow flashing wildly in the headlights, trying desperately to transport himself back into his mother's story, a different time, place, a story not about him, nothing that would affect his own life. He wasn't ready to take that step of somebody else's making into his own future. If only he could've realized that was the million-dollar question, the one that would change everything. *You'll want to be with me, won't you?* What could he have said that might have made a difference? What if he said no? What if he said fuck you, the hell with you both, *grow up*! shut off the engine and jumped out of the car into the night. Instead he said nothing. Didn't answer her, never answered her, just kept driving forward, his world unraveling behind him.

When they got home, opening the front door, shaking snow like dandruff off the shoulders of their jackets, Buddy's father stood in the hallway, burning like some oversized light fixture. "Go upstairs!" he roared, and Buddy did.

But he listened to them, for hours it seemed, standing behind the cracked open bedroom door. He couldn't make out their individual words so well, but the tone of it! His mother's voice was cold, colder than he'd heard any voice, colder than the storm pummeling snow like sand against his bedroom window. His father's a bellow of rage. Buddy heard the back door slam, the crunch of his footsteps. Then his father's Chrysler wailed out of the driveway, slipped on the icy road, stalled and screeched off again, tires spinning.

The silence from downstairs weighed on Buddy like a headache. Was he getting a headache? He felt like he might vomit. There was something different about this fight, something shut down. He didn't know what started it, never knew for sure what they were fighting about half the time when they fought. They were just two people who couldn't get along, couldn't control their anger and unfortunately had control over him.

Next day, Christmas, snow drifts piled so deep against their house they couldn't see out the downstairs windows, so high you couldn't make out the neighborhood, couldn't tell if the world outside even existed anymore. Once that would have been magic, waking up Christmas morning under so much snow.

"Like being smothered," his mother said.

Like having your whole life cave in on you, Buddy thinks now, staring out the rectangular windows of The Bus, Honolulu a hot green glimmer in the noon sun. He inhales a pungency of tropical growth and diesel fumes, still avoiding Marnie's eyes. Instead he stares at the other passengers, mostly older, Japanese and Chinese, aloha shirts and khaki pants, colorless, shapeless dresses. "Mamasans," Marnie calls the old women, a title of respect she said. A knot of local teenagers holed up in the back in oversized tee shirts and baggy pants, everyone is wearing rubber slippers, Hawai'i state footwear. Buddy gazes down at his old Filene's Basement Reeboks. They don't even have basements in Hawai'i.

"So?" Marnie asks, jabbing his elbow with a purple fingernail.

"For chrissake!" He rubs his elbow, scowls at her then looks away again. You can't keep looking at this girl's face, afraid of what you might find there.

"I don't sleep on beaches, Buddy-boy, and we can't keep hitting off my poor uncle who was in Vietnam. I need a daily shower, a full-length mirror and a real bed with sheets. Clean ones, the basics, huh?" She rides her nail down his arm, gently this time. His skin tingles at her touch. "Puh-lease?" she begs, tickling him now, her fingers scuttling up his arm like a spider.

"Are we really running away, Marnie? Nobody knows where we are." There's a fierce and sudden aching in Buddy's throat. Stares down at his Reeboks. Who would've guessed they'd turn out to be *real* running shoes.

She shrugs, puts her hand on his leg, tracing the outline of his knee through his jeans, purple nail like a crayon. "Maybe nobody cares where we are. Did you think of that? Like, maybe they just as soon we be wherever we are, where they don't have to deal with us. Out of sight, out of mind. We need your bucks, Buddy-love. For the motel. It's you and me, babe."

He sighs, gazes at her hand, curled up tenderly like a new leaf, small but determined, etching invisible hearts on his leg. Why is it things seem to get even harder when she's being nice? "Oh man," he whispers, "what happens now?" That tightness behind his eyes, in his throat. A flea can jump eight inches into the air, about a hundred times its height. If a person could do that, jump a hundred times his height, he could fly over a building forty stories high, disappear into the air and be gone.

So here's where things start getting prickly. Imagine this Honolulu night, moonlight so intense the ocean looks like it's painted, streaks of silver riding the waves like liquid lightning. Ala Moana beach bathed in it, the whiteness of salvation Buddy's mom might call it, the light before the end, just two crowded streets from where the Palm Gardens Motel sits at an intersection off Keeaumoku, leading into Waikiki.

OK, so he couldn't actually *see* the beach from their motel room, like he could afford a fricken ocean view? You could hear the traffic though, horns blaring like swarms of mosquitoes, cars surging back and forth. You could hear the drip drip drip of the bathroom faucet, TV droning from the next room, the in and out of Marnie's breath sleeping on the queen sized bed beside him, a barrier of towels and clothes she erected between them. "No way!" she hissed a half hour earlier, pulling away from his kiss, his hand strolling across her stomach.

Well fine, he wasn't so sure he wanted to either, to tell you the truth, not after the night they just had. He thought maybe she was expecting it, a *couple* in a motel and all. Like in the movies, right? But he knew she was still mad. Here's how that went: Earlier that evening they had taken a taxi to the heart of Waikiki, which Marnie insisted on even though Buddy told her he spent too much money on the motel. "I'm sick of The Bus," she whined. "It makes my head hurt." Right, he thought, like this girl would know a headache? But there they were, Aloha Cab, the driver listening to a Filipino radio station, words shot out like strings of firecrackers.

Buddy settled uneasily against the back seat. He was thinking about a man in a wheelchair he'd seen earlier in the Tripler Hospital lobby waiting for Marnie to collect her pay, silvery eyes like two minnows, friendly enough, smile wide as a mitt. That's what this man had asked him, "You like to play ball?" Buddy nodded yes to be polite, though these days he couldn't care less about sports. "Soccer, football, baseball, which?" he continued blinking those fishy eyes. Buddy just kept nodding, trying to ignore the wheelchair, the man's pant legs hanging empty as balloons. Something about him reminded Buddy of his dad. For a ridiculous moment he imagined tossing a football with this man, low so he could catch it from his wheelchair, this man throwing it back, a fierce and perfect arch. Not that Buddy's father played ball with him much. "Wait," he would say, or "Maybe this weekend."

The taxi got caught in traffic on Kapiolani Boulevard, horns bleeting, evening sky pink with a slant of gold that lit up the tops of a row of palms. They looked like a brigade of giant, feather-capped soldiers. "Check out the army," he whispered to Marnie, but she was plugged into her iPod.

Which gave Buddy plenty of time to think, and what he thought about was stealing his grandmother's money. Would she hate him even more if she knew, if she *could* know? He was pretty sure she didn't like him much, even before he became a thief. The last time he saw his grandmother before moving here was when she visited them in Maine, long time ago it seems now. It was winter, a *real winter* as they say in Maine, not the half-ass, global-warming ones they've had of late, and his grandmother bitched non-stop about the cold, the snow, spent more time attending to the weather than she did to Buddy. Every morning after a fresh snowfall she'd peer out of a frosty window, sour-faced, calculate the amount like she's adding up somebody's debts. "Well," she'd announce, "ground's four inches closer to the roof. One day, mark my words, it'll swallow your house." His mom said his grandmother complained about the heat and humidity in Hawai'i. "She's a person who never found her place," Gwen said.

And Buddy thought about his mom, whom he lied to. That kid in his English class, the one he told her he was staying with, probably didn't even know his last name. But he was tired of the way she was so consumed with his grandmother. OK, so maybe it wasn't very mature of him, but he wondered if his mother even remembered *him*, always saying how his grandmother couldn't remember things, how she had to be a mind for them both. Buddy missed the way his mother used to be with him when he was younger, when things were different. Sometimes he even wished she would touch him the way she used to. Head on her lap she'd tickle his ear, her finger tracing the rim as if it were some perfect shell.

His musings were interrupted by a sharp jab in the ribs. "Look!" Marnie pointed out the Aloha Cab's window.

"Damnit Marnie, stop poking me all the time! Am I meat or something?"

"What*ever*. Like you're lost in space, Bud-o, I need you back on planet Earth. Look!" she insisted again, grabbing his chin, jamming it in the direction of the window.

They were beside the Ala Wai canal, inching toward downtown Waikiki. He saw what she wanted him to see, on the lit-up grassy strip between the road and the water, a cluster of boys had surrounded and were taunting a small black dog. The Ala Wai glowed with patches of silver like floating coins, from the street lamps, and the lights from closely packed condominiums on the other side of the road. The driver turned up the radio, some mournful Filipino ballad ricocheted through the cab.

"You know what they're doing, right? They eat dogs in *certain* neighborhoods." She pointed significantly at the driver's skinny neck. "They think it's a delicacy," she whispered.

"For chrissake Marnie!" Buddy's cheeks burned. He prayed the driver hadn't heard her, visions of being locked up for eternity in an Aloha Cab, meter running, radio blaring a language that sounded like nails on a chalkboard to his haole ears, and he's not talking fingernails. There are glimpses of hell other than what you might read in the Bible. "Maybe that dog's lost and they're trying to bring it back, is all."

Marnie shook her head and a hunk of her hair drifted lazily across his arm. "Give me a break, Buddy babes. Face the facts. Lost dog in Hawai'i one night is barbecue the next. The black ones are best. Something about the way the sun sinks into black fur, gets absorbed, bakes the skin. Like a marinade."

He closed his eyes. Flashes of lights, shooting stars, the signal he's getting one of his headaches. Maybe he could stall it. Breathed deeply, tried to empty his mind of all the paranoid little thoughts that kept parading through it—kidnapped by the taxi driver for insulting his culture, forced to listen to Filipino radio talk shows 24 hours a day; tried to force the temperature of his skin down thinking *cool*, Maine in October, that sort of thing. He didn't bring his migraine meds to Honolulu. His mom would've packed them for him.

In Maine they shoot deer, even moose, but they don't eat dogs. Buddy's dog Blinky died in his mom's arms. Heart failure, couldn't walk anymore, even drawing a breath was almost too much trouble so they euthanized her. He missed her still. And he missed Maine. He missed his neighborhood, old houses standing staunch through all those winters. He missed the hills, giant evergreens that grow bigger in his memory of them, that craggy green land and no traffic.

He opened his eyes, staring at Marnie rolling about on her tight little butt to her iPod's playlist. But he didn't have Marnie in Maine, that was one thing he didn't have. Hell, he didn't have *any* girlfriends in Maine.

"Hey!" she nudged him, "there's the International Marketplace." Palm trees and Tiki torches, the brashness of ukuleles accompanying someone singing in a wobbly, high tenor, chaotic laughter, the buzz of evening activity all floating in through the open cab windows, along with the pungent scent of night-blooming jasmine mingling into whiffs of a woman's perfume.

"We here already!" the driver snapped, pulling up near but not inside the loading zone at the curb where a tour bus sat, engine idling. He turned around and stared expectantly.

Buddy dug deep into his pocket, his head then heart pounding. Where's the other fifty? Wiggled his fingers around, pulling at the lining, sand, grit, stickiness. Yanked his hand out, gazing dumbly at his empty fingers.

"Pay the dude!" Marnie whispered. "Like what the hell?" A line of cars were stopped behind the cab unable to pass, blowing their horns.

"Eight dollar fifty!" the driver barked.

Shoved his hands into both pockets just in case, inhaled a breath of the bus's exhaust, the violent heat of the traffic. A wail of horns made his head feel like there's a jack hammer inside, tearing up the concrete of his synapses, inching toward his brain. Wham! imagined the explosion, blood, bits of skin like confetti, no more headache. He whispered, "For chrissake my money's gone!"

Marnie stared at him, those yellowy-brown eyes glowering like a predator's in the near dark. Suddenly she throws open the cab door, jumps out into the traffic, grabbing his hand and yanking him behind her. "Run!" she shrieked.

Buddy didn't turn around to see if the driver, who rattled out a stream of something fierce and unintelligible, was coming after them. Head reeling, he followed Marnie's fleeing shape, darting in and out of the line of cars toward Kuhio Beach. "I wouldn't *never* have brought you to Honolulu if I knew you didn't have enough money!" she shouted, "what a loser."

They ended up walking back to the motel, Marnie forgetting whatever it was she had been so insistent that Waikiki could offer, a silence between them like the silence of death. Buddy counted his steps. He had learned this from his mom when the headache pain is unbearable. "Counting makes you feel more in control," she said. Made it to a hundred then stopped.

So shouldn't he have suspected this was only the beginning, tip of the iceberg, that sort of thing? Not just one night gone bad, but a life that somehow took a wrong turn? Iceberg looming in the blue-black darkness, his future careening toward it? Back at the motel Buddy's unable to sleep,

Marnie purring behind her barrier of clothes and towels, and he's staring at walls lit by the headlights of passing cars and the globe of a distant moon. Now he's a thief *and* a fugitive. Pretty uncool for someone who wanted to be an entomologist. Would he even be able to go home again?

5

Gwen

THE COUCH OF NO RETURN, Gwen thinks, sprawled face down on it, her mother asleep in her chair and Gwen remembering how Madge used to wait for him on this couch, after the police brought the broken surfboard home, after the Hilo Tribune-Herald announced "presumed drowned," after Auntie Violet held a memorial for her brother because his own wife wouldn't. "No!" Madge shook her head vehemently, sparks of her auburn hair. "He's probably having the time of his life in Tahiti." Then she ordered Gwen not to speak her father's name.

She seemed to believe he would walk into their house at any moment, pull up a chair, his sheepish grin. For a while Gwen too hunkered down on this couch beside her mother, mute, barely breathing. "Sit still!" Madge hissed. Was she listening for his steps up the lava path leading to their front door? Every evening Madge would make up her face like she was getting ready for a date, carefully apply lipstick, stroke of lime eye shadow highlighting those green eyes, change out of her Capri pants, zip on a sundress, brush that auburn hair until it glowed pink in the late light of the room.

Every evening the rituals more determined, a ferocious beating of the brush through her long hair splayed across the back of the couch. In the morning Gwen would find strands the color of fire, stretched and sinewy, glistening on the green upholstery.

This when childhood was still new, when an adult could tell you anything and you would believe them. Gwen imagined how he'd look coming up from the sea. Would he be covered with seaweed like some swamp creature? Would he speak the language of fishes? Would she get to talk to her father again? She felt this constant ache at the back of her throat that became a kind of burning, sitting beside her sullen mother, wind scratching about in the ohia trees outside. Later she'd tiptoe into the kitchen, try to drown that fire from her throat with ice water before going to bed, alone. Her mother no longer tucked her in.

Then Madge stopped waiting. She wore the silk kimono he gave her on their first anniversary every hour of the day and night. Face not made up, hair unwashed, unbrushed, she stopped waiting and started nagging Gwen: "Did you even out the rows of wood in the wood pile? Well, why not? Are you *shirking* because he's not here to witness? We'll need to work harder, prove that his absence means *nothing*."

Six months after her husband disappeared Madge took over his store, his debts, the trappings of his life. Gwen turned nine and her mother forgot her birthday, and it was then that she started seeing everything in terms of her father never doing these things again. On the day of her birthday she woke up shivering on the glassed-in lanai that had been in those days her bedroom, dawn leaking in, yellow-orange fragments through a cracked window. He won't see the sun again, she thought. She wished herself Happy Birthday in the bathroom mirror thinking he wouldn't give her a present. Brushed her teeth, he wouldn't brush his anymore; pulled up her shorts, thought how he couldn't wear clothes. Eating Cheerios, drinking the canned guava juice her mother made her drink, making a sour face until Madge said, "Don't spite me, missy, you drink it because I say so!" Gwen thought how her father wouldn't eat, drink, sleep, wake, *breathe* a single breath, anymore.

That night in the bathtub, after her mother's bath and using the same water—they're on catchment in Volcano, water tanks going dry as bone on a run of hot weather, so that it becomes habit to share a bath during any season, save water, be prepared—Gwen stuck her face down into the grey tepid liquid that still smelled of her mother, closed her eyes and inhaled until she choked. Sputtering, eyes pulled wide open in panic, the burning at the back of her throat suddenly quit and she could cry. Her father was not coming back.

And now Buddy is gone. But not *disappeared*, Gwen reminds herself. Sitting up she pours herself another glass of claret from the bottle parked on the coffee table, its contents clear as garnet. He's on O'ahu, staying with Marnie's uncle. "Todd's a Vietnam vet who thinks he's got that PMS thing," Marnie's mother told Gwen on the phone when she called.

"You mean PTSD, don't you?" Gwen asked. "Post traumatic stress disorder?"

"Whatever. The point is he doesn't really have it. Couldn't in my opinion, he was only there long enough to get a twig up his ass when he squatted down to do his business. They had to surgically remove the thing if you can believe that, your tax dollars at work."

"What on earth?" Gwen asked, not really sure what she was asking, or what she'd hope to hear as an answer. Her cheeks flamed. *Marnie's* mom.

"We were told a mine went off close by to where Todd's doing his thing, so he sits down real hard, startled like. They sent him home with a Purple Heart, but he gets it in his mind that in the meantime he was exposed to Agent Orange. Go figure. That's what I know."

"Well…" Gwen said. What was there to say? She waited for *her* to say something, the kinds of things mothers say to each other, reassure Gwen her son will be fine, that Todd is a parent himself, or he always wanted to be one, or at the least he's capable of being around teenagers without screwing them up even more than they are! The "mom" kinds of things none of them believe, but somehow makes them feel a little better, like they're in it together. Then again, did she want to be in *anything* with Marnie's mom? Gwen said goodbye and hung up.

She started praying hard, every hour, every night, for Buddy's safety and the return of his senses. It's all she had. What was she supposed to do? Fly to Honolulu, search for whatever wretched hole this Uncle Todd person is squatting in and scold her son out of there, as if he over-stayed his welcome and he's late for dinner, something *normal* like that?

When Buddy called the first time Gwen shrieked at him, told him she'd sic the police on him if he didn't get home immediately. Bad move, but it's not like you're thinking too clearly when your kid runs away. "For Lord's sake!" she told him, "you leave me here with an ill mother, all alone, tell me nothing about where you are so I'm worried sick on top of it all!" That was another mistake. He's not in the mood to hear how *she's* doing, taking care of his grandmother. "No *problemo*, Mrs. Winter," he snarked. "You want someone to depend on you. So she's a little old." Then he hung up, and when she star 69'd the number no one answered. Payphone, he'd told her, don't even bother.

It was three days before he called again. That was when he told her he'd be staying with Marnie's Uncle Todd. "I'll be working for the Pineapple Company," he said, "but I need money, just until I get my first paycheck. I'll pay you back."

"You don't have your migraine meds!" Gwen pleaded with him. "You've got to have your medicine, let me bring it to you!" Clunk, he hangs up and she's left wondering what he was doing, what he was wearing, what he was eating, and whether he was sleeping with that Marnie! Gwen wondered if he loved her more than she. It's tragic, the petty things a mind stews over even in dire emergency. No wonder you hear about people wanting to change their underwear when they're all but stricken on the floor with a heart attack, the ambulance on its way.

What she said to Rob when he called was, "He's got this job in Honolulu for the summer, with the Pineapple Company."

"Managerial?" Rob asked.

"Sure," she lied. He's managing. He's sixteen, he could drop out of school and she'll never see her son again! "He's doing fine," she said to Rob.

Of course, Gwen has to wonder if it's her fault. She's a mother and that's the nature of the thing, the job description. *Wanted, a weak-kneed guilt-ridden pushover-type person to assume full legal care of another until that other reaches eighteen, and then worry about him for the rest of her life, knowing everything that goes wrong in his life is somehow her damn fault!* There were times when she used to think how nice it would be if Buddy was grown up, living his life someplace else and she had her own life back again. Sometimes she wished it, for him to be grown up and gone, his sullen, defiant presence not such a constant reminder of her failures. But she never imagined he'd do it *now*. Was she that awful? Her own father walked into the sea, husband's filing for divorce, son runs away and her mother's headed off a damn cliff, Gwen swears, and seems to be basking in the stress she's causing, aiming to take Gwen with her.

Madge is awake now and staring out the window. Gwen wants to grab her mother, shake those intractable shoulders she tried so hard to nestle against when she was a child. She had to learn to depend on those shoulders, grown thinner now; what choice did she have? Snap out of it! Gwen wants to shriek. You think you're the only one who's been left? Simple things have become a nightmare of complexity. Just a month ago it was, I'll help you get dressed, Mother. Now Gwen's yanking Madge's pants up, tugging her shirt down over her head, jamming her fighting, waving, antennae arms into her sleeves, all the while Madge is shouting curses. "You sonofabitch, you rascal, imbecile, marauder!" Like she's testing vocabulary words for their fit. Gwen has to knot the ends of her shirts together, because Madge has torn off all the buttons. "Grow up!" Gwen screamed at her a few days ago, then drank herself stupid later that night. It's not her mother's fault. She knows that. She'll never be a candidate for the Rapture, that's for sure, not that Gwen figured she had a shot. If she were Catholic she could repent, go to confession, say Hail Marys, get absolved. What do you do when there's no one to confess to?

This morning she was forced to tie Madge to her rocking chair. Tying up her own mother has got to be the last straw, but yesterday at dusk Madge raced through the house, knocking things over, this diminished little hellion of a person yanks open the front door, then books it out into the field, an old wild woman disappearing into the pili grass like some ratty bird. "Don't let them get me!" she shrieked. Then she was gone. The rift! Gwen immediately panicked, her childhood threat: Watch where you run off to, behave yourself or you'll fall into the rift, get *swallowed up*!

It was growing dark and she had to call the police, a search and find mission, her mom as target, a helicopter hovering above the kipuka forest, lights flashing, propeller beating the air.

"Maybe your mother should be in a nursing home," one officer suggested, "where they'd take care of her." Maybe *you* should be put out of my misery! Gwen thought. "She's too young for a nursing home," she told him. They found her finally, hunkered down under a koa tree, trembling like a trapped animal.

So fine! Gwen thinks, glaring at her mother whose face is as flat and expressionless as the glass she's fixated on, she'll send Buddy what little money she has, pretend he really is just working there, a summer job on another island. Kids get them, summer jobs, and there's less to get on the Big Island, even less up at Volcano. Stands to reason he'd go to Honolulu. Normal as pie. She'll be cheerful when he calls. And oh so gently she'll remind him about school starting up again in September, mail him a ticket to fly home at that time. She won't send the police out after her son, maybe they'd want to put *him* in a home!

Lord she could ring that Marnie's neck! He was a mostly good kid who liked bugs and got headaches, before he met that girl. Let *her* put a cool washrag on his forehead when he's down with a migraine. Let *her* hold his hands when he feels such despair he begs for a knife, cut out the headache and be done with it.

6

Buddy

AFTER THAT NIGHT IN THE Palm Gardens Motel they had spent the next on Kuhio Beach. Marnie was beyond pissed; no money for food, hiss of the waves sliding up on the shore, Go home, Go home. Todd, Marnie's lunatic uncle, was in Tripler Hospital for a "treatment" and his hippie pals were using his place for the night. Marnie refused to stay there with his friends. "I'm a model," she said, "I don't spend the night with waistoid freaks. You're a fuck-up, Buddy, you know that, right?"

"You think the cops will come after us for stiffing that taxi?" Buddy asked her. He was too busy being stunned at the sudden and savage detour his life had taken, a train derailing, taste of its burnt metal at the back of his throat, to worry much about what she was thinking of him. At least at that point. First he's a thief, then a runaway, now he's a fugitive? How the hell could a fifty-dollar bill just disappear? That night on Kuhio he had looked at Marnie suspiciously, her profile unyielding as some goddess in the moonlight, stony and severe. He concluded she wasn't the type to bring misery on herself by making *any* money disappear. If she stole it, they wouldn't be sitting there together.

"*Hello*? Duh, they'll be after you. They'll catch you and lock you up in the Bad Boys Home. Ever seen it? They work them in the hot sun all day and at night the mahus throw raping parties. So there's a place where it's better to give than receive, wouldn't you agree, Buddy?" Of course, funny thing about that—remembering all of this now, lying beside Marnie on a mattress at Todd's place—*he* works in the hot sun all day in the goddamn pineapple fields, and at night she turns away from him like he's some kind of leper. Sometimes he imagines just doing her, rolling over on top of the clothes, the sheets, the shoes she has piled up between them, and taking her; like his grandmother's money, that easy. He's feeling really weird about that money at this point, and really weird about his grandmother. The money just flat out disappeared. Maybe she put some kind of curse on him for stealing it?

That night on Kuhio Beach he had reached for Marnie's hand. He needed the press of something real to soothe his fear and another head-ache coming on. The pain was ebbing and flashing directly behind his right eyeball, keeping time with the rhythm of the waves, flash in, slide out, in, out. She swatted his fingers like he's a fly. "No dude's ever made me sleep in some beach park, and you want to hold hands? Do I look like a wino, Buddy? Some pathetic loser? Do I push my life around in a Foodland basket for chrissake, mumble sweet nothings to my fifteen fuckin' selves?"

"Well sor-ry," he muttered, collapsing down on the sand, pressing his head into its grainy coolness. He wanted to cry but no way would he give her that satisfaction. Shut his eyes and pretended to sleep, pain ripping through his head like a gale's in there, and then he guesses he did sleep, world famous Waikiki Beach fading out behind him, sigh of its surf.

In the morning Marnie was sitting cross-legged on the shore like some beached chieftain, her yellowy-brown stare fixed into a distance of aqua sea. Mynah birds were chattering up a storm from the edge of the park's grass.

"I got it figured out," she announced, when Buddy inched down the sand beside her, "follow me."

He yawned, gazed longingly at the public bathrooms where a knot of puffed-up locals hung around the concrete entrance pointing at them, their crude remarks. They probably assumed he did something he didn't get to do. Decided to hold back his pee, hoping he wouldn't have to defend whatever honor Marnie might have. Buddy followed her off the beach and onto Kalakaua, mingling with the throngs of summer tourists already out. "I hate them," Marnie said. "I hate how they leave places I'll never even get to go to."

"Places like Iowa," he snorted.

"That's not the point, Buddy, duh. Like they have the freedom to do that, huh? To fly somewhere else, then they bitch about crowded restaurants, or the cab is late. They're clueless about us real folks who live here, they could care less. Like we're just a decoration, make it more real or something."

Buddy shrugged, grateful that for once she wasn't going off on him.

The morning was pink, mynahs cackled and doves cooed in between surges of traffic. He brushed sand off his shoulders and pants. His head still hurt but a few hours of sleep had taken the edge off. Marnie pulled out two pairs of dark glasses from Super Purse, the giant lahala bag she hauled around. Next she dug her hand in and yanked out a brush, pulling it through his hair as they strolled down the street, securing his hair into a tight mini ponytail using a rubber band she pounced on off the sidewalk. Then she rubbed Hawaiian Tropics oil into it, also a Super Purse find, dragging a few greasy curls over his ears. The touch of her fingers on his neck, and Buddy's eyes sprouted with tears; lucky he had on the sunglasses.

"Now you look more like a local instead of a mainland haole. The cops'll be searching for some shark-skinned tourist boy. Your mother will give them a picture of you, huh?"

"My m...m...mother?" he felt suddenly sick again.

"Yeah, your m..m..m..m..mother!" she mimicked, "shit yeah. Like the pigs will put out a all-points. She would've reported you missing to the Hilo P.D. Ah oh, busted! Can you grow a beard with that lilikoi fuzz on your chin? You'll have to snake a shirt, Maine Lobster Fest is a dead give-away, and anyway it makes you look a dork. A lobster festival, like wow, I'm so impressed. Lobsters are giant sea scorpions. How cool can that be?"

"*Snake*?" he asked, his heart going thump thump, a dog beating its tail inside his chest.

"Dude, get real. Like how did you plan on us grinding, buying food with the money you don't have? Honestly, Buddy, you're a sweet guy but you can be such a loser."

"I thought we'd stay at your uncle's, when he comes out of Tripler?"

"Well sure, be a loser, a bum *and* a mooch! How you think Todd's supposed to feed us? Huh? Ever consider that? He's got a disability. Grow up, Bud-o, and get this: your childhood has just come to a screaming end."

"Screeching," he sighed. "I think the cliché is screeching, not screaming."

"Whatever, ask me if I care. It's haole talk." She shrugged, and he had a sudden impulse to nibble a chunk out of her shoulder, suck in a mouthful of that satiny skin. Buddy had stopped walking then, planting his feet on the busy sidewalk outside the International Marketplace, twangy noises from ukuleles, throngs of tourists scouting for cheap souvenirs, shrieks of laughter echoing from inside. Inhaled a plume of diesel from a passing bus melding into the humid, flower-fragrant air and coughed. The sky above a lapis-blue, like it was spray-painted. "Christ Marnie, maybe we should just give this up and go home. My m..m..mother would send plane tickets, one for you too." He hesitated, sucked in a careful breath. She's staring at him, but luckily he didn't have to eyeball those yellowy-browns behind her own dark glasses. "I just don't get why we're doing this. What's the point? It was cool for a while, but it's becoming, I don't know, something else. Something hard."

Marnie grabbed his arm, boring her chipped purple fingernail into his still sandy skin. "You don't know what the hell you're talking about! You don't know what hard is! There are worse things and for me home's one of them. Let's just make this work, OK sweetie? I'm hungry. We have to snake us some grind. We're a couple aren't we? That means we stick together, us against them, huh, my love?" She breathed *my love* into his ear, her hot tongue flicking out those two magical words against his lobe, pulling her arm all the way around his neck, squeezing close enough where he could feel her breast pillow against his chest. He stretched his free arm around her, sliding his hand discreetly under her shirt. Sighed. He understood *my love* is just an expression, the way people sign love at the bottom of a card, even an email; love, my love. Still, when opportunity knocks, don't you just have to answer?

"And anyway," Marnie said leading Buddy into Tong's market off Kuhio, the two of them still side by side, Siamese twins, attached at her breast and his hand, "When I'm a famous model I'll pay you back double. I'll keep you, the way rich dudes keep their mistresses. You can sit around all day and study bugs while I nail the catwalk. You'd like that, huh? Nothing to do but bone up on bugs?"

He sighed again, still trying to concentrate on that breast. He thought better of correcting her *bugs* terminology with *insects,* in case it distracted her out of her mood that lets him do this. It didn't even concern him that the flagpole in his jeans announced his attachment; trying to hide it would mean breaking them apart.

"So the trick here," she whispered, strolling him through the dairy products aisle, its flickering fluorescent lights illuminating cartons of milk, haphazardly stacked yogurts, pink and yellow chunks of cheese, "is to act casual. Move like you got a purpose, but at the same time scout out the area for security cameras. Above all don't look scared. Know what you're nabbing, check to be sure nobody sees, then chuck it down your pants, under your shirt. Meanwhile I'll distract the cashier dude."

"Wait! Marnie, what do you mean? I have to do this? Why can't you?"

"Buddy, Buddy," she shook her head. "Look at me. Let's think this through. Do I have a t-shirt on? Just how much cheese can a tank top hide?" Then she was off, sidling up to the clerk. So now he's a fugitive and a shoplifter too? He inched through the narrow aisles, head and heart pounding. There were packages of foods with Asian characters scrawled on their labels, jars of sticky looking black stuff, Li hing moi, shredded ginger, dried squid, bottles of unidentifiable floating substances in thick liquid—not much he'd want to buy let alone risk stealing. The food looked to Buddy, this kid from Maine, like it was straight out of some sci-fi movie, like it could come alive in its cellophane, its scrubby jars, mealy liquid and all, rise up on scaly little legs and chase him out of the store. Either that or it was a parasitic brew, hatching something that would live inside him, his intestines its buffet, throw parties for its buds, maybe burst from his stomach one night like the Alien. He shuddered and rubbed his forehead, hammering its distress at his temples, damp with sweat, warm and clammy.

By the time Buddy reached the luncheon meats he was seeing colors. His migraine was back, full-on torpedo rush of a fast and furious supersonic jet, whooooosh! He had to grab something or Marnie would ditch him for sure, maybe latch onto one of those bleached surfer types that prowl Waikiki, hair drifting about their tan faces in blow-dried clouds, toting their boards under their arms. He wondered if they ever actually went into the water, wouldn't it ruin their hairdos? He knew if he didn't act quickly he'd end up vomiting all over the sand-encrusted vinyl floor. Heart thrashing in his chest, hand shaking like palsy Buddy snatched a package of bologna, the most plausibly edible thing he could see; shoving it down his unbuttoned jeans, he lurched back out the open door and into the sunshine.

They ate under a palm tree near the beach, white sand, aquamarine water, the warm breeze playing them like everything was oh-so-tropical and idyllic, just a couple of youngsters picnicking by the beach. Marnie plucked two cans of cream soda and a package of Ding Dongs from Super Purse. "My contribution. Next time get bread too. News flash, people eat bread with bologna, like that's the reason bologna exists, so you can eat it with bread. Mustard's a plus. Most folks eat bologna sandwiches with mustard. Maui Onion is ono-awesome. The trick to snaking quantity is you unzip your pants before you go in, stick out your opu so you look fat under your shirt. Nobody suspects fat people of being criminals, because they're fat people."

Buddy shook his head. "*Unbutton*, Marnie, these jeans have buttons. I can't unzip them for the ease of stealing, but I suppose you wouldn't have noticed that." What was he supposed to say? Tried to swallow a bite of Ding Dong, but it scratched like pebbles in his throat, and he spit it into the short grass. It occurred to Buddy he had no control over anything anymore.

LATER THAT AFTERNOON TODD TOLD them about the pineapple fields, after returning from his treatment at Tripler. They'd been hanging out on his front door stoop waiting for him. Marnie decided they had no choice but to impose on her uncle. "Give him whatever he wants," she commanded, "we owe him."

"They fight chemicals with more goddamn chemicals," Todd sighed. "I lie there and they just pump the shit in my blood. Makes me feel like a new man, for little bit anyway." He planted big wet "howzit!" lips over Marnie's. "Course you folks can live with me babe, we're family, huh? But you'll have to work because, you know, I can't." He shrugged. "Da kine chemical disability, yeah? It's what you call entrenched. These guys came back from Iraq and Afghanistan with new shit, and I'm not saying I don't empathize with the dudes and dudesses, but mine's been going down for years. Means I should get seniority or something."

Buddy peered around his new neighborhood, the Waikiki Jungle, clusters of termite chewed beach shacks and two story garden apartments all crowded together, flat yellow yards—the off-the-beach area the hotels hadn't catabolized, a scrappy little neighborhood in between Kalakaua and the Ala Wai. Todd stuck his hand out to seal the deal. Buddy shook it, fleshy and damp, then let it drop. He stared at Todd's big shirtless belly, which announced his presence before the rest of him, then back to his cavernous grin. "Maybe a grenade," Marnie told Buddy later when he asked her what happened to Todd's teeth. "He's our family's only hero. The only one who ever even got out of Hawai'i."

They followed him into his house, the darkened living room, blinds shut, peeling wallpaper, smells of historic food and the pungency of pot and rotting bananas. Mid-afternoon but some of the hippies were still passed out on the lauhala mat carpet.

"OK folks, aloha *o-yeah*, I got *renters* now!" Todd said. When nobody budged he kicked a torn chair, white stuffing drooling out like it's foaming at the mouth. "Incoming, wake the fuck up!" he shouted. "Have to let folks know what's what," he said, winking at Marnie, who grinned like he'd said something clever.

After everyone left in clouds of pot and patchouli oil, they sat down in the cramped room, its furniture "reclaimed" from sidewalk discards and Salvation Army showrooms. "Looks gnarly," Todd admitted, "but I'm not what you'd call a *Better Homes and Gardens* dude." Buddy studied a brown spider slowly spinning its web in a corner; at least it would never be disturbed by anyone dusting. "Blow?" Todd asked, digging into the pocket of his jeans, pulling out a scrupulously folded slip of paper. Buddy was reminded of a junior high school game where you write down names of girls, fit young teachers, rock stars, American Idol champs and other hotties du jour, fold the paper into different angles and when a kid picks a particular fold, that's the person he'll "do." If only it were that easy. "Care for a lick of candycaine?" he grinned. Buddy peered over at Marnie ogling her uncle, like his was a performance created just for her.

Todd grabbed an ancient *Penthouse* off a brick and board shelf, put it on his lap and dumped a portion of the white powder out of its paper onto Miss Whomever's pumped-up chest, chopping, spreading three even lines with a gritty looking comb he yanked from behind his ear. Buddy's stomach did that shrink-wrap thing, squeezing its contents. "Don't matter if I get hooked on this shit because they'll just shoot me up with some other god-damn shit at my treatments. It's called pick your shit, yeah?"

Buddy had intended to shake his head when Todd offered him a line, but then he looked over at Marnie glowering at him, those bobcat eyes. "Don't insult him," she mouthed.

"We can yak about the pineapple fields after we're amped," Todd said, "good opportunities there. I know a guy could get you folks right in, yeah? Trust me, it'll work out."

Now Buddy turns on his side away from Marnie and the barrier she erected between them. The night is humid with its mingling odors of pot, the stale mattress that's become their bed, and the canned chili they had for dinner. He thinks about carrion beetles, a smaller, flatter beetle than most people are familiar with. Carrions are scavengers who feed on decaying animal carcasses; nature at its best, nothing goes to waste. Buddy closes his eyes.

7

Gwen

GWEN TUGS MADGE OFF THE chair like she's a rag doll and begins dressing her. "For crying out loud, Mother, you got bones in your legs?"

Madge squeals, wriggles, curses, but Gwen's grip is firm.

"Well that's an ugly shirt. I don't look good in ugly clothes!"

"Now wouldn't you think that fashion is the last thing we ought to be concerned about here, hmmm?" Gwen shakes her head, stares at her mother. The sagging skin on Madge's forearms hangs out of the sleeveless top like two elephant trunks. "Jesus Christ," Gwen mutters, "with respect!" The pain of Buddy's leaving suddenly punches her hard. She sucks in a ragged breath. "I think I need a drink."

With Madge in tow Gwen heads toward the kitchen, Madge wagging her finger. "It's a little early don't you think?"

"Look around and tell me, is anyone missing? Am I a mother without a son here? Nothing is too early when your child is gone. I said I need a damn, excuse me, drink."

Madge snaps, "So drink then! Just what do you think you're doing with me?" She yanks at Gwen's hand around her wrist, makes a motion to unfurl it like dough.

"We're going out, that's what I'm doing with you. Since lately you've been acting like a child, I get to treat you like one and hold onto you." She pours her wine then lugs Madge out the door. *Guide her firmly*, Dr. Alvarez said, *but don't yank.* This when Gwen tried to haul her mother out of her office, after Madge engineered a sit-down strike on her doctor's desk. *Remember, inside a person afflicted is an adult who's known a lifetime.*

"What if Buddy calls? Shouldn't you be home? You don't have a cell phone."

"I can't afford a cell phone here! We're just going to take a little drive, that's all. I thought it would be nice, and I need to get out of this house for a bit."

"You need it? You, you, you."

Gwen sips from a plastic cup filled with burgundy, tart in her throat, plodding the familiar path, Madge pinching her arm. "OK Mother, *we* need it."

She fires up the Mustang after they've settled inside, the motor roars, sputters, chokes and stalls, then she does it again. "Jesus Mother, you ever get this thing tuned-up?" Madge sits in the passenger seat, brittle as straw. Gwen backs slowly out the dirt driveway, then heads up the road.

She rubs her aching forehead. "Jesus!" she whispers again, more like a plea. Her eyes burn and her stomach hurts. What she really wants to do is to curl up and sleep, pop two Xanax, maybe three, dreamless. She places her hand tentatively on Madge's leg, quivering in the passenger seat like something caged. Is she frightened? Gwen peers over at her mother's eyes gazing stonily ahead out the window. "Hell-o?" She waves her hand in front of Madge's face. No sign of life. Is she prepping for a *catastrophic reaction*, Dr. Alvarez's term for the way Madge can have a flat affect one moment, then suddenly she's grotesquely excitable and paranoid over who knows what?

They pass the Bird Park on the Mauna Loa Strip road, then continue winding as far up the mountain as you can get in a car. On both sides there are groves of koa trees, slim young ones and the huge towering 100-foot variety Hawaiians built their canoes from. Leaves are silvery and shimmer in the rare air that becomes sweeter and thinner the higher up they drive. They pass ohia trees with fiery red lehua blossoms, Pele's flowers, growing abundant in the old broken-up lava flows. Pele, the Hawaiian volcano goddess. Life amongst the ruins. Gwen stares out the windshield at the landscape, thinking how foreign she feels to it now, out of place and out of touch with everything she once loved. A bitter taste on her tongue, blinking back tears. *Buddy!*

Madge's eyes remain fixed ahead.

Gwen parks the truck at the top of the road, shuts off the engine and climbs out, then reaches in and slides her mother to the edge of the seat, carefully lowering her legs to the ground. Madge's once shapely calves are tent spikes now, spindly and bent. She makes a *Huuunh!* sound, scowls at Gwen. "Leave me be. What's wrong with you?" she sputters.

With Madge's hand locked firmly into Gwen's, they stroll over to the edge of the old pavement where a trail begins, shards of green olivines glittering in the dirt. Spread out below is Kilauea, its craters stark above the cloud-line. A quilt of clouds stretches over the rest of the island, a slap of violet ocean beyond. Pu'u O'o steams in the distance. Gwen sucks in her breath. The raw beauty of this land always made her long for something, and she's not even sure what, but there's that familiar ache.

"Goddammitall," she whispers, trying out the words almost tenderly; maybe if she runs them together it doesn't count as a swear? Forget it, it'll all be done soon enough. Though one must also prepare for the possibility of being wrong. The Lord works in mysterious ways. Maybe in the end nobody gets to reduce Him to a calendar calculation; maybe it's like predicting the end of the world by asteroid impact, even though some believe a particular culprit is already in orbit. You know those behemoths are out there, but who's to say for sure when one will crash? Maybe it will rain space-junk for forty days and forty nights; apparently there's enough of it out there to drown an entire continent in extraterrestrial trash.

A bright red apapane flies overhead, glides into a koa's sky-high branch, then dips down to a lower branch, dropping like an autumn leaf. Gwen thinks about Maine, autumn, and Buddy when he was little offering her the first fallen red leaf from the oak in their back yard. He loved doing that, claiming the first leaf, giving it to Gwen.

Madge stops suddenly, planting her neon pink sneakers into the dirt trail, then sticks out her chapped lower lip, glowering. "You can't make me!"

Gwen tugs, yanks her hand, then squeezes Madge's arm. "Geez you're a stubborn old wahine, Mother." She strokes Madge's tangles of hair, hot and strangely sticky as if the late morning sun had melted into it, a buttery goo. "We'll go home soon, I promise." *The Buddy-bribes when he was a toddler; I'll take you there if you behave here....*

Madge drops open her mouth and lets out a hoarse chirping, *Hnnnh!* Then suddenly she screams, shrill, hollow, a wail of despair. Gwen drops her mother's arm, presses her hands over her ears. "Mother, please stop. Please, you've got to stop this!" She grabs Madge's trembling shoulders feeling suddenly dizzy, her mother's screams ragging through her. Tries to quell her own rising panic, that sour taste of failure. *Catastrophic reaction. Temper tantrum.* The backwards world again, unable to control her own mother who's behaving like a two year old. "It's OK! We'll go back." Gwen tries to remain calm, counting steps through her clenched jaw.

Madge keens, squawks, her body swaying on its spindly legs like a bird, beak opened, beady eyes becoming murky and dark. Gwen pushes her toward the car. "A nice little drive, that's all I wanted. My life's coming apart and I'm on a goddamn mountain with my mother who's having a fit!" She helps Madge climb inside, buckles on her seatbelt, Madge's voice growing softer and softer, until it's a reedy wail stuck mid-scream, like a needle on a scratched and ancient album, an old song nobody would want to remember anyway.

8

Madge

THEY THINK YOU'RE CRAZY, OF course. You grow older, little bit sick and they pronounce you mental. She's mental? Gwenyth thinks Madge is mental! She's like a drug addict with her wine, may as well shoot it up and be done with it. Ah, so there it is, Madge remembers needles. It goes like this: Sky dark, clouds thickening, we are weaving our leis, Mama and Makela, white and purple crown flowers. Pierce the fuzzy little bottoms, pushing them onto the long silvery lei needles, skinny as a twig, bendable as a finger. Mama's humming as she finishes a lei, perfect circle like a cloud. "My crown flower princess," she calls Makela. A warm rain falls. We stay in it! We don't run from it! Grass squishy around their ankles, under bare feet. "Washes the poison away!" Mama hums, offering her glorious face up to the grey sky.

She *was* Makela. She *is* Madge. Her daughter was/is Gwenyth, freckles, tight as an icepick. So occasionally Madge gets stuck on a name, a relationship, a pronoun, *who are you now?* So what? It's not like that changes any of it. Better to sit by the window, study the mountains. When you look out, there they are.

Remember mountains. And volcanoes, Kilauea, Halema'uma'u, House of Pele. Mama who's called Ana calls her Makela. Father calls her Margareit, which is English for Makela or maybe French. Maybe both. If he's mad he'll call her Margareit Shirley. When did she become just Madge? The Artist called her that, *Madge my badge,* he said. Mama's little and light, has floaty hair, lacy as a cricket's wing, voice full of breath, puckered face like the skin of a lychee, the curve of her cheek. Lovely Ana. She was a child when Father married her, *then comes Makela.* Sometimes she talks-story to Makela in Hawaiian, words flowing soft as water.

Mama says, "I'm driving near Halema'uma'u one day and what do you think? Here comes Madam Pele, flowing white dress, flowing white hair, little white dog by her bare brown feet. I stay with my sister. *Auntie who?* We packed a picnic and we're going ohelo berry picking on the crater's slopes.

"Pele shares the picnic then disappears after drinking a bottle of gin, our offering, all *pau.* (You must *always* carry gin with you, warns Mama, in case you meet up with Madam Pele. It's her favorite.) We walk to the berry place. Bushes so loaded it takes all afternoon to fill the ten Naalehu milk jars, all gone, all pau. The jam we make lasts a year. We leave a jar beside Halema'uma'u with a branch of ohia-lehua, Pele's flowers, quills red as the points of matches."

She is Madge. Gwenyth undresses her, puts her to bed. Madge lets her. She will not scream, not even when the blackness comes. Is it a dream? Walks into a house, somewhere up the road. Finds a cowboy hat, so soft! Like velvet! Like a little boy's crew cut! Madge never had her little boy but she could feel his hair in this hat. Would The Artist be here if they had a little boy? Put it on. Tall as a mountain! Shoulders up straight! She's a cowboy, a paniola, galloping the fields, sun on her back. To be this free!

Gwenyth takes the hat, makes her little again. You're no cowboy, Madge. Turns off the light. She's tied her wrist to the bed's...wooden thing. Where is the language for this? Silk sash from her kimono; The Artist gave it to her so he could slip it off, so she could slide up pink and full as a petal, opening for him. "I'm sorry to have to tie you, Mother, honest to God, this sucks beyond belief! But I can't risk you wandering again. You might get lost."

She tries sitting up, leaning forward. *Lost?* She will untie it! Her free hand! Rigid, her own daughter called her. To Gwenyth this means she can't be moved easily, won't respond how she wants, like her puppet. For shame, daughter! Whose breast did you suckle? Madge trussed to her bed like a chicken.

Here is what rigid is. Every day a little more locked inside this odd old flesh. Lifts up her nightgown. Slides her hand down, the one not tied, touching the dried-up place, the empty trench where once there was life? Where baby Gwenyth came from, where The Artist loved? OK, so she danced a few clubs; she wanted to be a dancer, for crying out loud, she remembers that much! But the rest…was to try and forget. Madge, *his badge*, was lost a long time ago.

9

Meanwhile ... Buddy

MIDDLE OF JUNE AND STILL no hookup with Marnie. Honolulu, peaceful bay, sheltered bay; that's what the name means, so he was told. Peaceful... what he's feeling is anything but. Waves of horny blasting through him, hot yet so fricken needful he can hardly bear it. It's as if his body's on fire and drowning at the same time. Maybe he doesn't smell so good? It's not like opportunities to climb into a hot shower are abundant around here. Note use of Mother word. She has this refrigerator magnet that says God's love is abundant and His gifts (what you get) are too. So if you pray for something over and over, let's say a state-of-the-art wall-sized LED high-def TV, then maybe he breaks down like a worn out parent with a bratty toddler and gives it to you? What god works like that?

Todd's "pad" as he calls it, in the Waikiki Jungle, has one bathroom, a you-wouldn't-believe-how-disgusting toilet, a suspiciously booger-green sink, and a shower stall that no longer supports plumbing, home to a rowdy band of daddy long legs. "Chemicals," Todd shrugs, offering up his long yellow hands to the cracked ceiling. Like this explains a toxic bathroom.

Chemicals are the bane of Todd's life. His hair's falling out, he claims from Agent Orange, which also caused the prickly rash like lines of marching ants, up and down his arms. Plus, he informs Buddy one night after Marnie's asleep on their shared mattress behind her barrier of clothes, towels, old sheets, *balling* the babes is no longer on his to-do list. "Part of my dick's gone," he confessed, "eaten away by The Orange. Want to see?" Buddy didn't.

Half the time the water won't work in Todd's sink, and there's usually at least one giant cockroach in the green-encrusted basin, waving its tender antennae up at Buddy. No way is he going to get it wet. Do you know there are times when a roach is a better friend than a person? No games, you understand what they're about. Food: they want it, you got it, they'll find a way to get into it.

Some days they swim at Kuhio Beach, showering afterwards in the frigid outside showers, dank stink of salt and pee, half a dozen tanked locals eyeballing Marnie. Lately she's been lounging around in Todd's house smoking weed with him, windows shut, air stifling and gritty, like it's been sucked up by a vacuum cleaner then blown back through each little room.

Sometimes Buddy snags a hit or two, but mostly he watches, wondering where it's all heading, if he'll see his mother again, if he *wants* to see her again. Most of all he wonders when he will hookup with Marnie. He feels aching to burst, can hardly sleep, the scent of her beside him makes him crazy. He wants to suck her in, exhale himself back into her, blow on the parts of her need cooling off, burn deep inside everything else. "Reality check!" she snaps, "we can't hookup with my uncle here. Like is this his house or what? That's creepy, dude, my uncle in the next room. It's like incest or something. Stop thinking with your dick, honey. I swear, guys think their dicks are divining rods. Stick it in, magic happens. Not so simple, Buddums."

Then she tells him a story about one of her "dates" she called them, like this is some kind of a tuck-me-in bedtime tale? He's supposed to sleep easier because of this? She leans over the barrier between them; he can make out the glow of those yellowy eyes in the light from the street lamp outside illuminating them, owl's eyes, see in the dark predator's eyes, could she, *would* she, pounce? "I can trust you Buddy-love, you're not like the others. Makes me want to tell you things, yeah? Confide in you, like a friend." She says this stroking his arm, and he imagines her scooting over that barrier and climbing on top of him, so tight he would feel the beat of her heart against his. How one day in modeling school she meets this really fine older guy, *blazing* she calls him. "Modeling school," she laughs, "what a joke! I was skinny and spastic before my boobs came fully in, so my mom decides it'll give me some confidence."

Here's what it gives her. This guy, this *blazer*, is a designer from Honolulu, some kind of smokin' nightclub wear and he's going to take her out to dinner, he tells her, to a really nice restaurant where they can discuss her career as a model for his line. (His *line*, man! How do they come up with these things?) But first, detour to his hotel so they can smoke a blunt, get them pumped for this fabulous meal ahead. Prime rib, he tells her, lobster, mahi mahi, whatever she likes. Cherries jubilee for dessert, wink wink.

Marnie's telling Buddy this, his head on the unwashed pillow, stink of it mingling with her good grassy scent—like new-mown hay, he's thinking, even though he hasn't a clue what that would actually smell like. Buddy imagines her eyes fixed so trustingly, hungrily on this blazer, picturing the night, that dinner, her future as a model, getting her out of her house, schlepping her away to her brand new life. At the hotel he fires up, hands her the blunt (*rockin'* best weed and blow, he assures her); she's perched on the bed—where else can you sit in a hotel room? Then he eases her down, his hand slick and sliding and she gets that sinking feeling (she doesn't say this exactly, but what else could it be? still trying to convince herself maybe this is *the one*?). She'll need to remove her dress, of course, keep it nice for their dinner afterwards. Marnie still believes in that food, if nothing else.

Of course there's no dinner. He drives her home, rented car, stereo pumping, he's humming along to the Red Hot Chili Peppers, *Californication*—cruises into where her parents are partying, beers on their lanai, pupus, and like nothing out of the ordinary has happened, he tips back a cold one with them. As if Marnie isn't standing there, *like nothing's happened*, the throbbing between those ginger thighs, knowing this one too will leave and she'll be *here*, wake up *here*, that *here* is what she can expect out of life.

"The end," Marnie tells Buddy, squeezing his hand that had inched over the barrier between them. Tugging hard at his fingers she pops them into her mouth, one at a time, flicking her hot grainy tongue up and down until he feels that madness aching like an old hurt between his own scrawny legs.

10

Gwen

THE PHONE'S RINGING AND MADGE shrieks from her rocking chair: "Shut that blasted thing!"

"Buddy?" Gwen wails out of the bathroom, zipping up her pants. Glowering, she grabs the phone. "Ah sweet Jesus, whoever it was hung up! For Lord's sake, Mother, you couldn't answer the damn phone? You were right there."

Madge shrugs. "They aren't really my thing."

"Oh sure, wouldn't want to compromise your *thing*. Then again last time you answered the phone you told Rob I was an alien who inhabited the body of your *real* daughter." Gwen glares at Madge, who's cracking up about something, jabbing her finger toward the knotty pine shelving on the back wall, snorting like it's a private joke, something she sees that no one else can. *That's* the joke, Gwen supposes. She's seeing something no one else can, because it's not even there. "I need a drink!"

Gwen strides into the kitchen, grabbing her bottle of Merlot and a mug, pours then swallows, anxiety like ice freezing in her throat, her eyes an itchy, watery red. Pouring herself a second round she throws her neck back and inhales it; takes a third glass into the living room, drops down into the overstuffed chair, spilling a few drops on the pale pink arm. It fades instantly into the upholstery like old blood. Spits on two fingers then stabs at the wine stain for a second, shrugs and takes another chug. At one time everything in this room was bright pink, yellow or green, colors in a garden, shades of living things worn pale as puke now. Gwen's dressed in her mainland garb, faded jeans, tucked in pastel plaid shirt, blends right in.

Last night on the phone she told Rob that nothing can cure what Madge has. "It's a progressive illness. There's some evidence her own mother might have suffered from TIA's, then died of a heart attack before things could get worse," Gwen said, "lucky her." Now she peers into the white space filling the plate glass window, drums her fingernails up and down the rim of her glass. She likes the solidity of this sound. Announces *this*, anyway, is real. Gwen shakes her head. "I need to get more wine. We'll stop at the store after…" she hesitates, stares at Madge.

Madge pipes up, "Me too, I want one!"

"Oh for Lord's sake, you don't even drink anymore."

"By order of who? Where is it written?" she scowls, then gives Gwen a ghastly smile, made worse by the smear of red on her teeth from the lipstick she tried to put on earlier, forgetting what she was doing in the middle of the act, then licking her lips with her tongue.

"Christ!" Gwen mutters. She staggers over to the front door, grabbing her mother's glacier-blue parka off the hook beside it. There's drizzle today, fog, volcano weather as Madge used to call it, when she still had the spunk to complain about the weather, and everything else.

Madge squeals, "You can't make me! Don't think I don't know what you're up to here."

Gwen approaches her slowly, the parka held out in front like an offering. "Now look, we're going to see Dr. Alvarez and that's all there is to it.

You know we need to. We've discussed this. It's for your own good." She reaches for Madge who slaps Gwen's outstretched palm, a mean high-five. "Honest to God, Mother! You think this is some pleasure outing for me? It's for you, for Christ's sake, and I mean that with all due respect."

"Just who you think you're dealing with, sister!" Madge shouts. "I'm a grown-up. I don't need you or anybody else."

Gwen stares down into her mother's gaunt face, leaning over a little to hoist her out of the chair. Her body's gone rigid, her hands squeezing the rocking chair arms. The skin around her mouth is pinched and starved, the color of a watery make-up. Madge Johnstone once had an ample girth, *voluptuous* was the word in an admiring world before skinny was a trend, rather than a condition of impoverishment. Now she appears diminished, shrunken and pale, cheekbones sticking out like two little knobs under hollowed eyes. "After the apocalypse none of this will matter," Gwen mutters. It gives her odd comfort. A good excuse for failure, if nothing you do will ultimately make any difference anyway.

Something tightens in Gwen's chest. Madge's scrawny arms are wrapped around the rocking chair's arms so tight she can't lift her up without detaching, breaking her suction like an octopus. "There are thieves," Madge confides, "whose sole purpose is to steal your life right out from under you. I want my dinner."

"It isn't even lunch yet. Remember? You just had your cream of rice two hours ago." Gwen smiles encouragingly at her mother, who suddenly lunges, mouth pulled open in a viscous sneer, chomping down. "Sonofabitch! You bit me!" Gwen jerks up straight as a fishing pole, shoves her throbbing finger into her own mouth, pulling it out again to examine the carnage, storms into the kitchen, yanks open the freezer, her eyes tearing up at yet another insult, her own mother biting her! Returns with a dishtowel filled with ice cubes wrapped around her hand.

"You hid the damn ice pack somewhere, didn't you! You think you're putting things away but you put them in crazy-ass places instead. I found a stick of butter in your lingerie drawer yesterday, God! You hear me? Butter doesn't pair with underwear!"

"I'm not budging from this chair!" Madge announces, her whole body quivering. She looks surprised then gazes in dismay at her lap.

"Oh great, now you've wet yourself! You refuse to use those Depends, but then look what happens. Look what happens, Mother!"

Gwen cradles her sore finger against the ice, pondering this unlikely image, Madge Johnstone in diapers. "It's my damn turned upside down world," she sighs. "It's like you're becoming my daughter. I guess I better change your doctor's appointment, it's obviously not happening today. Maybe you just need an extremely long nap."

Gwen stares out an open window at the lava path. She feels suddenly lost, hollowed out, a nothing sort of person, the kind a father walks away from and never comes back. The late morning sun slips out from behind Mauna Loa for a moment, then is quickly obscured by another dark cloud, the mountain lolling purple as a tongue. She imagines a life where she is free to come and go as she pleases, no runaway son, no mother losing her mind, a husband who's maybe signing divorce papers at this very moment. Volcano smells green and sweet today. Honeycreepers trill from ohia trees, a nene reams out its raucous call.

Gwen helps her mother up, leads her into the bathroom, tugging Madge along like a slab of wood, an ironing board with feet.

"Why, Gwenyth? Have I been so awful?" Quiet words, Madge's sudden, tragic lucidity.

"It's OK, Mother." Gwen undresses her, running a silvery stream of warm water from the faucet then washing her carefully, touching her mother with the familiarity of her own flesh. Pulls a clean gown over her head, and then the kimono, a swoosh of silk, print of tiny gold butterflies that settle around her; you can almost hear the flapping of a hundred little wings.

Speaking of Wings… The Jody Johnstone Story

HE WAS A LONELY, SCRAWNY, bug-eyed boy who blossomed into a water-angel. At first it was just body surfing, an act of abandonment and forgetting, throwing his little body into the wave, willing its velocity, its mad rush of rolling motion to carry him away, do with him as it pleased, the thrust of its trajectory (like flying!) with Jody inside it an almost sensual experience, before he had any recognition of that word. He was a little boy who after his mother died was never kissed or held again by his father. His big sister, herself in shock over what happened to their mother, although not exactly blaming Jody, became suspicious and fearful of a world that would allow such a fate; she never touched Jody again either, not even to hold his hand in play. "Walk your little brother to the playground!" their father would growl, "I need some peace around here." And Violet did, instructing the boy to follow her. Then she would sit and watch him swing, slide, merry-go-round, mechanically engage the equipment the way Jody figured he was supposed to do, until they were allowed to go home again. Theirs was a house that had lost its play. When he came home from school it was to his sullen, fuming father, with only the memory of Jody's mother as something they could share between them.

But the waves! Jody was as happy getting spun and tumbled by them, his head smushed down into the sand below, as he was catching a ride and flying all the way to the beach, the world a blur for the minutes it took, the wave's rippling speed and the frenzy of its movement like a windstorm in Jody's ears. And when it pulled him under and twisted him about, the riotous tumbling of a rabbit in the jaws of a wolf, for that moment he was all survival—a gut, physical presence. Then and only then could Jody forget how his mother died trading plates with him, getting the botulism from the mahi mahi *he* had ordered then refused to eat at Rudy's Restaurant, where they used to go on Sunday nights, enjoying his mother's spaghetti to its last greasy bite.

"That fish is undercooked," his father had warned. His mother shrugged. "In Hawai'i we call it sashimi," she said, beaming at Jody, her last smile, and his too for a very long time.

Another talent the young Jody had, besides his adeptness in the ocean, was a way of recognizing a soul's essential loneliness, though not much of a clue what to do about it. *Sensitive*, his father called him, and it didn't sound like such a good thing when his father said it. "You may as well be an artist," his father would say dismissively, during the few times he tried to act like a father—pitching his son the occasional ball, and once taking him boar hunting in the Ko'olaus, a total disaster, with a twelve year old Jody accidentally discharging one of his arrows into the shoulder of the guide's hunting dog, who spun about, yelped then lay still. Jody sobbed the whole way home. "For crying out loud you just stunned the thing!" his father snapped. "Believe me you're no kind of a marksman. What will you be like when you're a grown man? *May as well be an artist!*"

What the boy saw in that injured dog was another living being whose destiny had been suddenly and tragically altered from an interaction with Jody. He felt things keenly, the jittery, nervy, random motion of the world's erratic spinning, and since he seemed powerless to affect this in any way, perhaps his father was right—he should become an artist and try to at least *paint* this thing, color its painful truth so others could know it too. His father scoffed, shook his head and reminded his son there was always juvenile detention, if he wanted to experience some *painful truth*. The Bad Boys Home.

One high-energy day, when he'd drunk enough beer to get him hyper but not yet unconscious, their father piled Jody and Violet into his Chevy sedan and hauled them out to the Waimanalo side of O'ahu, green as kale, like it's some pastoral Hallmark-does-Hawai'i scene, then he pointed out the juvenile detention homes, boys on one side girls on the other, long and flatiron pink, inhabitants working the land like they're slaves to it, broiling sun, no rest, nothing to look forward to except maybe when you get beat up later if you're a haole (their dad said Kalani High School, his alma-mater, had beat up the white kid days), a break in the routine. "Kids go *there* when they're not good," he warned, "if they can't tow the line." Then he took them out for ice cream telling them benevolently, "Don't worry, you're both good enough, so far." Violet quaked, tending her cone with timid little licks, just enough to arrest the dripping. Jody methodically devoured his, staring up at the Ko'olaus running parallel to the road, much more in-your-face than they were on his side of the island, where they functioned like a backdrop. If you had asked him what flavor his ice cream was, he wouldn't have been able to tell you.

When Jody was a junior in high school his best friend Blake was sent to *Juvie* for his aversion to shopping in stores, preferring Waialae Kahala's upper-class houses instead. After he was released Blake told Jody about a guy in there, who slept on the cot beside his and cried at night, whose name on the street was *Make*, dead in Hawaiian. He was quiet about his crying the way folks are who've been crapped on from zygote to pubes, didn't expect anyone to do a damn thing about it, Blake said. You almost couldn't hear it; maybe it's the wind or a weird kind of snore? Once he woke up and Make was sitting on the edge of Blake's mattress. Just sitting, didn't even look at Blake. Apparently he couldn't bear being alone on his cot that night, and he had nowhere else to go.

Jody nodded. He understood that, having nowhere else to go.

PART II

Summer

11

Buddy

IN MAINE THE CICADAS' THRUM would fill the air like the buzzing of an electric saw; summer air buttery and thick, like toast this air. Male cicadas make this sound with plate-like organs on their thorax. Buddy examined a dead one once, severing the wings with his tweezers, perfect and whole like it had just dropped out of the sky. Females chew slits in twigs and deposit their eggs, then the wingless young fall to the ground, burrow four to twenty years, surviving on juices sucked from roots. When fully grown they climb up a tree, skin splitting down their backs and the adults emerge, already humming. Hmmmmm, they mate, lay eggs, then die.

Summer in Honolulu and Buddy's hands ache from picking pineapples eight hours a day. Nose burns from the acrid stink of the fruit, the blowing red dirt from the valley where the fields are, at the foot of the Waianae mountains. Back aches from bending over the prickly green rows, straight as teeth. One night Todd made them a pina colada, cheap rum, pineapple juice, Buddy thought he would gag.

Marnie quit the fields after barely one week on the job, claiming red dirt under her nails is a lame image for a model. "Models don't *labor*," she said, "we pose." Then she did it for him, hand on hip, neck tossed back, kissed him when he was about to protest. For Buddy's own efforts he gets minimum wage. Part of that money goes to Todd for their rent, the privilege of holing up in his shack, the rest sucked down their throats. You see the scenario here: basically he's supporting Marnie, like a husband for chrissake, and they haven't even hooked up. Sometimes he wouldn't mind those old fashioned "pay back" mores, fair is fair, isn't it? You always reciprocate a gift, his mom used to say. Marnie whined, "be patient, babes, just wait." Just like his father.

Maybe she never forgave him for losing his money that night and this her way of punishing him? She was under the impression he had much more than he did, thought he nabbed his grandmother's life savings or something. "It's not worth it just to take *some*," Marnie said, "if you do a thing do it all the way." Apparently this philosophy didn't apply to having sex with *babes*.

So now it's night again, he's trying to sleep, and per usual not getting any. He sighs, tosses a bit, hoping a bounce or two might jar Marnie, roll her over a little closer. Through her barrier, the Great Wall of Chastity, he can inhale her scent; tonight she'd slathered her skin with plumeria lotion, purchased courtesy of Buddy's pineapple funds. He's starting to wonder about wasted youth, a wasted life, the kinds of things you aren't supposed to have to think about, care about, *wonder* about, when you're still a kid, when supposedly the world is wide open to you.

At first in the fields the local pickers ragged him because of his Maine accent, because he's haole and a geek. You think it would've done any good telling them he's a sixteenth Hawaiian, how else the crinkly curls on his head, hair the color of poured tar? Soon enough they lost interest, and now he's ignored, invisible, an aching, burned out absence. He rides The Bus from Waikiki every day at 7:00 AM, back at 5:00 PM, like some old person with responsibilities instead of a life. Sometimes Marnie fixes him supper, prying open a can or two, corn, chili, Dinty stew, heating up the contents in one of Todd's beat-up pans, but mostly she lounges about with her uncle in the front room, smoking weed, blinds still closed from the night before, Todd ranting about how the Vietnam War had altered his destiny. "I could've been anything," he laments, "a lawyer, even a goddamn professor. I would've been excellent at that, professing."

Buddy asked Marnie how come "the chemicals" kept her uncle from walking around the corner to Tong's for food, yet the day his disability check arrived he managed to hike two miles to his post office box. "Bud-o!" she snapped, her yellowy-browns boring into him, "he's our host and a war hero. He's even got a Purple Heart. So he's a little messed up, not all of us are born princes."

Here's what Buddy's thinking, lying awake on this grungy mattress: this, the life of a prince? He holds up his hand. Broken moonlight through a twisted slant in the dust-coated blind illuminates one giant callous, stained yellow from the pineapple acid.

But on the fourth of July Buddy gets the answer to the question he's been needling himself with, pinching, poking, stabbing: *Why don't I just go home?* Independence Day and the pineapple fields get a holiday, prickly little stinking green plants sleeping sweetly in their red dirt beds, even the Dole roadside stand is closed, no paws or jaws to maul them today. Marnie and Buddy get amped on some especially potent "warrior" crystal meth-laced weed. "More of a kick than Wheaties," Todd announced, "breakfast of champions." Buddy fretted about the meth part but Todd said, "Ain't no biggie, dude, your basic household chemicals. Good housekeeping seal of approval!" He chose not to think too hard about that, and after smoking the spliff Buddy couldn't think much about anything.

They decide to go exploring in the Ko'olau mountains, and Buddy feels like he could run the whole way there but Marnie snorts, "You're pupule like your tutu, crazy grandma!" Sticking out her thumb, she nabs them a ride almost immediately. "Sometimes," he tells her after thanking the driver (dirty old fart, had trouble steering and leering at Marnie in the rearview), "I think it's better to be a girl. Look how easily you get rides, for one."

She shakes her mane, rolls her eyes, "Girls don't have say in *some* things, huh? Like you'll know what I mean, soon enough."

He shrugs, grins, feeling excellent for once, not a pineapple in sight. Why ask for trouble? It'll find you anyway.

They hike up a moist, muddy trail, pungent odor of fallen guavas, spicy scent of the Norfolk pines, Ko'olau forest, gnarly as the spruce forests in Maine. Rushing sound of tumbling water, and suddenly the trail opens up beside a stream with an amazingly clear pool, a waterfall cascading down a stark black cliff.

Buddy sucks in a breath, "Holy shit!" Seizing his hand, Marnie smiles smugly like she's the one who created it. Around them are wild, overgrown tangles of plant life, the rampage of tropical shrubbery in a hundred glistening shades of green. The fresh flow of the mountain falls, so white it reminds him of the cocaine they've snorted, nostrils burning, eyes watering, head luminous as stars. "So maybe we don't need drugs, with places like this to hang out in."

"What, like you want to make my uncle feel useless? You're feeding us, so he needs to feel he's providing *something*. Think of someone else for a change, babes."

"Fine, so drug me!"

Marnie giggles, her hand tightening into his moist and tingling fingers.

They have the stream to themselves, no sounds except the roar of the waterfall, trilling of honeycreepers. Sunlight beaming through shadows of trees makes the water hop and sparkle with diamonds of light. Marnie lets go of his hand and strips off her clothes. All her clothes, just like that. Like she does this in front of him every night. Like they're some old married couple and he's seen her body a million times. Buddy's jaw drops open, feels like piranha are nibbling at his eyeballs, burning and feverish, the sight of her naked flesh brown as moss. Before this he's only seen a completely naked girl in the movies, Internet porn sites, a text gone viral by a soon-to-be-suspended senior at HJA, and in his dreams. The first girl who even let him cop a feel of her breasts, Selma Reid, a developmentally gifted seventh grader at Rock Harbor Middle School, made him do it in a playground tunnel, in the dark, under her bra, no flashlight allowed. He had tucked one inside his jacket pocket just in case.

Like a stoned goddess Marnie poses shakily on a rock, then dives into the pool, a perfect arch, the ripples from her gorgeous body cutting through the water like blades. "So come on haole boy!" she taunts, treading water, "whatcha waiting for, huh? Like you want me to send you an engraved invitation, or what?"

Buddy's suddenly afraid of his own white-skinned scrawniness. Awkwardly he tugs off his clothes, feeling cold and strange, a rise beginning between his legs, wondering if this means that maybe she loves him, a little? Taking off her clothes, diving in then asking him to do the same, she's beckoning *him* to her.

He peers down into the dark depths for a moment, praying there are no submerged rocks where he's about to land, but he doesn't want to parade his nakedness in front of her any longer than he has to. He thinks about other guys she's had, big, brown, six-packs where on him ribs protrude like chicken wings, then he jumps in anyway, paddling through breath-sucking cold toward her. Without hesitating, without even kissing him she pulls that urgency between Buddy's legs into her hands, positioning her thighs tight around his skinny hips, moaning into his ear. She doesn't put him inside her; they just rock like they've been frozen together in the icy black water, his heart jabbering so hard against his chest he's afraid it'll break out in its own language, start chatting with hers. Or else she'll feel its pounding and think he's scared.

Which he is, of course, and absolutely driven with what he believes has to be love for this girl, this horny tenderness. Marnie holds his dick in her hands, legs locked like jaws around him and they float like spawning fish. "Next time we'll hookup *all* the way," she whispers.

Buddy feels for an incredible moment, her hands stroking him where he's only dreamed them before, a part of something permanent as the rocks, the waterfall, the dizzy scent of the white and yellow ginger on the banks of the stream. Above them the mountain is erect, a giant boner, Marnie's breath warm and tickly in his ear. He shudders and floats free.

THAT EVENING FROM ONE OF the last payphones in Waikiki, breath of The Jungle on Independence Day—music beating out of opened doors, fire-crackers popping, exploding into the moist night air, mingling with the scent of pot, exhaust, trade winds swooshing through the palms—Buddy calls his mom and tells her he won't be coming back in September.

"What on earth do you think you're doing, son, you're in high school for God's sake! You can't make those kinds of decisions." Her voice sounds strangled. He can hear the clink clink of ice in a glass, burgundy on the rocks no doubt. "You drinking boogers on the rocks?" he snaps, which is mean and doesn't Buddy know it, his thirteen year old phrase for this, the way her wine consumption became more and more a fixture in their lives, predictable as the tarnished chandelier over their dining room table, one bulb perpetually dark, the tinkling sounds from a glass in his mother's hand as they consumed their dinner, punctuated by a strained conversation aimed at him—far be it for his parents to actually converse with each other at this point. His mother put ice in her glass when she felt a need to control the amount of alcohol she consumed. Who was she kidding? She drank twice as many glasses of it watered-down. But he was a smartass, boogers on the rocks. Listening to the jaggedness of his mom's breath on the other end of the receiver, he can hear Grandma Madge in the background howling, "Robbers, rapists, jewelry thieves, sneaking around, hiding under your bed. Invaders, I tell you!"

"She thinks we're not alone!" his mother whispers fiercely. "Jesus, Buddy, I couldn't be more alone. God, make my son get his head on straight!" Then she starts to cry.

Buddy feels bad for a moment, and it's like a chunk of that ice got stuck in his own throat. He clears his throat, trying to think of something to say, something reassuring, something sure. But then he thinks about Marnie, her hands on him. "Look, I'm sorry, but the thing is I'm old enough. I can drop out of school if I want to. It's bullshit anyway, you know that; you quit your-self and you were a teacher, for chrissake. I've got a job. I can take care of myself. You don't need me there, you've got Grandma. I just get in the way. You don't have to worry," he adds. Because worry is what his mother does.

"Come home!" her demanding tone again. "Please, Buddy. You're my son! Have I been such a bad mom you don't even want to live here? Come home, Buddy, please, for God's sake, if you love me at all!"

OK, so you think the Gestapo-guilt approach would work on *him*? He's a fugitive, a thief, a druggie, and he's in love with a goddess. Buddy hangs up the phone.

July inching closer to August, a rancid, humid heat, stillness of the Kona air and everything the same again, picking pineapples through the blaz-ing yellow days, lying on the mattress beside Marnie, black sweaty nights, untouched. One night he hurls the Great Wall of Chastity between them across the room, clothes, towels, sheets, shoes, thudding against the wall. Marnie howls, "Go ahead, rape me if you want it so bad; I'll hate you for-ever, you fuck!"

"When was it exactly I stopped having a life? It's like I'm my father, work all day come home to a bitch!"

"You're the only guy I can trust," Marnie says, her voice suddenly soft. "So just wait, OK? These things have to be right or they don't mean a thing. It's got to mean something or we end up hating each other. It would suck if that happened. I'd hate it if you hated me! You wouldn't want that, huh?"

Try me! he thinks, but he's silent.

Here's something Buddy remembers from being a little kid: hearing his parents, one of their fights, one summery weekend day. It was back when they first started their yelling at each other, their war, and he couldn't understand it, this thing that seemed to rage up between them, the coldness that crept into their lives when he didn't even see it coming; then it was there. That day, sun beaming so brightly it looked like you could cut the shadows it made with scissors, he carried his Garfield scissors outside to escape the noise of their anger. He took paper, a plastic bucket with his color markers, animal cookies and his Batman thermos filled with apple juice. He considered running away. Instead, he climbed up the oak tree in their back yard, cut out shapes with his scissors, colored them then released them to the breeze. He could hear his parents hollering from inside the house. They didn't know or care where he was.

Buddy slid down from his tree perch and sat on the grass, leaning up against the oak's thick trunk. Stuck his bare legs out from under its shade into the bright sunlight, then held completely still letting the humid heat cause perspiration to bead up on his skin. Eventually he heard them, the low buzzing sounds he was listening for, over him, around him, Sweat Bees. Small and brilliant, like they'd been colored by his magic markers. Their nest was in the ground near this tree, and they were attracted to the scent of perspiration. Buddy knew this. And he wasn't afraid. He loved the orderly ways of their world. He loved how everything they did, every movement had a reason. Several lit down on him and crawled up his legs, antennae sensing him, sweeping over him. They didn't sting. He knew they wouldn't. Pretended he was one of them. Closed his eyes. For a while he too had a purpose.

12

Gwen – Some Personal History

AT EIGHTEEN SHE LEFT THE islands swearing she'd never go home again. "I'm off this rock forever!" she muttered, in her knock-off designer jeans, Chucky-shod, her eighties big hair—or as big as her mouse-thin locks could fake. Hilo Airport, her mother at the gate, a silly, overdressed figure with her blaze of red hair, watching her daughter leave. This was an event; everything was an event, yet this one broke Madge's heart. She didn't wave, though Gwen did—full of relief, release, the sense of some kind of freedom about to finally unfold.

Now she's back. *The rock* is where she lives. Can it be home again? Wear this island like an old shirt? Love her without judgment, like a marriage, the kind that lasts? She *wants* to be part of Hawai'i again, but feels cut away from it, from her life in Maine, everything. Flops down on the sofa, faded to the color of dried grass. Gazes at her mother slumped over in her rocker, the tawny afternoon light through the plate glass window, crisscrossing her forehead, weaving the lines on her face into sunlit cobwebs.

"Mother!" she hisses, though she knows Madge won't acknowledge her. The daily struggle, search and find mission with Madge's TIA-afflicted mind the hidden object. How will she be today, this hour, moment to moment? Lucid? Insulting? Ridiculous? Desperate? Gwen doesn't know what to do with her, what to say, how to *be* with her. She's not uncompassionate. She just doesn't have a clue. She drinks and she doesn't have a clue, or she doesn't drink and she doesn't have a clue. She prays for a clue and comes up empty. What plays through Madge's mind behind that hollowed-out expression? What images of their life together, Gwenyth as daughter not caretaker, does her mother remember?

"You might want to start thinking about an assisted living placement for her," Juli Alvarez suggested, their last visit to her Mountainview office. "You're not looking well, Gwen, you look run down. You can't manage this exhausted. There's no shame. Your mother is ill."

"But how can I take her away from her home? Her house is sanctuary."

"Maybe you underestimate her, Gwen. Anyway, it could come down to being the only choice."

"How can I do that, Mother?" Gwen asks her now, knowing she's not going to answer. It's almost like a stubbornness takes hold, as if because she's sick it's OK for her to become less human, throw away any semblance of the manners that defined Madge Johnstone before, become something else, willful and self-serving. Not that she wasn't selfish before, but now she has permission to go as far down that path as she wants, to a place Gwen is not allowed to question. But does she extricate her mother from the life she's known, because somewhere in Madge's brain something has slipped? Maybe it's slipping in Gwen too. Lately she's felt a dull breath of *something* creeping up inside, something old. Last week she bought a bottle of hair dye, *Wash away that grey*. Like a disease, cleanse thyself of the visible effects of growing older. It sits in the medicine cabinet. She doesn't really care how she looks these days. She thinks about menopause, *the change* Madge used to call it; first you get *the curse*, then the change when your body can no longer do that, losing its ability to replicate itself, becoming... who? what? And what will it matter anyway, after the apocalypse? If it's on schedule, that is. Gwen's starting to doubt the veracity of even that. Maybe the upgrade punishment for their human misdeeds will be to force them to keep living in this mess they've created, wars, environmental disasters, economic starvation for all but the super-rich—*the rich get richer, the poor have children*, as her mother used to say.

Gwen studies her mother, her face, neck, the skin folding in rolls like Play-Doh. She loved her mother's neck, that sweet place her perfumed collars touched. Used to kiss her there to avoid her heavily lipsticked mouth. Gwen still kisses her there every night before bed, her mother's breath sour as old wine. No matter if she brushes her teeth, Madge's breath lately has become the smell of slowly rotting from the inside out.

Gwen tips her head back against the couch, closes her eyes. It's late afternoon, that lonely leaden time, sun's already slipped behind Mauna Loa. Summer will be over soon. Buddy won't be coming home. She can't believe she could be the mother of a high school dropout. They did the right things when he was little, read to him, took him to museums, educational games, Sesame Street. A few years later they held current events discussions at the dinner table, even when Rob and Gwen could barely stomach speaking to one another they bantered on with Buddy about Judaism, Christianity, Islam, Iraq, Afghanistan, terrorism, racism, sexism, classism, homophobia, gay marriage, gun rights, gun *wrongs*, immigration—all to inspire curiosity, critical thinking, a love of learning and civic responsibility in their son. The one thing Rob and Gwen did together they agreed was good. Their supremely intelligent son. When Buddy became fascinated with bugs, who was it led him out in their yard, the woods behind, searching habitats, charting behaviors, identifying numerous crawlers by their family tree? And bugs, in Gwen's opinion, are God's *second* mistake. "They're insects," Buddy would correct her, "not bugs."

When she was a teenager there was no question about where she'd live, with her mother, or that she'd finish high school, college, get a job, get married. "You have to be able to make your way as a woman first in this world, then a wife," her mother told her. "There's no telling what little tricks the future will cook up. I wanted to be a dancer. Look at me. Prima ballerina of the art supplies store."

Lately Gwen's teenaged years have been coming back in a remembered blur of Madge's demands: Pick up your clothes, do the dishes, sweep the lanai, your hair needs styling, that skirt is too short, your jacket is ugly, wear lipstick, *be someone else*. After Gwen's father *disappeared* her mother turned the telescope on her. Gwen was the record of Madge's life, proof she still had one. She shrugged away praise for making Art's Alive a success, heralding it forth out of financial ruin. "I have business sense is all," Madge said. "Either you have numbers sense or you don't. It's what you are with people that counts." In fact, Gwen's mother was a lot better with numbers than people, but who would tell Madge that?

Gwen lay awake during those chilly Volcano nights, listening to the wooden walls creak, counting familiar sounds year after year, a clock of sorts, measuring her time in the house until she was old enough to leave it. She counted the knotty pine patches on the ceiling above, shining in a striated moonlight through louvered windows. There were fifty-one patches, but each time she counted them as if maybe they'd surprise her by birthing one more. Curled up under the yellow and white Hawaiian quilt sewn by Grandma Ana, Gwen, who never knew her grandmother, imagined her grandmother's arms around her and she could finally sleep.

Once she dreamt her drowned father rose out of the rift at the back of their yard, arm bones stretched wide as branches to receive her. She rushed into her mother's room, flung herself down on Madge's bed and howled. "No no," Madge admonished, running her fingers stiffly through Gwen's hair, "don't tell it. It's bad luck to tell a bad dream, especially before break-fast. Might make it come true."

Fifteen and a sophomore in high school, Gwen started running. Every day after school she ran up the Mauna Loa Strip road, labored breath, pounding heart, squeezing inside her chest like a vice. At night she endured the burn of charley horse cramps. When they finally stopped her legs were tight, wired with hard new muscle. Runner's legs.

Gwen became Hilo High's girl track star, fastest mile on record, acrid scent of track dust in her nostrils, eyes shut, counting those final tortuous steps, running herself to victory and a full athletic scholarship to the University of Washington. Before leaving Hawai'i she took a last run up Mauna Loa. A brilliant day, the island spread out below, craggy edges, luminous sea, a crater stark with shadows: Kilauea Iki and the Devastation Trail, where she strolled with her father the morning before he walked into the surf.

Gwen met Rob Winter at the U.W. in her Architecture Appreciation class, one of those post-seventies "easy A" electives that still clung to the catalog. She'd never seen such a beautiful face on a man, skin clear as water, eyes the milky blue of sea glass, lips so pronounced they could have been drawn on. Later she would tell anyone who asked, she married him for his good looks and his politics. Rob was a "radical" in the late Reagan eighties, championing the downtrodden when everyone else was out for themselves, big hair, big houses, consumer brand identities. Gwen loved his vision of revolutionary chaos, how the Capitalist greed and grit of our world would be "washed clean." The perfect socialist society just a Maytag away. He was still at war when most everyone else had ended theirs, college kids educating themselves for lucrative jobs in the financial industry, expecting to shell out big bucks for a mortgage on a showcase home, interest rates high as those glass ceilings still firmly in place for anyone who wasn't a white boy like Rob. Reaganomics.

He watched her run every afternoon around the U.W. track, Mt. Rainier looming in the distance like a great white ghost. Afterwards they'd go to his basement apartment on Capitol Hill, she showered and he'd dry her off, telling her she smelled like she stepped out of a deodorant can—about as poetic as Rob Winter got, but this was OK because he was a radical. The first time they made love was the first time Gwen had sex, and she had felt ambivalent; *this* was what everyone was raving about? His penis poking about between her legs, his breath wheezing in her ear and then the deep shuddering sigh. The next day in class her vagina burning, he smiled at her so gratefully.

They smoked pot and made love on his mattress regularly, purple light bulb scrunched into the naked fixture dangling from the chipped ceiling over them, lava lamp on his night table, bottle of cheap Chianti (this, her first seductive taste for bad red wine?), Billy Idol on the stereo, scent of their sex pungent as the Northwest rain that fell most every day until you want to slit open a vein, she whined to Rob. Then they did it all over again.

Rob's friends came over, ex-radicals and radical pot smokers, and Rob ranted, "We got to get Reagan out, government for the people not the fat cat Republicans!" sucking an emphatic toke off a joint. He flunked spring quarter, spending more time plotting "taking over" classroom buildings than actually attending classes in them. "Like they did in 1970," he said, "protesting the Vietnam war." (Rob was impressed to discover that in 1968 Gwen's father, after being drafted, flunked his induction physical for psychological reasons, earning a 4-F classification. He asked her how her dad managed that, did he fake being gay or crazy? Gwen didn't think so, didn't think he faked anything.)

She wrote Rob's term papers for him, figuring she was doing her part for the "revolution," even though a part of her recognized the only revolution at the University of Washington those days was inside that handsome head. Rob was the *angry young man* and Gwen was content to let his public anger give shape to her own private hurt.

After they graduated Rob asked her to move to Portland with him. He had a job waiting for him, he said, a friend of his father's who owned an accounting firm. He'd make lots of money and give it to "the cause." This was the West Coast. It didn't occur to Gwen at first he meant Portland, Maine.

So what happened? What went sour after they moved, got jobs, bought a house, had a baby, did the *right* things? Maybe that was it, they did the *right* things. What happened to her husband's anger at the wrongs of the world? When did it focus on the wrongs of his wife instead? Rob quit his job as an accountant, couldn't stand the boredom he said, numbers whose only purpose was to make money for other people, and instead worked his way up the ranks in prison administration. No more chatter about the revolution; it was the nineties. When did her own love fade, becoming drab as the couch she sits upon now? A recognition of his presence, like this couch, a furnishing, part of the surroundings rather than the center of her life?

She thought the baby would set things right again, and their own house to be a family in. They borrowed the down payment from Rob's father, and Rob turned to her in their still furnitureless living room, her belly blown out like a blow fish, blank walls, bare floors, said solemnly, "We've bought into the American Dream. It's too late to turn back."

The baby became a competition between them: who would make little Richard smile first, whose title, Mommy, Daddy, would form itself first on those pouty little lips, who would he crawl to for comfort, who would he love more.

Their lovemaking went in much the same way as their double mattress on the floor became a four poster king-sized bed, matching IKEA bureaus. For a while it was just sex, a steamy release caught in between toddler feedings, grownup feedings, the daily grind. Who turned away first in that oversized bed, the habit of space between them on the Egyptian cotton sheets growing more pronounced every year?

They spoke civilly for the next year or two, inquiring politely, without interest, about each other's days. Gwen was the discouraged young teacher trying and failing to make a difference, Rob a prison administrator making enemies. His beautiful face tightened, hardened, lovely lips wrenched into a perpetual sneer.

Gwen felt sucked out, dried up, old before she could give up on being young. Unformed, like a papaya that never had the chance to ripen before being punctured by some bird, insides turning to mush. She felt how unattractive she'd become to Rob and shrunk away from him even more because of it. She felt a gulf of emptiness, like a condemned person, the kind whose father walks into the sea, who wasn't enough for her mother; the kind who deserves the loneliness life so readily dishes up.

One night, Rob locked up in his den, Buddy in his room, Gwen walked down to the cove near their house with a bottle of wine. A few years later she would begin the affair here that would end her marriage, justifying it then to the emptiness of her marriage. Rob made her unhappy, ergo she deserved to get laid. On this particular night the water gleamed silver in the moonlight, but over the Camden Hills dark clouds gathered. It occurred to Gwen that her world, so carefully constructed at one time, its adages for survival—wait quietly with Mother for Father to come home, be quiet around Mother so as not to provoke her, run herself off the "rock" and into a new life with Rob Winter—was like building with tinker toys: college, marriage, Maine, job, house, baby. The results fragile, momentary. Her world had come apart.

And this is what happens, she thinks, staring at her mother bent like a noodle over the silk sash anchoring her to the rocking chair; this is where the paths converge, where they all are leading. Madge has removed a pink sneaker from a bony white foot, and is attempting to paint her toenails, gnarly hands, fingers shaking with the effort of making that perfect swipe with the neon polish, her face almost tender with concentration. She's trying hard to remember how it was done, puzzled at how difficult it's become, frustrated. "Ahhhhh!" she moans, "dammitall!" as the brush with a glob of polish slips out of her pencil-stiff fingers. Then she seems to forget about it, gazing out the window, hands folded on top of her lap. Life has a way of doing you in the exact way you would not have chosen, Gwen thinks, remembering her pristine, glamorous mother to whom outward appearances, an elegant, precise grooming and the way it could disguise an inner mess, meant everything.

Tomorrow is the first day of September and Buddy hasn't called for several weeks. This is the time, a few years back, Gwen would take him shopping for new school clothes, new binders, notebooks, their clean sharp scents of possibilities. The Maine air would become crisp, and she'd plan a final outdoor barbeque, Labor Day's metaphorical end of summer, rhythms turning once again toward the year at hand. She did what was expected, didn't she? She did what you do, a mother, a son. In four days he's supposed to start school. If he doesn't come home, there's all the time in the world, too much time, yawning infinitely. She's lost any influence in her own son's life. "Quit mothering me!" Buddy shouted during his last call, when she suggested he could go live with cousin Timmy in Manoa, if he was so bent on staying on O'ahu, family at least, a safer harbor. Timmy studies things, Gwen told him, at the University.

She can call the police. She can still do that and she told him that, her ace in the hole. You *belong* to me legally, she told Buddy, you're not eighteen. I can report you as a runaway, she said. She's mulled over this scenario a million times, the police seeking out and dragging Buddy home the way they chased after her mother...*You should put your mother in a home!* He'd leave the moment Gwen's back was turned, and he'd never trust her again.

She hasn't told Rob. She's afraid in their divorce he'll use it against her. Not that he wants custody, but just to get it. Theirs isn't a marriage, it's a winner-take-all match.

Her mother emerges out of her glazed reverie and attempts to paint her toenails once again, fingers bent and crooked as twigs, hands shaking, a little muscle under her mouth twitching. "Oh this is so...so..."

"Impossible, Mother? I could help. Let me help you."

Madge ignores Gwen, mumbling to herself. Encouragements? Admonishments? Madge is barely seventy, yet her twisted, arthritic hands have aged beyond what Gwen recognizes as *Mother's* hands. Gone the cool long fingers combing through Gwen's hair, stroking her cheek before she crept off to bed. Her mother's words in those days may have been abrupt, but her hands showed her love. After her father was gone Gwen lived for those hands.

Finally Madge manages to finish the toenails on both of her feet, placing the brush back inside, capping the bottle. Looks triumphantly over at Gwen, eyes glittering like small stones. "Perfect, Mother!" Gwen tells her, her heart feeling like it could snap apart.

Madge's eyes blaze then cloud over. Gwen follows her gaze out the window, Mauna Loa and Mauna Kea indigo in the evening shadows. Regal mountains, nothing can touch their imposing volcanic beauty, their grace, giants in a world where most everything else is insignificant by comparison. She hoists herself off the couch and staggers to the window, stiff from doing nothing but sitting by that damn landline, waiting for Buddy's call. Gazes down at the lava path, the scraggly growth of wild orchids on either side. If you focus on this path, really focus, it appears to stretch out past the dirt road, over the pili grass field, through the tangled kipuka, rising on up the blue girth of Mauna Loa.

Gwen sucks in a breath. "You're still waiting for him, aren't you, Mother?

I'll be damned," she whispers. She feels suddenly utterly helpless, a chilled, skin-prickling sense that both of them, her mother and herself, are headed down a steep cliff with no footholds to crawl back up. Madge's health will continue to decline, and Gwen gets to be caretaker for this inevitability when she should be caring for her son, who's intent on marching off a cliff of his own crazed creation.

How could she still be waiting for him? Gwen thinks, watching Madge's intent focus out the window. As if her father after all these years could walk up the path, back into their lives. He'd be just an outline in her own eyes, like the path itself in the near darkness lined with the rowdy, unkempt orchids, the whiskers on his face. Gwen can't even clearly remember that face; only his eyes, those sad, olivine-green eyes.

13

Buddy

Did you know there's some 500 give or take different species of Click Beetles? He's the go-to when it comes to beetles. The eyed click beetle, this striking little number, when it falls or lands on its back, lies quietly there for maybe a minute, then all of a sudden with a loud click it flips into the air. If it's lucky it lands on its feet and is off; otherwise, it tries again and again until it gets it right. Some click beetle larvae feed on roots. The rest eat other insects. Cannibalistic little critters, aren't they? When Buddy was a child he used to watch other kids play with them, press on their abdomens making them jump and click. He felt bad for those beetles, being maneuvered and forced to perform by some sweaty kid's grubby little hand.

Now I'll bet you're all fired up for another Marnie bedtime story. Can we consider the affect these stories had on Buddy, sleepless and untouched beside her? That no matter how twisted, how perverse, how utterly debauched and even tragic these incidents were, they had the power to keep her sexual in his eyes, desirable in the way someone is who seems to live the life of the body beyond one's own virginal flesh. This little tale is a winner, and you might remember it when you hear the rest of Buddy's story. There's order to this madness.

OK, so Marnie's twelve years old and her stepfather, alias The Sleaze, is taking her to Honolulu for a football game. He's recently become her stepdad officially so he's probably trying to get in good with the fam. But this is no picnic in the park, involves a plane and Marnie comes from a poor family, they barely have working cars let alone extra money lying around for airfare; metallic skeletons of a VW van and a Chevy four-door something sit in their yard, propped up on cinder blocks for her stepfather to work on when he gets around to it. The object isn't really to get these running though, because then what would he do to look busy while her mother slaves as a fry-cook at the local dive for the family income? Yellow jackets make their nests in these cars, her stepfather's fighting roosters perch on them, scatter around them, zip under them, spots of red like old blood flaming through their combs. Broken-down vehicles are part of the Lo yard ecology.

So he takes her to Honolulu on Aloha Airlines, and it's not even pro-football, the Rainbows, nothing like that. It's high school, Roosevelt, the school her stepfather went to versus its biggest rival, Punahou, a school for rich haoles and smart everything else. No place her stepfather would've gotten into, Marnie assured Buddy, and even if he did you wanna make a bet his folks couldn't have afforded it? You pay major bucks to go there, almost as much as college. It's the school the president went to, before Harvard.

The game was in the old stadium, she tells Buddy. Rickety wooden bleachers, sparse grass and huge patches of dirt worn so smooth it's like walking on vinyl, that fried smell down where you get refreshments, the dank and greasy stink of popcorn, desiccated teriyaki meat sticks, hot dogs, and body sweat from the swarms of people crammed into narrow lines at half time to get their snacks. Marnie's only twelve, yet no doubt the hot young babe's beginning to bud from the little girl larvae, carving of future curves nestled in the baby fat at her hips, that lava colored hair even then almost down to her butt. Maybe she looked older than she was from behind—she'll give him that, she said, probably he figured she was a teenager already, that he was coming on to her, almost normal-like.

So there she stood in this crowded refreshments line, folks pushing in toward the counter so you could hardly even stand up straight, crackle of pidgin English around her, everybody seeming to know everybody else and here's Marnie Lo, pre-pubescent kid from the Big Island, her stepdad lounging in the bleachers like the waistoid he is, making *her* get the malasadas and Cokes. What kind of father sends a young daughter down into the bowels of a decrepit stadium?

She gets a strange feeling from behind, as if now the line is *really* pushing, leaning in on top of her and Marnie has all she can do to keep standing up. Makes her press in too close to the guy in front of her, not even an inch of space between her and whoever's behind her and it's too crowded to even swivel her neck around and see just who that is. Marnie doesn't know a soul in Honolulu, she reminds Buddy, only Uncle Todd, and he's not really a part of her life at this point. Nobody's a part of Marnie's life at *this* moment; she's in it alone. No space between her and the man in front of her, little man, her breath skittering into the heat of his shiny bald head.

That's when she feels it, or she thinks she does, she's not completely sure, line so tight can't help the innocent thrust of another's flesh? In the background the Roosevelt High School band is playing something snappy and she imagines the cheerleaders, *rah rah rah*, or maybe these are the song leaders, short red and yellow skirts swizzling about their perfect legs, red and yellow pompoms flung high into the oaky sky, stadium lights a lazy haze above, jerking about to the band's *fight fight fight* song, trying to get the crowd to join in too. No, it definitely isn't the push of just *any* flesh, it's a hand! fingers! slipping down the back of Marnie's elastic waist shorts, under the elastic band of her white cotton day-of-the-week underpants (*Friday, yeah!*) in cheery bright pink embroidery, hearts and flowers and a smiley-face, sliding down the smooth flesh of her pubescent okole like it's meant to be there. This hand, these hot wormy fingers inching their way into those deeper, deepest, never-before-touched parts of her.

Marnie's eyes burn, forehead, cheeks, sport searing marks like they've been scorched, knots of panic and sickness in her throat. She considers for a moment wailing around and hitting him, whoever it is, punching whatever her fist meets. But there's no room to even turn, angle sideways, force the hand out from where it's headed, hot fingers now rubbing smoothly against her, almost gentle like he's massaging her, slow and steady, a silkiness to it and she just knows she's going to vomit, but there's no place to do this, the bald head in front of her barking his order to the gum popping Portuguese girl, malasadas end of the booth.

Which means it's almost Marnie's turn, and she has to force herself to remember what it is she's here for, four malasadas, dripping with grease, sinfully sugared Portuguese donuts, two for her stepfather, two for.... *Who is behind her?* Fingers sliding up and down like piano keys, playing her, then suddenly one is inside her as if it belongs there, so gently though! like she's something precious; or maybe like she's nothing at all, just this hot moist flesh getting hotter, desperate under his touch. *Whose* touch? Because once she gets the malasadas and plunges out of the crowded line, will she see him? *Will she look?*

Marnie stutters her order into the flat unconcerned face of the girl, face, flesh, all things flesh, even the bulbous sugared malasadas cradled in their cardboard container like swollen brown fingers, severed off thumbs, juicy snap of the girl's gum. Marnie presses herself hard against the counter, as if maybe she could break through its plywood, behind its rickety barrier, back where the malasadas bubble in big vats of oil and everyone knows what they are about, fry them, sell them, go home. Then would she be safe? Could she go home and be the same?

They do go home of course, flying back to Hilo the next morning after spending the night with a policeman friend of her stepfather's, his Kailua ranch house, gentle lull of the surf off Kailua Beach in the distance, and Marnie on a pallet of sheets and an old canvas sleeping bag inside a cedar walk-in closet; her own little room the policeman told her, amongst the policeman's shiny black shoes, his slippers, under his hanging policeman clothes. Her stepfather and the policeman drinking in the next room, she can hear their voices growing louder, more animated, agitated, arguing about some ball game, some Hawai'i Rainbows player violation, while the violated Marnie Lo lies still as death in the policeman's closet.

Now, you'd expect her to be feeling...something, right? Maybe a kind of supreme loneliness, a cruel awakening to the inexplicable harm the world can so suddenly dish up: she's a twelve year old, for chrissake, who's just been molested by a stranger (she never did look back, plummeting out of that refreshments line, malasadas and Cokes clutched in moist hands, feet on fire), and now they've stuck her in some closet, away from her home, from the familiar, and maybe all of that's changed anyway? Maybe, you'd think, she'd be feeling a kind of betrayal, her new dad slapping those dollar bills into her hands for the malasadas, a treat at a game she probably wasn't much interested in anyway. Not many girls Buddy knows get a boner for football let alone it's not their school, not even their island, for chrissake! Those treats at half time were probably what Marnie looked forward to most. She's still a kid, so things like that carry some weight, a moment of joy you can anticipate, help you make it through the rest.

So here's the thing that gets him, the thing Marnie expected him to close his sweet little Buddums-eyes by, she said, and fall asleep, another night behind the chastity wall, chastised and untouched. Sure, Marnie admitted, she'd been feeling a little sick, lying there on that pallet without hope for sleep, rhythm of the waves beating in the distance, in and out like the ocean is the earth's heart and she's apart from even that. That's how she felt, Marnie said, set apart, separate in some unspeakable way. The way he touched her, like she was something else, like she wasn't even her—so impersonal, yet precious at the same time in its gentleness.

Now get this; here's the thing that kept Buddy tossing and turning, not a hope in the world for a wink of sleep: his *girlfriend* announces solemnly that this was her first sexual experience. Can you believe it? The girl counts this tragic, twisted, exploitive little incident as a sexual *experience*! And when she feels the urge to, you know—here's where Marnie peeks over the barrier at Buddy, smiles all flirty-like, *get off* she says—it's what she thinks about. That pathetic, desperate, dirty little moment, standing in the malasada line at the broken-down King Street stadium, a stranger's hand sliding down inside her pants. Sometimes she even puts a face on him, her molester, with a cool haircut and some indefinable need that only she could satisfy.

These days that stadium doesn't exist; tore it down to the ground, Marnie said, and built a new one somewhere else.

Speaking of a Hand in Someone's Pants – The Jody Johnstone Story

THIS IS WHAT WILL COME back to him—the touch of her inner thigh, that silky, sure skin when she guided his hand inside her pants at the Blue Cheer concert in the old Civic Center Hall. There ain't no use for the summertime blues. Ain't no need? He can't even remember the words exactly, just that it was like Blue Cheer had caught on fire with this song, even the rafters were booming and crackling and the thrumming of the floorboards under him was like riding on a roller coaster, or better yet a wave, swelling up under and around him, and he's in its tube, shooting through. Did he toke on a doobie before? Probably. It was 1968 after all, and Jody just weeks away from tearing open his draft notice in the mail. Everyone passed joints around in those days, the concert hall a haze of smoke, purple haze! in the lights, the strobe, and he didn't even know her name when she slunk up to him and started kissing him, her tongue, his tongue, his hand on her breast and she's guiding it down, him down, the two of them in a heap on the floor. She has those tie-waist, hip-hugger bellbottoms on, tie-dyed too, their electric blue print a swarm of fish or squid or protozoa for all he knew, something alive and swimming up the fabric. Only a matter of untying them and his hand is in there, sliding down her hips then stroking that velvet thigh, his hand on her inner thigh now, fingers slipping under the band of her bikini underpants, deeper and she's moaning, or maybe Blue Cheer is moaning, the world echoing with the sounds of a drawn-out hmmmmm…. Just when his fingers like naughty little caterpillars wiggle toward home base, a dark shape is in front of them, his ruptured face lit up in the strobe, a mad, pony-tailed Judas roaring, "Kiss her! Kiss her now motherfucker and you're done!"

Jody sees the silver wand in his hand, like magic! he thinks, not comprehending any of it, a magic wand? At a Blue Cheer concert? Then the girl's anguished scream, *Nooooo…* the sound of a firecracker exploding, POP! the wand pointed at Jody. Within that second or however many beats of a moment it took (he's reconstructed the infinitesimal steps again and again): girl throws herself over him—.357 fired in the nanosecond of her lunge— girl's body slumped against him, the bullet ripping through her chest, a bullet that was meant for Jody. The auditorium erupts, but they are far enough back from the stage where Blue Cheer doesn't hear it, the shouting, shrieking, *ohmygod*! Pumped up and amplified to the max, the band keeps blasting as Judas opens his mouth, releases a tortured wail like the death scream of a rabbit, then plunges the gun down his throat.

Jody doesn't find out her name until the next day, reading *The Honolulu Advertiser's* account of it, the "Blue Cheer Murder/Suicide" they called it. Even the police, when they questioned Jody that night after the ambulance left, after the concert hall shut down with yellow tape in front of the entrance, just called her *the victim.* Margo Malone. It didn't seem to matter to anyone that Jody had been the intended target; most likely a "domestic spat," the paper said, that the couple had been known to quarrel in public. Margo Malone, who knew Jody no more than twenty minutes, had *died* for him, his hand pressed against the satiny skin of her inner thigh. Had she been trying to make her boyfriend jealous? It certainly worked if that was the case.

Margo's mother gave Jody her daughter's blood-stained blouse when he stopped by her home a few weeks later, a manicured ranch house in a Pacific Heights subdivision—going there felt like something he should do. Pink with ruffles at the cropped hem, washed again and again after the police had returned it, but you could still see the stains, rust-colored clouds covering the front of the shirt.

"Nobody listens to me. This is proof of what happened, do you understand? Nobody cares until they see blood. Tell the world about her, don't let them forget her," Margo's mother said, staring vacantly at Jody, her eyes the color of slate, pouches of bruised looking skin under them. She didn't invite Jody inside, just handed him Margo's shirt as he stood on her lanai, shifting his weight from foot to foot, shrunken with guilt like he was the one who did it. He was the one who lived.

But what could he tell? The sleek touch of her inner thigh? He couldn't even remember her face, a blur in the lights, the haze, the smoke—this twenty year old girl, his own age (which he also found out from *The Advertiser*), who had traded lives with him. For the second time, after his mother ate the plate of poisonous fish that was supposed to have been Jody's, someone had done this. Jody was waiting for Strike Three.

Part III

Autumn

14

Gwen

On a bright October morning Gwen's cousin Kiki shows up at Big Volcano cabin, and before she has a chance to step inside Gwen's at the door, asking her to stay with Madge so she can go to Honolulu to see Buddy. "It's my only hope," she says. "I'm reduced to begging."

"No how you doing, Kiki? Do come in, because I have a BIG FAVOR TO ASK YOU?"

Gwen rolls her eyes.

"Fine, OK, tomorrow. Check out that sky! Today is not a day for babysitting pilikia wahines. How about I take you folks to Kalapana, the lava pool where we used to swim, remember? The volcano covered most of it but there's a secret place Pele left. You've been babysitting your mom since you got home. Need to get out and enjoy Hawai'i again."

Gwen sighs, "Sure, whatever," helps her mother put on a pair of capris and a sleeveless shirt, then they walk out to Kiki's truck.

But when they get to Kalapana Madge refuses to budge from Kiki's truck, punching down the lock on the passenger-side door the minute

Gwen grabs her towel and climbs out. "Jesus!" Gwen hisses into the half-open window, "Can't you just one time cooperate?" Madge stares out the windshield pretending she doesn't hear Gwen or maybe even know her.

"See?" Kiki winks. "Pilikia."

"Indeed," Gwen mutters. "Suit yourself, Mother. We'll be right over there by the water. I'll be watching you though, so no funny business!"

Madge remains inside, a monument to stubbornness, the truck parked under the sweeping shade of a banyan, its airborne roots like long caressing fingers. She will not be caressed. She's fierce, impenetrable as stone, head nodding, jerking upright, then finally slipping back against the seat, for a nap Gwen hopes. Perched on a warm rock, Gwen tips her face up to the sun, squirming her legs about in the lava pool's cool dark water. Old habits of the swim, a casually embraced day. But it seems she's lost the ability to relax, stomach churning, mushy as an old peach. She watches Kiki, sitting on a partially-submerged ledge opposite Gwen, neck slung back, her long hair dangling in the water. Her cousin's wearing surf-shorts and a t-shirt, which she doesn't seem to mind getting wet. Gwen's swimsuit hangs on her skinny torso like a rice sack with arm-holes. Note to self: eat!

Gwen stares at the landscape around them, formerly lush now a lava wasteland, pushing her legs deeper into the salty water until it reaches the tops of her thighs. She gazes at Kiki's wet hair shimmering, sunlight cutting over her cousin's tan face, then she squiggles her body like a tadpole over a jutting finger of worn-down pahoehoe lava until she's fully submerged in the shallow pool, throwing her head back until the water covers her head, nose sticking up like a beacon. Once they would've picked torch ginger to wash their hair with in the lava pool, conk-on-the-head ginger is what they called these giant red flowers. Squeeze the bulb over their heads letting the foamy-sweet juices drip down. That was back when they pretended they were nature-girls or some such thing. Gwen would go home later and re-wash her hair with Prell.

Now she crawls back onto the ledge above the pool, lifts her face into the afternoon sun. Sighs then stretches, making a circular sweep with her recently arthritic ankles, right knee cap pops then shifts into place, remembering those limber limbs back when she was a runner, when she could run and have little else on her mind.

"Remember that Christmas you came home from college and we smoked weed here?" Kiki says. "Our moms had us beat, though. They did stuff like that all the time in the seventies. Inhaled and saw all kinds of truths. Where are they now, those truths? My mom long gone and yours seems to be trying to check out too."

Gwen pushes her leg into the lava, rubbing against its roughness with her own sure flesh. She glances over at the truck, her mother's head still back against the seat, thank Jesus. "Yeah, I also remember you used to go clubbing with my mother, dancing with strange men until all hours. She thinks I didn't know. I always thought you preferred women."

Kiki laughs. "I did tell Auntie Madge the dudes in those clubs she sucked us into weren't doing it for me."

"I hope you don't think that made you any less of a slut in her book," Gwen sniffs, grins.

She re-positions herself, sitting cross-legged on the sun-warmed ledge. Roar of the ocean behind them, lavender stretch of sky. "How come you never left here, anyway?"

"Well *somebody* had to be in charge of my family! Timmy crawling inside his books. Violet drifting in and out. Getting her to be a mom was like holding down a helium balloon, let go and she'd float away. Like your dad, Gwen. The Johnstones weren't flesh and blood people, more like wraiths. Auntie Madge is at least real, even though she's a pain in the okole."

A high long wail, as if talking about her sent some sort of signal, then a shouted "Damnit! Where the hell?" announces Madge is up from her nap.

Gwen groans, slings her towel around her shoulders. "Hold your horses I'm coming!" she mutters, as they head back to the truck. Once inside she grabs Madge's wildly waving hand, presses it to her chest. Dr. Alvarez told her that sometimes the beating of another's heart can be reassuring to a disoriented person. Kiki starts up the truck and they clatter along a dirt road hitting ruts and bumps, creeping under a tunnel of halekoa, palm trees, ironwood, tangles of kiawe that lunge out, scratching the sides. The breeze blowing through the open windows smells of lilikoi and ginger, ripe and sweet. Gwen inhales deeply, a tang of salt water on her skin.

Throughout the summer, September and now October a drought's left much of the land parched, dried grass the color of wheat, no rain to clear away the vog, the land glowing yellow with an eerie sulfuric tinge. Crown flower bushes are being ravished by Monarch caterpillars. Normally this plant sustains both the insects and its numerous blossoms, but this year leaves are shriveled and the flowers sparse, dropping upon a cracked earth. One night at dinner, a few days before Buddy fled the island, he told Gwen and his grandmother if the Monarch food source kept drying up they'd be in big trouble. That they're already threatened.

Madge had scoffed and pinched his arm. "Never mind those insects. It's me! I'm threatened."

The next day, mid-morning, Gwen greets Kiki at the front door of Big Volcano cabin. She's got a glass of wine in one hand, hair brush in the other, dragging the brush through her wedge of hair, grey streaks like lint, alternating with glubs of wine down her throat. "I'm medicating for the trip, no Dramamine in the medicine cabinet, ya know? Come on in," she chirps.

Kiki follows her inside waving cheerfully at Madge glowering in her rocking chair, slumped over like she's about to huck a loogie, a fine line of drool dribbling down her chin.

"I have to remind myself none of this will matter after the apocalypse."

"Have you considered maybe it already happened, your apocalypse? You know, hell on earth, what with global warming, wars, terrorism, poverty—your basic human shit storm."

Gwen rolls her eyes. "One thing's for sure, Buddy's sick of being a pineapple field hand. He's too damn smart; he knows his future isn't in some fruit." She slides up to the counter, grabs the jug of burgundy, pouring more into her glass. "He refuses to come back to Hilo Junior Academy, tells me it's for retarded kids. Fine, I told him, so what about going to school in Honolulu? He could live with Timmy, get his father to pay for it. Personally I think he's getting some very bad advice from that Marnie. I'm going to stay with Timmy, check this thing out." Spots of color prickle Gwen's cheeks. She points at the counter where a spiral notebook sits beside the wine, then hoists a bulging maroon backpack over her shoulders. Buddy's pack; the heft of it against her own back is a small comfort. "I wrote out instructions for her care. Look in the notebook for what she eats and when, that sort of thing. She likes her meals at the same time every day, only sometimes she forgets and thinks it *is* that time when it isn't. Dr. Alvarez's number is taped onto the phone just in case."

Madge shrieks, lifts up her chin, pointing it at the ceiling, a long shrill *Ooooooh*. "Just where are you off to, young lady!"

"Oh for heaven's sake, Mother!" Gwen drops the pack, rushes over and circles her arms around Madge's gaunt neck. "I'm sorry," she tells her, stroking her hair...a little hard.

Kiki slips up beside them and gently removes Gwen's hand. "Auntie Madge is upset about you leaving, huh?"

"She doesn't get it. I tried to explain about Buddy needing me. She's never been able to see past her own needs. I told her I'd be back in a few days and you'd take care of her. A few minutes before you came she asked me to take her to the beach." Gwen's eyes tear up. "Christ, this is hard.

With due respect, it's goddamn hard!" she yells, then marches back toward the door, grabbing her pack. "Can you understand? I resent the hell out of it sometimes and then I feel guilty about that. It's so damn unfair! I waited all my life to know my own mother, my only connection to my father, to whatever we might've had and it's too damn late! God, to tell you the truth I resent the hell out of her for doing this."

"Doing what, getting sick? You think she plotted this to diss you or something?"

"Everything was her way when I was growing up, and here we are decades later and it's still her damn way! The focus is Madge Canada Johnstone, her needs, never what I need. Maybe *I* need a mother, damnit, *god*dammit!" She yanks open the door, turns back for a second and sees two silvery tears roll down her mother's cheeks. Gwen feels them inside like liquid nitrogen, freezing, burning, tearing her in half. Without another look at either of them she slams the door behind her. Crunch of her own steps down the lava path.

15

Madge

SHE IS TIRED, GETTING MORE tired, tired, tired, tired of it all. For starters, her body breaking down. Gwenyth thinks it's all in her mind, her brain, those little lapses that once they've lapsed leave less of her, Madge diminished. But what she doesn't get is the part that came before it, the body, her body! Same one The Artist couldn't keep his hands off, and when he was gone there were others. Madge's dancer's body with its towel bar spine, shaped legs and lush lush lush everywhere else drawing them in, cliché be damned, bees to her honey; then her body's deceit after sixty, everything going south, shutting down, ganging up on her. Take those intractable eyebrow hairs, the white ones that insisted on curling up in her eyebrows, even a couple in her eyelashes; no matter how many times Madge plucked them they'd sneak back like some little white cat you've let out for the night, turn around and she's worked her way back inside, curled up alongside the fireplace, purring, eyes opened, watching. Don't even think it, those purrs announce, I'm home.

Men look at you and you get that quickening in your gut—they're looking at YOU. But they're not, you know, you just happen to be in the path of their vision. You could have as easily been a tree, or a dog, though then they might have at least looked at you with some fondness.

It got worse. The bridge in her mouth spanning two failed teeth over the chasm left by another one yanked; the dentist recommends implants—when did she hit the age where "implants" meant teeth instead of breasts? Not that Madge would've *ever* needed the latter! The pain in her foot, burning heel like stamping on hot coal—plantar fasciitis, the doctor said, and she thought he meant *planter*, as in maybe her years of trying to garden the arid volcano soil had caused it. The popping in her ears that the ENT specialist claimed was her jaw; TMJ she said, a prick of pain every time Madge chewed like a needle got stuck back there. And her knees, lord! like trying to bend a Barbie Doll's, stiff as plastic, though once upon a time every bit as shapely. Left hip on its way out, a hip replacement in her future? No way was she letting them do that, take good bone out of her—those perfect hips back when she did the go go cage dancing and dancing with the psychedelic band, Madge and Violet slipping away to Honolulu for the weekend, strobe lights flashing, her body bending and swaying like a wind's blowing through, shimmer like a willow, electric singe of those guitars.

Violet, what a sissy, lived up to her name. Madge had to bribe her, pay for everything and still that *cluck cluck cluck* chicken-gal slunk behind her, never more than two feet away like some sort of growth. Better when Violet's daughter became old enough, Kiki more brazen, an adventuress in the ways a woman *could* those days, even the occasional slut! There were the concerts in the Waikiki Shell, Madge sprayed with gold lame right over her bikini so she looked like Goldfinger's gal, the shells of her hipbones poking out. If they did the replacement she'd look like one of those haole tourists off the old lady cruises, lurching down the streets of Hilo or Kona in their helmet hairdos, bodies like a flour sack and that rocking gait of the titanium hip.

Eyesight diminished, will her hearing go next? The bags of chips, cookies, whatever she could get her hands on, and not stopping with just one either; whole packages of them blitzed in one long and lonely volcano night, vog sucking at the ohia trees outside, lacing its fingers through dried up ferns, their tips curled from its sulfur-stinking breath. This was the worst, body be damned! confronted with that emptiness, the vacuous silence that drove her back inside her memories, and it wasn't just The Artist, though she misses him the most; it was all of them gone, all that remained slipping, a life lived in those memories getting eaten away by the damn brain farts or whatever these lapses are! To realize how much of it is done, finished, over, *pau*, too late. When The Artist disappeared they all thought she was so brave, the way she pushed on, chin up, made good on his business, raised his daughter—little R & R in Kona on the weekends, but she could be forgiven *those* needs—just don't mention his *disappearance*, because it was unbearable to contemplate any blame in this. Madge couldn't bear it. You do a stupid thing like that, step into the ocean during the monster waves, waving your board about like a flag, *come-and-get-me*! others shouldn't have to be dragged in too as an emotional accomplice.

A betrayal, your own body turns on you and then the brain thing. Or is that also the body? Begins in the brain of course, but doesn't it all? Frigid little blood vessels not getting their content to where its needed, something not firing up quite fast enough, or missing maybe—like trying to start a cold car, the engine rolling over and over then finally igniting; but each time it takes a little longer, the car that much closer to the junk yard.

SHE IS MADGE. WELL, WHO they think? Talk around her like she doesn't exist? Buzzing of voices like she doesn't have ears, like she's already dead? Doctor with the yellow skin, smells of soap, baby breasts half her size tells Gwenyth it can cause dementia, these little strokes, each one stealing a little piece of the *she* she was before. *I'm here, right here! Can't you see me?*

123

She is Madge. If she reminds herself, she is. Nobody can take her where she doesn't want to go, not that...what's her name?...that niece of hers. Niece *by marriage*, so what? As if Madge doesn't know what she's up to. *Babysitting* you, she says. You were a lot more fun as a slut, Kiki. Where is her Gwenyth? When she comes back Madge will ground her!

She is Madge. Move like the light, like wind, wind of the light! Where the grass grows wet around her. Touch the crunchy edges of ferns, *remember* ferns. Delicate orchids, little lavender ballet shoes swaying on their stalks. Ah to be the dancer, one more chance to be the dancer! Pokey ground edging under her toes, nobody in Kawela wears shoes. We wear slippers, thin little stretches of rubber like eel skins around our toes, our naked feet. The Artist and Madge rent the cottage from Father. We're happy, aren't we? In our naked feet? And wasn't she his perfect chick, his *old lady*, his wife? Sexy as all get-out, even had him convinced she *loved* fellatio, that she lived for his prick in her mouth. OK, show me the gal who would rather suck on that instead of a cherry flavored popsicle or a lollypop, or how about a *real* banana damnit, and Madge will show you a liar. But wasn't that what love meant? You lie to make him happy, to make him love you more....

Then comes our Gwenyth and things... they're not *right* anymore. 1969, civil rights, women's rights, a man on the moon, Vietnam, draft lottery, draft dodging (he was good as drafted—what kind of man fails his induction physical?—not that she wasn't delighted to have him in her bed instead of slogging through some outer Saigon jungle, but what's the psychological profile, the relationship portent in this...)? 1970 and it's Kent State (she remembers! Students shot by National Guardsmen, how young they all were, kids killing kids), students marching on freeways, taking over buildings, rioting in the streets, a progressive, aggressive, sex-and-drugs-and rock-and-roll world out there, but in Kawela it's Madge and that baby, weeping. Breasts swell up fist-hard with infection, leaking like hot water bottles you put on to keep the chills away. Chilled, so cold. Try to nurse her, she's crying, Madge's crying, a hungry infant mouth snapping open and shut, open and shut like Pacman. Is this where it begins, not being able to satisfy? Madge was the mother who was never enough. When did it get so dark? Thicket of ironwood shading the cottage, rains too much. Where did the blues disappear to, the greens, lemony yellows? Her story in color.

The Artist starts his wanting, wanting too much; he exhausts her, this want, the way she can't seem to fill it. She asks him, When did I become not enough? His breath smells sharp like the stuff he cleans his brushes in. Not enough money in art turns out, like Father warned. The Artist works in a shop, sells paints, canvas, grows sullen, skinny as a whisker, working for someone else. Magic, I need my magic, he says! Madge would do it for him this magic, if she had a clue what magic he so desperately needs. Makes leis like Ana did, pikake, plumeria, illima, crown flower, to sell to the tourists, *aloha* for people they don't even know. Do *you* remember plumeria and crown flower? Poisonous these are. She strings blossoms onto her needle, skinny and long as a humming bird's tongue, but the milk gets under her skin, fingers swelling like little balloons, burn, itch, pop! At night she cries into her pillow, at first so he can't hear and then so he will. It wasn't supposed to be this way.

Father's gone and The Artist wants the money to buy their *own* arts supplies store in Hilo; he will manage it, he tells her, and in *his* store there will be magic. Tricks? she asked—*illusions*! he said, supplies for magicians, *conjurers*. Anything to make him happy, so maybe he'll stop needing her to be somebody else. They move to Big Volcano cabin, but turns out he's a no good *conjurer* of income and the store sinks. She tells him *do* something. Do something, or she'll sell that store, get back Father's money! Do your damn magic *now*! she says. Picks up the yellow surfboard.

Madge. Makela. Margareit. Wife. Mother. Daughter. Paper cut doll, flesh bland as paste. Life flows inside, out, sometimes slow sometimes a rush, sometimes shut off like a faucet. Who is in charge, Father? They think because she can't remember where the kitchen is sometimes, how to turn the kettle off sometimes, even what a kettle is, screaming and steaming from...where? Think she doesn't know she's sick. That she's not going to get well. That every day is a little worse. Words don't always come out the way she remembers these days. Like the Spill and Spell game she played with little Gwenyth, shake the letters, toss them out. Not the words she imagined would form, not the same ones at all. Sometimes this makes her so mad she breaks things. The crystal candy bowl, for instance. Throws it on the floor, shattering, winks up at her, little bits glistening like tears. What do you get by destroying my grandmother's candy dish? Gwenyth scolds. Stay long enough in this world you end up scolded by your own child.

You weren't the best mother, Madge, the fact of this aches your heart. Chilled little olive in there just couldn't *feel* enough, sometimes. You tried, God knows you tried, and you *do* love her, you do. But it wasn't enough. You were never enough. Madge was two mothers, the one before, and then when he didn't come home. The way there were two marriages, before and after Gwenyth. Madge was going to be a dancer. She wants her daughter to know Madge *knows* she is sick. That she doesn't have to hide it, her disgust. You mustn't put me away, Gwenyth, you will be here too someday. You will be me.

She remembers her own mother, Ana, Crown Flower Queen, the neighbors called her, humming, eyes empty as two plates, stringing her leis from the thick bushes against their house, so thick and gnarled even the sun doesn't dare shine in *those* windows, Father's Headache Room, dark, smells of the earth, earth to earth, dust to dust, this cave, retreat like a bat. Father a bat. Ana the sun. She sings Hawaiian songs, mournful words, sings and strings her leis, the Crown Flower Queen, so many poisonous leis!

Ana Canada, long wavy hair like a shawl, sitting on cool grass the color of mint, tells Makela how when she was newly married, she and her sister (Auntie who?) were playing with a slingshot they made out of shards of bamboo, shooting stones at mynah birds, not aiming to hit them, not really, just playing—a too-young wife who still had the play in her then. But Ana hits one, knocking it down from the mango tree. Father made her and her sister (Auntie who?) eat it. Made them pull out the black dead feathers, impale the small dead body on a kiawe stick. Bare as a pig plucked clean as a napkin, they cooked the mynah on the back yard barbecue. "Maybe next time you don't kill so easily," says Father. "That's for God to choose." He's always right, he lets them know this, but who is in charge?

Ana becomes strange, a stranger, out of focus, like she isn't really with them, like she's already left. "They can lose it," Dr. Alvarez says to Gwenyth—to Gwenyth! And here Madge sits, naked as birth under her cold yellow hand—"TIA victims." Shaking her head, hair thin and straight as sea urchin quills.

Speaking of Drugs – The Jody Johnstone Story

COULD WE STRESS HOW MUCH pot he smoked at that Blue Cheer concert, and that this might have something to do with his inability to clearly remember just how much was "probably" consumed? They were called lids back then, maybe still are, he's hardly an authority these days. Stuffed into a sandwich baggie like your mom packed your lunch in, only by then of course Jody had no mom to perform this act of kindness and no father who would—it was much easier for the senior Johnstone to hand his son five dollars for lunch at Zippy's, or wherever the kid wanted to go, just don't bother Dad. And Dad was able to pay Jody in this manner since the settlement he got from the Rudy's Restaurant Botulism Case was of enough heft that the senior Johnstone didn't have to worry about working, or parenting, or pretty much anything at all beyond the full-time occupation of his own misery. He had loved his wife, that much was evident, a love so big from a little man who had drawn an even shorter straw in the emotional-capacity of his brain, such that there wasn't much left over for anyone else. All this to say that Jody had plenty of "lunch-funds" for the best local weed, Kona

Mona, Maui Wowie, and for dessert he'd developed a fondness for psilo-cybin mushrooms picked in the Ko'olau mountain valleys. No time for a hike? Daddy's botulism assets could purchase mescaline, LSD, whatever the brand. Jody wasn't so much spoiled as bought off, money instead of discipline, money instead of guidance, money in lieu of love, and rather than face that silent Kahala ranch house with his despairing, hostile father and twitchy, paranoid sister (who stuck around after high school ostensi-bly to care for their father, but more likely because she was scared as shit to go anywhere else), Jody reveled in his own S & S lifestyle—smoke and surf—sometimes a hit of acid on top, paddling out to catch those waves then riding them to oblivion. Even on flat, no swell afternoons, the humid Kona air heavy as wet laundry, he liked to float about on his board, his back crisped in the sun to a fierce, kiln fired brown, diving down occasionally to pick up heads of coral off the ocean floor, scrutinizing them for colors and subtle intricacies, as only someone as stoned as he might do.

So let's face it, Jody Johnstone was out of his gourd at the Blue Cheer concert, enough that his sinewy, dancing shape with its tight surfer butt, that fried, electrified swaying of his hipless hips could attract such a fox as Margo Malone (whose name you'll recall he didn't find out until after the fact), peeved at her own boyfriend, but not savvy enough to recognize just how mad her boyfriend was at her, and how if you take that anger and mix it into a jealous, controlling personality, throw in a flack jacket pocket sized .357—this before the days of metal-detecting security going into a concert or anywhere else—you get the last few minutes of Margo's short life, Jody's hand on her stomach beneath the pink crop top, her mouth pressed against his, liking that well enough and really so *pissed* at that boyfriend of hers, whom she witnessed dry humping Patty Yamaguchi in the girl's bathroom at Honolulu Community College, Margo yanks that stoned *cat's* hand off her stomach, sliding it down so its undoing her pants, so its on her thighs, that silken inner thigh, her sweet, throbbing flesh—the last thing she feels, the last he remembers, the last moment of *his* life forever changed when Margo instinctively throws herself on top of him, taking the bullet that was meant for Jody. Why would she do that? Didn't know him from Adam, except for his hand on her thigh and the promise of this that would never be fulfilled. How do you repay such closure, her climax, the grand finale of a person who didn't know you but died for you anyway?

You don't, of course, and Jody's drug use became even more prodigious, legend in fact, because now there were two sacrifices he could never repay, his mother's and Margo's—how do you live *sober* with this, or maybe the more apt question, why would you?

One day, high as clouds, Jody and Blake go to a magic show at the Waikiki Shell. Well, they didn't officially attend, as in they didn't pay for admission, but hung out at the top of the bleachers where they had shimmied up the poles from the lawn below, smoking and snorting and, if memory serves, a hit of Orange Sunshine licked off a blotter. Jody wouldn't remember who the performer was, or his tricks (*illusions* he would in the future correct anyone ill-informed enough to call such artistry *tricks*), which had all been bathed in the wavy, sparkling, liquid fireworks displays going off behind his eyes from the acid. What stuck with him was a conversation overheard, the folks in the row in front of them chatting about the great Harry Houdini, the ultimate *escape artist*, and how he had made an elephant and a man disappear. "No shit?" Jody whispered. Made them *disappear*? No shit.

Interlude – A Houdini Death

AUGUST 5, 1926, SWIMMING POOL at the Hotel Shelton in New York, a coffin-sized box containing the Illustrious Houdini is lowered into the pool then dropped to the bottom, where he stayed under water for one hour and 31 minutes, substantially beating the 19 minute record for the "underwater burial" set by the Egyptian magician (fakir!) Roman Bey. Houdini repeated this in other major cities during his final tour, until his untimely death in Detroit. His body was shipped back to New York in his "underwater casket," becoming the only box the great magician never attempted to escape from.

16

Buddy

FEEL THIS, BUDDY BABES! HIS hand a cold blade of moonlight slipping down the curve of her too-full belly. Marnie babes, are we getting fat here? Too much poi, sweet and sour cherry seed, manapua and laulau? Too much Coke, too much ice cream, too much weed, stoner hunger (what-the-hell's-she-been-up-to-while-he's-out-busting-his-butt-in-the-pineapple-fields!), grazing, scarfing, grinding everything in sight? What's a poor, starving model to do! Little worms his fingers, inching, squiggling, thrusting, their downward venture, smooth pulpy skin of a caterpillar, the hunch, the hump, little bump and lump of SOMETHING'S IN THERE! We're not alone, Buddy babes.

A tisket, a tasket, Marnie has a secret, green and yellow, brown or white? If it's not *his* secret, than whose...! secret can it be?

Bedtime story number WHO THE FUCK KNOWS HOW MANY THERE ARE! *Hey there little red riding hood, you sure are looking good....* Which one is this, Marnie Lo? The big bad wolf sees you, follows you home, knocks on the door and you call out, come *iiinnnn*! from your sweet little pure little bed. What nice eyes you have, what a big...? Or maybe you see him first, think you have it all in control, *under my thumb*.... Thumbelina, pretty Thumbelina, so tiny, so helpless, such a crock! Bedtime story number 69? He feeds you this time, popping that popper right under your nostrils, sizzle of coke up your little pug nose, on your long red tongue, his long red tongue, tongue-tied we are, couple of fab yellow E's to top off that high, ah *Ecstasy*, and you don't remember a thing in the morning, you swear. (GHB, some date rape drug with that latte?) Or do you? How much does it hurt, Marnie Lo, *this* much? This burning, churning ache of the inadequate, the never can be enough for this person yet you're stuck there like some kind of barnacle, a thorn, something that won't ever come off whole again, stuck, dried out, wasted, used-up, Ka put! Forever dependent on...what? What's it to you, Marnie Lo, *who's inside you now?*

The Rose Chafer, a slim hairy beetle, one of the many scarab beetles. Now this is a family! a huge one, over 20,000 species, diverse in size and appearance. Adults appear in late spring or early summer, eating the leaves and flowers of roses, grapes, other plants too. Larvae burrow into the ground, feeding on the roots of grasses. Rose Chafers are difficult to control. Hah, like we should! The arrogance of humans. Survival of the one best able to exterminate the other.

Fruit flies, now here's an interesting insect, their claim to fame due to their scientific uses, studies of inheritance in particular. You can view their entire life cycle in just two weeks, watch them mate, watch the female lay her eggs, watch the egg become a larvae, a pupae, a full grown male perhaps, a bearded-wing, or even—get this! our interest in them—a *mutant*. And then they die.

17

Gwen

THE STORY GWEN'S MOTHER TOLD her about her own mother's death had to do with butterflies. A slow story, how it lingered. She kept stalling the complete telling of it, revealing its various parts over a forty-year span of Gwen's life. Did those languid revelations help prolong it in her memory? Force her own mother to stay alive longer. "She was so brief," Madge used to say, shaking her head.

The gist of it: one minute Ana Kalamahea Canada was stringing crown flower leis, alternating the purple waxy blossoms with the white, the next she's dead. It was Madge who discovered her, chunky little Makela seven years old, grasping her Skippy Peanut Butter jar stuffed with pale leaves from the crown flower bush, a fat Monarch caterpillar hanging upside down off the top, wiggling out of its old skin, spinning its chrysalis to become something new.

Over the years Gwen's visualized this scene, frozen into a time frame that must forever exist in Madge's mind. Everything lifeless except for the sluggish movements of that caterpillar. Imagined her mother, bewildered, chubby and earnest, tugging her own mother's hand to show her this prize, this impending transformation, the ugly caterpillar's debut as a beautiful Monarch. This is what Gwen is thinking about now, sitting at a picnic table on the sprawling green lawn of Ala Moana Beach Park, staring at Marnie, her son's *girlfriend*, he called her. Transformation. Under a hot midday sun the grass smells like dried corn. Gwen inhales, wishing *she* could transform, be someone else, anywhere else. A park, Buddy's suggestion when she told him she was in Honolulu determined to see him, public territory for their meeting so that "nobody" makes a scene. Marnie's wearing the same petulant expression she had on her face when Buddy first introduced her months ago, but something about her is different, something changed. Gwen studies Marnie as she gazes out at the ocean, sunny white light splaying the dark blue surface. Her face looks bloated, cheeks bunching up under her heavy eyes, a roundness almost cocoon-like. The girl has packed on some pounds, that much is clear, brown stomach lunging out over a faded purple palaka bikini, thighs like bowling pins.

Buddy looks the same, the way Gwen has visualized him every night before she sleeps, when she sleeps—glass of wine, a Xanax chaser, whatever it takes. His curls need a good trim, squiggling over his forehead and cheeks like macaroni. Gwen had wondered if when she finally saw her son again he would appear thinner, marked by months of feeding himself, trying to care for himself without her. Had hoped, perhaps... and admits to feeling a little disappointed that he appears so usual.

Marnie flashes her grin, leaning in over the stained redwood table. Gwen can smell strawberry shave ice on her breath, her lips cherried from the sticky syrup, the empty paper cone popping and twisting between her fingers. "I'm hapai. That's why I'm fat. Saw you checking me out. It's due the end of January."

Gwen turns away from her, temples twitching, heart pounding, and stares at the deep green ridges of the Ko'olaus behind. Breathe! she orders herself. "Oh," she says stupidly. Sunday in the park activities continue as if nothing's been said, nothing altered, no worlds ripped apart. *Oh?* Feels like she's being lifted out over it all, to observe from some shocked distance kites, frisbees, dogs scampering, barking, kids jumping into the small, shivery waves, darting about the gleaming shore, tourists sprawled on top of the sand in their garish bathing suits, salmon pinks, tangerine, neon orange, banana yellows (who pitches them this look as *Hawaiian*, colors outrageous enough to make sure they get they're no longer in Kansas?) sunburned skin the color of a bruise. Smells of teriyaki chicken, luau, all a part of some Sunday world surely but not *her* world. She tries to catch Buddy's eyes but he's looking away, out to the pale place where ocean becomes sky.

Marnie's blubbery Uncle Todd had lumbered over to a hot dog stand and returns now bearing sodas, hot dogs, and greasy malasadas. Purchased with *Gwen's* money, along with the shave ice. "Kaukau for the keiki," Todd grins, his fat, rectangular face like a shoebox with lips. He hands Marnie some food, sticking his paw out and gingerly rubbing her belly. Gwen's own stomach curdles at this display. She glances at the hot dog he's put in front of her in its little paper dish, smothered in mustard and relish, and a sour bile creeps into her throat. "Preservatives, huh? *Whatevah*," Todd nods, watching her stare sickly at her food. Shakes his head. "Can't avoid them so may as well indulge." Pops half a dog into his mouth.

"Buddy!" she manages finally, voice cracking. "Is it yours? Is that baby yours?"

He shrugs, a drawn-out and sustained shrug, long as a yawn, avoiding her eyes.

"I think you at least owe me an answer! I enrolled you at Iolani, a good school Timmy told me, an *expensive* school that I paid for, and Timmy's all set for you to live with him, said it would be just fine."

"*Dad* paid you mean. Dad's the one who pays. You're there, I'm here, Dad's five fricken time zones away and he pays. It's the way things work in our family."

"What's the difference who paid, that's not the point!"

"We're not moving," Marnie chimes, shaking her hair, uncombed violence of it spewing about her shoulders and back. "We don't need school. School's bullshit."

"You don't speak for my son..."

"What the hell!" Buddy interrupts. "Nobody speaks for me, OK? Quit mothering me. If I go to school it's because *I* want to go to school."

"You can go to school and live with me, yeah?" Todd offers, sucking malasada sugar off one swollen finger at a time. Gwen studies his tongue, the color of Marnie's bikini, purple and unapologetically obscene. "Only you'll have to keep paying some rent. I can't work on account of The Orange...that's Agent Orange," he confides to Gwen, leaning over the table so close she inhales the sour odor of onions on his breath from the hot dog. "It ruined my life. What you see is a shadow of the man I used to be."

A very *corpulent* shadow, Gwen's thinking.

"Does Timmy have a bathroom with a decent mirror and a working shower? Would we have our own bedroom and a bed with legs, not just some mattress on the floor?" Marnie asks.

"Who do you anticipate will pay for this birth!" Gwen demands, deliberately ignoring her would *we* have a bedroom.

Marnie flashes her grin, those long white teeth. "Chill out there Mrs. Winter, have a beer. Todd's got some Primo in his pack. Your boy here says you get into an alcoholic bev-er-age now and then. No worries about the keiki, your tax dollars at work, huh? I can go on Welfare. Check this out, Buddy moves to somebody's crib I go with him. We're a couple."

"About to be a trio," Gwen mutters, gazing furtively at Todd's canvas pack parked on the bench beside him, the metallic taste of need in her mouth despite that Marnie's rudeness and her own son's betrayal, an ashy lump in her throat like a chunk of coal. Her food sits untouched, Todd eyeballing it like it could run away. She gazes longingly at the mountains, deep green

Ko'olaus, the color of something fresh, not broken, not the heartbreak she's feeling now. Turns back to Buddy with a vengeance. "You get up!" she roars. "Please! Can we please take a walk down the beach, alone? I need to talk to you, *alone!*" She glares at Marnie, challenging her, but the girl only shrugs and yanks back her hair, a greasy hunk of it kidnapped by her hot dog bun.

"I don't take walks," she says. "If folks were meant to walk, why the fuck did God make cars?"

"Can I score your dog and malasada?" Todd asks, already lunging for them as Gwen stands. "If you're not going to be eating them."

"Bon appetite," she replies, motioning to Buddy to follow her. Her heart pumps hard as they walk down to the shore, dodging cruising toddlers, scuttling dogs, ears pointed skyward, hoisted like sails. Feet sink into soft sand, the water clear and tepid around her ankles. That Sunday-at-the-beach feeling in the air, she remembers from when she was a kid here, a certain abandonment and brief freedom, curling waves, blue-hot sky, the world of Mondays doesn't exist for one glorious, golden afternoon. This time she doesn't feel a part of it; more like she's set apart. "One hot dog," Gwen whispers, "two malasadas, three dead fish, four broken shells, five screaming kids..." and the wrecked parents who if they're smart send them off to military school before they're teenagers! Count, count, count! she orders herself.

"Jesus Christ, with all due respect, Buddy, why can't you just say if it's your baby or not? If it is, obviously we need to take certain actions here. For Lord's sake, can't you just tell me? Clearly I'm not going to start moralizing, it's a little late for the *use protection* talk! Yes, I wish you'd never slept with that girl, and I wish you had enough sense to wear a condom, and sometimes I wish you were two years old, except I'd have all this to face again, by God! I wish it wasn't too late for a lot of things, but you've been living with that Marnie and obviously it's too damn late for whatever you *didn't* do."

"Oh so you immediately assume it's mine, huh? You don't owe me a damn thing, it's not your issue," he mutters, glaring.

"Well what does that Marnie say she wants you to do?"

"Will you stop calling her *that* Marnie! She's Marnie, just Marnie." Buddy hesitates, stops walking. He picks up a broken stem off a sun-bleached white coral, gazes at it for a moment, then hucks it into the sea. When he finally looks at Gwen there's a dampness around his eyes. "The thing is, I don't exactly remember it."

"Remember what?"

"*It*! We fooled around some, but...I just don't remember, OK?" He peers at her suspiciously. "Maybe it's not all what it's cracked up to be. I doubt insects feel important when they do it, they're just programmed that way."

"For heaven's sake Buddy, we're not insects here." She throws up her hands. "Are you telling me you don't *remember* having sex with that girl? Is that what you're telling me?"

"I'm telling you I don't remember that *part* is all. We've been doing drugs too, if you want to know. Maybe I wasn't completely conscious or something."

There's a rage and a helplessness beating inside Gwen, a fist of it. She wants to slap him, and she wants to grab him and never let go. "Jesus! Buddy, honest to God, who was it I should've been or done that might have made a difference here? God, have we been this *lacking* as parents, your father and I? Did that Marnie tell her parents? She needs to go home, that's what she needs to do."

He shakes his head, spits. "She said she's never going home. Anyway, by the time it's born she'll be eighteen."

"Son, you've got to listen to me. If you don't know you're the father you can't be serious about taking this on, you don't know what you're getting into. Your life will be over! Do you hear me? You have plans, college. Is this why you haven't come home? This is absolutely insane, I'm letting her mother know. We need to get a DNA test, is what we'll do."

He stamps his foot in the sand, a hollow, shivery sound. "Here's exactly why I wasn't going to tell you! Let me handle this, it's my problem not yours. Maybe I was asleep."

"Oh for sweet Jesus's sake, you wouldn't be asleep for that, trust me! God didn't your father tell you anything? Movies? Porn internet for crying out loud. What about the uncle, Todd? He's too old to be hanging around you two, but could *he* be the father, sick as that is?"

Buddy lets out a sharp sound like a yip. Gwen rubs her ear then tugs at one hand with the other. For some reason she doesn't know what to do with her hands. It seems she should be doing something with her hands.

"I doubt that guy could father an actual life form. He's pretty messed up, or didn't you notice? But hey, like we appreciate the incest accusation." Buddy bends down, scoops up a handful of wet sand, drizzling it thoughtfully between his fingers. "Something's pretty damn weird about Marnie's family though, all of them. You and Dad weren't exactly Dr. Spock, but you didn't completely screw me up."

"Well gee, thanks for the vote of confidence." She narrows her eyes at him, the lump in her throat slipping down further, poking like a chunk of caught meat. Tries to force a deep breath. "Buddy, I want you to come home. We're still a family, aren't we? I know you miss your dad but we're still a family, you and me."

"I'm staying with Marnie."

"Are you pitying her, is that it? You can't be with somebody because you pity them, it'll never work. You'll ruin your life."

"It's already ruined!" he snaps. "Christ, you call what I'm having a life? Nothing to do with Marnie either, she's the good part."

Gwen stares at her son. It's like she's talking to somebody else, some separate person, with an existence significantly apart from her own. Well, isn't that the way it's supposed to be? You raise them to be on their own, right? The ocean hums. Warm small waves swirl around their ankles as the tide pushes in. Tears sprout in her eyes and she blinks them back. *No!* It's not supposed to be like this. If only it were sixteen years ago, start over, do it differently somehow! She can barely remember what it felt like to be adored, trusted, accepted by her own son, the center of his life. "So, what kind of drugs have you been taking?" she asks flatly.

He shakes his head, "Worried about missing some of your pharmaceuticals? You really want to know why I stayed here?"

She nods, eyes tearing up again.

"There's this guy I met who was in a wheelchair. At Tripler Hospital, while I was waiting for Marnie to collect her so-called modeling pay. Like, he had no legs, but he reminded me of Dad. He gave me something, want to see?" Buddy reaches into the pocket of his cutoff shorts, pulling out a tapa print billfold Gwen doesn't recognize. He removes a photograph and hands it to her, an apple tree in a winter field. She can make out the desiccated fruit hanging unpicked, paralyzed on the branches. The ground looks hard and icy, a dry cold yellow. There's nothing else, just the tree, its gnarled shadow.

"Looks a bit like Maine in the off-season, huh? The guy said it was his folks' property somewhere in the middle of the country. He told me he'd never see them again. He's got shrapnel inside him, splattered about like BB's, and he gets these infections. He said the doctors took one leg and then the other. His arms don't work too good anymore he said, so they'll be whacked off next. He's rotting from the inside out, one goddamn body part at a time."

Gwen wipes her forehead. The sun beats down like they're standing in a desert instead of the shore. "Why are you telling me this?"

"Because I kept seeing this crippled, decaying man as my dad! He reminded me of *some* kind of a dad. I thought about playing ball with him, things like that, *dad* kinds of things. Even though I don't have a hard-on for playing ball I sort of thought he would, you know? I thought he was really nice, giving me his picture and all. I thought that *meant* something, giving me his photograph of home. Wouldn't it be great to have a dad like that, I thought? Giving you stuff that means something, instead of checks jammed into envelopes to pay for a retard school. Can't even write a fricken letter. But you know what?"

Gwen shakes her head, not sure if she wants to hear *what*. What she really wants is to stop looking at him, stare instead at the ocean, sailboats, paddleboards, windsurfers, parasailers, other people having fun. She wants him to know his father used to be different, used to have something to believe in. Something to live a life by, just maybe not a life with her. Because that's when he started locking people up. It's not that he doesn't believe in prisons, just doesn't believe in himself holding the keys. How could he? Rob Winter was a *radical*.

She's thinking these things as tears roll down her cheeks. Her son's expression...hungry, needful, so goddamn separate from her, makes her mute, even when she knows he's waiting for her to say something.

Buddy shrugs, twisting the corners of his mouth into a grin. "Get this. You'll like this part. I found out later that guy, that *dad-like* guy stole my money! While I was looking at his fucking picture he snaked his rotting hand down into my back pocket and stole fifty bucks. Tripler called Marnie's so-called modeling agency, that sends her on these lame-ass jobs to justify their existence, and that's how we found out. They discovered it in his pocket when they did the laundry; he didn't even care enough to hide it. Spent some on cigarettes, shoved the rest inside his goddamn pocket. I scammed a taxi, lifted food, clothes. I was ashamed to come home. Then I started thinking, what the hell difference does it make?"

Gwen reaches her hand out but Buddy reels toward the water. He makes a sharp sound, twists around and throws himself backwards into a small wave, photograph and billfold in hand, then stands up immediately, shaking himself out like a dog. "Hey, like don't feel sorry for me, because I'm no goddamn better! I stole the money from Grandma in the first place!"

She rubs her eyes, sucks in a salty breath. "It doesn't matter, the money doesn't matter! Please come home, Buddy. It's not the same without you. Being your mother is all I've got."

"No!" He flings water out of his hair, twisting his neck about violently. "I won't be your reason to exist, no way. You're not pinning that one on me."

She gazes at the curve of his spine as he bends over, thinness exaggerating the play of discs, a fall of dominoes down his back. Her son. Flesh of her flesh. And she can't touch him. Swallows hard. "Then at least...please, Buddy, go to school here. Don't ruin your future. Your dad paid the deposit to Iolani. We're still your parents. Let us do this for you, please."

He shrugs, his usually pale shoulders glowing with a light yellow tan. "What future? I thought we're either Raptured or handed a one-way ticket to Hell, and soon, according to your pseudo-scientific calculations. Anyway, who says you're put in this world to do for me just because you gave birth to me? I live with Timmy, Marnie comes too. *I* don't desert people."

Gwen nods her submission. Though you deserted me..., she wants to tell him. She feels beaten. Maybe she deserves it. Her son is no longer a child. Maybe this was stolen when they left Maine. "I miss being your mother," she says quietly.

He snorts, "Can't imagine why. You have Grandma to mother."

THEY WALK BACK DOWN THE beach, white-hot strip of sand, approaching the picnic table on the adjacent lawn. Todd and Marnie are sitting on top, Marnie scowling, her bloated legs crossed like some belligerent Buddha. "At least that Marnie won't be so vain with some extra pounds on her," Gwen mutters.

"She's still the prettiest girl I know. Trouble with you, you judge everybody according to your own standards. Like Dad. He didn't fit what you determined a husband should be, huh?"

Her cheeks sear a hot red. "And I suppose he fits your image of an ideal father, an *absent* father? It takes two to tangle or tango or whatever the hell that bloody cliché is! When you feel the need to blame, what about blaming us both for a change? All I meant was some women are at their best with a little extra flesh, like my cousin Kiki, or Grandma before she got sick. Marnie isn't like them. She's a thin person waiting to have a baby."

Buddy gazes at the table. Gwen fights back an urge to grab him, kidnap her son from this craziness his life has become. She stares at Todd and Marnie just ahead of them now, chins cupped vacuously into fleshy hands. Buddy's going back to them and leaving her. He's wrong about giving birth, what is she in this world if not for him? You squeeze out a baby who's been part of you for nine months, make sure he gets his shots, hugs, bandaids on skinned knees, eats right, sleeps eight hours, no uber-violent video games or x-rated shows, and learns to read. But when he grows up, how do you protect him from a disaster of his own choosing? Where are the bandaids for this?

"You know what I want?" she touches his bare shoulder, pretending not to notice the way he flinches, pulls away. "I'd like to take flowers to the graves of my grandparents and just sit. It's important to remember family, son, to understand where you come from."

"So do it. Nobody's stopping you."

She shakes her head, a slightly hysterical laughter building inside. Forces it back, swallowing hard. "Well, the thing is I can't. You know why? Maybe you've forgotten. Our family doesn't have graves, we don't *do* tombstones, funerals, any of it. Our people don't die, Buddy. They just disappear."

Buddy snorts, "That's bullshit. So bury them now, in a virtual grave. It's clean and cheap, won't even need to dig a hole for the corpse."

"What on earth are you talking about?"

"Marnie showed me this website one day when we were hanging out in the computer lab at the retard school. It's called Findagrave.com. You type in a cemetery and a name and they do a search for the dead guy. If he's not there you can put him there, inter him virtually. Write an obit, all of it, even put flowers on his grave—they have photos of roses, lilies, whatever. So you can visit your grandparents' graves and never have to leave your home."

She stares at her son, not sure if she's shocked, bewildered, appalled, quite what she's feeling. It's like he's become someone else entirely. "Buddy, you are really not getting it."

He shakes his head. "Nope, I'm totally getting it. Will you please just fricken let me go?"

Gwen thinks again about those Monarch butterflies, how when Buddy told them their populations were disappearing she'd asked him why. He had shrugged, gave her his *duh* look. "Climate change, habitat destruction, human greed, the usual suspects," he said. "One day the world will wake up and it'll be *Whoops!* One of nature's most perfect creations, vanished."

18

Buddy

THE WAY IT PLAYED OUT? His mom huffs back to the Big Island in a snit because he refused to show her where he's living. Could you imagine Gwen Winter hanging out in The Todd's living room? Delicately brushing cockroaches off her ankles while they chat about chemicals, or maybe over a serving of chemicals: her Xanax with a side of his warrior-weed. "I feel like everything's ending," she'd said. "Sure," Buddy agreed, amicable enough. "But not yet. 2013, remember? You said you'd one-up the fundamentalists, cut them off at the knees." Then Marnie refuses to fricken move from this hole. The upshot? He's screwed.

Here's how that goes: They ride The Bus to U.H. to meet Buddy's cousin Timmy, who plunks them down on folding metal chairs in the front room of his Manoa apartment. Timmy's perched on the edge of the couch, the only real furniture in there, like at any moment he might bolt. He's got this inane monotone chuckle like some alien laugh track commandeered his brain. "So! Hee hee. Here you are. Hee hee. So!" Glancing furtively at Marnie's baby bulge like a roll of dough under her tight black tank top, the grin tugging at his mouth, dropping his lower lip into something that on a less skittish man might be described as a sneer.

He's a scrawny little man, bone and sinew with a pointy face like a rat's, sunken rat eyes and sharp cheekbones. Kiki must've been gifted all the girth in the Violet Johnstone side of their fam. He hands them paper cups of guava juice and a plate of Ritz crackers with triangles of pre-sliced cheese product. Later, Marnie will decide he was dissing her. "Like I'm a thing to wipe his feet on. Models don't *do* fake cheese. I've given blowjobs to stars! Don't forget that, Buddy-boy."

Yeah, like he's going to forget *that*? Especially since, according to these job stats he's no star in Marnie's records keeping. So Buddy's stuck in Todd's "pad," taking The Bus every morning to school. He doesn't have any friends at Iolani, can't picture himself fitting in with kids who go home to real homes, real parents, dogs, a real kid life where someone feeds you, bosses you around, and you get pissed at them and behave like a spoiled brat because you know they'll keep you anyway. He's in a broken down little rental in the Jungle with a bitchy pregnant girl, her creepy uncle, a house that boasts more roaches than food to feed them—the kind with antennae *and* the kind that lie around in ashtrays.

Lately Buddy's been skipping school, a few days a week then a few more. Head throbbing he lounges about Todd's house, sucking Kona weather making everything stick, doors, windows, clothes to his skin, air stinking of old glue. He doesn't know how to do this anymore, and he doesn't know how to get out of it. He's even starting to miss his grandmother.

Does Buddy have a home? He's a caddisfly, building his own personal house, carrying it around on his back wherever he goes. Caddisworms hatch under water making a silky tube to build their houses on, using sticks, sand, leaves, little stones.... *Drugs, promises of sex.* Caddisworms stick their little caddis heads and feet out of their front doors, close themselves off into their private little worlds until it's time to become a caddisfly. *Whoosh, I'm outa-*

here. Maybe he's like a shipworm, chewing his way into the massive wood of ships, prisoner in a hole of his own making.

Marnie's belly is becoming colossal, profound, we're talking *Samurai-hapai*. Buddy's no authority on these things, but it's starting to look like maybe she's got a litter in there. Do they really get like this with only one baby? She won't let him near her, not even to hold her hand. "Fluid," she squeals, "I've even got it in my fuckin' fingers!" waving her swollen digits in front of his face. She's sluggish, puffed up and pouting, but still managing to chow down every bite of nosh his pathetic income can buy. Using an Iolani computer Buddy emailed his father for more money, choking back whatever pride he might have once had. "For school," his dad scribbled on the message line of the check, five hundred dollars *for school*. It was folded into a sheet of blank blue letterhead, Rock Harbor Adult Correctional in blocked letters at the top.

"He feels guilty so he's paying you off," is Marnie's response. "If my folks had money? Like I'd be a millionaire. Fathers feel shitty about who they are around you and they think they can just buy that away."

Buddy eyeballs her stomach. "I don't think I'd be that kind of father," he tells her, though he's not completely sure about this, not really sure about anything at this point except that for some reason it's like he's nailed to this person. They haven't even established *if* he's the father, though that seems less and less likely—the girl doesn't let him touch her fingers, for chrissake, like something's going to happen in their sleep?

"My baby doesn't need a father, only someone around to take care of it."

"Isn't that what fathers are supposed to do?" He pictures himself playing ball with Marnie's baby, making sure the baby doesn't run out into the street, that sort of thing. He wouldn't be so bad at it.

She snorts, "Who the hell knows?"

One thing they don't talk about is why Marnie decided not to have an abortion, a thing Buddy's wondered since she first told him she was pregnant. It's not like the girl has any morality issues in this department or any other, when you get down to it. The baby *is*. He's not allowed to ask about it or argue its presence. Here's what he thinks: If it *is* his baby he sure didn't have any fun making it.

Dead body dream again, really weird. She's on Kuhio Beach, brilliant day, as always she's reaching out those long arms. And what Buddy does is he takes off all his clothes in front of all those beach people, lies on top of the body and...what? It's like a conspiracy, he doesn't even fricken remember *this*! Some beach boy strums a ukulele. Whatever he did gave him no relief at all.

Wakes up with yet another migraine, ground zero behind his right eyeball, chiseling in. Like some crazy-ass surrealist painting enticing him into its degenerate world, he follows the path to where everything is blurred and unreal, almost seductive in a really sick way.

The next day, a fresh, blue Sunday, headache's gone and Todd insists on taking them to Hanauma Bay, saying it's time they "prove" their loyalty to him. Buddy arches an eyebrow; this doesn't sound promising.

"Sometimes I get that post traumatic thing," Todd explains, "so then I guess I'm just not sure who the enemy is."

They hitchhike, catching a ride through Hawai'i Kai with a truck full of locals, who laugh and joke around with Todd and Marnie. Todd slips them a loaded crack pipe for their efforts, everyone's ignoring Buddy. Which is fine by him.

Beautiful Hanauma, with its sparkling turquoise water, a sanctuary for tropical sea life from turtles to parrot fish, and a haven for posses of inexperienced snorklers paddling its shallows, is hot and crowded. Skinny brown local kids dart and weave around sunburnt tourists in their garish swimsuits. Marnie's in her bikini top with a pair of black Lycra biker shorts, her massive opu lunging over them.

They hike out on the jagged lava cliffs on one side of the bay, above a frothing ocean the purple of cheap wine, out to where a fierce current surges into a circular shaped indentation, swirling, sucking down, then dragging back to sea. "We call it the Toilet Bowl," Todd grins, "get it?" Scent of the wild salt air around them, the frothing, seizing, smacking of the ocean below. Buddy got it.

He thinks about his grandfather who probably drowned. They say it's not so bad once you stop fighting for breath, almost a meditation of sorts as the water fills your lungs, ferrying you back to ancient times maybe when we're all a part of the sea. He doesn't buy it. Suffocation couldn't be much of a hoot, wet or dry. Life wants to live.

"You have to jump when I tell you or you won't make it. This is the trust thing I'm talkin' about, yeah? Trust me, you survive. The way it is in the Army, where we only got each other to depend on."

"Wait, what?" Buddy asks, beginning to shake like he's already wet. "Why do I have to jump when *you* tell me?"

"Because you're dog meat if you don't. You don't come up again, you dig what I'm saying? This is not keiki play. I know how to beat it, so you got to trust that."

Todd didn't get it. Buddy was asking him about the bigger picture, as in who made *him* God? Marnie's uncle sees micro-shots, the edges not the depths of possible consequences. He saw action in the Army for all of about two minutes, and he's giving Buddy brotherhood protocol? Buddy watches a couple locals jump at the moment the tide swoops in, filling the indention like the swirling of, yup, a toilet bowl. Pop back up again in a froth of churning ocean, whooping. "Christ!" he croaks, "you can't be serious."

"Jump already!" Todd howls. Buddy looks at Marnie for a split second, her challenging smug grin. Then the damnedest thing, he does it. The cold hits him first then a mouth full of salt water, the ocean smacking him about, pulling at his trunk, twisting his legs, grabbing his groin in its frigid punch. He feels like a baby-doll in the hands of some demented Chucky, whose limbs are about to be severed. Above him Todd's laughing, taunting face rises up and down as the tide surges under Buddy, lifting him up then sucking him back. Grappling at the mossy, slippery rocks as the current works to drag him out to sea, Buddy thinks: I am going to die.

"You're OK, dude!" Buddy can hear Todd shouting. "You trusted me, you jumped when I told you, so see? You're OK!"

Buddy's not sure what he is. Sputtering and gasping as the cold water swells around him, clinging to the rocks like some mutated, overgrown barnacle, he's realizing he did this for Marnie, to prove himself to her in some incredibly stupid way. Because that vision of the "couple" he'd been holding on to, keeping him beside her at night, the Great Wall of Chastity growing ever larger between them despite the now irreparable proof she's none too chaste—more pillows, an abandoned bedspread, Todd's old Army fatigues, beach towels and her own generous belly—that vision keeps slipping further and further away.

It didn't help. Yellowy-brown eyes as fierce and accusing as before Buddy almost drowned for her. "You just want inside my pants, isn't that right? That's all you guys ever think about, *dick* divining rod your mentor or something. Like, you think I want to live this way forever? Can't you at least get a better job? If you really cared about me you would."

"Why, so you and Todd can smoke up more of my paycheck?"

"I don't smoke bud anymore Bud*dy*, for your information! Come on, don't you know anything about anything that means *anything* at fuckin' all? It's bad for the baby." Her nose in the air, sniffing him out like he's the idiot and she's the martyr just associating with him. There's a heaviness about her face that goes beyond the fleshed-out cheeks, a burdened look, the look of a really old woman; like his grandma sometimes, Buddy swears.

He quit going to school. What's the point? Sometimes when he's sure she's asleep he slides his hand around the barrier, reaches out and ever so lightly strokes her swollen breast. She's got some big-ass boobs now, he'll give her that, but Buddy supposes he doesn't much care. A semi hard-on, nothing that even begs relief. He's trying to remember the pleasure this used to give him, touching her breast. If he can remember at least that, then maybe there's still hope.

19

Buddy, Again

SATURDAY, EARLY DECEMBER, A FLAT, humid afternoon, and Todd has decided Buddy and Marnie must prove their loyalty again, to keep living with him. He had spent the previous night smoking crack, watching himself slog through a sloppy, insect-infested jungle filled with trip wires and explosives that shoot up and blow a man's balls of. "Nothing left but a hole," Todd said, "instant femme fatal." Never mind The Todd exited Vietnam so soon he didn't even catch jungle rot let alone had to worry about tripwires; sent home with a twig up his butt for chrissake, earns the Purple Heart for this so called war-wound. These days, Todd said, soldiers fighting in Iraq and Afghanistan sign pledges that if they step on a landmine and their balls get blown off, to kill each other rather than sentence another man to life without his dick.

"So what do we have to do?" Buddy asks, pretty sure he's not going to like the answer.

"Prove your grit, your macho and *machesse*, by spending the night in Kualoa Beach Park, in the path of the night marchers. A dude's got to be able to count on another dude," he says to Buddy, "and a wahine too, yeah?" He tickles Marnie under the chin and she lunges out of his reach, yanks a blanket off of Todd's own bed, motions Buddy to follow her then stumbles outside, slamming the door.

"What the fuck, I look like a narc, some low-life rat?" Marnie snipes, predator eyes, vehement. "Like, you know what this is about, huh? This is about drugs. Fucker's gotten so paranoid thinks he can't trust his own family! Thinks we'll rip him off, snitch him out, the shit."

They catch The Bus to the Pali Longs, then she thrusts her thumb into the Nuuanu Pali-bound traffic, sunlit ridges of the mountains like broken teeth on a giant comb poking up on either side. Waves her arm about forcing her body, its intrusive middle ever closer into the road, until a minivan reels over, occupants gawking. "What, you never seen a hapai girl hitchhike before?" she snaps, yanking open the sliding back door, batting off Buddy's hand like he's some annoying mosquito when he tries to help her. Marnie climbs in panting heavily, tugging him along in her belligerent wake.

She's silent throughout the entire ride over the Pali to the windward side, jaw clamped tight, then a second ride, a Buick with a chatty older woman who keeps asking when's her "due date dear," not listening for an answer fortunately, since you can bet one never comes. They head into Kaneohe town, a sprawl of smaller houses and two story garden apartments, dull little pearls in the beige light of the late afternoon. Buddy whispers to Marnie, "What the hell are the night marchers anyway?" She glares at him, says nothing.

Kualoa Beach Park is nearly deserted when they finally get there, a small brown dog stretched out in the short grass, the sea a slick of greys and blues, pulse of miniature waves tugging the shore. He follows Marnie who strides across the public lawn like she's claiming land-rights, then lowers herself down on the stained olive colored Army blanket, at the far edge of the grass adjacent to the beach. He sits down beside her, keeping his dis-

tance, half of him not even on the blanket, and stares out at the little bon-
net-shaped island beyond the rippling line of surf. Chinaman's Hat, people
call this island. Who knows what the real name is? Vestiges of the politically
incorrect to survive into the Hawaiian twenty-first century. "He's gone too
fucking far," Marnie mutters, eyes glowing like two yolks in the last of the
sun's light. "He'll pay for this, the shit! Just what I can expect from *family*!
Fuck them! I'll leave them in their own mud. Become famous and rich and
I won't give them one filthy penny, not even toward their own funerals."

"But what are the night marchers?" Buddy asks again, grateful to see the
burn in her eyes not directed at him for a change.

"You really don't know? Son of a local wahine and you don't know about
the night marchers? What'd she teach you, how to wipe your nose but not
your butt?"

"OK, you don't have to get nasty. I'm from Maine, remember? The *local
wahine's* been there most of her adult life, so sue me, I wasn't brought up
Hawaiian."

"Yeah, like you *could*. I should've left you in Hilo. I should've left you
anywhere but with me. Don't you ever wonder why *I* picked *you*? Like I
thought you'd be different, that's why, better than the rest. Thought I could
trust you. Well for fuck sure you're different, you're a bug-loving freak!"

Buddy turns away from her so she can't see she got him. He's blinking
back tears and hating himself for them. Wheels around, stares at the cliffs
behind them, rocky and erect, brooding in the silvery dusk. True, it's not
like he hasn't been wondering every bloody minute about why she picked
him, and about why the hell he stays with her when it's been so fricken
obvious for so long she could give a damn! A *pregnant* girl, for chrissake,
by definition a run don't walk scenario in your average guy world. But
what are his choices? A father who buys his love, if it *is* love, and he doesn't
even spend his bucks on anything Buddy would *want* to be bought with;
a mother who's become more of a mother to her own mother than to him,

and would probably sell them both for lifetime stock in California wine and pharmaceuticals; a cracked grandmother who doesn't even like him.

Marnie swivels around until they're facing the same direction, panting at her exertion, swearing quietly. She strokes Buddy's shoulder. "I'm sorry, sweetie. That was mean, but like I get so mad is the thing! The life of someone who's born with a dick, that's the only difference. Not smarter, not nicer, not better looking, just got himself a cock. Todd thinks because he has one he rules. Even when it doesn't work he thinks he rules, just because it's dangling there." She sighs, pats his shoulder. "It is what it is. I don't make the rules. If I did, goddammit, there'd be some who are gonna pay."

"If you think you're going to make me start apologizing for my penis, Marnie, it's pretty unlikely."

She shakes her head, puts her hand gently over his mouth, kisses his cheek. Buddy lives for any signs of tenderness from this girl, he swears. It's pathetic, little crumbs of niceness from her and he feels his goddamn eyes start brimming again. She points at the mountains. "See those cliffs? That's where they come down from. This is their path, right through Kualoa. They're lapu, spirits. Army of the dead. It's major bad luck for anything that gets in their way, and right now, guess what? We're in their way."

He stares at her, arching his brow. "You're talking about ghosts? *You* believe in ghosts?"

"Oh please! These islands are haunted, you dumbass, everyone knows that. I'd face a hundred butt-ugly dudes in the woods before I'd get in the path of the night marchers, huh?"

Buddy shakes his head. Marnie afraid of ghosts! "Christ, I can't even process what I'm hearing, Marnie."

"Whatever, jerk-off, you asked! You just go right ahead and go to sleep tonight, cozy up and close your innocent little Buddy-boy eyes, but not me. I'm wide awake if I have to rub the whole damn beach in my face to do it. I hear footsteps, see the flickering lights from their torches and I'm outahere.

I don't care if Todd kicks us out, if I have to drop this baby on Kamehameha highway it's OK by me. You can bet if there's a choice between them taking you or me *Buddums*, I'm not the martyr type."

"Well if you really believe all of this then why the hell are we here? Why don't we just tell Todd we stayed here but spend the night someplace else? I don't get it, Marnie."

"Because he'll know that's why. There's a thing called honor, you heard of it? I'm telling you, your mama may have some Hawaiian in her big toe but there's not *any* of it in your blood. Don't you understand? Can you be this thick? He'll find out; it'll be obvious because they leave a message. Like, you want him to think I'm a chicken, huh? No way! Todd's not a *real* hero, and I'm not going to give him the satisfaction of thinking I'm like him, a fucking coward. He shames all those soldiers who earned their Purple Hearts the real way, saving someone's ass and getting hurt doing it. Makes me sick how my family goes along with it, pretends he's some kind of genius just because he was there."

"Well you yourself told me he's a hero." Buddy scratches his chin, crinkles his brow at her. He still can't believe it, Queen Marnie Lo, *afraid*?

"Oh for chrissake, listen with your brain once in a while and not just your ears. Go to sleep Bud-o, this conversation is pau. That's *over* to you, haole boy."

BUDDY SLEEPS IN SPITE OF her warnings, warm muggy night lulling him, sweeping sound of the tide rushing up onto the sand, retreating with a sigh. He sleeps despite an uncomfortable sense of *something*, a sticky cloud of it hovering, that feeling of dread. Sinks down into the blanket covering a thatch of dried beach grass soft as a mattress, exhaustion a shroud over him. The weight of all this loss, his girlfriend—what he had hoped for in having a *girlfriend*, his mother, father, even his grandmother; sometimes he even misses his grandmother. Holding back tears, eyes squeezed shut so there's no chance that Marnie, sitting bolt up right beside him can see him cry, Buddy sleeps.

PINK LIGHT OF MORNING, BUDDY wakes up to a nauseatingly sweet scent of flowers like he had fallen asleep in a funeral parlor, waves shrinking off the sand, head pounding the rhythm of his own heartbeat. Marnie's at the shore, belly thrust out like some mad, pregnant superhero, her arms outstretched toward the lavender horizon, as if she can lift up and fly. Buddy stares down at his own arm, tingling like a little vibrator's worked its way under the skin; there's a red welt, a bruise in the shape of a human mouth. Could she have bitten him, this crazy girl?

They hitch a ride on a lawn care truck back to Waikiki that lets them off near the Ala Wai, then amble slowly through the Jungle. Something's wrong. Buddy can feel it. His arm with the strange mark burns. He wants to ask Marnie about this mark, but one look at her pinched face and he shuts his mouth.

When they get to Todd's yard, broken white fence, clutter of rusted lawn chairs, scattering of litter and mounds of dog doo (preferred toilet for the various neighborhood strays), a parade of PIGmobiles are parked at every angle along the perimeter, blue lights twirling. Several of Todd's overnighters are led from the house in handcuffs, then The Todd himself, fat wrists locked behind his bare back. "I want a lawyer!" he howls. "I got a Purple Heart, you sons of bitches, you don't treat a goddamn vet this way."

"Shit!" Marnie hisses, "get down!" She tugs Buddy's arm and they fall onto the uncut lawn. Like a snake he follows her, crawling low, wiggling under scrubby kiawe bushes toward the broken-down gardening shed at the back of the property. Heart hammers inside his chest, his breath dragging in and out making sharp, whining little noises.

"Shut up!" Marnie whispers, as they slip inside through the partially opened hinged door, slowly pressing it shut. Though he's said nothing. "Shut up!" she repeats, wheezing and cradling her huge stomach. He tries to catch his breath, roiling and jagged, a wild wind inside his lungs. She hunkers down beside him, her giant belly hanging like a slab of something that doesn't even belong to her, squatting on the dirt floor. The old shed is dark and stinks of wood rot. Hears the soft steady crunch of footsteps in the grass outside. Marnie slaps her hand tight over Buddy's lips. He has this insane urge to bite her fingers, but his heart's racing so fast if he opened his mouth it might jump out between his teeth.

"Miss Marnie Lo? You folks in there? Mr. Richard Winter?"

"Shit!" Marnie rasps, "Not a word!"

"Lieutenant Kealoa, Honolulu P.D. I know your dad, Marnie, remember? You stay at my place once after a game, Roosevelt and Punahou, yeah? He told me you two stay here with your uncle. Uncle Todd's bad news Miss Lo, we've arrested him, yeah? He uses folks like you kids. Free drugs and before you know it you're holding for him, then he gets you on the streets. I need you to testify, or he's right back out again pulling that shit. He plays with folks, that wounded vet bit, make them believe he's somebody. He's in Nam, what, a week? My brother went there. My brother didn't come back. Know where my brother is? Up on the memorial wall in Washington. Fight your country's war, end up on a wall."

A sickness surges through Buddy, reeking at the back of his throat. He peers dizzily into the space above, a ray of broken light streaming through a cracked and grime-smeared window. There's a huge black and yellow garden spider stretched out on a scraggly web that hangs from one corner of the window, to some shadowy place over Marnie's head. His arm with the red mark burns, and though he tries to stop them, tears stream from his eyes like somebody's turned on a faucet. Marnie squeezes his head against her breast like a vice.

"Miss Lo? You hear me? I'm telling you I'm giving you folks a break here. Walk out and everything going to be fine. We been watching this house for weeks, I hope you know, watched the drugs go in and out, watched you go in and out. You folks aren't clean, but I'm a friend of your dad's and I told him I'll do right by him if you testify. I'm giving you a break, yeah? You're not eighteen, I can slam you both in Juvie."

Buddy sobs soundlessly against Marnie's chest, shoulders shaking like he's caught a deep and permanent chill. He has no specifics about Juvenile Detention (*the Bad Boys Home!*), only that he doesn't want to go there. Not exactly an extracurricular on his college application, and suddenly that's where Buddy wants to be, back in school, applying to colleges. Life the way you grow up believing it's supposed to be.

"Quit being such a pussy!" Marnie mouths in Buddy's ear. "He's not even my real dad!"

"OK, keikis, last chance here!" the voice growls from behind the shed. "I can come in, haul your okoles out of there, but I want it to be from you, get it? Needs to be from you. Fine, I'm gone, which means when you do come out, if we catch you? I can't guarantee you won't be in deep Ka Ka, yeah? You know where to find me. Don't mess with me, folks. I haven't had a goddamn thing to lose for a long time."

Steps recede, crunching through the grass. Marnie releases Buddy's head but still grips his arm. She's so close he can feel her shivering, almost hear the erratic thump and bump of her heart. He wipes his forehead, letting his frozen breath whoosh out. "What the hell is wrong with you? Thank God he knew your father or stepfather or whatever, otherwise he would've handed us our asses. Getting busted in a crack-house will not look good on our resumes."

She yanks away from him, and for the first time since Buddy's known her Marnie's the one crying, huddled against the splintered wood of the shed, knees drawn up as close to her chin as that belly will allow. He stares, stunned. "Christ, like what's wrong now? I mean he's gone. We almost bought it but he's gone."

She opens her mouth, lets out a squeak. "You idiot!" she whines, pinching her knees even closer against her chest, overlapping ridge of her girth, straining against the extra large tee shirt, Buddy's shirt, nabbed off a Crazy Shirts discount rack, sunset shot of Waimea bay and a surfboard. Looks like she's trying to shrink into the shirt. When Marnie speaks again her words fall in a flat monotone that reminds him of locusts.

"She was asleep, she never knew. Took her sleeping pills every night, dropped dead from the world. At first it was a game. He'd be sitting on the floor, playing his guitar. I'd go, *I'm The Crab, gonna tickle you*. Then I'd crawl all over him tickling and he'd tickle me back. After a while the tickling got weird. One night he gives me a beer. He was like so impressed by my chugging it down, within minutes another's in my hand. "You drink like a guy," he said. I took it as a compliment. I liked him complimenting me. So it became a ritual, Mom zonked, guitar, tickling, beer, or we'd just cut to the chase, beer, tickling, no music at all.

"He whispered it in my ear when I asked him, told me yes, he loved me. We can't tell my mom, I said. No, he said, never. So then I'm starting to think maybe she *isn't* my mom, because wouldn't she know? Care enough to figure it out? So screw her, she can't be a mother when this is happening right under her nose and she doesn't care. Made it easier for us both.

"The night we did it his hand slaps over my mouth so the moaning doesn't come out. So she won't hear, he says. But now I'm thinking it wasn't *moaning*, more like a scream. Maybe it's still in there. I can feel it sometimes when *you* try to touch me, Buddy, stuck inside my throat. I mean, try this: He's the only dad I got, my stepfather, and I'm *fucking* him! All this time does my mom notice? Does she say anything, does she do anything? Could she *be* my mother?" Marnie shakes her head, the violence of her lava colored hair. "The Sleaze," she whispers. "The thing is, I thought it meant he loved me more than her."

She hesitates, wipes her eyes, blinking tears back. Buddy's got a freeze-squeeze on his breath, afraid to let it out, afraid to move, to say anything because he can't possibly imagine what you say to something like this. What the hell? This is like some skanky talk show, reality TV, Dr. Phil, not *actual* life, not *his* life.

Suddenly she's the old Marnie again, yellow-browns fired up. "So, like guess what comes of it all, Buddy-boy!" stabbing at her belly. "OK, so this is the part where you find out for real you're not the father. Not that I actually *said* you were, did I?" She peers into his face, a sly little smile, pink slide of teeth. "You're the one came up with the 'maybe we did it in our sleep or when we're stoned' scenario. Like, did I ever even let you tongue me? Sorry, but for a smart boy you're kind of a dumbass, Buddy. So here's the thing. It ended up I kind of liked it, not so much the sex, the sex was just sex, but the *idea* of doing it with my mother's husband. He chose me because I'm hotter; all my mom did was take her crappy sleeping drugs, sleep her life away. It's like she was already dead. Why would he want that? Like screwing a coffin plank. You can hardly blame him, going for me. Goddammit Buddy, don't look at me that way. What do *you* know? It's not like we're blood relatives, not incest. I could call him Dad or I could call him Joe, what's in the name? I could've been the one who met him in that bar, only if I was a little older, is all.

"Then all of a sudden she wakes up and decides she wants him! Stops taking her pills, starts making like a full-on ho and he *bites*. Tells me we have to stop, that he's sorry he took advantage of me. *Sorry?* Like that's what it meant to him, like I was just a kind of masturbation, as if it wasn't *me* who hooked up with *him* in the first place? So fine. They can have the bundle. I'm going to drop his baby off on their lanai, and I'll say, here! I think this is yours! Then I'm checking out, away from all you fuckers. I'll be so far gone you won't even know I went."

"What the hell is that supposed to mean?" Buddy asks, for lack of anything else to say. He feels like his head, or maybe his stomach, maybe all of him is about to implode!

Marnie opens her mouth, swallows a breath of air like it's a hunk of bone, blinks back the wetness in her eyes again then rubs them with her fists. Like a little girl, he thinks, and watching her do this it's Buddy who feels broken.

She sighs, leans into him a little, then pulls away. "Don't you see? I just wanted to be the one who's loved for a change. I've hooked up, sucked I don't know how many cocks. This time, just *this* one time, couldn't I have been the one who's loved?"

Speaking of Vietnam – The Jody Johnstone Story

ON A MUGGY SPRING DAY in 1968, Kona winds prevailing, Jody wore Margo Malone's blood stained pink ruffled crop top to his draft induction physical, not because he was trying to get out of going to Vietnam (in truth he was so filled with despair at his unworthiness for Margo to have died for him a few months earlier, a virtual stranger despite the intimacy of his hand on her thigh, that Jody may have looked at war as a way of tempting fate to prove the real worth of his skin); he wore it because Margo's mother gave him the task of making sure the world did not forget her daughter, and since Jody barely knew her himself, the best way he could think to do this was to wear the shirt she'd been wearing that night, given to him by her mother.

"You a fag?" the sergeant who handled his papers asked.

"No sir," Jody said.

"No *what?*" the sergeant snapped.

"No sir I'm not a fag, Sergeant."

"Why you wearing a pussy-pink shirt then?"

"So the world won't forget Margo Malone Sergeant, sir."

The Army G.P. requisitioned a psychiatric evaluation after the sergeant asked Jody if he was ready to waste gooks for his country, and Jody admitted he couldn't personally schlep a weapon, since the only reason he was alive and not blasted to kingdom come was by the grace of Margo Malone. "However…" and at this point he leaned closer to the scowling Sarge, his voice lowered into a confessional tone, "I'm studying something more effective than firearms, that could make the Vietcong vanish into thin air!" Two hours later Jody told the Army psychiatrist all about Harry Houdini who made the man and the elephant disappear. "Imagine if we did that to the enemy, sir, *poof*, no more war!"

Understand that Jody would've gone to Vietnam if he was told to. He didn't have the courage to go against the grain, and he didn't know how to say no. He hadn't many political convictions at that time, or really any convictions at all, certainly not enough to take any kind of a stand against an authority that claimed him. He was afraid to die, but worse than that was the thought of someone who might die for *him*, a fellow solider who takes Jody's bullet, steps on Jody's landmine, plays catch with the grenade that had Jody's name on it. Yet again he would be in a dead person's debt, and how do you repay that? How do you even *thank* someone for dying for you? Jody would wander the world with that craven guilt, knowing he probably wasn't worth the sacrifice. If he went to Vietnam, he told the Army psychiatrist, with his luck Strike Three would invariably happen; someone would die for him.

Jody Johnstone was officially classified 4-F: *Draftee not qualified for military service; incapable of performing duties as a soldier, even in a national emergency.*

Part IV

Winter, 2012

20

Gwen

ANOTHER HOT, DRY JANUARY NIGHT and Gwen yanks down her blanket then the sheet, sweating, sleepless, thinking about the affair that derailed her life in Maine, her mother in the next room and her son bunking with lunatics in Honolulu. It began three years before the end of her marriage, stopped half a year after she discovered what a loser the prick was, then picked right back up again when she realized she didn't care. Turns out it wasn't her emotional life Gwen was fixated on, whether she was still capable of having one; it was the sex that drove her back. Affairs are like that sometimes. Rob found out the Christmas everything blew apart. Cliché, but that's how the ship went down.

Go back four years, Buddy's an especially rude and hostile thirteen year old, and it seemed Rob and Gwen had permanently weaned themselves from any love in their marriage, just habit. The problem, as Gwen has come to see it, was that they had made each other up—he was her revolution and she his runner, his long-legged champion, and as time blew by and they weren't these things anymore, their fantasies evaporated like smoke into the ozone, leaving the waste of what might have been possible. Some live their whole lives without enchantment, grasp on to one or two sweet moments, and these are enough to feed a marriage, or at least keep it from starving to death. What was it that made the Canada/Johnstone/Winter clan demand more?

Gwen felt like she was withering on the vine. Mostly what she wanted to do was sleep; even breathing was a chore. Despair a fist inside her chest had replaced her lungs, squeezing, releasing, squeezing, releasing just enough to keep her alive. Rob accused her of drinking too much, not *totally* a drunk he clarified, but too much all the same. "You should quit," he said.

"You think that's going to change me, make me better, a perfect wife and mother, *cure* me? It will still be *me*, Rob, just sober."

It was a cold spring that year, ground still winter-hard when Gwen gave notice at the school. She couldn't bear it any longer, classrooms of children who would never go anywhere, be anyone, knowing she could do nothing to affect this; poverty had already marked them, stamped them with who they could and couldn't be. And then she had nothing. She was at Speedy's, the University's copy center having her CV run off twenty times to apply for God knows what twenty other jobs, twenty teaching positions she didn't want and wouldn't get, just to convince Rob she was trying. His creed was either you're in a job or you're searching for one, because, heaven forbid! you wouldn't want "dead space" on your resume. Alyn Crysler, Assistant Professor of Biology, was copying an article for Bio 101.

The article is what she stared at to avoid sliding her eyes at him, his cut face, tan drifts of hair breezing across a sure forehead, smile like some toothpaste god. *Behavioral Discrepancies In Arctic Animals.* Whir of the machines in the background, their chemical stench filled her nostrils. She pictured him an animal in her own bed, erasing Rob's turned-toward-the-wall spine. "I'm a flagrant violator of the copy rights law," he admitted, winking; "no tree is safe around me." Gwen had in mind a different kind of violation and blushed.

The next day she walked up and down the block in front of Speedy's like some shameless schoolgirl, until he approached from the opposite direction. A brief, strained conversation punctuated by the roar of the traffic; the following day he bought her coffee at Starbucks. She wondered briefly why he didn't meet her on campus—was he ashamed to be seen with her?—then dismissed it in the steam of her latte, the precise angle of his chin.

After their third refill he asked did she want to take a ride with him? He knew a beach, he said. Which turned out to be the cove. They drove down from Augusta in his cobalt Fiat, Route 17, hills like bones on either side, nonspecific conversation. Gwen felt something light up inside herself and was concentrating on it, this fiery new sense of her. She didn't have much to say. She wondered what she would do. Hadn't explored these limits before, the extramarital flirtation (she was calling it just that, at this point), didn't even know if she had any. His hands were anchored on the steering wheel, and Gwen wished he'd put one on her leg, then prayed he wouldn't. *What would Jesus say?* Though she'd have to confess: Jesus was not on her mind. Alyn parked the Fiat and like a puppy Gwen followed him on the familiar path, down a meandering wildflower-strewn cliff in the summer, barren of everything but dried yellow grass during any other season. It didn't occur to her she could be seen, exposed, this stark walk to the beach, that Rob might see her if he was driving home from the prison. (Three and a half years later this is in fact exactly what happens). And anyway, they hadn't done anything yet. *Yet?* It was as if she'd been shot up with a spinal-block of the mind, all that raw electric nerve energy flowing everywhere but her good sense.

The day was bright and cool, beach deserted, the bay a skin of grey. "Where I come from the sea's blue," she murmured, feeling instantly foolish. Filler talk. He didn't give a damn where Gwen came from. Best not to know too much. Knowing means thinking, and if *she* started thinking she might think her way out of this. He grinned and squeezed her hand. "Could be red or puce right now and that's OK by me," he said. A man who uses the word *puce*! Even Gwen's fingertips were sizzling; she tucked her hand into his, hoping he wouldn't feel its clamminess despite the chilled air. Sight of the ocean, its smell, the grainy tickle of salt air quickened Gwen's breath. Alyn's hair blew across his forehead, delicate and web-like. Probably this meant, when she thinks about it now, that he was already losing his hair, that broad uncluttered forehead.

They ducked under a ledge of deep green spruce, the final steep descent of the trail pouring them onto the rocky shore. High tide, a wind rising off the frigid water and small waves slid silkily up toward their feet, retreating over thousands of pebbles with a sound like a motorcycle backfiring. Gwen shivered and he slung his arm over her shoulder. "Cold?" Heart thumping she nodded, falling deeper into his arms.

Desire was a quivery, melting sensation, staggering and immediate. She pressed against him, the shadow of his face over hers blocking the white glare of the sun, his lips smothering hers, sucking hers inside his, the mingling tastes of mint and salt. Toothpaste god. Hers. His. Barriers becoming less distinct. His hand on her breast, feeling the prod of his erection in her groin. "I'm not always so impulsive," she whispered. Somehow Gwen needed him to know this, that this was her yet it wasn't. Then she didn't care what he knew, who he was or who she was. In the distance the wail of a ship pulling out of Rockland Harbor, gulls wheeled and soared.

That night Gwen examined herself in the bathroom mirror, Rob snoring from the bedroom, her thighs, buttocks, covered with bruises, darkening signposts of the rocky beach that had been their bed. Alyn Crysler. Ran her fingers over those bruises, their purplish heat, wondering who she had become.

January still, still hot, and Gwen again awakes after only an hour of sleep with the panicky sense of something wrong. It's a way of waking peculiar to the volcano area, animals can sense an upcoming eruption and act queer all day, but people, less sensitive in their daytime lives, going about their business oblivious to the troubling smells of things, are more open in their sleep, waking suddenly, fretfully, instinctively. Before falling asleep she'd been thinking about Alyn again, though she tried not to—a penance perhaps? She's not Catholic, can't go to confession and emerge absolved. Do you miss him? She'd asked her sleep-starved self. No, she concluded, not him, *it*. *Him* was an abstraction, a person who served a role in her life, EXTRAMARITAL LOVER. The *it*, a love affair, was what was alive, reminding her *she* was alive, a person with a heart, a pulse, genitals, desired, desirous. *It* gave her back her life, not him. She'd slept little hashing through all of this. Now she rubs her eyes, snags a deep breath.

It hasn't rained in months. The rain forest, normally pungent and dripping with moisture, beads of it like sweat in the fronds of ferns, appears to be shrinking, turning in on itself in the strange Hawaiian winter heat. Giant leaves of ginger sag to the ground, as if the weight of their own blossoms is unbearable. Ferns are hard and brittle at their tips from the vog, the acidic breath of the volcano, their leaves like fringes of decayed teeth. Her mother's anthuriums, planted years ago and cared for passionately until Madge's sickness became too distracting, are dried out and cracked, waxy colors fading like old lipstick. Their water tank is dangerously low. Water, the silvery thread of life pumped into the area's catchment homes has become a commodity, to be sold, bargained for, even stolen.

This time it isn't Madam Pele that's shaken Gwen awake so suddenly, however. She calls the Park Service from the landline on her night table and the recording says that Kilauea, erupting for years now, is presently a thin lava rivulet creeping toward the sea. Shaking off the sensation of wanting to fall back asleep she climbs out of bed, pulls on her bathrobe and moves over to the window. Something is wrong.

And there's Madge in the yard below, wild haired and butt-naked in the moonlight, arms outstretched as if she's sleep walking, zombie-like lurches heading straight toward the rift ahead, Mauna Loa a luminous giant in the moon-painted distance. Fear seizes Gwen's chest. She breaks away from the window, tears through the house and rushes outside wailing, "No, No, No!" A few more steps and her mother will tumble, sucked into the earth, its gaping trench sheltered by the abundance of ferns and ohia Madge once coveted, graceful, botanical courtesans decked in green, coyly disguising a mortal danger.

Gwen hurls herself down on the hard dry ground, tackling Madge around her ankles, her bird-boned body collapsing in front of Gwen's like pickup sticks. "Where in God's name do you think you're going! Why the hell do you do these things to me?" They lie panting in pili grass not even damp with dew, Gwen's own heartbeat crackling in her ears. "You're doing this on purpose, aren't you? Just to make my life more miserable than it already is. You don't care! You never cared!"

"This? What's *this?*" Madge shrieks. Then she's quiet, peering around the yard blinking.

She doesn't even understand where she is, Gwen realizes. Must have been having one of those brain episodes. She sits up, then pulls Madge up into a sitting position beside her. "You think I want this to be happening to you, Mother? This isn't exactly easy for me either. My life is crumbling like it's built on sand. Don't you think I need you? Don't you understand I've *always* needed you? For Lord's sake, it's always been you. When the hell is it ever about me? When's my turn for attention!"

Madge starts to cry, a shrill, tremulous keening. Gwen rises, yanking her up by her underarms, hollow as two empty flour sacks, then marches her across the parched grass back to the house. She's determined Madge won't wail her way out of this one, make Gwen pity *her*, not this time. Inside she sits her mother down on her rocker and examines her, for what she doesn't know—some kind of brokenness manifest on the outside, all the while Gwen understands what's damaged in her mother is too deep to see. Madge continues to cry, a little slower, softer, then a whimper like a hum, a disturbance of the air around her. Gwen covers her naked body with the pink and pale yellow afghan her Grandma Ana had knitted, baby colors. Madge's mother never had the chance to see her daughter grown up. She notices the stain of tears on her mother's face, her swollen eyes. Madge has been crying for a long time.

OK, Gwen's thinking, is hers the only broken heart? "So you figure you won something tonight getting out of the house? I didn't tie you because I thought I'd allow you a little dignity for one night, now look what you've done." God the cruelty of it! These little strokes, as though in erasing bits of a person's brain, the memory that charts who she's been, her very soul is rubbed out. "Do you see why I have to tie you, Mother? Do you get it now? You almost ended up in the rift, for Jesus' sake!"

Madge snaps her mouth shut, rolls her eyes up, tosses her head back against the back of her rocking chair and glowers at the ceiling, her belligerent, sulky *I'm not saying a word to you* look. Gwen sighs, closes her eyes for a moment, and then in the quiet she hears it. The faint, steady whisper of running water. Pops open her eyes. "Oh dear Christ! Tell me you didn't. Did you turn on our water out there? Jesus, why would you do a thing like that in the middle of a goddamn drought!" Gwen tugs the kimono sash still attached to the back of the chair around Madge's waist, knotting it tight— she doesn't care if it hurts her! snatches a flashlight off the shelf by the door and dashes back outside.

Under the yellow glow of the lanai light Gwen sees it, a stream of it like it's supposed to be there, natural and unassuming as a mountain brook, from the runoff hose at the base of their water tank. She shines her flashlight on the gauge after twisting the spigot taut. The tank is almost dry. Flopping down on the muddy ground where their water ran free Gwen sobs, her back pressed up against the aluminum side of the tank. They'll have to buy it from Hilo now, shuttled up in trucks when the drivers get around to it, *Hawaiian time, no sweat yeah*? Water, the price of imported beer. And where will *this* money come from?

At her mother's last appointment Dr. Alvarez suggested that maybe it was time to consider a nursing home. She pointed out Madge's thinness, eating like a moth these days. "It's her way of exerting some control. I could admit her to the hospital, put her on a feeding tube, but that just buys time, you understand?" Juli's slender fingers hooked over Gwen's hand, squeezing for a second, then let go.

Where will the money come from? Rob still sends a check for Buddy's schooling, a little extra now and then, nothing to depend on and nothing legally binding until they are officially divorced. Gwen's without a job so they're living off Madge's social security, her savings dwindling and soon maybe dry as the tank. She's struck with a sudden memory, an especially gentle moment between her mother and herself just months ago, when she seemed almost normal, accepting of the two of them together, wanting Gwen to be with her. It felt the way it's supposed to, mother and daughter, cooking then eating dinner, enjoying a cup of decaf afterward. Madge made Gwen promise she wouldn't put her away.

This is what occurs to Gwen, that she's living her life in myths: the myth her son will come home and nothing will have changed between them; the myth her mother can get better if she just finds the patience to give Madge more of herself, not resent her mother for taking it; the myth Rob might find life unbearable without his family and become the man he was when she married him. The myth she can somehow crawl out of this sinking life into a better one.

Two nights ago she found her mother on her bedroom floor weeping. Madge had fallen from her bed, but she didn't remember it. She was too weak to even pick herself up. Gwen helped her back into bed, tying her wrist gently to the mahogany bedpost with the kimono sash. "So you don't fall out again," she told her. Felt like some kind of criminal, tying down her mother when it was so heartbreakingly obvious that what Madge wanted was to be free.

Gathering herself up off the ground, trailing her hand over the scaly side of the tank, Gwen moves heavily back into her mother's house. There was a question she had asked herself after her affair with Alyn was finally over: What will she have to pay?

21

Madge

So she asked him: why can't you be satisfied? Transformation, he told her, like this was some kind of answer to some question she didn't ask. He said he needed to know it was possible. The Artist creates a butterfly garden: sluggish caterpillars metamorphose into the gentle grace of the butterfly, iridescent wings beating the air, orange, black, wings of the Monarch flit and flash in the sunlight. King of the butterflies. Madge remembers Monarchs!

Pua-Kalaunu, Crown Flower, Giant Milkweed, Butterfly Bush. Larvae of the Monarch feed on fat pale leaves downy as the fuzz of a peach. Handsome black and yellow caterpillars turned upside down, nature's eating machine, munching toward metamorphose on the silvery underbellies of leaves. They grow fat and slow, dangling from the underside of a leaf; skin splits becoming a tear-shaped cocoon.

The Artist watches. Madge watches him watch. "Transformation is about magic," he says, kissing her cheek. Her *cheek*, not even her lips. Who is this queen that no longer pleases her king? Where is her place, her cocoon? "If you look closely," he tells her, "you can see the markings of the former caterpillar and its future as a butterfly, the outlines of its wings taking shape inside the chrysalis." Like seeing the baby in the grown man, she thinks.

One day it emerges, wings still damp. "Perfect!" says The Artist. Slowly he dries his wings, this king, up and down, up and down, testing, testing, one two three. Then he's off, rising above the crown flower bushes, pua-ka-launu, flowers with their five curled back petals, pungent and beckoning. The Monarch dips down, lights on one for a moment, opens his wings and flies away. "Madge!" The Artist exhales her name like a sigh. "If only we too could do it."

"Transform?" she asks him, "Or fly away!"

She is Madge. Her daughter tells her that Kiki is here. The Artist's sister Violet's daughter. Which makes her... what?

"Kiki!" Madge calls out. Hah, nobody answers. "You slut!" she whispers. She remembers that concert in the Waikiki Shell, Jefferson Starship, Kiki's barely of age, collapsed on a blanket under the stars, drunk with lust and maybe too much 100-proof Vodka, Madge suspected, fed to her by the drummer of some local band (she forgets its name, no doubt history has too), someone Madge knew once upon a time, hugs offered, drugs offered, the way it was back then, love for humanity, as long as the music lasted. Madge could tell Kiki had a thing for Grace Slick, her tiny skirts, eyes riveted on those well-formed legs. Later, in a bathroom stall, on her knees in front of this drummer. "Kiki!" Madge had snapped, yanking open the door (well *someone* had to be the grownup), "you don't have to do that." Kiki stopped, looked puzzled. "I thought it's what we do?" she slurred.

"If you've come to *babysit* me forget it!" Madge chirps, just in case Kiki really is here. They don't fool Madge. Light flows in from the window, streaks of it this dusty pulpy light, circling like an elongated halo. Not this one, no angel this one. Their words, just talk, talk, talk. Madge has words too; it's just that the right ones don't always come out of her mouth anymore, teeth a barbwire fence.

Time has lost its boundaries, days become nights, more and more the swirling fog, impenetrable grey like clouds of cement. Can she no longer remember the perimeters? Before, now, tomorrow, the days the nights?

"Gwenyth, talk to *me*!"

"I'm here, Mother, it's OK." Like a butterfly, wings ragged, torn by the wind there is fear in her daughter. Madge would reassure her, but how? She feels so weak, like a helpless baby, but old, something the world no longer has use for.

Here is what's left, what we come to, where it begins, where it ends. *This she must remember.* Ana, small and brown, curled like a leaf, a cashew nut, a question mark, shriveled up in the middle of the hikie'e, little stuffed pillow of a person. The day is a wash of light, bright and hard, relentless light the kind that revels in itself, *light, light, light!* Light is the afternoon steaming in. Garish light, dizzy light, hot, aching light the color of everything yellow in the world light. Light that is the air, harsh, hard as the mummified caterpillars.

She is Makela. She collects them from the crown flower bushes, watches them dangle from the lids of her jars, shed their skins like snakes and become cocoons, emerging as butterflies. Then she sets them free.

Only this one time she forgot to put air holes in the jars and the caterpillars died. Fell crisp and hard as pennies when she dumped them onto the kitchen floor. She doesn't question it. Doesn't wonder why caterpillars curl into little balls and die. Doesn't understand *die*. It's a going away, Father said. Like on the Lurline? The giant white ship drifting in Honolulu Harbor like some moored ghost, an enormous floating angel, mournful pull of its horn shattering the air, taking the people then bringing them back, smothered with leis, swoosh of flowers, perfumed scents, sense of something special but not for her? Father said, *God's* Lurline has two directions, up or down. She asked Father, Who is in charge? Who do you think! he said.

Makela plucks more caterpillars off the crown flower bushes, grows like a thicket in their back yard. The leaves are soft, fuzzy as the yellow-black caterpillars hanging underneath; leaves like umbrellas protecting them from this burning light. The smell of the crown flowers, a fickle smell that sometimes is no smell, other times haunts the air like a spirit. Ana told her about spirit bites. Nahu akua. Wakes you with the scent of flowers, she said. You see the mark on your skin. Means someone will die. The crown flowers are pale purple, Queen Liliuokalani's favorite color, said Ana. When the Queen died, half turned white. But their milk… is poisonous.

One day the big fat caterpillars will become Monarch butterflies, black and orange markings, zebra stripes and butter sticks, wings fuzzy-soft as tissue. Makela peels them off the bottoms of leaves, the milk seeping out, *Wash your hands!* Caterpillars stick to the leaves like ticks. Puts them in jars. She won't forget air holes this time. She'll wake up one morning and the caterpillars are pale lime cocoons, which will become translucent, dark outlines of wings pressing against the chrysalis. "This," Ana says, "is what it's all about."

But today, this day of hard of hurting light, Makela steps inside to show Ana the new batch of caterpillars. She's curled up on that hikie'e like a little brown cocoon. Room glares in its hard yellow light, flowing in through the plate glass window that faces the sea. Room wants to trap that light, the sea, the sun, her mother! "Wake up, Mama!" Doesn't she know? Can't she see? There's never been so much light, such a hot, glowering, fierce afternoon. Makela has five fat caterpillars. One of them has already attached itself upside down to the top of its jar, ready to split its skin, become the chrysalis from which the beautiful butterfly will emerge.

Ana is curled up, doubled up as Madge comes to see it over the years, as she *remembers* it. Is haunted by it. What is the thing she could have said? It was all so…unfinished. Brown hands, fingers swollen from the crown flower leis, bent into little claws. They clutch at her little belly, her opu. Her mouth, her throat, shut tight, so tight! like nothing else will find its way down that dark tunnel again, no papaya, no laulau, no manapua, no avocados green and dripping with morning dew the way she loved them.

Nothing Ana loves inside that doubled-up stomach, through those lips shaped like O; oh! oh! "Mama!"

Ana's kitchen is yellow. Kitchens should be yellow said she, like lemons, like butter, like the sun exploding in. Her kitchen smells of the kimchi she made them for lunch. In the years to come Madge won't ever eat pickled cabbage again. Jude Canada towers in the yellow kitchen. Tall as the door, high as the ceiling, takes up all of the air, the light, what is left of Makela's childhood. He lets the people in; they flow through their house like light itself, yellow door, yellow light, bodies like shadows, words like wind, mumbled, whispered, cold. Makela shrinks down behind Father like she's not really there, like she's already gone.

Silence, dusk slipping into night, black like a cave, swallows you up so that in the morning when you are set free from its dark mouth you will never be the same. Ana, Crown Flower Queen, crown flower halo around her sweet head. A light unplugged, her body is here but she's not in it. Where is she, Father? Then even her body is gone. *Disappeared.* A cocoon, shredded, torn little shell on the top of the jar. Makela does not set the butterfly free.

Now she dreams of Ana, riding a boat on a sea of hot lava, black hair flowing behind like wings. The boat is cocoon shaped, a cradle amongst all this heat and destruction. Madge reaches out her arms to Ana but they can't hold on! The fire is too great! The lava too hot! She told him, *do something!* Yellow surfboard, ocean the color of a bruise.

Speaking of Love (and Magic!) – The Jody Johnstone Story

HE'S BARELY OUT OF MARGO'S blood stained crop top when he's into her pants, Margareit Canada, her first name way too reminiscent of Margo's. Madge, he calls her. Five years older than he, but she has an innocence about her, still those twitchy expectations about how her life might unfold, a girl who lost her mama around the same age Jody lost his. Not that these were the things that drew him in—let's face it she was, as they said in 1969, a stone cold fox. (A year later during a New Year's eve bender on their lanai, two bottles of champagne and a quart of rum eggnog, the Hawaiian night hazy with firecracker smoke, Madge will reveal to Jody that her mother may have been poisoned too. Jody found this too crazy to contemplate; what kind of karma pushes him into the bed of someone whose mother also died with her throat closing up, knives slashing her gut, every cell shutting down in betrayal? "Madge my badge," he slurred.)

Jody's first Madge-sighting was on Kalakaua Avenue a couple blocks up from the Ilikai Hotel, where she's teaching Dan Wallace Ballroom, would prefer to teach almost *any* other kind of dance, modern, even ballet, she'll tell him right off the bat, but there weren't many options in Hawai'i those days beyond the hula. He had thought she was hitchhiking at first, her muscular leg in a tight mini-skirt strung around a lamp pole, her long red ponytail rippling in the trade winds like a flag. He slowed down his VW, heartbeat knocking against his chest wall. When she extricated herself from the pole—just stretching her calves she'd tell him later, he shadows her—she's sashaying down the sidewalk, he's creeping along in the slow lane, until stopped at a red light, she suddenly turns around, making a circular motion with her hand to roll down his passenger-side window.

"You're stalking me," she says, leaning into the window, frankly examining his face like some answer is there.

His cheeks burn. He has no experience with this kind of thing, but when he looks into her eyes the color of Norfolk pines, he's reminded of that green place in the tunnel of a wave and he's hooked, his gaze flying across her face, already tumbling down the finely-honed planes of her neck, her collar bone, the curves of her shoulders, her voluptuous chest. He shakes his head, starts to mumble something but she's smiling, so he smiles too.

"Now you're checking me out," she tells him. "Do you dance? Because that's where we're headed." Then she climbs into the front seat of his car, whoosh of some sweet fruity scent, pointing them toward the Ilikai.

He parks, hands sweating and a tremor in his chin, hoping she noted his perfect parallel form between twin hippie vans, executed on the first try, then follows her into a high-ceiling room off the Ilikai lanai where a gaggle of reluctant boys and chattering pre-pubescent Lolitas are instructed to find a partner and line up. "One two three four, one two three four…" she goes, grabbing a tall Chinese boy and forcing his feet into the shape of a box. "The foxtrot," she announces, releasing the boy to a pimply-cheeked girl in bra-points she hasn't quite mastered. "Learn it if you learn nothing else; the foxtrot is the potty-training of dance." Then she holds out her shapely arms to Jody.

He hopes to God he'll be magically transformed into Fred Astaire or some such *gallant* in those darling arms, but instead immediately tromps on her pretty pink toes in their strappy high heels. She snaps her neck back, flinging her ponytail across her shoulders like it's a whip. "I've had more coordinated twelve year olds!" she groans, telling him he better plan on taking her to the Hendrix concert if he wants to see her again, because his dancing audition is over.

That night Jimi howls from the Waikiki Shell, *Are you experienced!* strutting off the stage with a bouffant-headed blond on his arm after setting fire to his guitar. Madge's face is rapt, like an angel Jody thinks with something skewed, sensual perhaps, though he still doesn't have a clear reference for that word. Jody's only experience with anything like love at this point is the lustrous touch of Margo's thigh, and the reverent, even sensual he supposes, sensations he gets inside his ocean sanctuary, the velocity of waves, tunneling through them on a surfboard. (Though when the desire for *reverence* becomes more about the need to forget, only his body thrashed down on that sandy bottom will do, the rush of the whitewater so strong he can't hear his own thoughts, and for those moments, breath held, eyes shut, he's not waiting for Strike Three.)

After the concert they stroll along Kuhio Beach, lights from the hotels playing across water the inky color of the night, and he reaches for her hand, hoping to erase the memory of those hot, nervously fumbling fingers on Margo's cool skin—vanish it with the fresh touch of Madge. Since watching that magician in the Waikiki Shell, Jody's been developing another crush of sorts, Houdini! The greatest escape artist of all time, how he could be thrown into the Hudson River, manacled, and float free; how he could walk through brick walls, saw girls in half, and most particularly, how he could make someone vanish off a sheet of plate glass. *Vanish!* Jody's been practicing Houdini's illusions while studying painting at the university, his dad's insistence that he go to college for *something*, even if it had to be art.

The following week Madge invites him home to meet her father, but on the day of their meeting Jody's VW dies. Frantic, he borrows Blake's motorbike, which Jody assumed he could ride just fine (if Blake could, how hard could it be?)—and anyway Madge's Kawela neighborhood was a straight-shot out on Kamehameha Highway, he argued when Blake tried to give him a hands-on lesson. The drive went fine until roaring up the Canada driveway, full of the confidence born from not crashing the first hour out, the bike slips on a pothole and comes reeling toward the house sideways, Jody forgetting in his panic that the rear wheel brake was out and the one that worked was on the handlebar, winding up in Jude Canada's prize hibiscus bushes.

Jude, tall as a lamppost storms out, surveying the damage to his plants while Madge fusses over Jody's scraped chin, elbow and a twisted ankle.

"What do you do for a living son?" Jude growls.

"I'm in the arts, sir."

Jude scowls, fingering a crushed pink petal. "Wrong answer. You believe in God?"

"I believe in magic," Jody offers. "But I keep my options open."

"What about my daughter, she one of your *options*?"

"No sir," Jody grins. "I think she could be necessary."

A few months later they were expecting a baby, which ended Jody's art studies, since a job would now be required to support his budding family. Madge growing rounder, fuller, her pregnancy making her more lush, voluptuous, more of the *abundant* woman Jody couldn't get enough of, and less like svelte Margo Malone with the silken thighs.

Interlude – This Could Happen in 1968

YOU MEET A GIRL AT a concert, not even meet her in the formal sense, as in anything so establishment as a name—maybe you're dancing and you sway into her, like a branch in the wind, your leaves trembling at her touch. Or, passing a joint around a crowded room your lips trace where hers have been, tasting the moisture from her mouth as you suck in the smoke. It was both more and less personal in those days, and you felt enough a part of a greater something such that it wasn't at all unusual to have her glide into your space, as it was referred to—and in ten minutes you're kissing, fifteen and your hand is in her pants, your fingers rubbing up against the velvet moleskin of her inner thigh.

It was that way in 1968, and in 1969 when just months after shadowing Madge on a Waikiki street Jody found himself married, a father-to-be. It wasn't ironic. They believed in it, this improvised love, opening themselves up to its possibilities, comfortable platitudes for the rest. War was bad. The Vietnam War Jody escaped (though he confessed to anyone who'd listen he'd been willing enough) was bad; peace, idealism, a certain stoned humanitarian acceptance of that which was not considered bad, and the ecstatic sense that these things could in fact conquer all the rest—this was good. It didn't occur to any of them then that they would get old, have mortgages, struggle to pay bills, lose their homes, their marriages, be under-employed at jobs they hated, watch Mother Earth become corrupted by greed, species disappearing, climate collapsing, endure overwhelming loss, become ill because they couldn't afford the treatments that might have saved them, die. That they too would have to die.

22

Buddy

SOME ENTOMOLOGICAL INFO FOR YOU, file it under trivia—unless you happen to be a moth, of course, not so trivial then. The female silk worm moth flaunts her horniness by giving off a substance called bombykol, the ultimate pheromone. Male moths can smell it diluted to one molecule in a quadrillion in the air, finest chemical sensing in the animal kingdom. Package that and you are president of perfumery, CEO of cologne. Some moths have the equivalent of an eardrum in the middle of their thorax. Spiders and crickets have them on their legs. Earwigs have short, leathery forewings and a pincer-like abdominal appendage, pincher bugs his grandmother calls them. She told him pincher bugs crawl into the ears of their victims, burrow in and pinch the flesh. They like children's ears because they're tender, she told him, so that's why children get earaches. Maybe that's how come you've got an earache, Buddy, she said. As if insects don't have better things to do besides giving brats earaches! Human beings are so selfish. Get this: he's nine years old, his grandma whom he barely knows comes to visit them in Maine, and she's telling him a pincher bug crawled into his ear and gave him an earache!

Here's the truth about earwigs. They spend their days in crevices or damp places feeding on insect prey, dead organic matter, fungi, pollen, plants, a sort of mini-recycling system. The cockroach also prefers moist dark places and slips out to devour his food at night. Sure, you might find him and his buds partying in your kitchen when you turn the light on late, but he's feasting on the crumbs you left, cleaning up for you because you were too damn lazy to do it yourself.

Consider lice, minute wingless parasites living and breeding on their host. That's what they do, what they're *supposed* to do. There's truth in that too. Biting lice feed on hair, feathers, fragments of skin. Sucking lice suck up the host's blood with their sucking mouthparts. Large burying beetles, a type of carrion beetle, dig under the carcass of a small animal until it falls into their hole, then they bury it, food for the larvae, eggs are deposited on the corpse. Nature at its finest, taking away, giving back. "God has an inordinate love of beetles," said the biologist J.B.S. Haldane. Buddy learned that from a book. What he's learned from life is this: there's always someone stronger and meaner, and they're the ones that usually win.

MARNIE, SIZE OF A LOLLING cow, left him two nights ago. "Sorry, Buddy, I can't do this anymore." Pushed her hand over his mouth when he tried to protest, shook her head. "I'm done." He wanted to tell her no one would love her. Don't even pretend anyone's going to *choose* you, Marnie Lo! Imagined her writhing in pain, having her baby alone in a pasture, on the beach, a street. Then wouldn't she miss him! He did everything for her, even tied her goddamn shoes. Marnie Lo, so enormous the rubber on her slippers wore clean through and he gave her his Reeboks. But he just stood there while she stuffed Super Purse with her shampoo, razor, a can of Hawaiian Sun Pass-o-guava juice, bag of Maui Onion Potato Chips, change of underpants, *his* t-shirt. She sighed, shrugged, then walked out the door.

Since the Waikiki Jungle bust they'd been living in a falling apart house on Sunset Beach, with a crew of Todd's *methengers*, along with some aging hippies—balding wastoids, the women in tropical print pareros, a road map of veins down their legs. These women could be his mother. Sometimes they'd hug him against their drooping breasts like he's their little kid, toking pot and sucking down puke colored protein smoothies, whining about whatever it is they figured they had coming that never came. Smelled like patchouli gone industrial, but he'd let them; no one else was touching this flesh of his! They smoked hash from homemade bamboo pipes, and before he went to bed they shared a pipe with Buddy, like a lullaby or prayer.

It's the methengers that were the problem. That's teenagers on meth, don't you know, a term *Totally Todd* coined. Methengers. Like they're a pack, too indistinct to warrant actual names. They did seem to come as a set—two ferret-thin dudes Buddy could barely tell apart, cutting scars up and down their arms, one sporting a bicep tattoo he made with a knife, looked like a rat—*renegade* it spelled, a Mother word. Two girls with scraggly hair, one bony, bad teeth, the other pudgy in her skinny jeans, serious belly overhang, who also had bad teeth. Meth mouth was the thing they all had in common, like it was some membership status. Todd introduced them soon as he was out on bail (funded apparently through methenger profits; whatever pre-bust secrets Todd kept from his niece about his drug dealings were out of the bag now), indicating his Waikiki pad wasn't cool anymore. Said he knew a house they could stay in at Sunset Beach, but they'd have to work. Pineapple fields? Buddy asked. He'd have done anything to get out of those; the moment Todd confirmed the job didn't involve fruit he was in.

Turned out these kids weren't just getting amped on meth or even amping and selling—they were manufacturing. Todd draped a lead apron over Buddy's chest and shoulders. "Will we be working with Xrays?" Buddy asked. Marnie's uncle winked and handed him this recipe, hand-scrawled and initialed, TT, *Totally Todd*:

HOW TO MAKE THE BEST HOT-DAMN, 20/20 WHITE CRUNCH, LA GLASS!

Wear a chemist apron and a gas mask, the shit's toxic as hell. One whiff can make you hurl, and that's the lucky thing, or you pass out and another couple snorts you're dead meat. It's the red phosphorous gas, makes an airborne poison when it's lit up from the other shit, can freeze your windpipe, scar your throat shut. You got to get this off matchbooks so be on the lookout for ones you can snag, like when they hand you a pack with cigarettes and you grab a couple extras. What, no smoke? Kicked the habit already? Nah nah, fire 'em up, dude! Or try just buy some boxes, Spartan rocks. You'll need glass beakers, measuring cups, a couple different sized flasks, and don't forget that full-face respirator, one gas mask. We got some of this shit already so check before you start. You'll be cooking the red phosphorous, iodine and pseudoephedrine, from Sudafed or sinus pills. This is harder to get now that it's behind the counter and even worse, you got to sign for it, which sucks (more governmental interference if you ask me; what's it to them how we use the goods, long as we pay for them, huh?), but you can get any shit you want on the streets for a price. You'll earn it back, one batch of the White Bitch. Serious methheads take an IOU, but don't fuck with them, get the product to them quickly or they'll mess you up bad. Iodine is a toughie because they'll put you on a list if you buy it from a chemical supplier. Try check out every drug store like Longs, Safeway, CVS, etc. and just buy a few bottles from each and if they ask say it's for your horse. Iodine Tincture rocks on hooves. Those are three main ingredients, simple, yeah? But you need other shit cause that's just one way to cook, plus you'll need a solvent for the process.

So, Coleman's Fuel, like what you used if you ever went camping. Muriatic Acid (HCl), they sell it in hardware stores next to the paint thinners. Acetone, Methanol—depending on what's around or how flush we are you'll need some of these to cause a chemical reaction, the magic bullet, yeah? changes the pseudo into methamphetamine. Now, I never took chemistry—Kalani High School tracked me with the born to lose bozos, meant we got shop instead, so I can't say for sure how this shit happens, just that it does. Different strokes for different folks, and different outcomes in the purity and form, but check out the possibles: Drano, Brake Fluid (careful, this shit can ignite then blow and you'll never even know it), you can try lighter fluid or Butane instead of the Coleman's, Hydrochloric Acid, Sodium Hydroxide (city workers douse roadkill with this and within minutes the carcass is yesterday's news), Ether, Battery Acid, Gasoline, Anhydrous Ammonia (which can take the place of the red phosphorous). This last one rocks for folks who live by a farm cause it's essentially a fertilizer. You folks are in Sunset Beach so we're most likely going for the phosphorous. But, whatevah! you need stuff that will cook, causing the chemical reaction that leaves you with those sweet crystals, Vanilla Pheromones, hottest-damn Hawaiian Salt—crystal meth! The end product looks a little like rock candy. Won't taste as sweet but stronger the taste, the better the shit. That's the American Dream in a nutshell: manufacture a kick-ass product, sell it, earn a respectable income from it.

You got to be careful though. Statistically 90% of all meth labs get busted by the narcs when they explode. And watch the stink, yeah? That's why I got you folks out in the shed for the cook, no poisons in the house, no cat piss smell, just that good beach air. Now memorize this and eat the recipe. You think I'm kidding? Chow down dude, or your butt buys my lawyer. Tiny strips shredded up and stirred into poi; yum, tastes ono-delicious with Tamari, yeah?

So the hell with Marnie! Buddy decides, burying his toes in grainy saffron beach sand, just who does she think she is, some demented goddess, queen of the cows? Marnie of the predator-yellow eyes. *But who am I?* Best not to look too closely into that these days. Sunset Beach house with its sagging steps, rotting clapboards, chipping paint, sloughing, termite-chewed walls, home sweet home. Hey, but not everyone gets *this*, wafting scent of bud in the AM (AM morning, AM most decidedly after their move), more fragrant than bacon to wake up to and served with a side of shrooms. A damn good thing too since the hippies are mostly vegans, and forget food stamps when you're living off the grid and can't even legally apply for them. Buddy's father used to say never trust anyone who doesn't eat meat.

Humans lose a part of their soul every day, he said, doing the things they have to do to keep alive; they need those little chunks of animal inside so they can remember who they are, be reaffirmed of their place on the food chain. Salty breeze through torn window screens and in front of the house the beach, waves thrashing, sweeping back. Sunset Beach is a world famous surfing beach. Envy him? Nothing he believed in before is possible anymore. Entomologist? Just bugs, like Marnie says.

Crystal meth was cooked in the shed behind the house per Totally Todd's instructions, but the hippies also had a hard-on about no chemicals in the kitchen, even buying green when it came to dish soap and oven cleaner. Not that oven cleaning was an A-list activity in that house. Lucy, the hippie most likely to hug, said she didn't approve of the methenger lifestyle. In the sixties, she said, they experimented with some grody things: huffing glue, chewing wood rose seeds, smoking banana peel, but never Drano, for crying out loud. But this was income, she recognized the value of that. And a high's a high, though she was skeptical of the methengers' behavior when they were tweaked, buzzing around all night like they're hyper-amped then balling like bunnies—she's heard them, she said, though she's never figured out which two go together, maybe it changes each time? Kids need a good night's sleep, she said. Plus look what it's doing to their teeth.

The methengers encouraged Buddy to sample their batch but he refused. He still had *some* principles. "I'm cool," he said, "the shit's for you." And Uncle Todd, of course, who collected a whopping cut of the sales, 90% after expenses. "You folks stay for free," he justified, "where else do tweaked tweens crash, the YMCA?"

Love's Soul Delivery—LSD—spell it in the thick sand, tracing over the sinking letters with a bleached kiawe stick. Purple ocean howls, smashing its surf against the shore at high tide. He managed to avoid LSD, until today. Used to be he had a limit here too, though at least it's sans the Drano. Used to be he had a girlfriend, or so he thought. This morning he ate it with one of the hippie gals, the one called Rebel who's wandered off somewhere. She had it on that disappearing rice paper, place it on your tongue, fizzy sensation like pop rocks. Rebel light, Rebel bright, Rebel, where you been tonight? Suppose he gets a headache in the middle of it, what if he flips out? Picks up a kitchen knife, something he's fantasized enough, hasn't he? Carve the headache out. But Buddy doesn't care, because now he's flying. "Hey!" Rebel calls out, "Check out the sand, each grain has its own groove."

She's down at the shore, short distance but it seems like miles, a stretch of desert wide and white as eternity. Lifting up the orchid print pareo tied at her waist, pale yellow thighs waxy as margarine, dancing at the edge of the ocean, giant whitecaps thrashing, foam rushing up those rippling legs. Intensely bright day, sand glistening like millions of mica chips, heartbeat romping inside Buddy's chest like something unleashed. Feel a part of the whole of things, this beach, its blue-black sea swooping down on top of Rebel who dives in, swimming under its glassy surface popping up like a dolphin. She's nude above her waist; must've taken off her halter-top in the surf. He can see through the translucent water breasts the color of clouds.

And that's enough to make him step carefully down this hill of sand toward her. He's having trouble negotiating it though, shifting sands this endless desert. Is the ocean actually a mirage? Like walking on a treadmill, shivery, uncertain, caving in around him. "Rebel!" Voice sounds like it erupted out of somewhere else; maybe he's not even him? Buddy used to ponder things like that when he was a little kid, when his parents began their war, ignoring him. He wondered if he even existed. What made him, *Buddy*? A part of them, beholden to them, lashed to them in some inscrutable way. Could he not just walk away, this separate flesh, these bones, organs, blood, *just walk*?

A knot of panic inside him now, stomach churning, calls out again but Rebel can't hear, aqua waves, white spray folding around her, her sleek head bobbing in between the sets. Buddy kneels down, pressing a hunk of the coarse gravely stuff against his face like he's washing his cheeks. A plunging, sudden thirst sucks at his mouth, sticky and dry, closing his throat. Forces himself to think of this as a normal thirst, think about tall sweating glasses of lemonade, with slices of lime like his mom used to fix them, blue-hot summer days in Rock Harbor, Mom, Dad, Buddy, united in thirst, if nothing else.

He wants to go home! Why did they do that, take away his home? Is home the place your parents are until they can't get along so they take it away? Whole body feels like it needs a drink, a six-foot glass of something. Skin's dehydrating, slurped dry in the burning air, itching like there's ants crawling on it. Tries to think about ants, something familiar, comfort in that. Fire ants of the Southeast attack baby birds, stinging them to death. Workers of the carpenter ant species are infertile females. Marnie so massively fertile she couldn't even tie her own shoes....

He's shaking all over, a bone-rattling shiver. Rebel is here, slipping up behind him then kneeling beside him, still topless and wet from her swim. She presses his face against her breasts and his fiery thirst in an instant becomes *want*. "Shhh," she hums, rocking, "it's just the drug. Tell yourself it's just the drug. It talks to us in special ways sometimes, tell yourself that."

"Just the drug," he mumbles, sliding his hand under her pareo, but then he pulls it back immediately. His dreams! The body! "Just the drug, baby," Rebel repeats. Gazes at him placidly, round eyes filmy and grey as car exhaust. She's sitting cross-legged now in front of him. No underpants! genitals spread, waxy as a drooping gardenia. Buddy shudders, shuts his eyes sways back and forth.

"Come on, baby," Rebel says, fastening her halter-top back on. "What you need is some exercise. We'll walk it off, this spooky drug talk." She spirals up then lugs him behind her like he's her little kid. Follows her blindly off the beach, through the broken-down neighborhood of beach shacks and the newer monstrosities built in the housing boom, half of them empty with foreclosure signs stuck into their overgrown lawns, toward the street. Clutching her hand, stepping high and deep over first sand, and now chunks of grass and pavement that seem like small mountains, like he should rappel them. "The drug just does it sometimes," Rebel says, "Can't tell you why. Maybe it reacts to people who tend to be a little nervous, you know, the way a dog smells out a person's fear? You nervous about something, baby?"

"Let me count the ways," he mumbles, remembering his mom, counting whenever it gets tough. *One, two, three...shit doesn't work for me.* Thirst back again but for nothing tangible. Swipes a hot tear out of his eye.

They cross Kamehameha highway toward Pupukea, Buddy tagging Rebel like some mutt down the side of the road, a snarly mess of long weeds, broken glass, cars blaring by. He's lost all sense of time, of direction, of *sense*, in the shadow of those lunging hips, like a palm tree these hips, fluid and wiry, a slim person garbed in a chubby woman's hips, singing "Just the drug," over and over like a mantra. "Tell yourself that, Buddy. I should've been a shrink or a counselor of some sort. Got a knack for this talking down shit, don't you think?"

They pass by a clutter of beach houses, dilapidated huts with brush in between, kiawe brambles, halekoa, plumeria trees sagging under the weight of their bloom. Cars with surfboards strapped to their roofs speed by, occasionally honking. Buddy's thinking how he has no control in his life at all anymore, or else he wouldn't be in this situation, cooking meth for a burned-out vet, LSD amped, following a hippie older than his mother, chanting *Just the drug* down Kamehameha highway. Just *who* is in charge?

At Pupukea they pant their way up a steep, winding road leading half way up the side of a deep green cliff, foothill to the Ko'olaus. "I told my mom I'd never do drugs," Buddy wheezes to Rebel who's beside him now. "She did some in college and her life is crap. Not that the drugs did that, but I told her I didn't want to do things the way she did them." He's listening to himself spew this nonsense; maybe if he keeps firing out the words his freaked-out thoughts can't crowd in? Why would an artifact named Rebel care about Gwen's life? Gwen Winter, former school teacher, former mom, creator of her own God, her own crazy-mother's babysitter, who drinks herself numb most nights just to get up and do it all over again the next day.

"What about chicks?" Rebel slips her hot fleshy arm around his waist. "You tell your mom you wouldn't do the ladies?"

He shakes his head, a sour taste of bile shooting up his throat.

They pant around a hairpin loop in the road and below them the whole north shore suddenly opens up, Kawela, Sunset, Pupukea, Waimea, spread out like knuckles on a giant rock hand all the way to Ka'ena Point, ocean a deep stretch of violet. He sucks in a whistling breath.

"Here's why, baby," Rebel grins, her earnest, bovine face, placid eyes sweeping over the view. "The reason for LSD. Seeing the world the way God sees it."

"Maybe God doesn't want us to see it his way," Buddy snaps, suddenly irritated. "Why does God always have to come into these things? What the hell's the point of being God if everyone else sees things the way he sees them? God has an inordinate love of beetles. A biologist said that."

Rebel shrugs. "I don't have nothing against beetles, beetles never did me no wrong. Some places they gob chocolate over them and eat them. Chocolate covered beetles, yum."

"My mom prays to God and her life sucks." This is an insane conversation, he's thinking, must be the drug, *just the drug*; she's talking beetles now and he's talking God!

Rebel lifts her round bare shoulders, sighs, her breasts rising like dinner rolls inside the thin fabric of her halter-top. "Your mom should do acid, some find God in it."

They continue up the road yakking inanely, anything to avoid any *real* thoughts, turning into a path overgrown with kiawe, knots of halekoa and a giant purple morning glory vine that lassos his ankles as he walks. "Down boy," Buddy mutters, kicking at it. He thinks of Blinky. Though his dog Blinky wasn't a boy. Thinks how he can't stand to lose what he loves, can't stand how you just keep remembering and the hurt doesn't go away. He's beginning to feel sick and clutches at his stomach, which isn't much of a stomach, taut layer of skin stretched between his hipbones like a drum. He used to imagine Marnie sliding down his body at night, licking his hipbones; saw that in a movie once. How many other guys did she do that with, how many *bedtime stories*? A sudden flash of Sunset Beach and how Rebel's body for a moment became the dead body in Buddy's dreams, vagina opening like it could swallow him.

"Look," Rebel announces, pointing up the path at a crumbling lava rock enclosure, "a heiau. Hawaiians worshipped here. Prayed for shit to happen, rain, revenge, people to die, those kinds of things. That big flat rock was for human sacrifices."

A chill creeps up Buddy's spine settling in his brain, fingers and toes go cold.

"Good place to get in touch with the spiritual element. Ever contact a spirit? See the Ti leaf wrapped bottles for offerings? There's even a couple of joints."

"I want to go now," he says, backing away from Rebel as she steps into the circle of rocks. She saunters toward the sacrificial rock and he hedges back even further. "Please, Rebel! What the hell? Let's go."

"What's the matter baby, you're not chicken are you? You're not afraid of...hmmm...ghosts?" She slaps her okole on the large rock swinging her thick legs off the ground, grinning her yellow grin; then she removes her top, flinging it into the air toward him. Buddy steps back again, making no attempt to snag it. Tugging off her pareo Rebel lies down butt-naked on the rock.

"Jesus!" he whines, "what the fuck are you doing?"

Splaying her pin-grey hair like a fan on the flat lava surface, Rebel stretches out slow and languorous like she's on some feather bed. "What would it feel like to be sacrificed?" Licks her lips, raises her fleshy arms toward the sky. "The ultimate sex, your body offered to a god, *consumed* by a god.

"Chrissake, Rebel!" A slug of vomit in his throat and Buddy wonders if he's about to spew. Please, not here! he thinks. Marnie warned him about Hawaiian spirits; they've got attitude, she said, you don't want to piss them off. The body dream flashes before him as he stares at Rebel's nakedness. Any flicker of desire he may have felt has turned to revulsion, and suddenly he's seeing her dead on that rock, bloodless, an ancient dried-out offering. He sees himself on top of her.

Barreling back down the path, booking full speed ahead like something's after him, and then he's certain there is. Footsteps! Behind him on the path. He twists his neck around without breaking his stride, nothing. Rebel's still on the rock, lolling about like some sun-stroked reptile. He runs faster and the footsteps do too, padded sounds of two pairs of feet trampling brush and dirt. A directionally challenged night marcher, lost from his brigade? Runs harder, breath pounding and wheezing, scratching the wall of Buddy's chest like something feral. He's screaming for air, or maybe he's screaming period. If a night marcher catches him maybe he'll be forced into his own dream, sex with that dead body who's young then she isn't, and in the end she's wearing his grandmother's face. *Oedipus* move over! Feels a terrible coldness, a chilled wind breezing through him, its glacial advance inside his veins. Then, thank God!—he breaks out of the path and onto the main road leading down the hill to Kamehameha highway.

"*King Kamehameha, ruler of the islands…*" singing that insipid song to ward off he doesn't know what, the kinds of insane thoughts that might try to knit all of this together, shape it into something real. Footsteps and nobody's there? Nobody of flesh, anyway! King Kamehameha pushed rival soldiers off the sheer cliffs of the Pali. More spirits roaming O'ahu out for revenge. He may become a believer yet. Walking at the side of the highway again, thumb stuck out, cars roaring by just like before only it doesn't feel the same. How can anything feel the same after you've been chased down the hill by some footless-footsteps? A small white car screeches to a stop just past him, backs up and pops open the door. "I've been looking all over for you! They said you took a hike, but I thought they meant it as a figure of speech."

Buddy gawks at her, still dizzy from the residue of the drug, stands stupidly chewing his tongue, a wash of afternoon sun lighting the air around her. "What the hell?"

"Well get in for Pete's sake, we aren't exactly at a rest stop," Gwen says.

Hesitates, swallowing hard then climbs in rubbing his eyes. "I'm still fucked up on acid, that's what this is about," Buddy mumbles to himself. "What are you doing here? How did you even find me on this street, for chrissake?"

"What am *I* doing here? More like what have you been doing here all these months driving me crazy with worry! I'm sick of it, fed up. You are my son. You are under-aged and should be living with me until old enough not to. That's what I'm doing here."

"Oh no, you're not going to start bitching me out are you? I've had a pretty bad day. I don't need a lecture about now!" He shoots her a look then shakes his head. "Christ!"

Gwen reaches over him and locks his door, a swoosh of cool air, then angles the car back into a line of beach traffic. "You seem a little edgy. And you're pale. You look like you've seen a ghost, Buddy. Why on earth were you hitchhiking? It's not safe, you know that."

He realizes he's trembling. Stares at his hands, skinny fingers at weird stuck-out angles. Looks at the dashboard, trying to concentrate on something. Island Wrent-A-Wreck, the plastic decal on the glove compartment. "You're renting a used car? Who rents a used car?"

"Never mind the bloody car. That Marnie told me where you two have been staying; that's how come I'm here, how I found you. *She* went home. Ran into her at the KTA. Looks like that baby's due soon."

He shrugs, stomach churning, throat burning. Marnie, that fricken traitor!

"She said she couldn't stand the way you were living, with a bunch of druggies, she said. You cold, Buddy? How come you're shivering like that?"

"So where are we going?" He musters so he won't have to answer her, remembering those footsteps! Plus, if his mom figures out he took acid, she'll make him read the Bible every day for the foreseeable future, her threat if she ever caught him using drugs. If Buddy can even *foresee* a future anymore. Some girlfriend, makes him stick it out on O'ahu all these months then she's the one goes and blabs where he is.

"We're going to that house so you can settle up and pack." Suddenly she swerves off the road, a dirt parking area in front of the Banzai Pipeline surfing beach, wail of a horn behind them, shuts off the car engine.

"Good one! Smart choice getting a used car, maybe." He stares out at turquoise waves curling like giant lips, and surfers, little black ant-like shapes riding them. "What's the deal?"

"Well, I've been thinking about something, cruising up and down this road by the ocean looking for you." She makes a ragged, breathy sound like dragging on a cigarette, twists a hank of her hair around her finger. "See those waves? Big, right? Well those waves times another twenty or thirty feet were a drug to my dad, your grandfather. Like alcohol to an alcoholic, heroin to an addict. You know anything about big wave surfers?"

Buddy snorts. "I'm from Maine, remember?"

"A crazy bunch, I'm telling you, they live for the adrenalin rush. They'll chat about sliding down the face of a humongous wave like it's something alive. They get smashed, bashed, and come up looking for more—if they come up that is. Apparently my dad couldn't resist the lure of these waves. But the thing is, where he went for his last ride wasn't the famous big wave places like Waimea, or right here at Pipeline. He was where waves aren't considered surfable, because of the reef, the riptide, the form, all kinds of reasons, so what was he even doing down Hamakua with a board, folks asked? Some thought he did it on purpose, marriage gone sour, business going under, but I'm starting to wonder if maybe he really did go into those waves just to surf the damn things. He probably looked at those giants thundering into a place that doesn't usually have them as magic, and my dad was all about magic. Auntie Violet said it's our genetic legacy, depressives, mood disordered, impulse control challenged, plum *crazy* for Pete's sake, pick your poison. Just words, son. So, what if he really did go in looking for a perfect ride?"

Buddy frowns, watching the surf. Even with the six to eight footers today you couldn't pay *him* to set foot in that ocean. "Well what's it to me? I didn't even know your father."

She nods, "Yeah, but could be you're like him. You do crazy things too, Buddy, like running away to O'ahu with a pregnant girl!"

He stretches and pops his knuckles. She's waiting for him to say something. He looks at her face, remembering a photo he'd seen of her, maybe a couple years younger than he is now, dark haired and pretty, unsmiling. She spent half her childhood without her father, and now Buddy is too, without his dad. "So I don't get why you're preaching at *me*, your dad's insane surfing doesn't have a thing to do with my life. And what makes you think I'll go back to the Big Island with you?" He stares out toward the horizon, low clouds, pale sky the color of bleached bone.

His mother sucks in a breath. "Son, listen to me. It's your grandmother; she isn't doing well. I mean it. I need you to come home and be with us. I really... I just can't do this alone anymore. Nobody should have to do this alone."

He feels uncertain how he's supposed to react, what he's supposed to say.

Should he even believe any of this craziness? *It's just the drug,* he imagines Rebel humming—though for all he knows she might still be on that sacrificial rock getting gang-banged by a brigade of night marchers! What he's feeling is something cold and squiggly in his gut like a fish flopping inside, remembering his dream, the woman's face that becomes his grandmother's face. "Why can't you just hire someone to help? Isn't that what people do, these sorts of situations?"

"My mother doesn't like strangers in her home. She'd hate that. It has to be us, son."

"I don't know what *I'm* supposed to do about anything."

"Of course you do!" Gwen snaps. "And what's up with that purple mark on your arm?"

"So? Maybe Marnie bit me. She can be something of an animal turns out."

"From the looks of that ghetto-house you've been staying in, just about anything could have bitten you. You know what the Hawaiians would say? That it's a spirit bite, nahu akua."

Buddy snorts. "So when did *you* go all native?"

Gwen sighs, starts up the car. "I don't know. I don't know about anything anymore. It's probably a spider bite. Forget the waves. He walked into the water, he didn't come out."

Interlude: Notes To Precede A Big Wave Moment

TECHNICALLY HIS DAUGHTER IS RIGHT about big wave surfing mentality, adrenalin junkies, like with any extreme sport where death can snag you as readily and arbitrarily as the thrill of escaping it, but that's not what Jody Johnstone was about. For him, the whole getting drilled into the sand routine was about forgetting that he had in fact escaped death twice already by the grace of two who didn't—not to have the ride of a lifetime he could write about for Surfer Magazine or brag to anyone who would listen. Penance initially, then it became a plan.

JODY'S NOTES - A LESSON *in the Physics of Monster Waves*

1. In order to get really large waves you need high velocity wind, say 50 mph give or take for, ideally, two days over a huge stretch of ocean (drum roll… our Pacific!), to churn them up.

2. As they enter shallower water, like over a reef, they start to slow down, but they also increase their height. I don't totally get why this is, just is.

That's the magic, maybe, right there.

3. What that does is lead to a formula. I'm a fan of formulas. No need to speculate when there's a formula. Frequency: how many waves are passing per second, times Wavelength, which is the length of the waves (duh). Tada! you get the velocity of the wave!

4. Then there's amplitude, which sounds like attitude—the *attitude* of a wave. Amplitude is a measure of how big. If you see a mini, followed by a tsunami, that right there is amplitude. There are three things that go into amplitude of a wave: wind speed, length of time its blown (like I said in #1, two days is optimal for giant *amplitude*, though 36 hours could work if the other conditions are good), and the distance of open ocean its blowing over. That's called fetch.

5. All of it has to come together to create a monster. The greater each of those three variables, the more monstrous the monster. If there's limited fetch, you might see six footers, but take an intense wind blowing for 48 hours over unlimited fetch, you get, yup… the giants.

JODY HAD ONLY FINISHED A couple years of college, plus he was an art major, not exactly your prototypical physics geek. But he was determined, and he had a plan, a formula, and the lost notes, or maybe we should say the undiscovered but fully imagined *rumored* lost notes, from his mentor-in-magic, the one and only Houdini, master of the great escape and the world's foremost (at *that* time!) disappearance artist. Jody had already determined the Hamakua coast, with its stretch of deep open water created by its long fetch, its shallow coral reef and submerged lava bed coastline, had the *potential* to create waves with a certain speed and velocity. What he needed was the right wind.…

Part V

Later That Winter

23

Gwen

IT'S LATE, A MOON-GLOWING NIGHT, insect sounds, and yet again Gwen is sleepless. She polishes off the last of the burgundy, then heats up a cup of milk in the microwave, cradling its warmth in her hands. Earlier this evening she had been searching for a marking pen that hadn't dried up, scanning the cluttered shelves over her mother's mahogany secretary, popping open overfilled drawers, her hand dragging through each, and she discovered a photograph of her parents' wedding buried in the grainy depths of a bottom drawer. When Madge destroyed so many of the family pictures, ones that had Gwen's father in them, could she have forgotten this? Or hidden it away! They were married under the avocado tree in Jude Canada's yard, so gnarled and twisted with age it no longer bore fruit. Shadows from the tree's branches patterning those hopeful faces, the bride and the groom, blaze of chaotic light behind, a camera that shouldn't have shot into the sun. Who wouldn't have realized that, or disregarded the wisdom entirely? Gwen's grandfather, Jude Canada. Instructions were for everyone else! Her mother wore a lacy white holoku with a white pikake lei, and her father too was in white, the traditional white Hawaiian wedding shirt, his sun-streaked hair shades of the moon. White, the color of innocence and hope. Gwen the size of a date already nestled inside Madge.

"Your mother yakked through so much of the service," her father once said, "almost didn't hush up long enough to recite her vows." Gwen thinks about the spectacle of this, a glib Margareit Shirley Canada about to become Madge Canada Johnstone. Her father, a surfer with his tan skin, his shaggy hair and boyish grin, her mother the beautiful auburn-haired dancer beside him. He must have thought he landed the catch of the century.

Jody Johnstone sold art supplies in Art's Alive, but what Gwen remembers were the magic aisles. Items right off of a Houdini playlist: cards, ropes, manacles, trunks, fish bowls, a bird cage (pigeon not included! the instructions announced), plumes, lamp bases, assortments of tubes, glass pitchers, dye bottles, slates, and a cabinet with a secret compartment, so the magician could make believe he was sawing a girl (they were *always* girls) in half. There was even a large packing box with a built-in trick panel, and instructions for Houdini's famous water-escape, that Gwen's father typed out with this precaution: "Unless you're a strong swimmer do not attempt!"

Was her dad an artist? He called himself one, yet he seemed obsessed with Houdini's magic, the *illusionist*, which was more about making things unreal *seem* real, than anything solid. Anyway how would Gwen know? Madge destroyed her husband's paintings, perhaps out of anger over his abandoning her, the store, his *disappearance*, who knows why! when she took over Art's Alive. And the magic. She got rid of the magic.

Nights at their dinner table that final year, her father sat tugging his hand through tufts of uncombed hair while Madge recited his wrongs. At what point did he give up? Wandering in and out of his studio that was also their laundry room, going in later each day to work; when the surf was up he wouldn't open the shop at all, leaving their house with his board on the roof-rack of his old VW. He became a breeze that could blow out of their lives at any moment. Why couldn't her mother see that?

Sipping at the cooling milk, Gwen frowns at its blandness, reaching for the ceramic chicken sugar bowl, center of the kitchen table. Dumping in a clump of sugar, she attempts a tender taste then pushes the cup away. Stares at the chicken, a silly piece yet no doubt with some designer name stamped under its fragile rump. Madge Canada Johnstone, glamorous in a place where glamour was greeted by a raised eyebrow. *What's she up to?* Curvaceous, graceful, at ease in her expanse of skin. Gwen shot up tall and bony like her father, raw, awkward, big feet. "Eat too much poi your hips blow out and you'll waddle like a duck," her mother scolded when Gwen developed a preteen obsession for poi, dipping in hunks of raw sugar cane, slurping, chewing, sucking. For a while it was all she'd eat, some sort of power play with Madge who made her sit at the dinner table until bedtime, staring belligerently at her cold plate of "real food": slab of overcooked flesh, soggy vegetables and a "starch," a potato no doubt, since everyone else here eats rice.

A couple months after they moved to the Big Island Gwen came home from third grade and discovered the house in the field opposite them on fire. "Look!" her mother handed her binoculars, pointing at the great tongues of flame licking out of the windows, a hungry arch toward the roof. "Will you look at all those people watching, those parasites. Where are they when life is normal? When there isn't a tragedy? Sirens draw them like flies to a picnic."

Gwen stared at the black curling columns of smoke, red and blue twirling lights, her mother clutching her so close she could barely breathe. Firefighters were running about, coats flapping like penguins. She noticed the boy who lived there, a fifth grader, sitting at the end of his driveway, out of the way of the commotion or anyone's concern. He was bouncing a basketball between his open legs, gazing intently toward the hoop on the garage. So far the fire had spared the garage. "That boy just lost everything," Madge announced, "and he wants to play ball." Years later Gwen would get it, the admiration in her mother's words: she had been indicating (or maybe lamenting!) that Gwen should be like that kid. We press on.

After her husband *disappeared*, after those months of waiting for him to come home, Madge stormed into Bank of Hawai'i one morning lugging Gwen in tow. "So how do you expect us to live now!" she demanded of Mr. Yamamoto, the bewildered manager. As if the answer was a secret kept deliberately from her.

Perched on a chair opposite him, upright like her back's nailed to a board Madge poured through her husband's banking records for Art's Alive, clucking her tongue, twisting her fingers, slapping Gwen's knee once when she started to fidget on the chair beside hers, then banging her fist down on Mr. Yamamoto's desk. "Must I sell leis for us to eat? What am I supposed to do? No Canada has ever bankrupt and I won't do it, I tell you I won't!"

"Well Mrs. Johnstone, nobody's suggesting you file Chapter Seven here, I mean certainly that would be premature at this time." He gazed at Gwen, as if a fidgeting eight year old might offer a clue. "I'm sure your husband didn't expect for you to have to go through his financial doings. I'm sure he didn't expect...what happened to him, you know."

"Financial *doings?*" Her mother glowered at the puzzled man shrinking behind his giant koa desk, her green eyes sour as olives. "No body, no dice! He could've broken his board himself so it would *look* like he drowned, so that *I* would be forced to save his business. Which is exactly what I intend to do. I will not be a lei seller, not ever again."

After they left the bank Madge marched across the street into Liberty House, bought a black silk suit for herself and a navy blue sailor dress with a stiff white collar for Gwen. Gwen hated it. She wanted a black dress like her mother's. "Little girls do not wear black," Madge said firmly. "These are our mourning clothes, so that it looks official, so we can get on with what needs getting on. How typical," she muttered, shaking her head, red hair whipping about like a firestorm. "Can you see how it is, Gwenyth? The things people do so they don't have to admit they're a failure? Pride makes man a foolish thing. Pride goeth before a fall, so it's been said. Remember this, Gwenyth. Some day it will be an important lesson."

For the second time in as many months after finally falling asleep, Gwen wakes up immediately with a sense of something terribly wrong. Lies in her bed, the misty light of dawn, heartbeat erupting in her throat. She's listening to the sounds of her mother's heavy breathing from the next room. She's breathing, Gwen's thinking, she's alive. But there's a cloying, nagging hollowness in Gwen's stomach as if she hasn't eaten for days.

She listens to the scolding and chattering of mynah birds, the raw screech of a pheasant then a nene, the throaty cooing of mourning doves. She hears the slurping, dripping sounds of the damp heavy fog, harbinger of rains they so desperately need, she hopes. Stretching, she pulls her legs out from under the covers, sliding them down on the floor. Feet touch the hook rug Grandma Ana made, years before she would have become her grandmother. *Nothing's wrong, everything's fine,* whispers it to the rug.

Pulls on her bathrobe, sucks in a deep breath and strolls into her mother's room. Madge is lying in her bed, eyes glittering up, dark and muddied like patches of wet soil. The green has gone out of them, Gwen notices this immediately, but she's awake, most certainly, eyes fixed on Gwen. "Good morning, Mother!" She says it crisply, a healthy no-nonsense kind of daughter after all, sharp and competent. The woman who made her wear navy might picture her in a black power suit now.

Madge drops open her mouth, twists it into a prunish shape and lets out a chirping sound.

Gwen frowns. "Speak up, Mother, what is it?"

She does it again. Gwen notices as she bends down a trace of tears in her mother's eyes, and the strange fluttery movement of one hand over her quilt. Heart does that flip-flop thing. "OK lazy-mazey Madge, let's get you up and start our morning routine, shall we? Hmmm, what do we want for breakfast? The usual? Cream of rice? The usual it is, comfort in the usual, right Mother?" She's babbling and tugging at Madge's arms, and her body isn't following like it usually does, however reluctantly, it feels weighted to the bed like a bag of sand.

Gwen yanks the covers off, slides her arms under those swizzle stick legs. "Now Mother, this doesn't make sense, uh uh, no sense at all. You're skinnier than me these days, but you feel heavy as a horse this morning. What's the deal?" Gwen plops Madge's feet straight down on the floor, drags Madge up on her feet, grunting and groaning under this strange new weight, this leadened inertia of her mother's body. But the minute she's in a standing position she collapses back down on the bed, like a wet noodle. Makes a croaking sound, eyes glistening.

"Oh goddammit, with all due respect, what the hell!" Gwen hooks her hands under her mother's armpits, yanking her up again and again she collapses. Tugs her flaccid legs straight out of the bed and she falls back against her pillow, arms flung out like she's being crucified. For a brief moment Gwen thinks of a snow angel, Buddy back when he was still her Richard in the new Maine snow, small arms stretched over his head, grinning up at her. She starts to cry.

Racing out of her mother's bedroom back into her own, Gwen grabs the phone off the night table, knocking it over; slamming it back down again she picks up the receiver and dials the number scorched in her mind, who needs speed dial! "Juli?" she howls into the receiver. "Get Dr. Alvarez on the phone! It's very important!"

"This is her answering service; confirm your phone number and I'll have her call you back. If this is an emergency please call 911."

"No! No emergency. But urgent, very urgent." Gwen hangs up, waits, counting empty seconds by tens to make them move faster, ten, twenty, thirty...staring at the inert landline, listening to those earlier sounds, birds, suck of the fog, her breathing...all changed now. Thinks how she should have gotten a new cell phone when they moved here, or better yet a smart phone—why didn't she take the time to do that? Oh yeah, the money. But now they're dependent on this ancient landline! Not even the number has changed from when she was a kid.

When it rings she jumps, snatches at the receiver almost knocking the whole thing over again. "Gwen? Juli Alvarez here, everything OK?"

"OK? OK? No, it's not OK!" There's a bitter taste in her mouth and she knows what it is goddammit; it always comes back during times like this, the worst kinds of times, fear and that goddamn lie...*pretending everything was OK*. All the while she knew. She's a child, but she knew, and she couldn't say it, wasn't allowed to speak the words. He wasn't coming back. "My mother can't walk, Juli! I can't get her up, her legs are like, I don't know, wood. I can't deal with this!"

"Call 911 immediately. They'll get there faster."

"No! It would scare her. Please just come over here, Juli. Please! I don't think it's life threatening; I mean she's alive, but something's going on here. Please?"

Gwen hangs up the phone, pressing her hand over her heart, thrumming through her fingertips like it's about to implode. Count! she orders herself, then she's so thirsty for a drink of something tart and mind-numbing she can't stand it, about to march into the kitchen, the hell with what time of the morning it is, when she hears Madge groan, and then a cry that could be her name. She remembers she left her mother flung out on the bed and strides into Madge's room, a retching at the back of her throat. "All right Mother, I told you this would happen, didn't I? You're weak from not eating, that's what, I told you you have to eat! Remember how you cursed me? You cursed me, said damn you to hell! Well damn you too, Mother, we're all probably going to Hell anyway!"

Gwen massages Madge's legs briskly, roughly; maybe it's a circulation problem she's thinking. Maybe she's not getting enough Vitamin D since she's not eating, can't stomach milk, and she's developed rickets; though she could get that vitamin from the sun, but she isn't going outside anymore either! So maybe that's it. "Rickets, Mother! I bet you have bloody rickets." Gwen remembers looking at pictures in *Life* magazine as a child, other children in places so removed from her own reality they seemed remote as the moon, their little legs shaped like bow ties made of twigs. *See how lucky you are,* Madge would say.

"Well," Juli Alvarez says, running her long hands up and down Gwen's mother's legs, "it's not her legs."

"They're wooden!" Gwen insists. "Just try and swing them down on the floor, they won't support her weight and she weighs like a hollowed out stick these days."

"Say my name, Mrs. Johnstone. No, OK then can you say your name? Can you speak your name to me, Mrs. Johnstone? Can you count to five?" Juli Alvarez, sharp eyes and shiny hair smiles her sweet smile at Madge. Holds out a slender hand. "Would you squeeze my fingers please?" Madge is immobile, eyes fired on her doctor's face. Juli motions Gwen to follow her out of the room.

"All my life people have left me," Gwen tells her, her steps tiny, half-frozen, a buzzing like a cloud of bees whirling inside her brain. "My father, my husband, well that was mutual, my son. My life is a chronicle of desertions, Juli. Do you want some tea? Why don't I make us some. If my cousin Kiki were here she'd fix the herbal kind that tastes like the remains from a vacuum cleaner bag, though I must say I prefer Earl Grey myself."

"Gwen. I want you to stop right here and take a deep breath." Juli wheels around, planting her hands firmly on Gwen's shoulders. Gwen's taller than she, and she looks up, her eyes leveling into Gwen's until it seems like Juli's the one who's taller. "Listen now, I know this is difficult for you. Your mother has had a major stroke. A debilitating stroke. Her left side is...not working, and it's unlikely she will regain speech. What we can do now is make her comfortable as possible. I'm going to step up her Heparin and add more low-dose aspirin for clotting. I'd like her moved to an appropriate facility, but I know she told you she doesn't want that. I'll assess her condition further in a couple days. We may need to consider tube feeding, which of course can't be done in your home. For now I recommend hiring a CNA. If she's bed-ridden she'll need to be turned regularly or she'll develop bedsores. We'll get you a wheelchair so you can move her out of bed for a while each day if possible, as this will help with circulation and muscle motility, but it will be hard for you to lift her in and out of it on your own. Some patients recover partially from such a stroke, with speech and physical therapy, but Madge was already in a deteriorating condition from the TIA's, you know that. The protocol would be to call an ambulance and admit her at the hospital, but realistically there isn't anything more we can do at this point. Our tests will confirm the obvious, and in her weakened state the upheaval and exposure could make things worse. I'm sorry." She releases Gwen's shoulders.

"What about that new stroke medicine, they've made it sound like some wonder drug!"

Juli nods, "Sometimes, yes, but she would've had to get to the hospital hours ago. Timing is everything with that one."

"Are you telling me, what, that it's *hopeless*? Is that it? That you've given up on her?" Gwen's voice is shrill, a siren in her ears, the wail of a wounded beast and she can't control it. "OK, fine, I don't have a life anymore, do I? I don't need this, always having to worry if she's in her bed, tie her up. God, what am I, a jailer? Jesus, how ironic. I've turned into my ex-husband, a warden for my own mother! She's like a kid, and God knows I'm not so good with kids, you know my own son ran away?" Gwen glares at her.

"Yes," Juli says, "I'm sorry."

"Don't be, he's back. Though he may as well not be for all the time he spends around here with us. So she should just go ahead and check out, right? She'll be better off!"

Tears are careening down Gwen's cheeks; she doesn't even bother wiping them. Juli reaches out again but Gwen reels away from her. "Hey! Allow me this, I'm owed at least one fit; we all get to lose it occasionally, don't we? You think I'm manic, is that it? Lithium for the Johnstones? Goddammit, you're essentially telling me my mother's *dying* and I think I'm allowed a reaction!" She spins around in the direction of Madge's room, then stands there shaking in the hallway. Stares into the familiar room that is suddenly unfamiliar, suddenly named; a *dying* place, place of death, death will happen there. No *disappearing*, not this time.

"Do you know, Juli," she begins, quieter now, "she hid her grief when my father was presumed drowned. Who would've known? That's the way she wanted it to appear. She pressed on. Made *me* press on, hiding any fear, pain, sorrow, despair for God's sake, I was just a little girl! Made me pretend I too believed he'd come back. A goddamn lie, but I admire her ability to pull it off. She lost everything in her life but me. Imagine, being the kind of person who loses everything, but keeps on making the whole world think it's all just fine. That Madge Johnstone, so *akamai*, everyone said. Then you end up in bed turned over by a stranger. How will she bear that?"

Juli places a cool hand on the back of Gwen's neck. Gwen wants to cry at the touch. Nobody's touched her in so long. "You've got to get some help, Gwen, this is too much to handle alone. You told me your mother didn't want to be in an institution, so the only choice is to bring someone in. She may need oxygen at some point to make her more comfortable. A CNA can do these things. It's not your fault. It's just the way it is."

24

Buddy

THERE'S A SPECIES OF FLY called Empidids, where the male bears gifts for the female he wants to hook up with, a juicy young midge let's say, all wrapped up fine in a white silk balloon he spins himself. Secured to his abdomen, held shining in flight, he offers this wonder to her. If she accepts he nails her, and she's OK with that, bargaining her sex for this beautiful prize. The crazy thing is entomologists have recorded stages of this gift, from the delectable insect inside, to the next where the midge is all wrapped up, but the male has sucked it dry first, to a beautifully spun package with nothing in it—all presentation, no substance. In each of these behaviors the female accepted the gift, giving herself to the male in exchange.

Entomologists don't know what to make of this: is the female tweaking on the package itself, and whether or not any meat's inside didn't matter? The male cunning and the female not so much? The female's turn-on was watching the male labor over that balloon just to impress her? Maybe it's all about the presentation dance, the two of them drifting in motes of sunshine, the package sparkling like jewels it may or may not be carrying. Or maybe it's just that humans can't apply their Hallmark values to the insect world, that whatever instinct the female has for accepting the male's gift, and the male for downgrading it, it's been working that way for millions of years.

One of his teachers once asked Buddy why he was so *enamored* of insects, and Buddy detected that shudder of the human who finds insects unsettling because they aren't human: they don't respond to love or any emotions humans recognize; they don't do bad consciously so there's no possibility of redemption. Worse than indifference and it's unfathomable to folks. So they off them, or some of them, because they can—even though they know they can't ever get them all. That scares the shit out of people.

Empidids will thrive long after the apocalypse, whatever form it takes: his mom's revisionist version; the fundamentalists' with four horsemen and wailing zombies; climate collapse; asteroid annihilation; or maybe humans just nuke themselves out of existence. But the insect world is ancient and has run all this time on instincts wired for survival, flawless for what they do to ensure species success. Whereas people muddle along, their trite thoughts in their arrogant brains, their pathetic politics, weapons, advanced technologies and meaningless toys, fractured families, failed love, their so-called evolved consciousness that knows the despair of its own mortality, stumbling if they are goddamn lucky into some kind of grace. The real question is, why *wouldn't* Buddy be enamored of a fly? As eager to embrace the remains of someone's picnic as they are his flesh, and when that one's gone they'll as readily find someone else.

HE'S DRIVING DOWN THE VOLCANO highway toward Hilo, grocery shopping at the KTA for his mom, a way to get the car, get away from that house. He thinks about Marnie, watching the metallic flash of tin roofs on the same Quonset huts they passed so long ago it seemed, on their way to the airport, to Honolulu, when everything still seemed possible. Zoom in seven months later and picture this: Buddy with Marnie at the Sunset Beach house, before she concocts her disappearing act. There's not even a mattress to sleep on, to erect that wall of chastity. It's nighttime, late. Marnie's on the couch, and Buddy remembers being down on the floor trying to get comfortable on the ratty old Army blanket, the one they nabbed from Todd's busted place, beside her. His world is caving in on him and he doesn't try to touch her anymore, doesn't even fantasize about it much.

She leans over the edge of the couch, "Buddy? You awake?"

He sighs, because how in the hell is he going to sleep, just a moth-chewed blanket for some kind of creature comfort on this sand-encrusted floor that slopes no less, as if even this house would like to give up on itself, roll gently down the beach and into the sea. He's counting the ways his tender young life has flushed down the toilet and doesn't bother answering her.

So she lifts up his arm, he's thinking to punch it or twist it; Marnie doesn't like it when people don't pay attention to her. Instead she moves it oh so gently on top of her belly—she's on her back, of course, has not been able to sleep any other way since her pregnancy took over her middle, depriving her of a waist, hips, even a side, this girl is all front—and fans his fingers out over her opu, under her shirt. He feels the hot tautness of her stretched skin, feels suddenly weak, because the baby is definitely in there, and mad as hell to come out it seems, like a hooked marlin, flopping hard against his reluctant hand.

"You want to hear the story about how I lost my virginity?" Marnie whispers. Which is the last thing he expected her to say, his hand still on her stomach, and he's trying to pull his arm back down with the rest of him, but she pounces on his fingers, locking them firmly against her.

Your fucked you stepfather? is what he'd like to shout so the whole fricken household can hear, wherever they are, stink of incense, weed, chemicals drifting in from the bushes under the windows where the methengers toss their empty butane canisters—how did his life become *this*? But he's mute. Waves sweep the shore. Such a sad sound at night, rhythms of the sea, back and forth, in and out, regular as a heartbeat, nothing about our own insignificant lives will affect this. Unless we factor in global warming, glaciers melting, the seas' temperatures growing warmer, rising tides swamping the coasts, but Buddy's not going there, his own broken, pathetic self is about all he can contemplate at this point.

"No," Marnie says, as if she can hear what he's thinking, "not *The Sleaze* you idiot. Like I'm talking metaphor, you remember those, Buddy babes? From the retard school English class? I'm talking about giving up something, offering it to somebody special, abandoning your childhood, becoming a WOMAN." Marnie says this last real loud and he cringes. It's not like she was ever a WOMAN with him.

"Listen," she says, "I feel like sharing this with you." (Note that *Buddy babes* is still stubbornly silent at this point, so you get to hear it from her, the way she told it to him.)

"It's pre-retard school, I'm fourteen, a freshman at Hilo High, where most everyone else my age goes or doesn't go and I've about decided to become one of the ones who doesn't. I mean like what's the point? Where's algebra going to get me in the end? Shampoo girl at some beauty shop calculating her tips? I'm a model, remember? Models don't need to know if X equals Y on the catwalk. Algebra is not a fashion standard. My mom drops me off every morning on the way to whatever diner she's strutting her frying chops in, Job of the Month Club. I walk the High School walk until the Fury disappears around the corner, then I book out to where the cool kids hang. Melvin's house, of Melvin and the Fuck Punch, awesome band. Kind of post nineties pop retro-metal-punk, totally tight. You've heard of them, huh? I was like in love with Melvin's little brother, Marty.

"Your name sounds like mine, he said, first time he met me. I thought that was something, that he listened to my name so carefully. He's younger than me, thirteen, and sometimes when I watch him I can see he's still like a little boy. Does little boy things, picks up frogs and inspects them, rides his bike when everyone else just lazes about smoking bud, meth, crack, doing E, hooking up, dissing folks that don't do these things. Something about this makes me long for... I don't know what but I get this kind of ache when I look at him, like something that should be in my life maybe but isn't.

"So one day I meet him at the corner by his house, near a grove of papaya trees and the kipuka forest. I step out in front of him on his bike so he has to stop, and I ask him to come with me into the forest. I want to show you something, I tell him. He follows me, expecting I don't know what, Hawai'i's first snake? A dead body? I'm giggling, thinking how surprised he'll be. When we're in among the ferns and ohia, nobody from the road or the houses can see, I make him close his eyes, then I take off my shirt, unhook my bra, lift it up and turn toward him. You can look, I say.

"Marty's face goes all red, which is pretty hard to do when your skin's the color of a Hershey bar. I can tell he wants to look away, but he doesn't want to look away. I like the feeling of that, a kind of power. So I tell him he's the one I want to do it with; you know, I say, for the first time. Then, know what he says? You're not going to believe this, Buddy babes. This thirteen year old dumbass, doesn't even go to school, just rides his bike around like a loser, he tells me: I don't do virgins! Can you believe it? Like, what the hell kind of an answer is that? There I was, baring my boobs for the little twit!

"So I yank my shirt around me, twisting it until it's covering me like a towel, don't even bother putting it back on. Run all the way back to his house, face blazing, mad as hell. I know Melvin and the Fuck Punch are practicing there, and I've seen the way Melvin eyeballs me when he thinks I don't see—he's a rock star, thinks the cunts are supposed to come to him, huh?

"They're taking a break, Melvin's on the lanai sucking off a smoke. So I walk over, still clutching that shirt against me like I'm holding in my heart. I go right up to him, lift his hand to my mouth and take a drag off his cigarette, wet from where he sucked. He smells like hair grease, and something sticky-sweet like guava jam.

"Melvin takes me out to the papaya grove and when he's done, which was pretty quick, even a fourteen year old could figure that out—I'm not even sure he hit the mark!—this time I put my shirt on the right way, buttoning every damn button, even the one at my neck. Zip my jeans wishing I could just keep on zipping, stomach, chest, boobs, neck, my whole head swallowed up inside. As Melvin reaches for his own shirt, yanking out another smoke, I tell him: Make sure your little brother knows, OK? Tell him Marnie's no virgin, not anymore."

Speaking of Virgins – How to Make The Girl on The Plate Glass Disappear

THIS WAS IT, THE ONE Houdini worked on for years, would've been his coup de grace if he had lived to see it through, the vanishing of a girl on a sheet of plate glass. His notes specified that in his illusion no stage traps would be necessary, wanting to one up the famous Chinese Wizard, Chung Lee Soo (who was really the American Billy Robinson, former stage manager for Hermann the Great). Soo was known for his Vanish in Mid-Air illusion, whereby a board would rest on a platform, and Soo would introduce an assistant who would lie on top of the board, fastened by straps. The board was then placed on a metal frame at the back of the stage inside a cabinet, tilted so that the audience could see the assistant on it. The magician aims a gun at the cabinet, a puff of smoke and when it clears the assistant has disappeared. The illusion was created using a special board that's actually a double, and a cabinet with an escape hatch activated by the firing of the gun. There were pivot rods, releasing devices, complex mechanical mechanisms—an elaborate effort, you better believe it, and

Houdini's quest was to do it better. In Houdini's diagrams the curtain rises and the audience sees two assistants holding a sheet of glass between them. Enter a pretty young girl in a scanty costume. She lies down on the glass and the magician covers her with a cloth stretching from assistant number one to assistant number two. After the cloth has been placed on the girl for two drum-rolling minutes, the magician lifts the cloth and the girl has disappeared—nothing but a glistening sheet of glass.

How Houdini *would've* pulled it off: one of the assistants is actually a hollow dummy figure, and under the taut stretch of cloth the girl unzips this dummy and slips inside.

How Jody Johnstone pulled it off (as you will see in Jody's own notes bye and bye): *MRI, or Molecular Reorganization Invisibility*... one-upping the master himself.

25

Madge

IF A PERSON COULD KNOW something will happen that changes everything else that happened before, what would she try to hold on to? What would matter most? Was she loved? Is that it? Would she recall the day he told her, hiking the Ko'olau mountains under a sky so pale it looked frosted on, air pungent with fallen guavas, green pines swaying, jagged rocks over them and around them like ridges of teeth, like being inside the mouth of the world? They loved! Him, her, him inside her. In two months they'd be married and expecting a baby, but they didn't know this yet, just their love. So why was that not enough? Where is the thing to hold on to? She must come to it, must remember it, quick! Things are freezing up, memory like ice chips, bits of it frozen hard.

Would it be this?

The Artist's koi pool, lava banks, hole dug, water pumped in from the water tank. *Do your damn fish need life more than us?* Why did she say these things? His *projects*, always his projects. When you're failing at business, these are the things you do. One day she sees him face down in the pool with his hands roped behind his back, goes wailing into the greasy fish-stinking water after him and he pops up grinning. Houdini's underwater escape, he tells her, shrugging, as she pummels him, kicks him, hugs him, holds on to him for dear *please*! life. As in, *Duh*! shouldn't she have guessed this? Houdini said to practice, so that's what he's doing; she's sputtering, weeping, clawing at his darling rock-hard shoulders. He just smiles that smile.

Madge, he sighs, demonstrating how he can tie the rope around his torso, his hands, then scissor kick up from the bottom. He's becoming a pro, he says, practicing his deep breathing, working on how long he can keep his head underwater, versus how long it would take to escape from the rope, learning to expand his lung capacity. Unless you are an absolutely fearless swimmer, Houdini warns you to avoid ropes underwater, he tells her, like this is the thing that mattered. Golden, red, orange, twitching, flashing, all around them the carp swim frantically, faster and faster like they are trying to liftoff, almost as if they can fly.

Or would it be this?

Long black hair her rope, her lifeline. She washed it Saturday mornings, unwound it down, down, little black bobby pins like ants on the yellow kitchen table. Mama Ana's hair tossed into the metal sink, an animal tail of it, Castile shampoo beading up like frog eggs. Makela rubs her hands together, this itch, this yearn, this *something* burning between pudgy fingers, errant little wiggle-worms, these fat fingers, squirming ever nearer.

One day Ana slinks down beside the sink, grabbing her chest. *My heart!* she moans. They pick fruit from the Noni tree in the front yard, pale yellow and bitter, smells *pilau*, leaves thick with deep veins like the veins in Mama's wrists...BUT WHAT ARE THESE? White trails, broken paths, swirls of little white snakes. SCARS? Hands the color of wood, scars the color of snow, she squeezes the Noni juice into a glass of water, drinks it every day. For your heart.

On Saturday Makela is naughty, those itchy fingers creeping up, ladybug scissors, handles shaped like wings gnaw through a clump of Ana's hair, *shhheelp*. Her hair's never been cut, the Hawaiian way, Ana said. Stares sadly at Makela's small hands folding over it like a prayer. *Are you trying to keep me here, little keiki?*

Father says it's her heart, that blinding day. They don't talk about it, never again. Makela sees something else. She sees that rosebud mouth twisted, *O*; she sees the crown flower leis, piles of purple and white, a crown flower crown on Ana's little head, hair floating out across the hikee like she's drowning. Ana's little head, little mother, little mouth twisted, *O*. "Little bit crown flower can heal," Ana said, "but too much is deadly."

Or maybe this?

The Club in Kona takes half a day to get there, but step inside its dark interior, electric Tiki torches and indoor waterfalls, the scent of wet earth pumped in through air conditioning vents, and you wipe out everything else, everything you are, were, might have been, dissolving into the first double Mai Tai the bartender makes you, darkest rum and all of it melts away: you are new, no history, unformed, undone. DJ playing "In a White Room," her body a vision in gold lame, inside the glitter-cage decked in mini-traffic lights, stop go stop go, mindlessly whipping her head about, limbs reeling, muscles undulating, flowing like a liquid lava lamp, gyrating to Clapton because nothing else matters: eyes shut, hair wild about her face, hips on fire she becomes the music, all nerve, shooting through the hollow of those vibrating notes like riding a wave. Clapton becomes the

Stones becomes the Eagles becomes Donna Summer and a flashing disco ball. Close your eyes, sling your hips, slide through the years into the Electric Slide; dance because you can, because your heart is broken, because you have those hips.

This one's a surfer too, his graspable shoulders; like a cliff you climb these shoulders and remember that frosted sky! His body a longboard underneath, and afterwards speeding through the vast and empty Ka'u lava desert, like driving on the moon (they trained the moon-walking astronauts here), all the way back to Volcano in time for Gwenyth to wake up: fix her breakfast, Corn Pops and that guava juice she whines about erupting with Vitamin C. *Because I said so!* If she was nothing else Madge was still a mother.

Nothing creeps up. Nothing comes upon her. Terrible touch of Nothing like the fingers she can't see can't feel can't move, but Nothing knows she is here. Squeezes round your neck, pries open your mouth, slips down your throat. Nothing says, now you are mine.

26

Gwen

LEGS STIFF AS TWO MASTS, two boats sailing in two different directions. Schlep her mother to the bathroom every morning over the bedroom's wooden floor, splinters are not a concern, what's a splinter in two downed logs? Ease her onto the toilet thinking maybe she'll do it this time, this one little dignity. Refuses all solid food. Gwen gives her Ensure, encourages her with a straw like a toddler, then spoonfuls of it shoveled against those rigid lips.

Buddy is at the far perimeter of their lives, in and out of the house like a shadow, mostly avoiding his grandmother and Gwen. He's as closed off since he came back from O'ahu as he was in the months before he left. It's as if nothing's changed, except Gwen's knowledge that he no longer needs to depend on her, could leave again at any moment, the unspoken threat between them. She treads delicately around him, says noncommittal things, when really what she wants is to shake him, shout in his face, DON'T EVER DO THAT TO ME AGAIN. She wants him to swear to her he won't leave, that he still needs her to be his mother. This much seems to have ended. What they are to each other now, how their new relationship will be defined is unclear. If only she could hear him say it once in a while, *Mom*, instead of calling her...nothing. Last week Madge had a panic attack of sorts, screaming, moaning, batting Gwen off like she's some pestering fly, her one good arm weakened, haphazard as a slinky. Attempted to dissolve a Xanax in a glass of water for her mother but Buddy caught her at it. "What the hell?" he said, so Gwen chugged it herself.

Now Gwen's sprawled on the living room sofa, staring at her mother propped up in her rocker. Madge is dozing, head lolling about one side of her neck, the side that still works. Gwen thinks of a sunflower, its big daffy face, wilting. Part of her robe has slid down revealing a prominent shoulder blade and a blue-white slice of her once fabulous breast, now flat as pie. Didn't bother dressing her. What difference could it make?

She thinks about death—the word, one syllable sharp as a gunshot. Why couldn't it be described more lyrically, serene-sounding words like mel-o-di-ous, har-mon-i-ous? Instead of a syllable like a stab. Death, the word, was not spoken in the house she grew up in; like *sex*, *death* seemed to bear the weight of its possibility. Last week she had this insane urge to drive down to a tourist bar in Kona and pick up somebody, anybody as long as he lived at least three thousand miles away and she would never have to see him again. What stopped her? Disease. Possible death. Ridiculous because if the world's going down, why even worry? What's a little STD or HIV-positive to an apocalypse? Jesus' blood the atonement for the soul. In the end Jude Canada would atone only for not being God. "I lived the best I knew," he said to Madge, and then he died.

She studies her lightly snoring mother, like purring her snores, like it's some sign of contentment, sleeping more and more these days, longer naps, more frequent naps, napping the focal point of any day. Sometimes Gwen doesn't get her up in the morning until 10:00. What can she do awake that she can't do as well, perhaps more comfortably, asleep? She can't read, can't talk, if the TV's on she stares into the dark space above its light. Gwen prays that somewhere deep inside where her mother's locked away there's a livable life of sorts, memories reminding her who she was. Either that or total oblivion so she's spared realizing what's happening! Gwen is losing her mom, and with Madge go all the old resentments, fears, all the things they never spoke of, any chance for a better love between them.

Is Buddy frightened of his grandmother dying? This word, *dying*, difficult to even think it with the image of Gwen's mother attached, how can she speak of it with Buddy? His only experience with death was his dog Blinky. The memory of that day comes flooding in, its unwanted illumination the blinding headlight of a bulleting train.

That morning Gwen opened the closet to pull out her silk blouse, a stirring inside her, the brush of his name on her tongue, *Alyn*, buzzing through her like an electric current. She had been with him for a couple hours the night before, the memory of this sweet and funky on her skin. And there was Blinky stretched out on the floor on top of Gwen's shoes and a pile of dirty laundry, breath raspy, scratchy, unable to even lift her head in greeting. Her stomach was swollen, tender and full, as if she were finally bearing the puppies they deprived her of, taking nature into their own hands. "No infant canines," warned Rob when he agreed to let Buddy keep her. Now nature was taking Blinky.

Fortunately, or so Gwen thought at the time, Buddy was in school. She hoisted Blinky heavily into her arms, carrying Buddy's dog to the car wrapped in her own bathrobe. For some reason she felt responsible, like there was something she did or didn't do or could have done that might have changed things, might have saved her son's dog.

Wasn't that her life in Rock Harbor? A plethora of should haves and shouldn't haves, the childhood admonishments of her own mother becoming her adult inner voice. Thinking about this now she can't help it, a quick jaunt into the kitchen, nab the burgundy from the cupboard. Plops back down on the sofa, her mother still snoring, slugs down a few gulps of wine. It's the taste, she tells herself, she drinks it for the taste, relishing its tart comfort. She keeps it *in her control.*

There's something to work out here, something she's got to remember that feels unfinished, feels wrong. Sometimes a glass of wine or two helps clear the memory, loosen things up a bit. She wasn't that bad a mother, Gwen thinks, but not all that great either and, admittedly, during the years of her affair when everything was breaking loose, not much of a wife. At that point she didn't even have the what-it-takes to do her daily run, which had devolved into an every other day power-walk, then an occasional not so powerful walk, then no activity that produced even a sheen of perspiration—except for compulsive snacking on spicy salsa and chips. Gwen hadn't figured out what she could be good at anymore, until meeting Alyn and making love to him! Surely there's a price to pay, a sin that must be atoned for, but was it really such a crime?

"I think we'll have to call it a day," said Dr. Genoit, Blinky's vet. She avoided Gwen's eyes, stroking Blinky's tender pink belly, scratching gently behind her ear. Blinky panting lethargically on the long metal table like she's already half gone, small whine, the dull, grateful gaze into Dr. Genoit's own eyes. "She's an elderly dog. She's having heart failure, it happens to older dogs. If she were younger I'd suggest trying Digitalis. She's not very comfortable right now but we can remedy that. I think we have to know when to quit."

"Can I hold her? I should be with her when you do it, shouldn't I?" Gwen had read somewhere that this was the caring thing to do for a pet, hold it when they put it to sleep. She thought her son would want this.

Tears were careening down Gwen's cheeks, falling on Blinky, who didn't even blink. "That dog blinks a lot," Rob observed, when they brought her home from the animal shelter, back when Gwen could be everything for Buddy and this, her gift to him. "Do normal dogs even blink?"

Gwen wondered if Blinky knew who was holding her, as Dr. Genoit readied the shot, Gwen wondered if *she* knew. She put her arms around the big soft neck while the vet injected her, poor dog, not even the energy to whimper, intrusion of the needle bearing its lethal cocktail. Her head grew heavy in Gwen's arms. She smelled Blinky's old familiar smell, dog fur, dog food, the sharp odor of the barbiturate as she released her last breath. "You were loved," Gwen whispered into her ear, though she couldn't hear it and wouldn't know its language anyway.

Gwen peeled out of the vet's parking lot, a ragged sense of loss firing its neurons into her her brain, her heart, and headed toward the University. A fog was rolling in, she remembers that. Fingers of it, thick and smoky, stretching over the islands in Penobscot Bay, obscuring their perimeters. Last night with Alyn, as always that unspoken question, when would they see each other again? An affair is like that. No regular rhythms, no particular events, dinner, movie, a concert; just that carnal want driving them back again and again. Today Gwen needed more than that. Foghorn moaned and she felt it inside her, its wail the memory of that navy blue dress, after her father didn't come home. And not being allowed to say it: My father is dead.

Alyn's old Fiat was parked in front of the duplex he rented. "This car's traveled more miles than you and me," he said once, squeezing her knee. Gwen had laughed. It wasn't funny, but everything about being with Alyn was filled with that tense elevated lightness, luna moths in her stomach flitting about with their giant, ghostly wings, wanting things to be the way she wanted them, yet at the same time always expecting them to end. It was a pumped-up kind of nerviness, like mainlining a gallon of coffee.

Gwen walked up the three wooden steps to his porch, heart hammering. Surely he'd want to see her? Once she had told him she'd do anything he wanted. They were lying on his bed and he gazed at her, eyes steady. Suddenly he stood up, pulled her off the bed, then planting his hands firmly on her shoulders he guided her down until she was on her knees before him. "I like it like this," he said, pressing her head between his legs.

There is this Alyn admired about Gwen: "So lean, not an inch to spare," he'd say, pinching her hips, her butt, her plate-flat belly. Of course her life was pretty lean too, but couldn't Alyn be enough? Risky, a professor and a married, unemployed schoolteacher. But as he said, "Love's heightened when there's something risked." It was understood that *love* for them meant sex.

Gwen swallowed hard then knocked, and Alyn's voice sang out, "It's unlocked." She opened the door, stepped into the front room, and there he was, naked on his daybed, paisley coverlet, sheets, matching curtains closed against the dank afternoon light. Lingering odor of a meal, curry, wine, and a young woman's nude body stretched out asleep beside him, straight spine, buttocks like halved apples, a muscular, lean body. "Oh, Christ!" Gwen whispered.

Alyn flung his hand over his eyes as if that might make her disappear. "Good God, Gwen, I don't know what to say. You were supposed to be somebody else, my neighbor picking up his key."

"You'd let someone else come in and see you this way?" she asked inanely, as if she cared. As if she could care about anything else at that moment, his body, *her* body.

"It's on the shelf by the door, he knows to reach in and grab it there, wouldn't have had to come inside at all. Jesus, Gwen, what are you doing here anyway? You're supposed to call first." He sat up then and lit a skinny dark cigarette from a pack on the cluttered table beside the daybed. "I don't know what to say. Those are our rules, aren't they? Call first." He stared almost mournfully at the still asleep (or the civility to fake it) shape of the young woman beside him. Were the cigarettes hers? He never smoked with Gwen. This girl had some influence on him, clearly. Gwen felt ignorant and foolish. Her face burned staring at them. Was she a student? An *independent study*, he mentioned a few of those! Gwen realized she knew nothing essential about Alyn Crysler, Assistant Professor of Biology. She knew how he sucked in a breath then moaned it out when he made love; she knew the feel of that place at the base of his spine, his thatch of hair there and the encompassing way he held her under him, his limbs around and over her like mangrove roots, her body a canoe, trapped for a moment before sailing through. Those were the kinds of things she knew. Her stomach rumbled out a warning. If she stood there a minute longer she was going to be sick. "You make me want to vomit!" she shouted stupidly, half hoping the girl would wake up, see the kind of man she was with. Maybe she already knew. Maybe Gwen was the only one who never seemed to know these things. Her feet stumbled out his door.

"Listen, Gwen!" he called out, "It's just an affair. You know that, no exclusivity, those have to be the rules. My God, you're married. *I'm* supposed to keep an empty bed?"

By then the air was thick with fog, burdened with it like the whole world had lost its boundaries. She switched on the headlights, opened the car windows wide letting the push of cold air slap her cheeks, her chest, her fingers stabbing at the steering wheel, her fist pounding against it. *Just* an affair. Gwen never even saw her face. For months she imagined it though, sometimes scarred, ruined; other times, when she really wanted to torture herself, sculpted to perfection. Blinky was dead. Gwen thought about her last minutes alive, grey and white head drooping, eyes closing, the weight of Buddy's dog in her arms. This day had turned into a spectacularly bad one! OK, so she had no claim on Alyn, did she? He was right, her initials weren't embroidered on those paisley sheets. Who was she? An affair, *just* a woman who cheated on her husband. Here's something for the resume, Rob! Killed son's dog, cheated on husband, the *cheatee* cheats on her.

Inching down a shrouded Route 17 back to the coast, Gwen remembered the last time she saw her father, a day that also began in fog, but when it lifted became such a strikingly clear morning, it was as if her memory of it had been staged with spotlights: wandering the Devastation Trail, ferreting out small tongues of shiny lava smooth as glass, and olivines for her third grade class. "You know," he had said, "folks aren't supposed to take things from Madam Pele. She's a goddess. She has powers. Bad luck maybe."

"But I have a good reason to," Gwen insisted.

Her father laughed, brushing back a hank of hair off his forehead, squinting his olivine colored eyes. "So that's how it works! You think people are forgiven things long as they have a good reason for doing them, huh? Well I hope you're right little one, I most surely do. We're all going to need forgiveness for something." He said this stroking her face, but when she gazed up into his she saw he wasn't looking at her, green eyes fixed on some faraway place.

By the time Gwen pulled into her driveway it was dusk, dinnertime in some *normal* family's world. She felt that crunch of sickness, like returning from a crime, trying to creep back into a kind of normalcy all the while knowing something's forever changed. Turned off the engine, headlights, sat observing her house in the darkness, that cozy look houses have from the outside, lit up bright and warm, secrets hidden safely away in the unseen corners.

When she went inside finally she told Buddy about his dog. He was sitting at the kitchen table, skimming through his Algebra book for a test the next day. At thirteen Buddy had become disdainful, but at the least Gwen expected him to cry, and then she would comfort him, comfort them both. Instead he gave her an icy look, his eyes in the harsh kitchen light glinting like bullets. "It was *my* job to hold Blinky and be with her, she was my dog. Why did you do it, why didn't you wait for me!" He hurled his book down on the floor, bolted up to his room, slammed shut and locked his door, staying there for the rest of the night despite her begging him to come out. Rob was somewhere else. He was always somewhere else during any family crisis, she thought. She hated him for that. And she hated Alyn, of course she hated Alyn! Most of all though Gwen was hating herself, for while she knew something had irrevocably altered between them, she knew even then she would see Alyn again, that she would still long for, be grateful for, needful of his touch. That's what it was, not *just* an affair, but a needful touch.

It had been ages since Gwen was touched by Rob. Used to be when they were still having sex she expected things to be different between them the next day, illuminated in some way. It shaded her day, the rose-colored glasses thing, but it didn't seem to do the same for Rob. Everything for him was as it always was. Nothing special, nothing glowing, and so it became that way for her too. What was the use?

Gwen was alone and her guilt took on a life of its own, that cavernous place inside where things skulk about, waiting to release their torments at our most vulnerable times. Over the next three years this guilt would help her understand something: that she would never, no matter how deeply she tries to love, no matter what kind of mother she is, daughter, how much she drinks or even how well she prays, fill that empty place inside. And since the world will probably end anyway, why the hell should she even try?

Speaking of Devastation ...

1968, TET OFFENSIVE, AND THE Vietnam War turned dark, shocking the American public who'd been effectively convinced by their government that the communists were incapable of launching such a devastating attack. The war became increasingly unpopular and a perception grew that it was America's unwinnable war. In 1968 Jody Johnstone, garbed in Margo Malone's blood stained top, was classified 4-F, unfit to fight the war, as we've previously established.

At some point during the waning of that year it occurred to Jody that draftees who had dressed like *normal* young men for their induction physicals at Schofield, classified 1-A and sent to Vietnam, were coming home in a box, and Jody began to wonder if in fact *this* might be considered Strike Three. Were the soldiers from Hawai'i drafted at the exact time he was, then shipped off with the 25th Infantry Division and killed in Vietnam, dying *instead* of him? Jody contemplated this possibility, but eventually came to the conclusion that he avoided this fate coincidentally, a fate that was the consequence of a previous fate, Margo Malone dying instead of him, and therefore those unfortunate soldiers most likely did not. After all, the only reason he'd been dressed in Margo's crop top was to honor her mother's wishes that nobody forget her daughter, so probably the connection wasn't strong enough for Jody to consider himself having dodged *this* bullet that was meant for him, and for the rest of his life Jody would have to bear the guilt of having a life instead of some luckless draftee.

For eight years Jody pondered this linkage of fates, whereby he'd been classified unfit to die in Vietnam because Margo Malone had died for him, enough time for the war to end and for Jody to have a daughter he loved with an expansiveness of heart he hadn't known possible, and a terror that seized him awake in the middle of the night, his lungs a fist trying to squeeze in a breath, that *she* might be the one to take the bullet (metaphorically speaking) meant for him.

These were his thoughts on the Devastation Trail with eight-year-old Gwen that day, his last as her in-the-flesh dad, clutching her hand as they stepped over jagged bits of crumbling a'a lava, Pu'u Pua'i cinder cone a yellow dome in the near distance rising like the sun—as though somehow they'd left the earth and were walking among stars, the desolation of the lava field a huge and riotous expanse of darkness on either side of them, heading toward the light.

He'd explained to her why they shouldn't take lava souvenirs to her third grade classroom, how Madam Pele gets offended, he'd said, with testimonials from folks all over the globe who'd stolen her lava, Pele's diamonds, her hair, her tears, and had tragic things happen to them, *awful* things until they sent it all back. His daughter—how proud he was of her!—argued just as passionately that it was for an educational purpose, and therefore Pele should make an exception.

The air had a sweet, charred tinge, but not from the volcano—Kilauea's non-stop eruption wouldn't begin for another seven years, and the term *vog* for the sulfuric poisons it would spew into the lovely volcano air hadn't yet been coined. He remembers inhaling that air in gulps like he couldn't get enough of it, just in case it would be his last. For today was the day he would put his plan into action, a day that would culminate years of study and preparation. That afternoon a giant swell was due in off the Hamakua coast, he'd been tracking its progress using weather maps and tidal charts. The projected wave height measurements with wind-driven velocity were just about perfect.

But now it's morning, a crisp volcano morning, the sky that rich, pure azure the Hawaiian sky gets, blasted by trade winds and high enough up on Kilauea caldera to have little else to distract from the gingery air, stripy white cirrus clouds like dandelion wisps, and a fierce golden sun, its giant eye glaring down. Just in case Jody's plan didn't succeed after his years of working toward it—holding his breath underwater for so long he could become an Olympic swimmer by now; reconstructing Houdini's lost notes, as well as practicing his various illusions—particularly the ones having to do with making things vanish, Jody held onto his daughter's hand and reveled in being alive. He had successfully vanished several inanimate items: a pen, a carton of eggs (admittedly one by one), even an old bicycle. Jody didn't have the heart to vanish an animal, typically a rabbit though in Hawai'i more likely a mongoose, just in case he couldn't figure out how to bring it back. Not that animals couldn't exist quite happily on another astral plane, but Jody felt that if an animal didn't specifically request this, it really wasn't fair to intercept its life on earth and vanish it to another plane of existence. Who was he to make this choice?

Walking with his daughter Jody was feeling nostalgic for what he'd be missing—the touch of her small hand in his, their talks together. Jody's image of the father he had wanted to be for Gwen was the exact opposite of his own. Those silent dinners after his mother was gone, his sister twisting her napkin, wringing it in her hands between nervous, mosquito-sized bites of a meat their father had bought frozen hours before, then thawed on the counter and tossed into the oven without seasonings, baking until any remnants of pink flesh were as dried out as old glue. And his father either staring at his plate or at Jody, with a look Jody couldn't quite interpret, like he was vaguely displeased but didn't care enough to figure out what it was exactly about his son that made him unhappy. Jody didn't ask. You spoke when you were spoken to in the post-Hilda Johnstone family; it was their mother who'd been the life, the core, the center. Like one of those roundabout Lazy Susan centerpieces, she would twirl from one to the other of them asking about their day. Their father's days after she was gone were as dull as his food, and he didn't expect—or care—for his kids' to be any different.

Of course in some subverted, convoluted way Jody's father held Jody accountable for his wife's death, the poisonous fish that had been earmarked for his son by virtue of Jody having ordered it, but would he have thought this out to its twisted conclusion, replacing his son's green eyes with Hilda's hazel ones? He wasn't a monster-dad, just an emotionally AWOL one, and thus the vague dissatisfaction, and the father and son's shared sense of the better part of them both forever missing.

Jody had wanted to be the kind of dad who was more present in his daughter's life, but a few years after she was born he spent some time in upstate New York, cleaning out his grandmother's house after she died. Jody's grandmother, his father's mother, had lived like a hermit on twenty acres of land, and according to his father the family's rumored craziness was all about her. "The buck stopped there," his father said, "garaged and thrown away the keys." But his grandmother tended her land, grew her own food, slaughtered her own chickens, subsisted on sweat and cunning, whereas Jody's father sat around and did nothing at all, until even that became too much, and one day after Violet and Jody had families of their own he simply stopped breathing, with not even the TV turned on.

Jody's days were spent packing his grandmother's meager belongings, shampooing carpets, scrubbing vinyl floors, painting walls, repairing cracks in the ceiling, sanitizing her house to sell for the back taxes she neglected to pay, to wipe the slate clean. During the evenings he sat on her back porch and watched the deer that appeared in a herd behind her house, chowing down on vegetation in his grandmother's abandoned fields, and he became particularly interested in a doe with a withered foreleg. If she had been a human born of a certain generation, he might have figured her mom took Thalidomide—the leg was reminiscent of what that disastrous morning-sickness drug did to babies, their shriveled, curled up appendages. The doe got around pretty well on three legs, although clearly she would never be able to outrun a predator, or a hunter for that matter, though probably none would waste a shot on her, imperfect as she was. She had twin fawns, and what fascinated Jody was how little time she seemed to spend with them, wouldn't let them near her except to nurse, and then she'd hobble off leaving them on their own. It wasn't usual doe behavior, he gathered, as the other does in the herd kept their fawns with them. Jody determined that somehow the doe understood she couldn't outrun a predator, and if one was attracted to her scent, she couldn't escape and it would get her fawns too. (Fawns are born without a scent so they don't attract predators.) She instinctively knew not to let her damage bring danger to her young, but she kept an ear out for those fawns—if they mewed she was there.

Jody decided after he was back home again in Hawai'i, that maybe *this* was a model for the kind of dad he should be, the kind who wouldn't let his damage affect his daughter. If he stayed in their home at some point Strike Three would happen, and what if the sacrifice was his darling Gwen? He needed to figure out a way to watch over her like that doe, even if he was no longer an *actual* presence in her life.

Then there was Madge. A vision of her one night, Jody had awoken before dawn and couldn't get back to sleep, tossing about in their bed, trying not to disturb her, then going to the window when he realized she wasn't beside him. There she was, like some ethereal night bird in the moonlight, arms spread like wings, gyrating to a rhythm he couldn't hear. In her head? Or perhaps she had dragged the stereo speakers out on the lanai—this being pre-iPod and even pre-Walkman, a boom-box maybe if he could recall when those were popular. Whatever it was Madge had turned its volume down so that he and their daughter would sleep undisturbed, and she'd have the night to herself.

He was transfixed by her beauty, swaying in their yard like a night-blooming flower; he could imagine the scent of her, that deepening musk, and how in the early years of their marriage her skin smelled fruity and fresh. He had promised her the world, but in the end was unable to deliver, not even their home could've been purchased without her father's money. She wanted only to dance, she said, even though when he married her at twenty-seven they both knew the window for doing this professionally was closing. He was mystified how much she seemed to love him then, and how soon that turned to something else, when she understood how little he had to offer. His paintings, magic, surfing, and the memory of his hand on a dead girl's thigh, were what Jody was about, and none of it could be reconciled with Madge's own expectations, the life she believed they were supposed to be sharing.

They were like reverse magnets, polar opposites, the more remote one got the further the other drifted away. The law of entropy, the tendency for everything in the universe since the Big Bang to move from order to disorder increases with the passage of time. Degrees of messiness in nature will devolve to more messiness, and the difference between past and future was this ever-greater spin toward chaos. Thus in the larger cosmos, and at the heart of Jody and Madge's marriage, was this universal: everything moving away from everything else, expanding ever outward. The best thing Jody could do for his wife and daughter, he concluded, was to push this one step further: molecular disintegration and reorganization, or MRI, *Molecular Reorganization Invisibility*. In a few more hours the giant swell would reach the coast. Jody was ready.

Molecular Reorganization Invisibility

CRAZY BIG WAVE SURFER... WASN'T that essentially what his daughter suggested to his grandson? It wasn't like that. Nor was he ruminating over a failed business, failed marriage or even his failures as a dad—those sorts of shackles to the physical plane are not predictors of a successful MRI. Happiness, non-happiness, any sort of emotion whatsoever given the massive waves that were rolling in off the Hamakua meant distraction, meant physical death. And Jody had spent too many years preparing for this moment to simply die in it. It required clear-headed thinking and an accurate accounting to the most miniscule electron of a wave's force, times velocity, times size at the lip and inside the tunnel, its space-time continuum assessment; for there wasn't just one of these monsters smashing down upon the craggy shore, there's never only one.

Jody paddled like a madman in that breath between sets of behemoths to make it safely past where they broke. He had to battle a powerful riptide that tried to suck him out further, roiling in the opposite direction from where he needed to watch for *his* wave. He was reminded of the rubber duck his daughter played with in her bath when she was a baby; you wound it up and it paddled about furiously in a circle going nowhere—the way Jody's legs and arms fought to hold his board in place. Think of this, he told himself, whenever the bile shot into his throat, that crazy duck and his little girl. This was his best, a way to watch over her with no sacrifices, no Strike Three with her as possible victim. And what if it was Madge? First Margo, then her? What kind of a husband would he be then? His best for Madge was to set her free.

The day a wash of blues, a sky the intense sparkling indigo of the deeper sea, but where Jody waited the ocean swirled with a turquoise purer than stone, an electrified aqua like an illustrator's brush-strokes for a fantasy book; and here he was perched on top of his board, the mountainous swells rising up then shooting him downward like he's riding a giant's snore. The problem was if Jody assessed incorrectly and took the wrong one of these monsters, or worse tried and missed, he'd get caught in the impact zone of its brother behind it, and with a forty foot wall crashing down on top of you, you're a goner—human flesh was not built to withstand the force of all those furiously spinning molecules at such a height. If you paddled for the one you thought was it but caught its edge instead of its middle, you'd tumble down its face, like jumping from a forty-foot building which then collapses on top of you.

Jody rose up and down the mountainous range pondering these possibilities, waiting for the one he would catch. He would have to paddle furiously to position himself in its middle, then fly across its face, a sharp turn to its bottom, and releasing his board he'd dive down under at the exact moment it broke into a billion shimmering, spinning molecules, velocity times size, entering its massive centrifuge of frothing water.

Meanwhile, let's recreate what it's like to be adrift in an ocean alive with bubbling, boiling, reverberating, crashing sets of humungous waves. Most noticeable is the sound, each one a freight train hurdling through with the roar of an earthquake, something that will rise then fall, smashing itself spent upon the beaches, lava coast, then hissing back again like machine gun spatter across the rocks, then the thunderous clap of backwash greeting the next foaming whitecap. There's the spray from so much water at such a high velocity, your vision so occluded at times you'd think you were lost in a fogbank. And the smell! A broth of salty seawater cooked into the good clean Hawaiian air, with what waves that size drum up from the bottom, and not just the bottom where they crash—the deepest part of the ocean where they first began to build, calling from its depths the breaths of whales, prehistoric fish, krill, the teeming dream of the farthest reaches of cavernous places even our submarines won't find, where life is a thousand little critter eyes glowing in a darkness profound as space. All this was behind, above, under and around Jody Johnstone, when in that breath between sets, the proverbial calm before the storm, he spied it out there, bigger than all of the rest, a giant's giant, rogue amongst rogues, the last in a five-wave set zippering in at what Jody clocked at 30 miles an hour, the perfect speed, driven by a wild wind, rising even as he watched: his wave.

Oh save me! he whispered, or maybe shouted—who would hear him either way, as the first four waves in the set rose, unfurled, boiled over and broke. Then came number five. Jody paddled ferociously, his biceps burning like they'd been replaced with lit coal, to hit in its center where it lifted him up, a monstrous mechanical crane with the force of forty feet of ancient history, water from a sea as old as God, shooting out to the side, launching Jody down its face like a skier dropped from Everest. At the calculated moment he dove from his board 25 feet before feeling the concussion, the pressure that would force him into the ultimate spin. He could see the white boils of foam and froth as they dumped down on top of him, and he immediately grabbed his knees shaping himself into a human ball. It was critical not to straighten out, as then like a screw he'd be drilled into the lava-rock bottom and his neck, his entire spine would snap like a twig.

Jody felt the crash of a billion molecules of water, but rather than crush him, shaped as he was in a sphere with no edges—even his elbows tucked in—it threw him into a fast and furious roll, the supersonic spin like being wrung out in God's own Maytag.

This was the part that could go either way, *MRI* or death by broken spine and drowning, and just in case it went the latter, Jody forced himself to think the thoughts people think in those final moments before leaving this life: his wife? his daughter? Margo Malone's incomparable thigh minutes before it was she who would desert him? Surprisingly none of that came to him, but instead a strangely placid image: Easter, before Hilda ate the poisonous fish, and they would pack the family into their silt-grey Chevy and drive to her parents' house on Waimana Street, its flat expanse of coolness (their grandmother kept the drapes closed so the sun wouldn't fade her furniture), and Jody and Violet would take their Easter baskets outside where there was a little brook, the auwai their grandparents called it, with two flat rocks where they could sit and listen to its gurgle, smell its dark water smells, munching on the foil wrapped chocolate eggs their grandmother gave them. Doves cooing, honeycreepers trilling, the sun would be out, was *always* out, warm and clean on their shoulders, their bare legs and shoeless feet, and the world seemed as bright as it would get. With that image in mind Jody clung to his knees, as if it were these that would save him, and let the velocity of that colossal wave, the roar of its wild wind, bear him.

Interlude: MRI For Dummies – A How-To

SUMMARY: THE POINT (AND YOU geeks can peruse his notes, or as much as Jody's willing to share—magicians always preserve their top secrets for the brotherhood) was to let the huge mass of water spin and tumble him outside the space-time continuum, where he could become his own law of physics, into a state of molecular reordering, life albeit in its gaseous, anti-physical matter, not death, not drowning, invisibility!

JODY'S NOTES:
- Quantum physicists speculate that everything exists due to fluctuations in quantum particles.
- The mathematical equation for this indicates that somewhere along the line an initial zero separated from its greater nothingness and became a +1 and then the corresponding -1, forming matter and antimatter.
- The molecules take up the energy from the pulse, which sets the

electrons in motion (in this case the velocity of the wave times its size, breadth and depth).

- The electrons start rearranging themselves, which causes the electron cloud to oscillate between two different shapes for a very short time, before the molecules start to vibrate and eventually decompose, then *recompose* on a different physical plane.
- Begets the quintessential disappearing act pondered obsessively by the Great Houdini, perfected by his Humble *Highness*, Jody Johnstone. The ultimate escape, *transformation*, antimatter. Strike Three can't happen without a body.

I am the one who disappeared....

PART VI

Spring

27

Buddy

THERE WAS AN APRIL DAY in Maine when a Nor'easter swept up Penobscot Bay, tearing at leaves, winter's dregs clinging crazily to the trees in their yard, pale gold, old tan, dead brown. He remembers coming home from school, and he's noticing these trees, stripped clean as icepicks, their few remaining leaves spun to the ground, branches swaying and clacking like dentures. Dropped his backpack and stared at them a full minute before going inside. Didn't know why, but he felt this stabbing fear in his gut, the kind that sweeps through with no warning, all but paralyzes you for the moment. He shouted for Blinky, forgetting she was gone.

Now he's feeling it again, swallowing down his panic, that fear, that loss, standing on the buckling, termite-feasted steps of Marnie's front porch. She's leaning toward him just inside the screen, staring out, not opening the door. Behind him the late afternoon pales, a watered-down light; makes you sad, this light, there's no turning back—sun goes and then the night. He peers into her cramped living room, airless, curtains shut. He can hear her mother's cats slinking about, smell their cat smells. Marnie's stepfather's fighting roosters are trapped inside their tiny chicken-wire cages at the side of the cluttered yard, shrieking. "Shut the fuck up!" she screams out at them. "I hate those fucking cocks."

"Why haven't you called? And why don't you answer your phone? I've tried the landline, your cell, even texted you."

She snorts. "*Texting*? Like I thought we had a pact at the retard school not to be part of that. Even the methengers, cooked up their Drano like mental-defects, then sprawled about the living room watching South Park, texting each other for chrissake. Maybe my folks didn't pay the goddamn phone bill again, maybe Hawaiian Telephone cut us off."

"Why'd you leave like that, anyway? I thought you said we were a couple? I thought you said...shit, I told you I would've been the father!"

"Well you're not, so what're you peeing your panties about? Most guys won't take responsibility for the dirt they make let alone someone else's. What makes you so high and mighty? What makes you think you're the one who gets to play God?" She presses her face against the screen, flattening her nose.

"So, like, are you still going to be a famous model?" he says sarcastically, but he doubts she'll pick up on that; Marnie's head is irony-proof.

"Hey Bud-o, reality check! Models are born into *blond* families. Their folks teach them table manners and take them to dance classes. We don't even have a dinner table. We eat when we damn well want to and we watch TV while we're doing it, each of us separate. That way there's no fights over what we watch. We like it like that. If I want to go someplace I go. And I just as soon dance on somebody's face then take lessons."

He frowns. "Stellar image. So where is it? The baby. You had it, right?"

Marnie stares over his head into the white sky distance. Then she shoves open the door, steps out onto the porch. She's thin again, too thin. "Named her Martin."

"*Her*? A girl? You had a girl and you named her Martin?"

"You deaf or something? Yeah. Martin."

He shakes his head. "That's a pretty weird name for a girl. So, can I see her?"

Marnie's shrugs. "Suit yourself, but you'll have to ask The Sleaze. They took her to some folks to hanai.

"*Hanai?* Do I get a WTF moment?"

Marnie snorts then rolls her eyes. "Good one, Buddums, *WTF?* You sound like fricken Facebook. Thought you were supposed to be the intellectual. To you haoles it's an illegal adoption. For us it's just somebody who takes a kid we don't want." She leaps down off the rotting steps, paces about the small yard.

He follows her like he's still attached. The pungent red smell of plumeria from two heavily laden trees pulses into the muggy air, prickly overgrown crab grass stabs his ankles. When he gave Marnie his Reeboks he bought a pair of rubber slippers. Now he wishes he had his shoes back. It's not like he'll ever fit in here, whether shod in Hawai'i's preferred footwear or mukluks. "Try look in the mirror. You're only a little less haole than me."

"Oh, is it like a genetics discussion you came over here to have? Maybe we could sit around, sip Jasmine tea and categorize your bugs too!"

"Hah hah. I don't get it, Marnie. Why don't you just move the hell away from here? You're eighteen now, what's the deal?"

She whips around, those hard yellow eyes. "Yeah? So what's in your future, Buddums? Bug College? Fascinating! Hey, like I have a real bed. At least I have that."

"You *love* him? Your stepfather? How can you even look him in the eyes!" Buddy feels a punch of pain behind his own eyes, sweat breaking out on his forehead, seeping down into his eyebrows.

Suddenly she jumps on him, tackling him down onto the grass like he's an oversized football, flopping on top of his stomach, a ragged, wheezing sound. "It's not exactly about love, is it?" She exhales into his face and he can smell her last meal, onions, Poke, tangy and raw.

"Christ, take it easy! I just thought we had something. Didn't we? I didn't force you to do anything. I lived like a monk beside you in bed, and I still would've taken care of you and the baby, I told you. If you never let me touch you I would've been its father. I could've tried to be who you wanted me to be, goddammit, if you'd have just told me who that was."

"Yeah? You want to be some kind of savior, is that it? Bit of a Jesus complex here?"

He can barely breathe with her on his stomach, and then she starts bouncing, rolling her hips about in a wave of flesh. "Goddammit Marnie, I'm going to hurl!"

A whining sound squeezes out of her throat. "Give me a break, it's not about love in the end."

"It's so sick! He's supposed to act like your father, that's what a step-father is and he gets you pregnant for chrissake!" Head's pounding, heart pulverized, a roaring in his blood. He tries to shake her weight off his chest and at the same time he's mesmerized by her. She's lifting up her shirt, rubbing her hands on her stomach, rolling about on *his* stomach like she's floating on some tube in the ocean, like he's the ocean. He watches her butterscotch-colored fingers fiddle the buttons at the waistband of her shorts.

"A fling, Buddy, we just had a fling together that's all and it's over now."

Buddy's heart is a snare drum set. He's not sure if she's talking about her stepfather or him. Did Buddy have a *fling* with her? He wouldn't know what to call it, if they had anything at all. Stares hard into those yellowy brown eyes, except what he's seeing is not so much yellow at this moment, mostly a plain, dulled brown, the color of clay. He seizes Marnie's hands, pushes her off him, forces himself up clutching at his stomach then his head. "You know it wasn't any good! You can make it right, you can leave now. Where are your goddamn guts, Marnie Lo? I loved your goddamn guts, goddammit!"

She whips her head around, away from his scrutiny, but not before he sees a tear roll down the shallow of her cheek. "Do you even know what it feels like to be fucked? No of course you don't, do you, bug boy? You waited for *me*. Little virgin-boy, saving it for his Marnie. Thing is, sorry, but you just didn't disgust me enough. I've got to be good and disgusted by someone, and then I let them fuck me."

"I can be plenty disgusting," he mutters. He has this insane urge to huck a loogie at her, maybe smash that smug face into the dirt, swipe it around, would that be disgusting enough?

Turning back toward him, her full frontal glare, Marnie snarls, "How do you even know I was telling you the truth? Maybe I hooked up with other guys, maybe I don't even know who the father is, have you considered that? Every time I did it something in me died. I like it enough, don't get me wrong, having a dick in you is like being numbed from the inside. When you're slowly dying there's less of you left to hurt. That crip who copped your wallet at Tripler? He was dying, one piece at a time, so you can be damn sure he didn't feel a fucking thing for you. Why should he? You think everything is about *you*. He didn't give a damn about you, Bud. So here I am, slab of stone, a tombstone. What kind of dude wants to love something like that? Nobody *I'd* want, I'll tell you. Sometimes when you touched me? Nothing personal but I thought I'd throw up. I never asked you to love me. You know why they sent me to that *special* school? Cause I'm smart, that's why. I'm too damn smart for my own good, that's what my mom always told me. So, like you're not the only genius child around here, huh? What fucking good does it do being smart? What does smart get you in my kind of family? In this house I've got my things, my clothes, a bedroom that's mine, furniture, stuff that belongs to me. So I'm going to get really pissed if you say another word about me leaving, Buddy Winter."

His head's spinning, the migraine reeling in. Pain flashes in starts, boom! fragmenting, dissolving into a throbbing darkness then another blasts in all over again, like some kind of sonic reaction. Clutching his head, Buddy rolls on the grass away from Marnie so he's facing the cages with the fighting roosters, their grand displays. Which one becomes the bloody sacrifice, broken and sliced up from a blade tied to the skinny leg of another, neck hanging to one side like something wrung out, squeezed dry, a used-up rag? Which one the martyr? He's thinking how just like these cocks there's people walking this world with invisible blades around their ankles, slashing up other people, winning from the sheer surprise of their violence. Stares at Marnie sitting cross-legged in the grass, eyes empty as plates. "I should call the goddamn cops," he mutters.

"Yeah? Half of them probably do their daughters too. Maybe half the world's doing their daughters. Pretty convenient, got to admit, cost effective, like raising your own meat. Anyway he and I don't hook up anymore, if we ever did. You can't know for sure, can you? Like I told you, maybe I lied." She smiles, a slow languorous movement of her lips. He notices these are chapped, a thread of skin hanging down off the top like a crumb. No smile in those eyes. "Want to know why I named her Martin? Middle name's David. White boy names. You guys get all the luck."

Buddy rises quickly, head pounding like a wrecking ball's in his skull, staggers toward his grandmother's Mustang. What is the thing you say here? Tugs open the door, falls in, rams it shut, squeezes his head. "Ever hear of Martin Luther King?"

Marnie follows him, leaning into the open window. "So what?"

He gazes at the tops of her breasts, pendulous under the loose neck of her shirt, still with milk maybe and not a soul to nourish. "Not your lucky white boy, that's what," he says quietly.

She touches his forehead for a moment, strokes it with her warm hand. "Guess I never took care of you when you had your headaches, did I? Look Buddy, I know I wasn't always nice to you. Sometimes, I don't know why, but I just couldn't help it. In a lot of ways you're the best guy I've ever known. I mean it. That's why I wouldn't let you marry me or anything.

Your mom was right. You'd ruin your life with someone like me. Then you'd start hating me and I couldn't stand that. I was doing something nice, not letting you have me, if you come right down to it. You still think I'm hot though, huh? Who knows, maybe someday you'll check me out on the catwalk, Fashion TV. Don't I still look like a model even though I squeezed out a kid?" She peers at him anxiously.

Buddy starts up the car, yanks the shift into reverse then stares into her face. "Why'd you tell my mother we were living in a drug house? Now I have to pee in a test tube just to go to fricken school."

She laughs. "Wow, can you hear yourself? Like you can actually say *mother* now without stuttering! See, I told you your childhood was over."

"Yeah? Ask me if I wanted to grow up! You didn't answer my question, telling her we were living in a drug house."

"Well that's what it was, an effing glorified meth lab. Not *even* so glorified. It wasn't good for the baby."

"You didn't keep her!"

"Doesn't mean I wanted her born with Butane in her blood for chrissake. Me having to be anywhere near those toxins meant she was breathing them too."

"Well aren't you the moral compass all of a sudden."

She grins. "Just because I'm no Virgin Mary doesn't mean I don't know what's right for the baby, Buddy. Look, I know you're probably expecting me to turn into a nice person or something, learn from my mistakes. I'm just being honest here. I'm telling you, I don't have it in me. Maybe I'm defective or something, but not all of us can be *nice*."

"Do you even miss her, Marnie? Do you?"

She gazes through the Mustang's passenger side window into empty space. For just a moment she looks like she might break, but then she shakes her head. "I hardly knew her, like how could I miss her? She's an infant for chrissake."

"Inside you for nine months."

"So? Your intestines are inside you forever; you got some kind of a personal relationship with them?"

Buddy rubs his eyes savagely, like he can pop them right out of his head and then the pain would go too. "Why didn't you just get an abortion if you cared so goddamn little?"

She scratches one ankle lazily with the opposite foot, then shrugs. "And miss the looks on their faces when I came home ready to drop! Does this belong to you? I asked them."

"You always meant to come back here, didn't you? You were never going to stay with me beyond the months it took being pregnant with that baby."

"Oh my God!" she snarls, eyes mud-colored and fierce again. "I did her an effing favor. The folks who got her love her and they'll give her a decent life. Could be the most unselfish thing I'll ever do for the rest of *my* life short of booting your ass, so give me some goddamn credit here. You try shove a watermelon out through an opening the size of a pickle and then just give it away."

Buddy pushes Marnie's face out of his car window, angling the Mustang around so he's facing the street, slips the shift into drive. "Kids aren't supposed to be born to teach somebody a lesson, that's a pretty lame reason to add to the world population!" he shouts back to her.

"Well I didn't ask to be born, did you?" she howls. "I don't recall no *in-uteri* invitation, nobody asked me if I wanted a piece of this shitty world!" In the rearview Buddy watches Marnie shake her fist at the squawking roosters. "Shut the fuck up!" she shrieks. He peels out of the long dirt driveway dodging potholes the size of carp pools. He's feeling that loss, but not as sharply as he would have expected. No rage in his gut, not even a slow burn. Just this sort of...hollow. Those roosters will kill each other if she lets them out of their cages. No reason, it's what they're trained to do.

28

Buddy – That Evening

HIS GRANDMOTHER IS DYING. HE'S not entirely sad about it. She's not particularly likable and she's never much liked him. His mom refused to consider hospice care, insisted her mother wouldn't want a stranger in her home, yet he's a stranger to his grandmother. It's weird, living with a person who's dying. It hangs in the air, a cloud of it like smoke, invisible letters spelling it over their front door, DEATH IS HERE. He feels like he should hold up his head, look at the shapes on the ceiling, not at her, avoid breathing the same air. In case it's catching. He wishes she would get it over with. He knows that's bad, but he wishes it anyway. He doesn't care anymore if she forgives him for stealing her money; he just wants things to be normal again, or at least what passes for normal in his family.

It's over with Marnie, *pau*, that's what he keeps telling himself, driving the Mustang back up the Volcano highway. He can't show up in that scraggly yard again, climb those rotting steps, watch TV in her house, her mother's lazy cats splayed about like fur pillows. He should probably murder her stepfather; he'd be a hero in somebody's idea of a moral order. If, that is, she's told him the truth.... He can't understand it, and he can't seem to feel the despair about it he figures he should feel. It's rampant, the hurt we inflict on others. Every time you turn on the news somebody's done something terrible to somebody else, kidnappings, rape, terrorist attacks, mass shootings, and what banks and big corporations do in the name of greed, sinking people like the Lo's further down into a life where they get to choose between lights or a phone.

Sun slips below Mauna Loa, the mountain heavy and bruised, a swollen, beat-up look. He's supposed to stay with his grandmother tonight, so their cousin can take his mother out to the Volcano House for dinner. His mother's been losing it, and he supposes this is Kiki's idea of doing something helpful. But not to Buddy, it isn't helpful to him.

Back home he parks the Mustang exactly how his mother likes it, the less interaction with her the better, shuffles up the path. When he opens the door the first thing Buddy sees is his grandmother lying flat on the couch, stiff as a popsicle, cloaked in a banana yellow and pink blanket, one bony shin poking out. Is she dead? He inhales a breath of outside air deep into his lungs, steps all the way inside, switching on the overhead light. She blinks, not dead.

"Hey Grandma!" he calls out. No response, not that he expected any. "Guess what? My ex-girlfriend had a baby and she gave her away, how you like them apples?" He doesn't know why he said that; it's one of those incredibly dumb things you hear people blather, *them apples*, probably originated with the Three Stooges. He waits for a reaction. Nothing. This has possibilities. He can tell her all sorts of crazy-ass things, some of them even true.

Kiki billows into the living room, swish of her hips, her long slippered feet poking out from under the hem of an orange mu'umu'u. "Hey, kiddo."

Buddy immediately starts his lobbying, before his mother enters the room, so that maybe he has a shot at calling the thing off. "Why do I have to stay home tonight? If Grandma Madge can't do anything but lie here anyway, it's not like she'd be wandering around getting into trouble."

Kiki gathers her long hair into a bun at the back of her head, sticks a chopstick through it to hold it. Her spicy scent envelopes the room. "Your grandma should never be alone. You think she won't know the difference? Try abandonment issues. Her mother dies when she's a little kid and her husband walks into the surf. Then her daughter moves to the mainland far as she can get and still be on American soil. Not a lot to ask that you be here one night for her just in case, huh?"

Buddy shrugs, watching his mom make her way down the hall, eyes needled straight ahead, her calculated unsteady steps. She's been drinking more than usual, by the looks of her. On the koa mantle there's a photo of her at his age, Gwenyth Johnstone accepting a giant gold trophy for the regional track meet, placing first in the Mile Run. Where's that winner now?

"Be good!" Kiki says, as he holds open the door for her and his mother; he's brought up to do stuff like this and amazingly he does it. "Be with God," his mom mutters. Is she suggesting Buddy spend the evening with him? Do pizza or something? When she opened her mouth there was a smell like her own private grape orchard fermenting down her throat. He peers back at his grandmother. Buddy doesn't have a good feeling about this night.

A COUPLE HOURS LATER HE wakes in a panic, sweating, heartbeat drubbing out a drum solo. He fell asleep watching Survivor on TV, in the chair across from where his grandmother lies still as death. He listens for her breathing; she lets out a mini snore. He sighs, wipes his forehead with a sweaty palm, shuts off the electronic assault.

Dreamed the dead body dream again, weirdest ever. Caterpillar Hunters of all the crazy-ass things, large, striking beetles so green they look black, a line of deep red around their thorax. They're a predecease insect, their larvae attacks and feeds on caterpillars. Some of the adults can squirt an acrid fluid at predators, or people like Buddy who might try to pick one up and examine it. The bizarre images hammer inside him, her body, creamy skin on the black lava, hand clutching a glass cylinder that looked like a jar of some sort and these behemoth Caterpillar Hunters are crawling up her arm.

Buddy shivers, a clammy sensation, pinpricks of sweat down his spine, then peers again at his grandmother. She's awake and staring at him, head riveted in his direction, eyes bright as dimes. "You want something?" he calls out, pulse racing. Like she's going to answer. He grins, feels foolish. Gets up, stretches, casually walks over to her and squats down so they are at eye level with each other. "Guess what, Grandma. I'll bet I know what you looked like when you were young. You were pretty good looking. I'll bet Grandpa thought he scored a babe."

Her eyes glitter, a dampness to them like she's been crying. Something tugs at Buddy. What does he say to her? She never played much of a part in his life or he in hers, yet here they are. He's feeling something else too, something he can't make sense of or put words to. "Bullshit!" he whispers. Cheeks flush, he stares down at his feet in the alien rubber slippers.

She makes a chirping sound.

Buddy jumps. "What?"

Her head lolls, jerks to one side, eyelids shut then peel open. She makes the sound again, like some bird. "Did you just try to say something?" He waits for it, another chirp, peep, or maybe a full-on canary trill! But she's silent.

Buddy stares at her, then over at the wheelchair Dr. Alvarez left, perched like some metal monolith in the corner. Rises and waltzes over as if he knows exactly what he's going to do, unlocks the brake and wheels it back, his grandmother still gazing into the space he inhabited. "Hey Grandma!" he says, forced cheeriness, "want a ride?" Reaches under her arms before he can think better of it, armpits doughy and empty like two hollowed out bags of flour, light as something already half gone from this world. Lifts her into the chair. She doesn't resist.

He wheels her down the hall into her bedroom, still without a clue why. Feels driven by something, almost like his grandmother's leading him, though she's half unconscious so that's impossible.

"Drrrr!" she says, and this time he's certain he heard her try to say an actual word. He parks her beside the huge mahogany dresser that belonged to his great grandfather, Jude Canada. Buddy pictures him like his dresser, towering, woody and dark. He was *akamai* as the Hawaiians say, smart, but apparently not particularly nice. "He was a man of God," Buddy's mother said.

Face burning he tugs open the top drawer, his grandmother watching him. Has he determined this is what she meant? *Drrrr*, as in dresser, or drawer, or maybe dumbass! She's not objecting anyway. Can he make these decisions, become the conduit for his grandmother's voice? "You said drawer, right?" Like she's going to respond. He pulls open the next then the next, as if this is what he's supposed to do. He's ransacked her room before for money, what's a little bureau invasion? She makes a strange licking motion, tongue flicking over her bottom lip which is cracked and dry, from the stroke he's guessing; stroke victims get weird around the mouth, he's seen it in the hospital shows on TV. There's lingerie in this drawer, billowy nylon underwear and bras that could cozy soccer balls. Peers furtively at what were once his grandmother's supposedly prominent breasts, sunken into the cave of her chest.

The fourth drawer is a mishmash of different clothing, *accessories*, his mother's word, scarves, handkerchiefs, stockings, belts, puffy velveteen slippers. The drawer after that is more of the same, random items, and a beaded *evening purse* his mom called it, that probably saw some good times. One afternoon not long after they moved here, his grandmother napping on the couch, his mom had showed him some of Madge's *outfits*, as if he could give a damn. He didn't, of course, but did he have to act so disdainful? Grandma was a beauty and quite the dancer, his mom had said and Buddy snorted. He

269

feels sad about this now. What would it be like to have most of your life in the past, so far from your present reality that maybe you couldn't even trust its memory? Could his grandmother remember any of it, the person she was?

When he tugs open the bottom drawer, swollen tight from Hawai'i's humidity, it makes a squealing, prohibitive sound like it's daring him to keep opening it, and he sucks in a whistling breath. "Jesus, Grandma!" Her eyes gleam up at him. "What the hell, I thought old ladies were supposed to be neat!" A world is in this drawer, kitchen items, basting brush, skewer sticks, an ancient steel rotary beater that looks like it's a survivor of the nineteenth century, maybe earlier, a medieval torture implement; God knows what it would have beaten, that which laid the egg instead of the egg? Dried out soaps in various stages of unwrapped, a can of Lysol spray dotted with flecks of rust, pins, thread, dried-up and crusty glue containers, a poetry book (since when is his grandmother a Ginsberg fan? *Howl*, it says!), yellowed pamphlets, desiccated tubes of either a butt-ugly flat paint, or maybe face makeup for a vampire, business ledgers, lava bits, hunks of coral, old black and white photo note cards of some tree, some woman, some car, some beach, chunky cowry shells, a few still whole, the rest in pieces, melted stuck-together peppermint candy canes…. Buddy stops there, yanking out his hand in disgust, swiping it on his jeans. He can understand why his mom wouldn't have gone into this drawer to take care of the mess; she's a freak about things disorganized but likes cleaning them up even less.

His grandmother stares up at him, eyes spirally and intense like two whirling tops, like she's challenging him. He can almost hear her… *Chicken*! *Scared of fifty-year-old candy goo?*

"Christ!" Buddy mutters, plunging his hand back down again under a stack of ancient newspapers, and that's when he feels it, smooth and cool, cylinder shaped. "Oh no!" he whispers. Pulls the jar out, heart unraveling. "What's this Grandma, a *jar*, a fricken *jar*?" Weakness in his knees, a coldness in his stomach.

An old Skippy Peanut Butter jar, the top rusted on. Tries to twist it open but it won't budge. "This is too weird," he mumbles, looking at his grandmother, and he swears she's smiling out the side of that dried-up mouth, unless he can decide that for her too—when and if she smiles. A prickly chill plays chopsticks down his spinal discs. What could it mean, dreaming about a jar then finding one an hour later? Buddy peers in through the clouded sides, holding it up to the glass lamp on top of the dresser. The contents are lumpy, indistinct, but looks like a butterfly wing, Monarch by the markings. There's a shriveled up leaf of some sort, milkweed or crown flower probably if the butterfly's a Monarch. And...hair?

Buddy stares at his grandmother. "Hair?" he asks, making a face. She peers up at him, and while he can't say for absolute certain, he would almost swear he's seeing those old dry eyes tear up. Feels like his heart's going to snap apart. Kneeling down in front of her, Buddy places the jar on her lap. He thinks about his grandmother over the weeks since he's come back from O'ahu, since her major stroke, wheeled from her bed in the wheelchair then positioned in her rocker every morning by his mother, positioned on the couch most every afternoon. Positioned...as if the person is furniture. She won't touch her meals, breakfast, lunch, dinners pulverized into liquid for her, or just an Ensure, straw stuck in, cold on the tray. Every day she's got the pink shawl her own mother knitted around her bony shoulders. Breaks Buddy's heart that shawl, those sketchy shoulders poking through.

He lays his head on his grandmother's lap beside the jar, coolness of the glass against his neck. Imagines her hands, one of them useless and the other fluttery and strange, stroking his hair. Buddy would like to think she might do this, if she could.

Buddy's mom wanders around the kitchen, pouring wine into her glass, chugging it, pouring more. She keeps asking, "Grandma's asleep?" nodding her head. Twisting the top off the jar with industrial-size pliers, Kiki peers inside. "Wow, check this out, Gwen!" His mom glances at the contents, wrinkles her nose, frowns. "Dead leaves? Not to mention the dead butterfly, and if that's not disgusting enough hair of all things! Sick, really sick. This confirms it. My mother completely lost her marbles." She collapses down on a kitchen chair, elbows on the table, rubbing her head. "God, why am I even here, what's the use? Juli was right. She'd be better off with a real nurse. Should've just let them cart her away to a nursing home. Sure she'd be furious, but she couldn't give me crap, can't say a bloody word that makes a lick of sense so what would it matter?"

Bright patches of red under her eyes glow like fever. She's wasted, Buddy's thinking, and pretty fired-up. This could get ugly. He sighs loudly so his mom will remember he's here, maybe behave a little more sanely the way parents *sometimes* will around a kid, believing they're supposed to set some kind of an example. Plunks himself down on a chair opposite her, the table conveniently between them.

Gwen slugs down half her glass of wine. Buddy avoids his mother's eyes. This is that delicate state she gets in, a particular drunkenness where complicity is not a good idea, but you don't want her to think you're against her either. It's a no-win; usually she holes up in her own room before it gets like this. But not tonight. Tonight it seems they're in it for the long haul.

He stares at his grandmother's jar sitting in the middle of the table like it's a condiment. Gwen sighs, followed by a slurp of wine. Outside a sudden shower pelts against the window like tossed pebbles, rush of sound then the green smell of the Hawaiian wet. "Thank God we're finally getting rain," she whispers, resting her head between her arms on the table. For a moment Buddy feels sorry for her. She's exhausted, his grandmother waking her up every night, calling out unintelligible things that his mom assumes is her name, her duty.

"So," Kiki says, slipping fluidly into the chair beside Buddy's. "The thing to do now is figure out whose hair is inside the jar."

"That's a no-brainer," Gwen chimes without lifting her head. "Ana Kalamahea Canada, my grandmother. Madge told me how she cut a hank of her own mother's hair once when she was a kid and saved it. Good move, because after my grandmother died my grandfather swept through the house and removed all her things. She doesn't have much that was her mother's; about all she has is the shawl, couple of blankets, a rug and that hair, apparently, despicable as it is. Nobody could accuse Jude Canada of being a sentimental man."

"Yeah but did you know she was saving the hair in a jar with a butterfly? That's maybe the important part. Because what that might mean is she was keeping her mother's spirit with her, not letting it fly free to Po."

His mom pops up her head again, rolls her eyes. "Oh Jesus! It's hocus pocus time, folks."

"What's Po?" Buddy asks.

"It's like the locals heaven. I took a Hawaiian Studies class at U.H. They believe if somebody keeps something from your body, hair, a bone, even toenail clippings, you can't fly free to Po when you die. You're trapped here. Unihipili, spirit of a dead person kept by the living. That's why a lot of Hawaiian burial places are secret. Could be the reason Madge is holding on. She needs to let her mother go. I guess she was too young to bear it when her mother died."

Gwen snarls, "Maybe I don't want *my* mother to die either!" She slubs down the last of her wine, rises and roams around the kitchen, throwing open cupboard doors, searching for another bottle Buddy's guessing. "God, nothing in my life is the way I ever thought it would be. People around me can't even *die* like they're supposed to! The lord giveth and the lord taketh away!"

"How do you release her spirit?" Buddy asks, trying to avert the course his mother's on, about to erupt in Bible verses and religious clichés from the perspective of one who's read the Cliff Notes. Can the eleventh hour apocalypse spiel be far behind?

"It's no big deal. You just drop the contents of the jar over a sacred place. South Point on this island's always been a jumping off place to Po. I think folks can go to Pele in Halema'uma'u too."

His mom groans. "You make it sound like choosing an airline, will she get frequent flier miles?" She triumphantly yanks out an unopened wine bottle from the back of the compact, barely-used cupboard over the refrigerator, returns to the table cradling it tenderly like it's her own kid. "What knuckle-head tried and failed to hide this?" she asks, glaring at Buddy. "So my mother saved a piece of her own mother's hair. I saved Buddy's teeth, so what?"

"You did? You saved my baby teeth?"

"Yeah, so? When did you stop believing in the tooth fairy? I'm not that pathetic. I wasn't trying to keep the spirit of you as a baby with me. Well... maybe." She laughs.

Buddy feels a tugging inside, that his mother would save his baby teeth! It's not something he would've expected. "What about Grandma Madge? She said a word that sounded like drawer, and that's where I found the jar."

"Oh for heaven's sake, Grandma makes noises. That's all she can do since her stroke, sit around and make noises. Sometimes they sound like they mean something but, sorry, I just don't think they do."

"Yeah well what about my dream then? I dreamt about a jar an hour before finding this one." He's saying most of this for the sake of argument, but for some reason at that moment he felt like the defender of his grandmother's sanity.

His mom sighs. "Buddy, you've always had strange dreams. When you were little you'd wake up from one in the middle of the night, and I'd have to check your closet, lie on your bed with you until you fell back asleep. Once I woke up and you were under *my* bed! You have thin boundaries, so your dreams seem significant." She shakily pours yet another glass from the new bottle, a Riesling the label says, makes a face. "God I hate white wine. Who bought this? Why would somebody buy white wine when they know I drink red? It's like they drained the blood out of it, the *essence* of the grape!" Lets out a winey, sour breath.

Now *he* groans. He wants to grab that bottle from her, but of course he just sits. Buddy's the kid here, isn't he?

Gwen stands, staggers, is about to pitch foreword then catches herself and holds out her arms to him. Buddy pulls back in his chair, but his mom, who if she's anything can be damn persistent, steps closer. "I want to hug you! I swear, I just want to put my arms around you. Forget all the hocus pocus, helping some ghost out of an old, crappy jar. Let's help ourselves, you and me, son. Before it's too late. Not many get this, you know, a chance to start over."

29

Buddy - The Rest Of The Night

HE'S HAVING TROUBLE SLEEPING AND there's no meds to assist, no chemical intervention. What Buddy wouldn't have done for a couple of Totally Todd's Quaaludes, killed the meth buzz when it went on too long and the methengers needed to get cooking again. Went to the medicine cabinet to look for his mom's stash and discovered an empty Xanax bottle. The Ativan was gone too. Definitely not a good sign. Now he's tossing about in his wrinkly sheets, pulling them this way, that way, finally off. Sits up. The house has that burdened silence of late in the night, except for the rain, softer now, playing on the roof. Usually his grandmother starts up about this time, and for some reason he decides to check on her, maybe save his mom, whom he figured collapsed into a winey sleep, the trouble of being woken with a hangover so soon. Buddy's feeling sort of OK about his grandmother now, and he wants to tell her that when Kiki left she took the jar. She knows what to do, he'll tell his grandmother. He's not saying he bought into any of this, but what if his grandmother believed it? The woman had a peanut butter jar in her dresser with a chunk of her mother's hair and a dead Monarch in it, for chrissake! You just know here's a person who's going to hang on to every thrum of that weakening heart, until the thing's resolved. Buddy wanted her to know she didn't have to fight anymore.

But when he goes into her room his mother's there, standing over her, a shadowy shape swaying back and forth like a small wind's blowing through. Only it's very still. Just the thick raspy sounds of his grandmother's breathing, as if she's struggling up from deep water, a painful little whine after each shuddering exhale. Buddy feels a squirm of something cold in his gut.

"You don't know what's it's like," his mom sighs, not even looking at him as he stands at the opposite side of his grandmother's bed. "It's just that she's always been here. Even in Maine, 6,000 miles away I knew she was here." Buddy can smell the rancid sourness, the wine leeching from his mother's pores. Maybe she's never had so much wine inside her, almost pickled, fermented into something solid; you'd almost expect her to have chewed instead of chugged. Coupled with the anti-anxiety drugs? Let's count how many she took, how many glasses of wine, all of it co-mingling, hooking up in her blood stream!

His grandmother makes a sudden, cluttered sound and they both lean down toward her chest. But then she pulls out of another breath, shallower, a high soft wheeze. His mother turns toward Buddy. "I've been thinking, it's a funny thing about kids. You feel this satisfaction when they're little, imagining you're providing them with a good home, and then what do you know they grow up hating you anyway." She lets out her own breath in a whoosh, starts pacing about the room. "So Kiki took my grandmother the hunk of hair to *Po*, huh? Good thing you'll turn eighteen next birthday, son, this is enough to lose a custody hearing. The sanity thing, you know? Hair inside jars and jumping off places to the next world aren't exactly what they look for in a stable home environment. And you know there's always been that suspicion about us Johnstones maybe not being quite *right*. My own dad paddled into waves the size of a five story building! God, I guess I'm not much of a mother, am I? I need a glass of wine."

No! Buddy wants to shout, but he doesn't. He doesn't even meet her eyes, stares instead at her hands, the way they're shaking. She marches over to the bureau, flips on the small glass lamp on top and the room is immediately tinged in a dingy yellow glow. Tugs the dresser away from the wall, reaches down and drags up a bottle off the floor behind.

Holy shit! His mom's hiding alcohol around the house?

"OK son, I know what you're thinking, I've been hiding bottles, huh? Isn't that one of the twelve signs of an alcoholic? Didn't you tell me that once? Or was it twelve steps *curing* an alcoholic? I'm not sick, I don't need a cure. What I need is some wine!" She fumbles at the cork, yanks it out (clearly it's been opened before), tips back her long neck and slugs it. Buddy feels powerless. Who is he? A kid, standing by his grandmother's bed, her eyes glittering through eyelid slits occasionally but mostly they are shut. She breathes another ragged breath.

His mom starts to cry. "You don't know what it's like, losing your own mother. The spirit's gone out of her eyes, did you notice? That snappish thing she did with them, you'd look the other way not to meet those eyes. Nobody got the best of Madge Canada Johnstone I'm telling you, nobody. I put her in her chair every morning, facing her toward the mountains, she loved those mountains! She doesn't even look anymore, Buddy. She's not there inside, I'm telling you. And listen, her breath just keeps struggling in and out. It's a horror show I tell you!" His mother drops the wine bottle suddenly and it spills, a red mess flowing across the wood floor easy as blood.

Buddy rushes over to her, "Take it easy, Mom!"

"Oh Buddy, Buddy!" she fumbles at his cheeks, his chin. "You called me Mom! You called me Mom."

"What would I call you, *Bob*? Christ, look at this mess!"

"Do you think she's afraid?" his mother whispers, bending in towards his ear, her fetid breath. "I see it in her eyes sometimes, do you? Let's go look together and you tell me if she's afraid. If she's not then OK, I won't be either. I've got you, don't I? You called me *Mom*. I was scared all those months you were gone I'd never hear that word again."

Buddy dabs at the spilled wine with his grandmother's kimono, but likely as not she won't need it, and at this point he's afraid his mother, unsteady as she is, will slip and fall in the wet. He follows her to the bed, perching at the edge beside her. "There's so much we never said," she sighs, stroking his grandmother's grey fingers. Her fingers look like old beef, he imagines they'd feel clammy. He doesn't want to touch them to find out.

"When you came back, refusing the medicine for your headaches, I thought for sure you'd crossed over some line away from me. I got you that medicine remember? I was the one who took you to the doctor, sat with you when you first started getting the migraines. I was the one who was there."

His grandmother sucks in a haggard breath. Buddy shrugs, what can he say?

"Do you think the breath is the soul? When I was a kid I used to believe I'd stop breathing if I didn't concentrate on it. That's when I started praying to God and Jesus, to keep me breathing while I was asleep. I figured when I was awake I could stay on top of it, but who takes care of me when I sleep? So I started praying, even though I wasn't exactly sure they were listening since we never went to church—I think because my grandfather was a religious man, so of course my mother had to have it her own way. Touch her, Buddy, have you touched Grandma's face? Her skin is still so soft."

He shrinks away, changes the subject. "How come she never had a feeding tube? She's been wasting from not eating you know."

His mother laughs. "Ever seen a person hooked up to those? Not very attractive. Grandma's a vain woman. She wouldn't like those things stuck in her, right Mother?" She leans in toward Madge's mouth. "If you think

279

your grandma was babbling about a drawer she's sure not talking now. She keeps slurping those awful breaths, Buddy. It sounds like they're hurting her, what do you think? Like she's trying to breathe something toxic." His grandmother's eyes flutter open then close again. His mom leaps off the bed, pacing back and forth.

Then she leaves the room, returning before he had to fret over how to fill the silence, his grandmother maybe dying and what's he supposed to say about any of this? She's clutching a small photograph in an ancient-looking frame, some kind of gilded, tarnished metal. "Meet your great grandparents, Jude and Ana Canada. I've kept it hidden figuring it might upset my mother. She's not one for old family pictures. I guess when members of our family *disappear* they're supposed to vanish from genetic memory too. What a beauty, don't you think?"

Buddy gasps, almost chokes, staring at the picture, aged and yellowed behind the glass but the resemblance is clear, Ana Canada, his great grandmother, long black hair, sharp cheekbones, slender as a shadow looking suspiciously like the dead woman in his dreams. He rears back, waiting for either panic or clarity to set in but nothing does. Leans forward and gazes furtively at the photo again. Nah, he's just creeped out from all this craziness—he's a kid who believes in entomology, remember? The orderly biology of insects. It's not her, but an uncanny resemblance you might say. Buddy sighs, and this time he checks out his great grandfather too. It's obvious Grandma Madge got her fierce bearing from him. Besides, dreaming about your naked dead great grandmother could have some serious psychological implications. There's crazy, then there's CRAZY. He wouldn't want to set foot down that road, not even a toe. Could be his mom is right about his bizarre dreams; for sanity's sake let's give her that.

"When I was a child my mother used to talk about my grandmother like she was in the room with us sometimes. Freaky, I thought. She used to say, Beware the poisonous crown flower. My grandfather said Ana had a heart attack. She may have also been having the same TIA's that afflicted Grandma Madge, there's indication of some pretty strange behavior. Well, crown flowers, heart attack, whatever, I think they're wrong. I think she died of a broken heart."

"Why?"

She shrugs. "That's a no-brainer. Ana Canada loved the wrong man." His mom walks shakily over to the window and Buddy gets up and follows her, still afraid she might fall. Dawn is beginning to pale the sky. Soon they'll see the field beyond the rift, with its wild orchids like little purple berets, pili grass, ferns and ohia. No crown flower bushes at this elevation, too cool for the giant milkweed, pua-kalaunu. "Are we keeping a vigil?" she whispers.

"A *what*? Another one of your words?"

"Vigil, you know, family gathers around when the loved one's about to..." she leans in close to him, her intense winey breath, whispers, "So she won't be alone."

Buddy stares at the bed. His grandmother's still pulling in and out of those nasty breaths. He doesn't see or hear any change in this. The sound is starting to annoy him, and he can tell for sure it's bothering his mother because she suddenly claps her hands over her ears. "Jesus! I'm ready, I've finally convinced myself I'm ready and nothing's happening!"

Then she gets this strange look.

Now, here is what Buddy will wish in the weeks, months, even years to come: that he had time to interpret that look, think about it, *ruminate* on its ramifications as his mom might put it, maybe even sit with her over a glass of her wine and discuss it. Just talk, let the morning come in. "You believe she's suffering?" Gwen asks him softly. "You do, don't you? She wants to go and she's suffering because she can't. She made me promise I wouldn't let her suffer. She wanted to be at home, and to not suffer."

Buddy shrugs. He didn't know. He doesn't know. They both look over at his grandmother, snaffling those breaths, almost a sobbing sound in between when he thinks back on it. Maybe she really was crying. Maybe his mom was right. "It's the cruelest thing, son, ready to go and nobody takes you." When all is said and done, Buddy will hope to hell she was right.

His mom, her slow pinched voice, "Buddy, I want you in bed, it's late."

"But it's almost morning, why bother?"

"Don't argue with me now, I'm still your mother, right? We established that much. I want you to go to bed. I'm telling you, go to bed!"

"But Mom...." he lets it trail off, what could he say? Was there a thing he could have said that might have kept him in that room? If there was he didn't know it. He was the kid, following his mother's orders. He walked over to her bed, took his grandmother's hand in his for just a moment, those meaty fingers, then placed it back down on the sheet. And Buddy left.

30

Gwen

Don't be afraid, Mother, it's you and me, no arguments, no regrets, no trying to figure it out anymore. I prayed for you; don't know what you believe in beyond yourself but figured I'd cover all the bases. Are you cold? Your breathing is so loud! It's thundering in my ears, like a waterfall. We can pretend it's water, into the water, the Living Waters like your own father's church. Then you can speak the language of the fishes. My father spoke it. He spoke it to me when you wouldn't let me speak his name. Do you want to speak the language of the fishes? I didn't think I could bear this, but it's not so bad. It's OK, Mother. My head's all fuzzy but I'm clear on this. Your breathing is so awful, I just know it's hurting you trying to pull through all that water gasping for air. Do fish breathe air? I don't think they do. I'm going to stay right beside you and we can sleep, if we could just quiet that loud noise from your mouth; and the smell of it, I'm sorry, but it smells like something died in your throat. You'd hate that, knowing your breath stank.

Can you read my thoughts? When I was a child I believed you could. You seemed almost super-human to me, like you were sheathed in invisible armor.

Like a robot in a way, but a really perceptive one. I'd sit on that couch beside you, and I'd dare to think it, that he wasn't coming back, and you'd call me out on it, tell me not to think my negative thoughts.

Look, the silk kimono sash is still tied to your bed. He gave the kimono to you; remember how you loved its butterfly print? You loved it and kept wearing it years after he was gone. I would've given anything to remember him the way you must have. You rubbed him out, erased him from my life, not letting me even speak of him. I don't believe he walked into those mammoth waves just to surf. Some people fight to stay alive and some don't. I don't know why, but I know you're a fighter. Damn how you fought. But we're tired now, Mother.

Let's fall asleep with an image we can share. Remember how you used to tell me to think good thoughts before I slept and I wouldn't have bad dreams? I'll think it and you can read my mind, know it was true. The Lehua blossom lei I made you after I graduated from high school, before leaving the island for college. I knew you were heartbroken, and even then you couldn't show it. I made it myself, because of course no one else would, no lei seller would dare carry it—these are Pele's flowers after all, and if you pick them she'll want revenge, at the least she'll make it rain. Was I wishing this on you? Your own private raincloud to dump on you after I was gone? I'm not sure what I was thinking—I was never sure when it came to you. But it was beautiful, the scarlet quills of her flowers like flames, like your hair was, like you, my mother. And when I gave it to you, throughout that long silent ride to the airport you wore it, even though it might have been bad luck, even though you never believed in saying goodbye.

Madge

Fit of his uncombed hair, his sweet, clean shirt. Something moved her! Something snapped. Jody, Jody. Very core of her buzzing, your touch your smell taste of ... Jody. Storm blowing in. Pelting the house. Thunder snarls a warning. Wind wailing like it's alive, shrieking, moaning, sobbing. TV announces: Giant swell from the south, capable of generating the biggest waves we've seen off the Hamakua since the 1969 tidal wave.... Did she do it? Did she, could she, send her Jody into that surf, broken board, burning sky, fiery mouth of the sea? Jody! She didn't mean it, you understand? He says...yes! Madge, my badge. Yes. Afraid? Yes. Alone? Not anymore. There's a clarity never before...no, once before but she didn't know, how would she have recognized it? And who imagines its weight? Look for the light and it's yellow of course, like blowing wheat, blowing sun, yellow light, that yellow light! it is that yellow light. Beating of a hundred wings he comes, and he is the lead, Monarch, the King. Roaring air stirred up by so many wings, but such a weight in her chest, how will she move? Too late! this roaring, this light, and she is bold enough to do it right, the glide of their perfect black and yellow wings; who needs air to breathe when you can fly?

Buddy

So he does it. He leaves that bedroom, and he's thinking maybe she really does need to be with her mother, maybe there are words that need saying, or maybe she'll just sit beside her, stay with her so she doesn't have to be alone. He's the kid, remember? *Who is in charge?*

He can't sleep, we've established this much already, so he sits there on his bed, his head leaning in the direction of his grandmother's room down the hall, listening...for what? He can't hear that breathing, only imagine it, the gruff throaty sounds, the way it gets high on the exhale, whistle of air squeezing through whatever is left in there. It could drive anybody insane listening to that, what remains of a person already half gone, who maybe no longer wishes to be dragged along with that air, in and out. He'll come to believe this. Will have to believe it, that life was no longer her wish. However much he didn't like his grandmother in the past, Buddy needed to believe she would have wanted what happened to her.

Dawn through his window, a salmon colored sunrise obscured by a grey mist, then opening out above it, buoyant as fire. Hoarse cry of a nene. His head hurts. Buddy realizes sitting there he's been growing a migraine, but it doesn't hit him until he stands. Dagger of pain behind his eye and he bends over and vomits on his bedroom floor. Fine way to greet the day.

Walks the walk that no longer feels familiar down the dark hallway to her room, clutching his head. He's wondering if it was just a little later, maybe a half hour or so, considering the first signs of a new day leaked in while they stood there together, Buddy and his mom, hint of its beginnings, a pale light and his grandmother still breathing those awful breaths. Inhales deeply thinking if ever he was going to start praying this would be the moment, then breezes into her bedroom. First thing Buddy sees is his mom on his grandmother's bed, lying beside his grandmother, her arm flung over his grandmother's shoulders. His mom's shoulders are shaking, there's a dry heaving sound coming out of what Buddy's hoping is his grandmother, but the closer he gets he knows it's his mother.

"Oh Jesus, Buddy, that you?" Gwen whispers, lifting up her head. "I must've fallen asleep. Grandma's here, isn't she? She's still with us, right?" He stands beside them, his throat filling with a chalky, dusty, gravely stuff like a mouthful of blacktop. Swallows hard, the migraine pumping its thousand beats behind his eye, his head pulsing with pain. And this is what Buddy sees, the truth, what he hasn't told a soul because who the hell would believe him? He swears to God, Buddha, Pele, Po, whoever the hell is out there, when his mom slides her arm off his grandmother Buddy sees that damn kimono sash she used to tie his grandmother to her bed, to her rocker, to hold her down... knotted around his grandmother's throat.

"She's still breathing, poor thing, and it's hurting her so. A woman of a certain dignity, she wouldn't want this, I know she wouldn't!"

Except she isn't. She isn't breathing. He knows it immediately, you don't have to be a fricken genius to figure this out; no awful sound of it, his grandmother's wasted little body frozen as the Arctic in January, a purple bruise on her neck fanning out under the sash like wings. Buddy yanks his mother off his grandmother's bed, wiggles his fingers down under the sash, cringing at the touch of that cooling skin, doesn't even feel like skin anymore, like something plastic and inert, the Tupperware of flesh! He loosens the knot, a quick tug and the sash slithers into his hands like a centipede. Stares at his grandmother's face and she's staring back, but not seeing him, not seeing a thing. Ever seen a dead person stare? Nothing behind it, doll's eyes, flat, a darkness that isn't any color at all, the absence of it; eyes like buttons, sewn in, nothing that could have possibly been real. There's a small smile on her face though, almost a smirk when he thinks about it, remembers it in a certain way. He likes to remember it this way, a smirk. As if even in the end when she wasn't in control, she was. His grandmother would want it like that.

Buddy tries to lead his mom away from the bed, but she plunks herself down at the end, starts massaging his grandmother's feet under the covers, tenderly rubbing each little toe. He thinks how rigid those toes will become, how icy. She's humming and not looking at his grandmother or him, gazing out the window into the cold light of morning. Buddy leans over, away from the bed and spews. The migraine has its own agenda inside him, and loosing the knot around a strangled person's throat doesn't exactly appease it.

"Oh Buddy, do you have another one of your headaches? Let me get a cool washrag and I'll rub your forehead. I'll be right back. Don't worry about the mess. I'll take care of that later, what's a mother for if not to clean up her son's mess?"

"She's dead, Mom." He thinks he said this. Wanted to say it, thought hard about it but it seemed like the words might not take shape on his tongue.

She rises, sways, then collapses back down on the end of the bed causing his grandmother's body to jerk in Buddy's direction. He jumps back, head reeling. "Oh dear, I guess I had a little too much wine last night, did I son? I'm sorry, but I can't seem to move. Maybe you're right; maybe I do need to cut back on the drinking a bit. I don't remember, did I have too much?"

"Did you understand me? She's not breathing! Her bathrobe sash was in a knot around her neck!"

Gwen stares at him blankly. "Well people sleep with their robes around them, sometimes they do. Some don't use pajamas at all, just their robes.

Your father was never a pajama person. I don't think the entire time we lived together I ever saw him put on a pair of pajamas."

"Mom!" he wretches it out then starts to cry. He doesn't know why he's crying exactly, except that he can't seem to stop. He wants someone to come here and rescue him, take him away from this ending that can't ever change, his grandmother dead on the bed with a bruise on her neck, and his mother who will not remember. Buddy's never been near a dead person, not even his dog. They're so...final. His mom is muttering how she really is going to try and control her drinking, she's going to make a new start, she's saying, won't be a wife anymore but BY GOD she'll be one helluva mother. When the apocalypse comes, BY GOD she'll have nothing to hide. And she's mumbling ... "*The Lord is my shepherd I shall not want...He maketh me lie down...He restoreth my soul...Yea though I walk through the valley of the shadow of death...*" missing more than half the words, even Buddy knows that, and he's moaning, wailing. Then he's vomiting again and again until it's bile, until it's nothing, his throat a burning hole.

She didn't remember. A blackout is what it's called, but what Buddy understands is this: If his mother ever does somehow remember, knowing it will kill her. The rest of what happened is the way you recall a dream, a blurred sketchy vision of some kind of craziness that seemed perfectly rational at the time, then you wake up in the psych ward of Hilo Hospital, pumped full of antipsychotics, antibiotics, the *anti*-meds like the Antichrist of pharmaceuticals, and they're telling you you've had an "episode," that they have to keep you until you've been "evaluated," to maybe stand trial for the strangulation death of your grandmother.

His head was hurting bad. Boiling lava spewing inside his brain, rivers of it coursing through his blood, and his mom muttering about her drinking, chanting Bible passages and not even looking at his grandmother on the bed, her poor old life snuffed out. At some point Buddy started screaming, clutching his head, and then he ran out of there, his grandmother's bedroom, *dead* room he's thinking. He remembers this much, racing down the hall like it's some kind of marathon, his mother's son, a *runner's* son, like he's being chased, only his mother's not moving, frozen into her murmuring catatonia.

He's heading for the kitchen, his standard image, cutting the pain out with a knife propelling him forward. But when he gets there the first thing he sees is the giant pliers, still on the kitchen table from when they pried the lid off his grandmother's jar, and he thinks of butterflies for an absurd moment, how for Hawaiians the butterfly was a symbol of freedom.

Putting a hole in your head is an ancient practice, it even has a name, trepanation, comes from the Greek *trypanon*, meaning "a borer." Buddy knows because his mother looked the word up, after the fact of course. It's the oldest surgical procedure and it's still performed worldwide, so if he's crazy he's in damn good company. It involves geysers of blood and the removal of a chunk of skull, relieving pressure on the brain. Let the demons out. Hippocrates endorsed it for light head wounds. Some do it to relieve depression, the dullness of living. Some do it to take away the voices, or maybe that one particular voice that's always in your head, condemning you, voice of malice, of fear, of *you'll never be enough*. Lets the tide of peace flow in, the silence.

Buddy did it to take the headache away. Simple as that. Not with the pliers of course, he's not *so* cracked. The pliers reminded him of the other tools in the hall closet, his grandfather's tools, old as dust, but tools don't have expiration dates, and his grandmother could reportedly pound a mean nail herself. Yanked open the closet door, rummaged around a second or two, hauled out the electric drill and four bits. Buddy's own father taught him how to assess a situation for the correct tool, the right sized bit. They didn't play ball, but they used tools. This one a *bit* rusty, otherwise right as rain as they say.

Most people take an anesthetic, inject it or at least get very high so you don't feel the pain. But he was in pain already, a terrible searing in his head and gut, something else in his heart, something open and raw. It's the head he was concentrating on when he plugged in that drill, flipped the switch, the electric whirring blending into the scream that was already in his ears, his own scream turns out, because when Buddy started wailing in his grandmother's room apparently he didn't stop. And that was the problem right there; he wouldn't have known when to stop. Soon as the drill breaks through the skull membrane you're supposed to hear a gurgling. He couldn't hear anything but his own yowling and the high-pitched whine of the drill.

Things got shadowy then, Buddy believes he must've passed out. Remembers his mother's face over him, "Buddy! Buddy!" she's shrieking. "What have you done?" He's lying on the hall floor and there's blood all around him. He can smell its metallic stench, feel the warm river of it running down his face, pooling in his ear—which is maybe why everything's sounding so hollowed out, like he's not even there, like he's watching it all from a great and cavernous distance. For a moment Buddy wondered if he was the one who died. Maybe he did. Maybe he's the ghost, not even a part of his own wounded, ridiculous flesh.

The paramedics stopped the bleeding, and a shot of something quieted the scream in his head. Another, an antibiotic to fight infection; the third, Tetanus, then a fourth plummeted him into a chilled darkness spiraling in like a migraine, only no pain, no sensation at all. Blessed black, silence. If you can't get the hole far enough into the skull to let the demons out, well then you just pump the drugs in, right? Murder? Mercy? Madness? Who is killing whom?

Part VII

Ten Months Later

31

Jody

THEY LET BUDDY OUT, ACCOMPANIED by an attendant, for his grandmother's memorial, the scattering of her ashes on Mauna Loa. He's not considered a criminal, their lawyer assured his parents. The shrinks doing the sanity eval didn't buy the part of Buddy's story that implied his mom did it—what with a kid opening up his scalp with a drill—not much in there to incriminate her in their learned opinion. It's what we expected. Like Buddy said the truth would kill her, and our family doesn't do martyrdom.

They've got him on a plethora of labels, psychovitamins, antipsychotics, antidepressives, little white ones, nasty yellow sucker, paper pill cup, his faithful hookup perpetually waiting for him in the meds line. Drugs for when he gets his headaches, but the funny thing is he hasn't had another bad one since the aborted hole in his skull, hidden for a time under a white sterile bandage, his shaved head an urban-cool look; Marnie would've approved. Maybe it went deeper than they think. Maybe there are holes in us that nobody can see, they never really heal but they let some of the pressure out so you just don't hurt as much. Like a hole in your heart. Try bandaging that.

His parents' lawyer plea bargained for insanity over voluntary man-slaughter. Mercy by temporary madness. Buddy didn't know what he was doing, a *psychotic break*. His grandmother wanted to die at home, free of ventilators, feeding tubes, life prolongers; she was ready to go. "Her breathing was so labored, so painful, so *awful*," Buddy's mother testified, "could've sent anyone over the edge."

THE FIRST TIME HE NOTICES me is in the dayroom. I'm washing windows, swiping at the plexiglass with my dampened handkerchief, pretending to be a janitor, but he wouldn't know the difference. Later that day I'm at the game table and I motion him over—"Want to learn some card tricks?" I ask. I can tell from the way he looks at me he isn't sure what I'm doing here, because after all I appear perfectly sane. I look like a surfer, with my long blond hair, it *is* still blond, blunt cut in a surfer shag to the shoulders. One of the plusses for invisibility is when you molecular reorganize back into flesh, the whole time you existed on another plane your body didn't age at all. How could it when the cells are reordered in the space-time continuum, where things are so compressed you are antimatter, and only matter can *matter*, in what aging does to the body. I don't look that much older than my grandson, my own modest assessment, since I first molecular reorganized when I was just shy of thirty. Which is why, heart wrenching as it was, I had to let Madge leave this plane without seeing me in the flesh again. We weren't supposed to get old after all, we flower-kids of the sixties, but we do, our generation did, Madge did, and I didn't. She wouldn't have appreciated the nuances of that. Still, to my grandson at eighteen now, I look old enough.

He moves slowly, a lilt on the diagonal, drag to the center, the Thorazine Shuffle they used to call this walk, though I'm not sure Thorazine is still a drug du jour—Lithium Lurch, Klondopin Clog, endemic in a place like this. "The name is John Stone," I tell him, "have a seat."

He raises an eyebrow—at the name, I wonder, too much? Then he shrugs and collapses into the chair opposite me. We're sitting at one of their dandy cemented-to-the-floor Formica block tables, on cemented-to-the-floor benches, so the inmates can't pick them up and play toss at each other.

"John Stone the *Magnificent!*" I wink, shuffling my card deck. "We'll start with a classic. This is simple and easy to begin your repertoire. Pick a card, any card."

Again he raises that eyebrow, dark and fuzzy as a caterpillar—he didn't get the red or blond genes from Madge and me—our daughter is darker, shaded in more concretely. He looks like Gwen. Buddy picks his card and I tell him not to show it to me, then hand him the deck, which meanwhile I'd been shuffling in such a way as to bend it just enough, so that when he puts the card back—anywhere I tell him—I can detect the one not bent and voila, present him with his card.

He's not impressed. I submit a box of kitchen matches, which of course the Gestapo emptied its contents before they'd let me have it, I assure him, sliding the top off just enough to show Buddy it's empty then slipping the deck of cards inside. I invert the matchbox, open it and tell him to shuffle the cards, then to put them back in the box. I ask him to select the first six cards from his shuffled deck in the box, which he does, albeit a bit shakily from the meds, and then I name each one of them. Now both eyebrows raise half-mast. "What's the deal?" he asks.

I explain that the box has a secret compartment, and I removed those six cards from the deck prior to our session, memorizing their faces and order. When I inverted the box the compartment opened from the pressure of the rest of the pack, causing the selected cards to fall on top. "The box only looks like it held actual matches. I was pulling your leg, which is of course the point," I tell him. "You can buy it anywhere they sell magic supplies."

"I'm not so big on magic," Buddy replies.

"Sure, so why are you here?" *We* know, of course, but I want to see what he says. I can't be a narrator anticipating his response in my physical body. I have the same blindness and self-absorbed limitations as every flesh and blood man born of woman, when I'm schlepping about this carcass. That's what it feels like after you've been weightless, like a ghost dragging the metal chain of his life's mistakes, a hundred and seventy pounds of flesh and bone.

Buddy shrugs, peers at me sharply for a moment, those dark perusing eyes fogged from the meds, but it's still obvious this kid is smart as the dickens, then stares out the window where the late afternoon light on the thick plexiglass refracts like its plowing through a clear, shiny mud. We hear chatter from the outside lanai, shrieks and chirps—damaged souls emoting like myna birds; it's recreation hour at the loony bin, or the Pupule House as we Hawaiians call our State Hospital. Buddy has defaulted to the day-room even though it's a nice afternoon; good choice on a day like this as we are mostly alone, just brain-blitzed old Roberts nodding off in the corner, and OCD Takahashi pacing back and forth the perimeter of the room, counting his steps as he goes—my daughter would approve.

"They think I killed my grandmother," Buddy says quietly, leaning in closer to where I'm re-shuffling my Houdini deck. He stares at the cards, avoiding my eyes.

"Uh huh," I nod, scrunch my forehead a bit. "So why aren't you in O'ahu Prison?" I wonder if he'll notice my olivine-green eyes, the way his mother always described them, and start putting things together. In my former shape, which was *non*-shape of course, I could have jumped into his perspective, had him peer into my eyes and detail them as olivine green, olive green, green as spinach or not *even* green, depending on what a kid like him would see and, more importantly, deem worthy to comment upon. The benefits of narrator—pure empathy—the ability to completely lose yourself inside another's perspective and tell their story.

Buddy lowers his head and points to the crown where his hair, in a fashionable buzz-cut now, can't grow; clipper-cut they're calling this, the way it stops at the perimeter of his silver dollar shaped scar, still an angry looking red but pretty much healed, the skin welted and knotted over the scalp, clenched like a baby's fist. "I did this," he says, soft but succinct, "with a drill."

"So they think you're nuts?" I ask, because I don't know what else to say; my eyes, mouth, the back of my throat are brimming suddenly with a burning, liquid substance. The sight of my grandson's poor scalp, the broken place where even his own hair refuses to touch has filled me with such an overwhelming love for him, this vulnerable child with the wounded head! It occurs to me that maybe *this* could be it, Strike Three—Buddy, flesh of my flesh though a generation removed, this beautiful boy with a heart bigger than all of the rest of our family's crammed together, but injured, hurt and afraid, has taken the fall for his own mother, my daughter, and is here, locked up in an asylum, when he should be out chasing girls, starting college, a future limitless as the sky.

Suddenly I'm seized with a kind of convulsion, nothing to worry about, I get them—a body can be such a burden to bear. I shimmy, shake, rattle and roll, like a dog blowing off water from a swim. "You'll be fine," I tell him when it's over, six seconds tops, I doubt he even noticed. "Just play along like you think they're right, and eventually with all that affirmation and your own good behavior they'll let you out. They diagnosed me a head-case too, a concussion from a monster wave, forty feet of water crashing down on my head like a ton of bricks, if you'll pardon the cliché. I came here without ID long after the incident in question—a good illusionist never reveals his full repertoire, didn't I tell you I'd teach you some tricks? So I'm something of a mystery to them. TBI they called it, Traumatic Brain Injury. They like to bandy about those initials—at one point they were throwing in PTSD, figuring I was the right age for Vietnam, even though I wasn't ever in the war, but they thought I might have been, combat amnesia they hypothesized. They call TBI and PTSD the *invisible wounds* because soldiers get them, warriors." I tell Buddy all this to make him feel better, so he sees that he's not the only one in here with a diagnosis that isn't true.

"I'm not mental," Buddy insists, his voice a bit snappish. "I don't have any of those things."

"Right," I nod. "I believe you. But let me tell you something, and it's kind of personal. I failed at almost everything that meant anything, jobs, people, particularly people, the obligations you have to your family. Failed at them all *except* for madness, and that, according to the learned folks in here, I've done supremely well!" I grin, wink. Wink wink.

Buddy frowns, shrugs. "Not sure that's something to aspire to."

My turn to shrug on the outside, but inside my excited little electrons are dancing to my grandson's intelligence and acute perceptiveness. "By the way, is Blue Cheer still around?"

"What's that, a laundry detergent?"

"Hah! Why young man, do I detect a sense of humor? Can't imagine where you got that from. Blue Cheer did a particularly rousing rendition of Summertime Blues." Start to hum it and immediately feel the slide of Margo Malone's sweet inner thigh, swallow hard and shudder—will this moment plague me for the rest of my eternity? All those years when I should have been ruminating on Madge's incomparable chest, yet it's Margo's thighs that still make me quiver. I never even saw them unclothed. In fact, I barely saw her face, except for the ruptured slide-show of her forehead and cheekbones through the in and out of the strobe light, the electric blues and purples from the black lights flashing off the ceiling of the auditorium. Could we have loved each other? Who knows? I loved Madge and look where that got us! "Avoid their concerts. That's what I wanted to tell you.

"OK," I say, "I'm going to show you one more trick—in the biz we prefer the term *illusion* by the way—but when they chime that dinner bell in fifteen minutes I want you to know you may not see me in the cafeteria. In fact, let me tell you a secret: you won't always see me at all, but know I'll be here, watching over you."

"How come I won't see you?" he asks.

I wink and shake my head, resisting the urge to ruffle his brillo-pad hair, a grandfatherly sort of gesture. There's plenty of time for the truth about who I am. And I will be around to do this. This time I'm going to do it right. "Now Buddy, didn't I just tell you it's a secret?

"This one is called Vanishing the Card. It's Houdini's, he was famous for making things disappear and for escaping—an escapologist, one of the greatest in the world and my esteemed mentor. You'll need to make or purchase this special box, which I just happen to have handy." I remove it from my magic case on the floor by my feet, cleverly disguised as a zipper-less nylon gym bag with Hawai'i State Hospital inscribed on its sides, along with an envelope big enough to hold the box. The box has metal cutouts that look like prison bars—in fact the official name Houdini called this illusion was The Imprisoned Card, but I don't want to say this to Buddy. He's a newbie to the Pupule House—they held him at the Youth Center until he turned eighteen—and he's probably feeling a little wary, being trapped and imprisoned himself. Though it's not so bad here in Adult A. There are degrees of madness, and in this unit we're not considered a danger to anyone but ourselves. They can medicate for that.

I tell my grandson to pick a card and place it in the box while I seal the envelope; he can clearly see the card through the slats in the box. Then I throw my handkerchief over the box, say *Ta Da*! lift the handkerchief (still damp from its clever disguise as my window-wiping rag this morning) and the card is gone. Buddy's eyes get big for real now. "Wow!" he declares.

"Want me to show you how?" I ask and he nods, almost enthusiastically, or as enthusiastic as it gets around here, doped up as they've got us. I grin the grin of someone with teeth—invisibility doesn't cut it when it comes to smiling at someone you love. "Watch closely," I tell him. "Contrary to popular belief, what you *see* isn't always what you get."

EPILOGUE

DINNER DONE, TV WATCHED, SLEEP meds swallowed, overhead lights out and the loonies all abed, I visualize him, my grandson: hair shorn, eyes shut, all worry, grief, despair, the markings of our physical lives we drag about with us in the daytime, eased, his face smooth in sleep. Like an angel he looks, if I believed in that sort of thing. The ward is fairly quiet tonight—the usual coughing, moaning, men calling out to the ghosts of their pasts, or maybe their futures—it's all elastic, isn't it, this space, this time?

Here is the dream Buddy would dream if he still could: dawn coming in again over the orchids, that smoky gold sky. So golden this light, the way it flows into the windows, the room, the ceiling, walls, leeching up through the floorboards, splayed through cracks in the earth like hell's heaven and it's all the same—this light, this ending. In Buddy's dream he doesn't leave his grandmother's room, his mom falls into a good and gentle sleep; in this version she doesn't drink so much, her pill bottles full. He watches over his grandmother. He is in charge.

Picture that ancient Monarch in Madge's jar, still perfectly formed, the curled up lock of hair lying beside it like something sleeping. Whether my niece really took that jar to Po doesn't matter; whether you believe in the trapped spirit of Ana Kalamahea Canada, or that maybe this was all just the celestial manifestation of a badly needed butt-kicking, doesn't either. Ever watch Ruby-Throated Hummingbirds? The ultimate dysfunctional family. Buddy's mom used to put out a feeder in their Maine back yard every summer and they'd come in droves. But the males, the ones with red on their throats like a bloody gash, would claim their territory and *whoosh,* down they'd come like fighter jets on any female or adolescent who tried to drink the nectar, who'd then turn around and do the same to each other. You'd wonder how the species survives. But survive they did, and every year more of them returned.

In this dream Big Volcano cabin surrounds him like a cocoon, creaking of the knotty pine floors, the walls, and he's listening to its stories about the ones who've gone, Jude and Ana, and soon, Madge. He imagines her like one of those ballooning spiders, spinning their aerodynamic threads to travel the air currents thousands of feet above the earth. She's poised and ready, waiting for the wind, the perfect updraft that will lift her into that golden dawn, and carry her up on her kite of silk, a glint of gossamer in the morning's new light, until she's no longer visible and his dream is over.

As for me? Next time you see those big boys roll in to Waimea, Pipeline, even the Hamakua (though that's rare and let's face it, a death wish), imagine me on the lip of the forty foot monster right before it crashes, flying across its shiny face. Though you won't see me of course, as I will have already gone inside the tube, burning through its darkness like a shooting star, before I too disappear.

Acknowledgements

Some time ago I wanted to write a novel about a sensitive teenage boy obsessed with insects and a Hawaiian healer. That novel began, finished, began, put aside while I wrote three more books, began again. At one point the healer became a ghost. It was Marc Estrin's excellent editorial chops that helped me shape this final version of Vanishing Acts; but I'm not buying the ghost, he said. Now we have a big-wave surfing, Houdini-obsessed grandfather who believes he can make himself invisible, and a novel I am finally delighted with. Thanks to the Fomite folks: Marc Estrin, and Donna Bister for her fantastic production skills, and for being available to answer late-night email panic attacks. Thanks to my wonderful publicist Sheryl Johnston, and to Susan Hyde for her eagle-eyed copyediting. I am honored and so very grateful for Lee Upton and Jack Driscoll's beautiful cover endorsements, and thanks to Binghamton University and my colleagues in the Creative Writing Program for their support. Maile Colbert, my amazingly talented daughter, generously gave us the beautiful cover art, which couldn't be more perfect for this story. Finally, a very big thanks to all of my family, for believing in me.

Photo by Marisa Wriston

Jaimee Wriston Colbert is author of five books of fiction: *Wild Things*, a linked story collection, winner of the 2017 CNY Book Award in Fiction and finalist for the AmericanBookFest Best Books of 2017; the novel, *Shark Girls*, finalist for the Foreword Magazine Book of the Year Award; *Dream Lives of Butterflies*, gold medalist in the Independent Publisher Awards; *Climbing the God Tree,* winner of the Willa Cather Fiction Prize, and *Sex, Salvation, and the Automobile*, winner of the Zephyr Prize. Originally from Hawaii, she lives in upstate New York where she is Professor of Creative Writing at SUNY, Binghamton University.

Fomite

About Fomite

A fomite is a medium capable of transmitting infectious organisms from one individual to another.

"The activity of art is based on the capacity of people to be infected by the feelings of others." Tolstoy, *What Is Art?*

Writing a review on Amazon, Good Reads, Shelfari, Library Thing or other social media sites for readers will help the progress of independent publishing. To submit a review, go to the book page on any of the sites and follow the links for reviews. Books from independent presses rely on reader to reader communications.

For more information or to order any of our books, visit
http://www.fomitepress.com/FOMITE/Our_Books.html

More Titles from Fomite...

Novels
Joshua Amses — *During This, Our Nadir*
Joshua Amses — *Raven or Crow*
Joshua Amses — *The Moment Before an Injury*
Jaysinh Birjepatel — *The Good Muslim of Jackson Heights*
Jaysinh Birjepatel — *Nothing Beside Remains*
David Brizer — *Victor Rand*
Dan Chodorkoff — *Loisaida*
David Cleveland — *Time's Betrayal*
Paula Closson Buck — *Summer on the Cold War Planet*
Roger Coleman — *Skywreck Afternoons*
Marc Estrin — *Hyde*
Marc Estrin — *Kafka's Roach*
Marc Estrin — *Speckled Vanities*
Zdravka Evtimova — *In the Town of Joy and Peace*
Zdravka Evtimova — *Sinfonia Bulgarica*

Fomite

Fomite

Poetry

Fomite

Fomite

Odd Birds

Micheal Breiner — *the way none of this happened*
J. C. Ellefson — *Under the Influence*
David Ross Gunn — *Cautionary Chronicles*
Andrei Guriuanu — *The Darkest City*
Gail Holst-Warhaft — *The Fall of Athens*
Roger Leboitz — *A Guide to the Western Slopes and the Outlying Area*
dug Nap— *Artsy Fartsy*
Delia Bell Robinson — *A Shirtwaist Story*
Peter Schumann — *Bread & Sentences*
Peter Schumann — *Charlotte Salomon*
Peter Schumann — *Faust 3*
Peter Schumann — *Planet Kasper, Volumes One and Two*
Peter Schumann — *We*

Plays

Stephen Goldberg — *Screwed and Other Plays*
Michele Markarian — *Unborn Children of America*

CPSIA information can be obtained
at www.ICGtesting.com
Printed in the USA
LVHW112345101019
633894LV00001B/1/P